"You will think of using atomic sterilization upon the targets of my revenge. Don't do it. I will turn against you if you do. The plague must run its course in Ireland, Great Britain and Libya. I want the men to survive and to know what it was I did to them. You will be permitted to quarantine them, nothing more. Send their nationals home—all of them. Let them stew there. If you fail to expel so much as a babe in arms who belongs in one of those nations by reason of nationality or birth, you will feel my anger."

The President finished reading O'Neill's atomic warning...

FRANK HERBERT
THE WHITE PLAGUE

ACE BOOKS, NEW YORK

The author gratefully acknowledges permission from the following sources
to reprint material in their control:
Macmillan Publishing Co., Inc., for lines from "Sailing to Byzantium,"
by William Butler Yeats, from Collected Poems, copyright 1928 by
Macmillan Publishing Co., Inc., renewed 1956 by Georgie Yeats; and lines
from "Remorse for Intemperate Speech," by William Butler Yeats, from
Collected Poems, copyright 1933 by Macmillan Publishing Co., Inc.,
renewed 1961 by Bertha Georgie Yeats.
New Directions and David Higham Associates Limited for lines from
Poems of Dylan Thomas by Dylan Thomas, copyright 1939 by New
Directions Publishing Corporation.

This Ace book contains the complete
text of the original hardcover edition.
It has been completely reset in a typeface
designed for easy reading and was printed
from new film.

THE WHITE PLAGUE

An Ace Book / published by arrangement with
the author

PRINTING HISTORY
G. P. Putnam's Sons edition / September 1982
Berkley edition / December 1983
Eighth printing / May 1986
Ace edition / July 1987

ISBN: 0-441-88569-1

Ace Books are published by The Berkley Publishing Group,
200 Madison Avenue, New York, New York 10016.
The name "ACE" and the "A" logo
are trademarks belonging to Charter Communications, Inc.

PRINTED IN THE UNITED STATES OF AMERICA

10 9 8 7 6 5 4 3 2 1

To Ned Brown
for his years of friendship

PRECEDE

There's a lust for power in the Irish as there is in every people, a lusting after the Ascendancy where you can tell others how to behave. It has a peculiar shape with the Irish, though. It comes of having lost our ancient ways—the simpler laws, the rath and the family at the core of society. Romanized governments dismay us. They always resolve themselves into widely separated Ascendants and Subjects, the latter being more numerous than the former, of course. Sometimes it's done with great subtlety as it was in America, the slow accumulations of power, law upon law and all of it manipulated by an elite whose monopoly it is to understand the private language of injustice. Do not blame the Ascendants. Such separation requires docile Subjects as well. This may be the lot of any government, Marxist Russians included. There's a peculiar human susceptibility you see when you look at the Soviets, them building an almost exact copy of the czarist regimes: the same paranoia, the same secret police, the same untouchable military, and the murder squads, the Siberian death camps, the lid of terror on creative imagination, deportation for the ones who cannot be killed off or bought off. It's like some terrible plastic memory sitting there in the dark of our minds, ready on the instant to reshape itself into primitive patterns the moment the heat touches it. I fear for the shape of things which may come from the heat of O'Neill's plague. Truly, I fear, for the heat is great.

—**Fintan Craig Doheny**

*May the hearthstone of hell be his
bed rest forever!*

—Old Irish Curse

It was an ordinary gray British Ford, the spartan economy model with right-hand drive customary in Ireland. John Roe O'Neill would remember the driver's brown-sweatered right arm resting on the car's windowsill in the cloud-filtered light of that Dublin afternoon. A nightmare capsule of memory, it excluded everything else in the scene; just the car and that arm.

Several other surviving witnesses commented on a crumpled break in the Ford's left front wing. The break had begun to rust.

Speaking from her hospital bed, one witness said: "The break was a jagged thing and I was afraid someone would be cut if they brushed against it."

Two of those who recalled seeing the car come out of Lower Leeson Street knew the driver casually, but only from his days in postal uniform. He was Francis Bley, a retired postman working part-time as a watchman at a building site in Dun Laoghaire. Bley left for work early every Wednesday, giving himself time to run a few errands and then pick up his wife, Tessie. On that one day each week, Tessie spent the morning doing "light secretarial" for a betting shop in King Street. It

1

was Tessie's habit to spend the rest of the day with her widowed sister who lived in a remodeled gatehouse off the Dun Laoghaire bypass "just a few minutes out of his way."

This was a Wednesday. May 20. Bley was on his way to pick up Tessie.

The Ford's left front door, although appearing undamaged by the accident that had crumpled the wing, still required a twist of wire around the doorpost to keep it closed. The door rattled every time the car hit a bump.

"I heard it rattling when it turned onto St. Stephen's Green South," one witness said. "It's God's own mercy I wasn't at the Grafton corner when it happened."

Bley turned right off St. Stephen's Green South, which put him on St. Stephen's Green West, hugging the left lane as he headed for Grafton Street. There were better routes for him to make his connection with Tessie, but this was "his way."

"He liked to see all the people," Tessie said. "God rest him, that's what he said he missed most when he quit the postal—all the people."

Bley, slight and wrinkled, had that skin-stretched cadaverous look that is common among certain aged Celts from the south of Ireland. He wore a soiled brown hat almost the exact shade of his patched sweater, and he drove with the patient detachment of someone who came his way often. And if the truth were known, he rather liked being slowed by the heavy traffic.

It had been cold and wet through most of spring and, while it was still cloudy, the cloud cover had thinned and there was a feeling that there might be a break in the weather. Only a few of the pedestrians carried umbrellas. The trees of St. Stephen's Green on Bley's right were in full leaf.

As the Ford inched along in the congested traffic, the man watching for it from a fourth-floor window of the Irish Film Society Building nodded once in satisfaction.

Right on time.

Bley's Ford had been selected because of this Wednesday punctuality. There was also the fact that Bley did not garage his car where he and Tessie lived in Davitt Road. The Ford was parked outside beside a thick yew hedge, which could be approached from the street along a path shielded by a parked van. There had been a van parked in this covering position the previous night. Neighbors had seen it but no one had thought to comment at the time.

"There were often vehicles parked in that place," one said. "How were we to know?"

The watcher at the Film Society Building had many names but he had been born Joseph Leo Herity. He was a small, solidly fleshy man with a long, thin face and pale, almost translucent skin. Herity wore his blond hair combed straight back and hanging almost to the collar. His light brown eyes were deeply set and he had a pugged nose with prominent nostrils from which hair protruded.

From his fourth-floor vantage, Herity commanded an overview of the entire setting for the drama he was about to ignite. Directly across from him, the tall trees of the green formed a verdant wall enclosing the flow of vehicles and pedestrians. The Robert Emmet statue stood opposite his window and, to the left of it, there was a black-on-white sign to the public toilets. Bley's Ford had stopped with the traffic just to the left of Herity's window. A white tour bus with blue-and-red stripes down its side loomed over the small Ford. Traffic fumes were thick even at the fourth-floor level.

Herity checked Bley's license number to be certain. *Yes—JIA-5028.* Then there was the crumpled left front wing.

The traffic began to inch forward, then stopped once more.

Herity glanced left at the Grafton Street corner. He could see the signs of the Toy World shop and the Irish Permanent Society on the ground floor of the red brick building soon to be taken over by the Ulster Bank. There had been some protest about that, one ragged march with a few signs, but it had died out quickly. The Ulster Bank had powerful friends in the government.

Barney and his lot, Herity thought. *They think we're ignorant of their scheme to make a peace with the Ulster boys!*

Again, Bley's Ford inched toward the corner, but once more was stopped. There was heavy foot traffic where Grafton took off from St. Stephen's Green.

A bald-headed man in a dark blue suit had stopped almost directly beneath Herity's window and was examining the cinema marquee. Two young men pushing bicycles threaded their way past the bald-headed man.

The traffic remained stopped.

Herity looked down at the top of Bley's car. So innocent-looking, that car. Herity had been one of the two-man team to emerge from the yew-shrouded van near Bley's parking spot the previous night. In Herity's hands had been a molded plastic package, which they had attached like a deformed limpet under Bley's car. At the core of that package lay a tiny radio receiver. The transmitter sat on the windowsill in front of Herity. A small black metal rectangle, it had a thin wire antenna and two recessed toggle switches—one painted yellow, the other red. Yellow armed it, red transmitted.

A glance at his wristwatch told Herity that they were already five minutes past Zero Time. Not Bley's fault. It was the blasted traffic.

"You can set your bloody watch by Bley," the leader of their selection team had said. "The old bastard should be running a tram."

"What're his politics?" Greaves had asked.

"Who cares about his politics?" Herity had countered. "He's perfect and he'll be dying for a grand cause."

"The street'll be full of people," Greaves had said. "And there'll be tourists sure as hell is full of Brits."

"We warned 'em to stop the Ulster boys," Herity had said. *Greaves could be an old woman sometimes!* "They know what to expect when they don't listen to us."

It was settled then. And now Bley's car was inching once more toward the Grafton Street corner, toward the mass of pedestrians, including the possible tourists.

John Roe O'Neill, his wife, Mary, and their five-year-old twins, Kevin and Mairead, could have been classified as tourists, although John expected to be six months in Ireland while completing the research called for under his grant from the Pastermorn Foundation of New Haven, Conn.

"An Overview of Irish Genetic Research."

He thought the title pompous, but it was only a cover. The real research was into the acceptance of the new genetics by a Roman Catholic society, whether such a society had taken a position to cope with the explosive potentials in molecular biology.

The project was much on his mind that Wednesday morning but necessary preparations required his attention. High on his list was the need to transfer funds from America to the Allied Irish Bank. Mary wanted to go shopping for sweaters "to keep our darlings warm of an evening."

"There y' go," John teased as they left the Shelbourne Hotel, stepping into the rush of tourists and businessmen. "Only four days in Ireland and already you sound like a local."

"And why not?" she demanded. "And both my grandmothers from Limerick."

They laughed, drawing a few curious stares. The children tugged at Mary, anxious to be off shopping.

Ireland suited Mary, John thought. She had pale clear skin and dark blue eyes. Jet-black hair—"Spanish Hair," her family called it—framed her rather round face. A sweet face. Irish skin and Irish features. He bent and kissed her before leaving. It brought a blush to her face but she was pleased at his show of affection and she gave him a warm smile as they parted.

John walked away briskly, humming to himself, amused when he recognized the tune: "Oh What a Beautiful Mornin'."

John's Wednesday appointment for "transfer of foreign funds" was at two P.M. at the Allied Irish Bank, Grafton and Chatham streets. There was a sign just inside the bank's entrance, white letters on black: "Non Branch Customers Upstairs." A uniformed guard led him up the stairs to the office of the bank manager, Charles Mulrain, a small, nervous man with tow-colored hair and pale blue eyes behind gold-framed glasses. Mulrain had a habit of touching the corners of his mouth with a forefinger, first left side then right, followed by a quick downward brush of his dark tie. He made a joke about having his office on the first floor, "what you Americans call the second floor."

"It is confusing until you catch on," John agreed.

"Well!" A quick touching of lips and tie. "You understand that we'd normally do this at our main office, but . . ."

"When I called, they assured me it was . . ."

"As a convenience to the customer," Mulrain said. He lifted a folder from his desk, glanced inside it, nodded. "Yes, this amount . . . if you'll make yourself comfortable here, I'll just get the proper forms and be right back."

Mulrain left, giving John a tight smile at the door.

John went to the window and pulled back a heavy lace curtain to look down on Grafton Street. The sidewalks were thick with people all the way up to the arched gateway into St. Stephen's Green two short blocks up Grafton. The motor traffic was two abreast filling the street and crawling along toward him. There was a workman cleaning the parapet on the roof of the shopping center diagonally across the street—a white-coated figure with a long-handled brush. He stood outlined against a row of five chimney pots.

Glancing at the closed door of the manager's office, John wondered how long Mulrain would be. Everything was so damned formal here. John looked at his watch. Mary would arrive with the children in a few minutes. They planned to have tea, then John would walk down Grafton to Trinity College and begin work at the college library—the real start of his research project.

Much later, John would look back on those few minutes at the bank manager's "first-floor" window and think how another sequence of events had been set in motion without his knowledge, an inescapable thing like a movie film where one frame followed another without ever the chance to deviate. It all centered around Francis Bley's old car and a small VHF transmitter in the hands of a determined man watching from an open window that looked down on that corner where Grafton met St. Stephen's Green.

Bley, patient as always, eased along at the traffic's pace. Herity, in his window vantage point, toggled the arming switch of his transmitter, making sure the antenna wire dangled out over the sill.

As he neared the Grafton corner, the crush of pedestrians forced Bley to stop and he missed the turn of the traffic light. He heard the tour bus gain clear of traffic off to his right, trundling off in a rumble of its heavy diesel. Barricades were being erected on the building to his left and a big white-on-red sign had been raised over the rough construction: "This Building to be Remodeled by G. Tottenham Sons, Ltd." Bley looked to his right and noted the tall blue-and-white Prestige Cafeteria sign, feeling a small pang of hunger. The pedestrian isthmus beside him was jammed with people waiting to cross over to St. Stephen's Green and others struggling to make a way through the cars stopped on Grafton and blocking Bley's path. The crush of pedestrians was particularly heavy around Bley's car, people passing both front and back. A woman in a brown tweed coat, a white parcel clutched under her right elbow and each hand grasping a hand of a small child, hesitated at the right front corner of Bley's car while she sought an opening through the press of people.

John Roe O'Neill, standing at the bank manager's window, recognized Mary. He saw her first because of her familiar tweed coat and the way she carried her head, that sleek cap of jet hair. He smiled. The twins were screened from him by the hurrying adults but he knew from Mary's stance that she held the children's hands. A brief break in the throng allowed John a glimpse of the top of Kevin's head and the old Ford with the driver's brown-sweatered elbow protruding.

Where is that damned bank manager? John wondered. *She'll be here any minute.*

He dropped the heavy lace curtain and looked once more at his wristwatch.

Herity, at the open window above and behind Bley, nodded once more to himself. He stepped back away from the window and toggled the second switch on his transmitter.

Bley's car exploded, ripped apart from the bottom. The bomb, exploding almost under Bley's feet, drove him upward with a large piece of the car's roof, his body crushed, dismembered and scattered. The large section of roof sailed upward in a slow arc to come crashing onto the Irish Permanent Society Building, demolishing chimney pots and slates.

It was not a large bomb as such things went, but it had been expertly placed. The old car was transformed into jagged bits of metal and glass—an orange ball of fire peppered with deadly shrapnel. A section of the car's bonnet decapitated Mary O'Neill. The twins became part of a bloody puddle blown against the iron fencing across the street at St. Stephen's Green. Their bodies were more easily identified later because they were the only children of that age in the throng.

Herity did not pause to glance out at his work; the sound told it all. He tucked the transmitter into a small and worn military green pack, stuffed an old yellow sweater onto it, strapped the cover and slung the pack over his shoulder. He left the building by the back way, elated and satisfied. Barney and his group would get this message!

John O'Neill had looked up from his wristwatch just in time to see the orange blast envelop Mary. He was saved from the window's shattered glass by the heavy curtains, which deflected all but one of the shards away from him. One small section of glass creased his scalp. The shock wave staggered him, driving him backward against a desk. He fell sideways, momentarily unconscious but getting quickly to his knees as the bank manager rushed into the room, shouting:

"Good God! What was that?"

John stumbled to his feet, rejecting the question and the answer that rumbled through his head like an aftershock of the blast. He brushed past the bank manager and out the door. His mind remained in shock but his body found its way down the stairs. He shouldered a woman aside at the foot of the stairs and lurched out onto the street where he allowed himself to be carried along by the crowd rushing toward the area of the blast. There was a smell of burnt iron in the air and the sound of cries and screams.

Within only a few seconds John was part of a crush being held back by police and uninjured civilians pressed into service to keep the area around the explosion clear. John elbowed and clawed his way forward.

"My wife!" he shouted. "I saw her. She was there. My wife and our children!"

A policeman pinned his arms and swung him around, blocking John's view of the tangled fabric and bloody flesh strewn across the street.

The groans of the injured, the cries for help and the shouts of horror drove John into insensate rage. *Mary needs me!* He struggled against the policeman.

"Mary! She was right in front of . . ."

"The ambulances are coming, sir! There's help at hand. You must be still. You cannot go through now."

A woman off to John's left said: "Let me through. I'm a nurse."

This, more than anything else, stopped John's struggles against the policeman.

People were helping. There was a nurse.

"It'll be cleared up in a bit, sir," the policeman said. His voice was maddeningly calm. "That's a bad cut on your head. I'll just help you across to where the ambulances are coming."

John allowed himself to be led through a lane in the crowd, seeing the curious stares, hearing the voices on his right *ooing* and the calling upon God to "look over there"—the awed voices telling John about things he did not want to see. He knew, though. And there were glimpses past the policeman who helped him to a cleared place against a building across from the green.

"There now, sir," the policeman said. "You'll be taken care of here." Then to someone else: "I think he was hit by a flying bit; the bleeding seems to've stopped."

John stood with his back against a scarred brick wall from which the dust of the explosion still sifted. There was broken glass underfoot. Through an opening in the crowd to his right he could see part of the bloody mess at the corner, the people moving and bending over broken flesh. He thought he recognized Mary's coat behind a kneeling priest. Somewhere within him there existed an understanding of that scene. His mind remained frozen, though, frigidly locked into limited thought. If he allowed himself to think freely, then events would flow— time would continue . . . a time without Mary and the children. It was as though a tiny jewel of awareness held itself intact within him, understanding, *knowing* . . . but nothing else could be allowed to move.

A hand touched his arm.

It was electric. A scream erupted from him—agonized, echoing down the street, bringing people whirling around to stare at him. A photographer's flash temporarily blinded him, shutting off the scream, but he could still hear it within his head. It was more than a primal scream. This came from deeper, from some place he had not suspected and against which he had no protection. Two white-coated ambulance attendants grabbed him. He felt his coat pulled down, shirt ripped. There came the prick of a needle in his arm. They hustled him into an ambulance as an enveloping drowsiness overwhelmed his mind, sweeping away his memory.

For a long time afterward, memory would not reproduce those shocked minutes. He could recall the small car, the brown-sweatered elbow on the windowsill, but nothing afterward. He knew he had seen what he had seen: the explosion, the death. Intellectual awareness argued the facts. *I was standing at that window, I must have seen the blast*. But the particulars lay behind a screen that he could not penetrate. It lay frozen within him, demanding action lest the frozen thing thaw and obliterate him.

Despair and grief suit the Celtic mind more than do joy and victory. Every Celtic joy has its mixture of grief. Every victory leads to despair.

—Fintan Craig Doheny

STEPHEN BROWDER read about the Grafton Street bombing while sitting on the grass of the quad at the medical school of University College, Cork. As a third-year student Browder had learned enough about school routine to provide himself with a long lunch hour and a chance to crack the books and catch his breath between classes. He had chosen this luncheon spot, however, because some of the student nurses shared it and Kathleen O'Gara frequently was among that lunching troupe.

It was a warm day and this had brought many others into the quad, all of them preferring the green to the gothic stone monstrosity of the school, which often seemed to partake more of the old jail that once had occupied this spot than of a modern medical facility. The Cork *Examiner* in his hands was only a prop but he had been caught by the picture of a screaming man—"American Tourist Loses Family"—and he read the story, shaking his head now and then at the horror of it.

Browder's attentions to Kathleen O'Gara had not gone without notice among the student nurses. They teased her about it now.

"There he is, Katie. I'll loan you a handkerchief to drop in front of him."

Kate blushed, but could not keep herself from looking across the green at Browder. He was a skinny, gawkish young man with sandy hair and widely set blue eyes. His whole bearing gave promise of his becoming one of those stoop-shouldered general practitioners who inspire so much faith among their patients by their towering benignity. There was a persistent thoughtfulness about him that she liked. The shyness was sure to become learned diffidence and a down-the-nose austerity that would go well with his finely chiseled features.

Browder looked up from his newspaper and met Kate's eyes. He looked away quickly. He had been trying for two weeks to work up his courage, seeking a way to ask her to go out with him. He berated himself now for not smiling back at her.

He could not really define why she attracted him. She had a youthful figure, a bit on the sturdy side, but comely. Her skin carried those fine surface veins that gave a rosy hue to the complexion. Her hair now—that was a shining red-brown, part of the Viking legacy, and her dark brown eyes were set rather deeply under a wide brow. He knew she was recognized as a good worker, bright and cheerful, and he had heard another nursing student say about her: "She's no beauty but good enough to get a husband."

She is beautiful in her own way, he thought.

Again, he glanced at her and their eyes met. She smiled and he forced himself to smile before breaking the contact. His heart was beating strongly and he bent over the newspaper for distraction. The picture of the screaming man seemed to stare out at him, chilling him. The poor fellow's entire family gone in that blast—the wife and two children. For a moment, Browder had a fantasy picture of himself married to Kate O'Gara—children, of course. And them gone like this. All of them. Without any warning. Everything that had gone into Stephen Browder's choice of profession felt outraged by that bombing.

Was anything worth it?

Even the reuniting of all Ireland, which he solemnly prayed for on holy days—could that justify this act?

A splinter group of the IRA, the Provos, was claiming credit, according to the *Examiner*'s story. Browder had friends in the IRA. One of his fellow students made explosives for them. The sympathies of the University College student body were not hard to discover. They wanted the Brits out.

Damn the Brits!

Browder felt torn by his Republican sympathies and his shock at what had been done to those people in Dublin. Thirty-one dead; seventy-six maimed and injured. And all because some people in the dail were reportedly wavering, talking about an "accommodation." There could be no accommodation with the Brits. Never!

But would the bombs ever solve anything?

A shadow fell on his newspaper. Browder looked up to see Kate O'Gara standing there looking down at him. Hastily, he scrambled to his feet, spilling an anatomy textbook from his lap, losing part of his newspaper. He looked down at her, suddenly conscious that he was more than a head taller.

"You're Stephen Browder, aren't you?" she asked.

"Yes. Yes, I am."

She had a lovely soft voice, he thought. And he had an abrupt insight into what a powerful asset such a voice would be to a nurse. It was a calming voice. It gave him courage.

"And you're Kate O'Gara," he managed.

She nodded. "I saw you reading about that bombing, the one in Dublin. What a terrible thing."

"'Tis that," he agreed. Then, before he lost courage: "Must you go back to classes now?"

"I've only these few minutes."

"And what time do you finish?" He knew he was blushing as he asked.

She lowered her gaze. *What long lashes she has,* he thought. They lay like feathers on her cheeks.

"I would like to see you," he said. And that was God's own truth. He couldn't take his eyes off her.

"I'm expected home at half five," she said, looking up at him. "We could have a tea perhaps on the way."

"Shall we meet here after classes then?" he asked.

"Yes." She smiled and hurried off to join her friends.

One of the other student nurses, having watched the two of them, whispered to a companion: "God! I'm glad that's finally done."

Holy Ireland was just a name, a myth, a dream that had no connection with any reality. It was our tradition, a part of our reputation, at one with the myth that we have only the honor gained from glorious battle.

—Father Michael Flannery

JOHN ROE O'NEILL awakened to see a priest standing beside him and a doctor standing at the foot of his bed. He could feel the bed under him and smelled antiseptics. This would be a hospital, then. The doctor was a tall, older man with gray at the temples. He wore a green street jacket, stethoscope in the pocket.

Why am I here? John wondered.

It was a hospital ward, he saw: other beds with figures in them. It was a blankly impersonal room, a place designed with malice to negate the personality of the occupant—as though someone had worked consciously and with a great deal of hate to create a place that would reflect no human warmth. If this room uttered any statement it was: "You won't live long here."

John tried to swallow. His throat hurt. He had been dreaming about Mary. She had been swimming away from him in the dream, a great blue expanse of water all around and no sound in her movements even when he saw the water splashing.

"I'm going for the children," she said. He heard that, but still no sound of swimming.

His dream self had thought: *Of course. She must go for the children. Kevin and Mairead will need her.*

In the dream, he could sense Mary's mind as though it were his own. Her mind conveyed an oddly crystalline quality like the aftermath of fever. "I can't feel my body," she said. "Poor John. I love you."

Then he was awake, his eyes burning, and the priest and the doctor there. It was a green place with a carbolic smell that separated it from the memories of American hospitals. There were bonneted sisters bustling about and, when one saw him awake, she hurried away. The shade was up on a single tall window to the left of the doctor: darkness outside. It was night, then. Light came from unshaded bulbs dangling on long wires from a high ceiling. The doctor was examining a clipboard that was attached by a string and hook to the foot of the bed.

"He's awake," the priest said.

The doctor let the clipboard fall back onto its string and looked down the length of the bed at John. "Mr. O'Neill, you'll be all right. Fit as a fiddle by morning." He turned and walked away.

The priest leaned toward John. "Are you Catholic, sir?"

"Catholic?" It seemed an insane question. "I'm ... I'm ... St. Rose's parish ..." Now, why should he tell the priest the name of his parish?

The priest put a gentling hand on John's shoulder. "There, there. I quite understand."

John closed his eyes. He heard a scraping of a chair on the floor and, when he opened his eyes, saw that the priest had sat down, bringing his face close to John's.

"I'm Father Devon," the priest said. "We know who you are, Mr. O'Neill, from your things. Would you be related to the O'Neills of Coolaney, by the way?"

"What?" John tried to raise himself but his head started spinning. "I ... no. I don't know."

"It would be good to have family around you at such a time. Your wife's body has been identified—her purse. I'll not go into the particulars."

What particulars? John wondered. He recalled a bloody mound of tweed but could not place it in time or space.

"It's very bad news to be giving you, Mr. O'Neill," Father Devon said.

"Our children," John gasped, grasping at hope. "The twins were with her."

"Ahhhhh," Father Devon said. "Well now, as to that, I don't know. It's been quite a few hours and all the nasty work done but... Were the wains with her when..."

"She was holding their hands."

"Then I would not hold out much hope. What a terrible thing! Shall we pray for the souls of your loved ones?"

"Pray?" John turned his head away, choking. He heard the chair scrape, footsteps approaching. A woman's voice said, "Father..." then something that John could not make out. The priest responded in a low, unintelligible murmur. Then the woman's voice, clearly: "Mother of Mercy! His wife and the two little ones both! Ahhh, the poor man."

John turned back in time to see a nursing sister departing, her back stiff. The priest was standing beside him.

"Were your wife and children Catholic as well?" Father Devon asked.

John shook his head. He felt feverish and dizzy. Why these questions?

"Mixed marriage, eh?" Father Devon, having jumped to a wrong conclusion, sounded accusatory. "Well, my heart goes out to you all the same. The remains have been taken to the morgue. We can decide in the mornin' what's to be done with the remains."

Remains? John thought. *He's talking about Mary and the twins.*

The doctor returned and moved down the side of the bed opposite the priest. John turned toward the doctor and saw that the nursing sister had reappeared there beside him as though by magic. She wore a white apron over a green dress and her hair was contained by a tightly hooded cap. Her face was thin and commanding. She held a hypodermic in her right hand.

"Something to help you sleep," the doctor said.

Father Devon spoke: "The Garda will be in to talk to you in the morning. Send for me when they've gone."

"We'll have the lights down now," the doctor said.

"And high time it is." The nursing sister had a demanding voice with considerable tartness in it, a protective voice. He held to that thought as sleep enveloped him.

Morning was the sound of rattling bedpans on a cart. John awoke to see a uniformed police officer standing where the priest had been.

"They said you'd be awakening soon," the officer said. He had a mellow tenor, a square face with prominent veins. His hat was held stiffly under his left arm. He pulled a small notebook from a side pocket and prepared to write. "I'll not trouble y' overmuch, Mr. O'Neill. But I'm sure y' can appreciate there're things we must do."

"What do you want?" John's voice remained a croak. His head still felt fuzzy.

"Would you be telling me what you were doing in the Republic of Ireland, sir?"

John stared up at the officer. *Doing?* The question wandered aimlessly in his awareness for a time. His mind felt thick and clogged. He had to force a response.

"I was . . . foundation grant . . . doing research."

"And the nature of this research?"

"Gen . . . genetics."

The officer wrote in his notebook, then: "And is that your occupation, researcher?"

"I . . . I teach . . . molecular biology, biochemistry . . . and . . . " He took a deep, trembling breath. "School of Pharmacy, as well."

"And that would be in this Highland Park in the state of Minnesota? We've seen your papers, y' understand?"

"Near . . . nearby."

"You've family here in the Republic of Ireland?"

"We . . . were going to look."

"I see." The officer wrote this in his pad.

John labored against a tightness in his chest. He found his voice presently: "Who . . . who did it?"

"Sir?"

"The bomb?"

The officer's face grew stony. "They're saying it was the Provos taking the credit."

A chill shot through John. The hard pillow under his neck felt damp and cold. *Credit?* The murderers were claiming credit?

Later, John would look back on that moment as the beginning of the rage that took over his entire life. That was the moment when he promised:

You will pay. Oh, how you will pay!

And there was no doubt in his mind at all how he would set about making them pay.

> *Do you realize that this one man is changing the political map of the world?*
>
> —General Lucius Gorham, U.S. presidential foreign affairs advisor, speaking to the secretary of defense

THE WARNING letters began arriving during the week before the first anniversary of the Grafton Street bombing. The first one was timed to reach Ireland too late for counteraction. Others went to world leaders, where they were treated as crank letters or were bucked along to specialists. The letters were numerous at first—to radio and television news departments, to newspapers, to prime ministers and presidents and church leaders. It was determined later that one of the first letters was delivered to a newspaper editor on Dublin's O'Connell Street.

The editor, Alex Coleman, was a dark and vital man who covered his drive with a generally mild manner even when he was being most forceful. He was considered an oddity among his peers because of his strong temperance beliefs, but none doubted his penetrating alertness to a good story.

Coleman read the letter several times, glancing up occasionally to look out his third-floor window onto the street, where Dublin's morning traffic already had begun to congeal into its usual frustrating crawl.

Crank letter?

The thing didn't have that feeling about it. The warnings and threats made his skin crawl. Was this possible? The words had an educated air about them, sophisticated. The thing was typed on bond paper. He rubbed the paper between his fingers. Expensive stuff.

Owney O'More, Coleman's personal secretary, had clipped a note to the letter: "I hope this is a crank. Should we call the Garda?"

So it had worked its disturbance on Owney.

Once more, Coleman read through the letter, seeking some reason to disregard it. Presently, he put the letter flat in front of him and keyed the intercom to Owney.

"Sir?" Owney's voice always had a military abruptness.

"Check out the Achill Island angle, will you, Owney? Don't stir up any hornets. Just find out if there's anything unusual afoot."

"Right away."

Coleman returned his attention to the letter. It was so damned direct, so clear and straightforward. A mind of power and . . . yes, terrifying purpose, lay behind it. There was the usual warning to publish "or else" but then . . .

"I am going to wreak an appropriate revenge upon all of Ireland, Great Britain and Libya."

The expressed justification rang a bell in Coleman's memory.

"You have wronged me by killing my loved ones. By my hand alone you are being called to account. You murdered my Mary and our children, Kevin and Mairead. I have sworn a treble vow on their memories. I will be avenged in kind."

Coleman again keyed the intercom and asked Owney to check on those names. "And while you're at it, call the College Hospital and see if you can get me through to Fin Doheny."

"That would be Fintan Craig Doheny, sir?"

"Right."

Once more, Coleman read the letter. He was interrupted by the telephone and intercom simultaneously. Owney's voice said: "Doctor Doheny on the line, sir."

Coleman picked up the phone. "Fin?"

"What's so all-fired important, Alex? Owney O'More sounds like he's been scalded."

"I've a threatening letter, Fin. And there's some technical

stuff in it. Mind listening a minute?"

"Get on with it." Doheny's voice had an echo quality, suggesting a speaker phone.

"Is someone else with you?" Coleman asked.

"No. What's got the wind up?"

Coleman sighed and returned his attention to the letter, extracting the technical references for Doheny.

"It's hard to say from just a letter," Doheny said. "But I find no fault with his references to the recombinant DNA process. You know, Alex, it is possible that way to make new diseases . . . but this . . ."

"The threat could be real?"

"I'd give that a qualified yes."

"Then I shouldn't disregard this thing?"

"I'd be calling the Garda."

"Is there anything else I should be doing?"

"Well, I'll give that a think and be back to you."

"One thing, Fin! Not a word on this until I've had a go at it."

"Aw, you scramblin' newspapermen!" But there was a hint of laughter in Doheny's voice that Coleman found reassuring. A *qualified* yes. Doheny wasn't too worried then. It was still a good story, though, Coleman thought as he replaced the telephone in its cradle. A bomb victim's vengeance. Medical expert says the thing's possible.

Owney's voice came over the intercom: "Sir, that bomb at Grafton and St. Stephen's Green. You remember that?"

"That bloody thing!"

"Sir, three of the victims had the names in this letter. There was a Mary O'Neill killed with her twin children, Kevin and Mairead."

"From America, yes, I remember."

"The husband was at the window of a bank down the street and saw it all happen. Name of . . ." Owney paused, then: "Doctor John Roe O'Neill."

"Medical?"

"No, a professor of some sort. He was here on one of those foundation grant things they're so fond of—studying the state of genetics or some . . . yes, that's what our story says. Genetics research."

"Genetics," Coleman mused.

"According to our story at the time, sir. This O'Neill had

something to do with physical chemistry—a biophysicist—and he taught at some school of pharmacy in the States. Says here he also owned a pharmacy there."

Coleman suddenly shuddered. He felt that something evil had crawled beneath the surface of his land, a thing more venomous than any snake the Sainted Patrick had banned. That IRA bomb could come to be known as the most awful mistake in human history.

"Any luck getting through to Achill?" Coleman asked.

"The lines are jammed, sir. Should we dispatch an aircraft?"

"Not yet. Get on to the Garda. If the Achill phones are jammed, they may know something. Did you copy this letter?"

"Two copies, sir."

"They'll want the original . . ."

"If they don't have one of their own already."

"I thought of that. I just don't like tipping our hand. We may have a head start on this. Well, we'll just have to chance it." He glanced down at the letter on his desk. "I don't suppose there's any chance of getting fingerprints off this, anyway."

"Are we going ahead with the story, sir?"

"Owney, I'm almost afraid not to publish it. There's something about it. And singling out Achill this way . . . 'a demonstration,' he says."

"Sir, you've thought of the panic we might . . ."

"Just get me the Garda, Owney."

"Right away, sir!"

Coleman picked up his phone and called his wife at home, making it brief and imperative.

"There's going to be trouble over a story we're about to publish," he explained. "I want you to take the boys and go to your brother's in Madrid."

When she started to protest, he cut her off: "This is going to be bad . . . I think. If you're here, I'm vulnerable. Don't waste any time; just leave. Call me from Madrid and I'll explain."

He replaced the phone in its cradle, feeling somewhat foolish but relieved. Panic? If this thing proved to be true, there would be worse than panic. He stared at the letter, focusing on the signature.

"The Madman."

Coleman shook his head slowly, recalling the tale of the Irish coffin-ship survivor who, making a cross of shovels over his wife's grave at Grosse Isle, Quebec, had vowed: "By the cross, Mary, I swear to avenge your death."

O'Neill's wife had been named Mary. And now, if this was O'Neill, he called himself simply "The Madman."

> *They are a torture, my memo-*
> *ries—a lovely torture.*
>
> **—Joseph Herity**

THE PATTERN of change built itself slowly in John Roe O'Neill. It set him trembling unexpectedly at odd moments, his heart pounding, sweat breaking out all over his body. At such times, he thought of the old beliefs in possession. It was like that— another personality taking over his flesh and nerves.

Much later, he came to a personal accommodation with this Other, even a sense of familiarity and identity. He thought of it then as partly his own making, partly a thing rising out of primal darkness, a deliberate creation for the task of revenge. Certainly, his Old Self had not been up to such a deed. The kindly teacher-of-the-young could not have contemplated such a plan for an instant. The Other had to come into being first.

As the change progressed, he came to think of himself as Nemesis revived. This Nemesis came out of Ireland's bloody past, out of the betrayals and murders, and even carried with it a retaliation against the Celtic extermination of the First People, the Danaans, who had been in Ireland before the waves of invaders from Britain and the Continent. He saw himself then as a spokesman for all of the accumulated wrongs suffered in Ireland. It was Nemesis blaring:

"Enough! Let it end!"

But the Other asked: "Why should Ireland shoulder it all alone?"

The terrorists who had killed Mary and the twins had been trained and armed in Libya. And there was England's filthy hand in the whole mess—eight hundred years of cynical oppression—"Ireland, the guilty conscience of the English ruling class."

As this change became fixed in its purpose, John saw an astonishing alteration of his appearance. The old almost plump self went stringing down to a slender, nervous man, who avoided old friends, refused to answer the telephone and ignored appointments. People made allowances at first—"The awful shock of such a tragedy..." The foundation that had sent him to Ireland gave him an unrequested extension on the project with a polite letter asking if he wanted to turn it over to another researcher. The school extended his leave of absence. Max Dunn, who managed the family pharmacy, took over more of the business decisions and told John not to concern himself with anything except getting his life back in order.

John merely noted these things in passing. The change within him had become an obsession. Then he looked at himself in the bathroom mirror one Saturday morning and knew he would have to take action. Mary and the twins had been dead and buried four months. The Other was strong in him now; a new face, a new personality. He stood in the upstairs bathroom of the home he and Mary had bought when they had first learned of her pregnancy. The sounds of the old college town drifted up to him through the open window. There was a feeling of fall in the air but the forecast was for another two weeks of "warmer than normal" weather. John could hear Mister Neri down the street running his power mower. A bicycle bell went jingling past. Children shouted on their way to the park. It was September already; he knew that. And he remembered how Kevin and Mairead had shouted at play in the yard.

Neri shut down his mower. Mrs. Neri had been one of the most persistent callers. "You're wasting away to skin and bones, you poor man!" But Mrs. Neri had a younger sister, unmarried and getting anxious. There had been a matchmaker's look in Mrs. Neri's plump face.

John leaned close to the mirror and looked at himself carefully. The changes... not quite a stranger, but strange. *They won't have any photographs of this face,* he thought. But they would make drawings and spread them far and wide. At that moment, the thought still in his mind, he knew he was going to do this thing, knew he was capable of it and would certainly do it. That scream at St. Stephen's Green had set something in motion, like the slow beginning of an avalanche. *Let it come then,* he thought.

That morning, he put his house on the market and, because properties near the college were much in demand, he had it sold two weeks later to a "nice young assistant professor," as the Real Estate Woman called him. All of these people were like dream faces to John. His thoughts had gone questing ahead to the thing that needed doing. The Nice Young Assistant Professor had wanted to know when Doctor O'Neill would be returning to his post at the school.

"We heard about your tragedy of course, and we understand why you're selling—all of the memories."

He doesn't understand at all, John thought.

But the transaction put a clear $188,000 in John's pocket. The Real Estate Woman had tried to talk to John about his "tax obligations" and had worked to sell him "a much better investment a bit farther out but on land sure to increase in value dramatically over the next ten years."

He had lied to her, saying his accountants already had the problem in hand.

The contents of the house had brought an astonishing $62,000, but then Mary's father had left her some valuable old books and two fine paintings. Her family's furniture had included several antiques, a thing John had never even thought about before. Furniture had always been only something to fill the spaces in a house.

The college fund they had set aside for the twins yielded another $33,000. There was the McCarthy annuity from John's mother, against which the bank loaned him $56,000. Their small portfolio of stocks brought $28,900. The bank accounts over which Mary had worked so hard brought $31,452. Almost $30,000 remained in the grant for the Ireland project, money he had not transferred to the Allied Irish Bank, keeping it in a high-interest brokerage fund that the foundation had approved. His salary, reduced by the sabbatical's requirements, produced close to $16,000 more.

Friends and associates had seen only the surface of this

activity, taking it as "a good sign John's finally getting back to normal."

The most delicate parts of the transition involved dealing with the Internal Revenue Service and the sale of the pharmacy that had been in his mother's family now for two generations. Max Dunn said he understood that John might not want to publicize the sale, "and besides I'd want to keep the McCarthy name over the door." From family sources, Dunn produced a $78,000 down payment and agreed to a one-year deferral on starting payments on the balance—none of which John ever intended to collect. The $78,000 was what he wanted. Cash!

The IRS he put off with a token payment of $5,000 and a letter from his accountants explaining that due to the tragedy and attendant problems, time was required to settle the taxpayer's affairs. The IRS, mindful of the sympathy for John and wary of adverse publicity, granted a six-month deferral.

On the day he left Highland Park in his station wagon, John had almost $500,000 tucked away in the back in the fireproof box that once had held his will and property deeds. The rest of the wagon was crammed full of the carefully packed elements of his personal laboratory, including his computer. Two suitcases of clothing had to be secured under the safety belt beside him on the front seat.

Friends accepted the story that he was going to look for "someplace farther out, a place without these memories."

Late that evening, he ate supper almost four hundred miles away from the place he no longer called home, sitting in a roadside café that smelled of rancid grease. He chose a booth that gave him a view of the car parked outside, noting the gray film of dust that gave it a rundown look. That was good. The grille still showed a shallow dent Mary had put there while trying to maneuver out of a supermarket parking lot. John left without finishing the meal and could not even remember what he had ordered.

Later, he found a motel with an alcove parking place beside his room. He transferred the fireproof box to a place under the bed, put his father's old .38 Colt under the pillow and lay down fully clothed, not expecting to sleep. He could feel the presence of that box under the bed. The money represented energy for the thing he knew he had to do. Every sound outside brought him to alertness. Headlights sweeping across the window draperies set his heart pounding. Activity outside subsided as the night wore on and he told himself he would nap a bit. Someone starting a car awakened him and he opened his eyes to gray morning light around the edges of the draperies.

And he was hungry.

> *Those two wains dead will not win us friends. Could you not have waited just a bit?*
>
> —Kevin O'Donnell
>
> *Me standing back out of the window I could not see them down there.*
>
> —Joseph Herity

IN THE months after their first meeting in the quad, Stephen Browder and Kate O'Gara moved slowly from tentative acquaintance to what her mother called "an understanding."

"She's walking out with this young man who'll be a doctor," Kate's mother told her next-door neighbor.

"Ahhh, that's a fine catch," the neighbor said.

"Well, my Kate's no slouch around, and her almost a nurse."

"It'll be a fine thing, two medical people in the family," the neighbor agreed.

On a Friday, late in October, Stephen borrowed a fellow student's car, having arranged to take Kate to the Blackwater Hilltop south of Cork for supper and the dancing afterward. He had been saving for a month to afford this outing and it was a daring thing to do. The B-H, as it was known in Cork, had the reputation of a "fast roadhouse," but their Guinness was the best and their chef brought regular customers from as far away as Dublin.

The car was a six-year-old Citroën whose offside showed a long series of scratches from scraping a bridge abutment. It had once been silver-gray, but the student owner had repainted it a garish fluorescent green.

Kate, suppressing serious guilt feelings, told her mother they were going with other students to the harvest fair at Mallow, and that they planned to stay for the fireworks, the late supper and the music.

Her mother, remembering similar outings in her own youth, admonished: "Now, Katie! Don't let your young man make any advances."

"Stephen is serious, Momma."

"Well, so am I!"

"We'll be back by midnight or soon after, Momma."

"That's very late, Katie. What will the neighbors think?"

"I'll be giving them no cause to think anything, Momma."

"You'll be with the others all the time?"

"All the time," Kate lied.

Once she was in the car with Stephen, the guilt feelings made Kate angry and there was only one target. The sky was still luminous with the long twilight and there was a large moon low on the horizon, almost full, heavy with orange and the promise of a bright night. She stared out at the moon, intensely conscious of Stephen beside her and the privacy of the car, which purred along accompanied by a faint smell of burning oil. Stephen was not an expert driver and he compensated by holding down his speed. Several cars roared around them and cut in sharply, forcing him to swerve.

"Why're we going so slow?" Kate asked.

"There's plenty of time," Stephen said.

His calm, reasonable tone maddened her.

"We shouldn't be doing this, Stephen, and you know it!"

He took his eyes off the road to stare at her and the car followed his gaze, rolling off the left edge of the paving onto gravel. Stephen jerked the wheel and they swerved back onto the paving.

"But you told me you wanted . . ." he began.

"No matter what I said! It's wrong."

"Katie, what's the matter with . . ."

"I lied to Momma." Two tears rolled down her cheeks. "She'll be waiting there, worried. It's not been easy for her, Stephen, since my father died."

Stephen pulled into a lay-by and stopped the car. He turned and faced her. "Katie, you know how I feel about you." He reached for her hand, but she jerked it away. "I'll not have you sad," he said.

"Then let's really go to the fair." She looked at him, her eyes glistening. "That way it'll not really have been a lie."

"If that's what you want, Katie."

"Oh, it is, it is."

"Then that's what we'll be doing."

"It'll save your money, too, Stephen," she said, reaching for his hand. "You can buy that new stethoscope you've been wanting."

Stephen kissed her fingers, realizing that he had been maneuvered and this likely was a pattern that would be repeated many times in their life together. More than anything else, this amused him. He had no doubts they would be married after his graduation. And how like Katie it was, thinking of saving the money and the benefit to himself. He had mentioned the need for a new stethoscope only once. Again, she pulled away her hand.

The headlights of an approaching car bathed her in a brief glare, leaving him with the image of her sitting stiffly, fists clenched in her lap, eyes tightly closed.

"I love you, Katie," he said.

"Oh, Stephen," she sighed. "Sometimes I ache with the love of you. It's just . . ."

"It's the waiting," he said.

"Shall we go to Mallow?" she asked.

He started the car and turned back the way they had come, thinking as he drove how lucky he was to have found Kate.

"Let's go around Cork," she said. "If someone should see us . . . well, we shouldn't be seen coming from this direction."

"I know a shortcut to the Mallow Road," he said.

She smiled in the darkness. "Is that where you take all your girls?"

"Katie!"

"It's bad of me to tease," she said.

They drove in silence while Stephen turned off onto a narrow lane with high hedgerows on either side. This brought them presently to the Mallow Road at the eighteen-kilometer signpost.

"We'll be stopping at the Bridge House for petrol," Stephen said. "They've a restaurant."

"There'll be food at the fair," she said.

"You're not hungry?"

"Now that I think on it, a sandwich would be fine."

And cheaper, he thought. Kate seldom stopped being practical. It was a trait he admired. She'd be a good manager.

At the Bridge House, he bought two beef sandwiches and two bottles of Guinness, passing them through the open window to Kate before paying for the petrol.

"The man says it's going thin, the left front tire," she said.

"I've had a look at your spare," the attendant said. "Would you be liking it changed?"

"No." Stephen shook his head. "We've only a little ways to go."

"I'd be traveling it slow like," the attendant said. He accepted Stephen's money and made the change. "Slow as a peddler's cart and the horse ready for the knackers."

Stephen hesitated, then: "Slow 'tis."

He eased the car gently out of the Bridge House driveway behind a long lorry, which pulled away from him as he held his speed to forty kilometers an hour.

Now that there was a reason to go slowly and they were headed for Mallow, Kate found herself content. She rested her head against the back of the seat and looked at Stephen. It was good to be here with him. She could see a whole lifetime of interludes such as this. They would start saving for a car, she thought. It was none too soon, automobiles being so dear. She was about to say this to him when the left front tire blew. The car swerved onto the verge, bumped over a curbing stone and slewed sideways on grass, coming to a stop with the headlights illuminating a grass-grown private driveway between two broken-down gateposts. The gate itself lay on its side against the right-hand post, leaving the driveway open.

Stephen took several deep breaths through his open mouth, then: "Katie, are you all right?" His hands ached where they clutched the steering wheel.

"Shaken a bit," she said. "Should we be pulling off the road?"

Stephen swallowed and eased the car ahead into the grass-grown driveway. The way turned left almost immediately and his headlights revealed the burned-out ruin of a cottage, all the charred roof beams collapsed into the center. He stopped the motor and they sat there a moment, listening to the insects and the faint murmuring of a nearby brook. Moonlight poured over the hills behind the ruined cottage. There was a forlorn feeling about the place.

"Well, I'd best be changing the tire," he said.

"I'd like a sandwich first," she said.

He agreed and found an old blanket in the back, spreading it on the grass beside the car, then turning off the headlights. The moon was bright.

"Almost like day," Kate said as she brought the food to the blanket.

They sat facing each other, chewing in unison, clinking their bottles of Guinness in a toast to the blown tire, the moon, to the folk "who lived here when it was a happy house."

Presently, Stephen finished his sandwich and drained his beer. Kate grinned at him. She didn't know whether it was the drink or just being here with Stephen, but she felt an enormous sense of contentment. This didn't stop her from saying as he stood up:

"You'll get your jacket all dirty. Take it off and the shirt with it now."

She stood up and helped him, folding the garments neatly and placing them on the edge of the blanket. He wore no undershirt, and the look of his bare chest in the moonlight she thought one of the most beautiful sights in the universe. Almost of its own volition, her right hand went out and his chest was warm beneath her caressing palm.

How it all happened she could never fully explain afterward, even to her best friend and fellow student, Maggie MacLynn.

"Ohhh, he was so strong, Maggie. I couldn't help m'self. Nor did I want to. That's shameless of me, I know, but it . . ."

"Well, join the club, Katie darlin'. Will you be marrying now, I suppose?"

They sat alone together the following Monday on the quad, having an early lunch. Maggie had drawn the story out of her, having noticed Kate's quiet withdrawal. It had taken only a reminder of their childhood pledge "never to lie to each other about important things."

A tall, slender woman with hair the color of old gold, Maggie was considered one of the campus beauties. Some of the nursing students whispered that Maggie had chosen Kate as a friend "to set off her own looks." But the truth was they had been close friends from childhood, since their first day of primary school.

Maggie repeated her question, then: "Didn't he even propose?"

"I don't know what I'll say in confession, Maggie," Kate said. "God help me, what'll I do?"

"What you say is this: 'Father forgive me. I've had a sexual experience.' Tell him it was the drink and the great power of the man and you'll never do it again."

"But what if we do?" Kate wailed.

"I try to go to a different priest," Maggie said, matter-of-fact. "It saves the explainin'." She studied Kate a moment. "I know you, Katie. Will you be marryin' now?"

"Don't be stupid!" Kate flared, then: "I'm sorry, Maggie. But he was at me about that all the way back. And you know we can't marry until he graduates and maybe not until he has his own shingle out. We're not rich, you know."

"Then be careful, girl. You're the marryin' kind, the both of you. And there's nothing like a little pregnancy to hurry things along."

"You think I don't know that?"

> *There was this Irish brain surgeon ... (pause for laughter)*
>
> —British music hall routine

By the time he neared St. Louis, Missouri, on his third day on the road, John had decided on the name under which he would first conceal himself. There would be other name changes required later, he realized, but a new one was needed immediately.

It was early afternoon and already there was color in the deciduous trees along the highway. The hills were brown and a nip could be felt in the air. The cornfields were a rubble of cut and broken stalks. Billboards advertised "winterizing."

There would be a world-wide hunt for John Roe O'Neill before long. That name had to be abandoned, he thought. McCarthy—that had been his mother's name and it felt comfortable. Someone might make the connection but he would have abandoned it by then. His first name, that he felt he would have to keep; too late to learn to answer to anything other than John. John McCarthy, then, and to give it the proper Irish-American flavor, John Leo Patrick McCarthy.

He entered the city and was enclosed by its living movement without much noticing. His awareness was goal-oriented: ordinary lodging. A Central District motel rented him a room and he still had time to lease a large safety deposit box in a nearby bank. The money went into this box and he breathed easier when he emerged onto the street, which was busy with its evening foot traffic.

As he drove out of the parking lot, he glanced at his wrist-watch: 4:55 P.M. Still plenty of time to take those first steps on the identity change. A newspaper classified advertisement led him to a rental room in a private suburban home. The landlady, Mrs. Pradowski, reminded him of Mrs. Neri: the same heavily weighted and cost-accounting watchfulness in her manner and behind the eyes. It was too soon to become John McCarthy. He had to leave a few "footprints" for the blood-hounds to follow. He showed Mrs. Pradowski his O'Neill driver's license and said he was looking for a teaching post.

Mrs. Pradowski said he could have the room tomorrow morning. She gave no sign that she recognized his name from the news stories, now months old. The Grafton Street bombing was, after all, many tragedies back in time and far distant from St. Louis. Her conversation revealed a primary interest in advance payment of rent and noninterference with her "bingo nights."

Now, to find out if the choice of St. Louis was correct. A pharmacy customer had warned him the previous winter: "They got a regular factory there making phony ID papers. You gotta watch it when you're cashing checks."

It took him six days and uncounted glasses of beer in seedy bars to make contact with the "factory." Eight days later he paid five thousand dollars and received a Michigan driver's license and assorted membership and identification cards in the name of John Leo Patrick McCarthy. Another thirty-five hundred dollars got him an intensive lesson in altering passports plus a kit for making the alterations.

"You got a real talent for this," his instructor said. "Just don't set up shop in my territory."

Next, there was the problem of the car. Honest Andrew's Previously Owned Cars on Auto Row gave him twenty-two hundred dollars cash, the dealer sighing: "Boy, them big cars don't move too fast anymore."

The next morning, he took a bus to Marion and bought a used Dodge Power Wagon. It was one of Mrs. Pradowski's "bingo nights" and she was gone when he returned. He parked in the driveway, the wagon's license plates obscured by mud, and loaded his gear. A note with fifty dollars "for the inconvenience" went on the kitchen table weighted by his house key. His note said a family crisis called him away unexpectedly.

John spent the night in an outlying motel, collected his money from the safety deposit box in the morning, and John Leo Patrick McCarthy headed west.

The transition had gone much more simply than he had anticipated. There remained one more essential detail to complete it. Over the next three days, he removed the hair from his head. There had been a choice—shave or do something more permanent. He chose the latter course, not an insurmountable task for a biochemist, although it proved painful and left a fine network of pink scars, tiny veins that he knew would fade in time.

The mole on his left cheek vanished under an application of liquid nitrogen, leaving a scabbed sore that would in time become a puckered dimple.

The change fascinated him. He examined it carefully in the bathroom mirror of a Spokane motel. The flashing neon of an adjoining hamburger stand cast a baleful stroboscopic glare across the side of his face as the light flashed on the bathroom's drawn shade. He smiled. John Roe O'Neill, rather plump and with a rich matt of brown hair, a distinctive mole on his cheek, had become this bald, slender man with eyes of a burning intensity.

"Hello, John Leo Patrick McCarthy," he whispered.

Four days later, the first Friday in October, he moved into a furnished rental house in the Ballard suburb of Seattle, Washington. He had a one-year lease and only a bank with which to deal. The owners lived in Florida.

The Ballard house suited his purpose perfectly. The ease with which he had found it struck him as an omen. The owners had painted it a muddy brown with white trim. It sat anonymously in a mishmash row of other houses equally anonymous. The houses had been built on a long, low embankment, some sporting rockeries, some steep lawns. Most of them possessed daylight basements and garages under the main floor. John's garage opened into the basement with ample room to unload the power wagon.

The furniture was garage-sale jumble and the bed sagged. Old cooking smells permeated the house and persisted in the draperies. There was an odor of stale tobacco in the bathroom. He flushed the toilet and caught his reflection in the mirror over the sink.

None of his old mildness had survived. The *Other* was driven from within. He leaned close to the mirror and looked at the puckering scar where he had removed the mole. In that pitted void he sensed a final break with his past, the past of Mary who had called the mole his "beauty spot." He tried to remember the sensation of her kiss on that place; this memory, too, had gone. The shifting of his memories, the unchecked displacements, sent a shudder through him. He turned away from the mirror quickly. There were things to do.

In the next few days he made essential changes in the house— translucent film over basement and garage windows to shield him from prying eyes, burglar alarms, a substantial stock of food. The fireproof box went into a bricked-over secret cache he built behind the furnace. Only then did he feel free to start setting up the purchase routine for the special equipment his project required.

The thing that surprised him the most over the following weeks was the ease with which he acquired esoteric necessities. Telephone calls and money orders from anyone putting a "Doctor" in front of his name appeared to be the only requirement. He had everything sent to warehouse and accommodation drops, using different names, always paying cash.

While he was busy, memories remained tame and manageable. At night in bed, though, the shifting kaleidoscope in his mind often kept him awake. It was an odd thing, he thought, and not easily explained. John O'Neill had found it impossible to remember the fatal bomb's explosion. John McCarthy remembered it in detail. He remembered the newspaper clippings. O'Neill's screaming features in the photograph. But that person of the photo was gone. John McCarthy could remember him, though. He could recall the talks with police, the accounts of witnesses, the cadaverous figure of Father Devon, who had never corrected that initial mistake, believing that John had fallen into "a mixed marriage."

John McCarthy found he could put it all together—the sisters at the hospital, the doctors. He could remember his Old Self standing at the bank's window, the orange blast of the explosion. His memory replayed the scene at the slightest provocation—the little car, that brown elbow on the windowsill. There was Mary smiling and laughing as she hustled the twins across the street, the package clutched under her elbow. Odd, John thought, that they never found the package. Obviously it had contained the sweaters for the children. The cost of them had shown up on a credit card bill, Mary's scrawled signature on the receipt.

The entire incident at the Grafton Street corner assumed in time the nature of a movie. It was locked in a sequence that he could call up at will—the crush of people around Mary and the twins, her stopping beside that old Ford . . . and always the orange explosion peppered with shards of black. He found that he could control the flow of it, focus upon particular faces, mannerisms, gestures and bits of personality in that macabre companionship.

And always the orange explosion, the sound thumping in his skull.

These were, he knew, John O'Neill memories, somehow removed from John McCarthy. Insulated. It was like having a television screen in his mind with descriptive pictures and voices.

"Good God! What was that?" the bank manager shouted.

They were a historical record, accurate but failing to touch anything within John McCarthy except that fierce determination to visit horror upon the authors of John O'Neill's agony.

As he grew accustomed to this play of memory, he found it could be expanded backward and forward. The punctual bomb had exploded during their first day in Dublin after an obligatory three days in a castle guest house near Shannon Airport. The three days had put heads and bodies into Ireland's time zone after the flight from the United States.

"Now we have our Irish feet," Mary had said as they registered at the Shelbourne in Dublin.

John had awakened early that first morning in the city of the Black Pool. There had not been one whiff of premonition. Contrast, that was what it had been. He had begun the day with an exuberant feeling of health and happiness—all of which only amplified the later anguish. Tragedies of that dimension should be anticipated by omens, he told himself later. There should be warnings, ways to prepare.

There had been nothing.

He awakened beside Mary in one of the two bedrooms of their suite. Turning toward her, he found himself intensely aware of her loveliness—the tousled hair, the eyelashes brushing her cheeks, the soft rise and fall of her breasts as she breathed deeply in sleep.

The O'Neill thought was clear and simple: *Ahhh, the fortune of this marriage*.

There had been peripheral awareness of the twins sleeping

in the adjoining bedroom, the sounds of morning traffic on the street outside, a smell of baking bread in the air.

A suite, b'gawd!

The McCarthy grandfather would have been proud. "We'll go back someday, lad," the old man had often said. "We'll return in style."

We're here in style, Grampa Jack. You didn't live to see it, but I hope you know about it.

It had been a sad thing that Grampa Jack never made it back to the "old sod." *Back* was probably not the correct word, though, because he had been born on the ship to Halifax.

"All of this for seven hundred rifles!"

That had been the McCarthy family plaint during the "poor times." John had never lost the memory of Grampa Jack's voice regretting the flight from Ireland. It was a story told and retold until it could be called up in total by John O'Neill. The McCarthy silver, buried to keep it from piratical English tax collectors, had been dug up to finance the purchase of seven hundred rifles for a Rising. In the aftermath of defeat, Grampa Jack's father, a price on his head, had spirited the family to Halifax under an assumed name. They had not resumed the McCarthy name until they were safely into the United States, "well away from the thieving British."

In his Dublin hotel room, John O'Neill sat up quietly in the bed, aware then of how Mary's breathing changed as she started to waken. She cleared her throat, but her eyes remained closed.

Mary O'Gara of the Limerick O'Garas.

She had loved Grampa Jack. "What a sweet old man. More Irish than the Irish." None could sing "The Wearing of the Green" with a more stirring voice.

"From your father's people, John Roe O'Neill, you're descended from the Ui Neill. Ard Ri, High Kings, they were on the Hill of Tara."

The grandfather had begun the genealogical litany the same way every time.

"And from the McCarthys, well now, lad, we were kings once, too. Never you forget it. Castle McCarthy was a mighty place and strong men built it."

The O'Neill grandfather had died when John was two. John's father, Kevin Patrick O'Neill, turning away from "the Irishness," had sneered at Grampa Jack's "McCarthy stories." But John's young head had been filled with Troubles and Risings and an abiding hatred of the British. He had particularly enjoyed the stories of Hugh O'Neill's revolt and the rebellion of Owen Roe O'Neill.

"Roe O'Neill, that's part of my name, Grampa."

"Indeed 'tis! And you'd be advised to live your life in a way that gives honor to such illustrious ancestors."

"Burn everything British except their coals!"

How Grampa Jack had laughed at that.

In the Dublin hotel room bed, Mary spoke beside John: "We're really here." Then: "I still miss Grampa Jack."

> *I believe it was Tacitus who said there is a principle of human nature requiring us to hate those we have wronged.*
>
> **—William Beckett, M.D.**

AN EVEN one hundred copies of the first "Madman Letter" went out and the following letters were more numerous. The first letters, all sent from an agency drop in Los Angeles, went to government officials, newscasters, editors and to important scientists. Their message was clear: quarantine the infected areas. To that end, some of the letters carried an additional page calling on scientist recipients to explain the gravity of the situation to their political leaders.

Dr. William Ruckerman, past president of the American Association for the Advancement of Science, received one of the letters with the additional page. It arrived at his San Francisco home with the Monday morning mail and he opened it over breakfast. He realized at once why he had been selected to receive this letter—his own DNA researches were not exactly secret in the scientific community. This letter had been written by someone on the inside or close enough to the inside that the special nuances of Ruckerman's project were known to him.

Ruckerman reread the references to "back translation from the protein" to determine the RNA, "thence to the DNA transcription." That was ordinary enough, but the writer of this letter also made it clear he had used a computer "to sort through the restriction fragments."

That was a bit more esoteric, a bit more inside.

What sent a chill up Ruckerman's spine was the reference to using sterioisomers in translating the RNA sequences in the protein molecules.

"Superimposition to determine the patterns."

Those were the Madman's words.

Ruckerman suspected immediately that the man had used alkene polymerization for part of his breakdown series, conjugation and resonance . . . yes. The man implied as much.

"The letter shows a full understanding of purification and subunit composition techniques," he said to his wife, who was reading over his shoulder. "He *knows*."

There was enough information to convince a knowledgeable reader, Ruckerman realized. This, in itself, said a great deal about the author.

There had to be more to it, Ruckerman knew. The Madman fell short of revealing key facts. But he led up to those facts with chilling accuracy. That, coupled to the threats, stirred Ruckerman to action.

He thought carefully about how to handle this, then sent his wife to pack a suitcase, following her to the bedroom where he placed a call to the President's science advisor, Dr. James Ryan Saddler. Even then, Ruckerman was forced to press his way through a barrier of secretaries.

"Tell him it's Will Ruckerman and it's important."

"Could you tell me the nature of this important matter?" the secretary asked, her voice sweetly insistent.

Ruckerman took two deep breaths to calm himself, staring at his reflection in the bedroom mirror. There were new lines in his angular face and his hair definitely was going gray. His wife, Louise, looked up from the packing, but did not speak.

"Listen, whoever you are," Ruckerman said. "This is *Doctor* Ruckerman, past president of the American Association for the Advancement of Science, a close friend of Jim Saddler. I have important information that the President of the United States should know. If there's any need for you to know, I'm sure someone will tell you. Meanwhile, you patch me through to Jim."

"May I have your telephone number, sir?"

She was all business now. Ruckerman gave her the number and cradled the telephone.

Louise, who had read the Madman letter over his shoulder, asked: "You think that's a real threat?"

"I do." He stood up and went to the bathroom. Returning, he stood beside the bedroom phone and tapped his fingers on the dressertop. They were taking ungodly long about it. He knew they would get through to Saddler, though. Jim had laughingly explained it once.

"The presidency of the United States runs on communication. Not on facts, but on the intangible thing we like to call 'information,' which is a kind of bargaining token exchanged at high levels. Carriers of this information always recognize the value of it. You'd be surprised at how many official reports begin with or include 'We have information that...'. That's not the royal 'we' but the bureaucratic 'we.' It means someone else can be blamed or share the blame if the information proves wrong."

Ruckerman knew he had put on enough pressure that the White House communications system, a military operation, would find Saddler.

The telephone rang. Saddler was at Camp David, a male operator informed him. The science advisor's voice sounded just a bit sleepy.

"Will? What's so damned important you have to—"

"I won't waste your time, Jim. I've received a letter that—"

"From someone calling himself 'The Madman'?"

"That's right. And I—"

"The FBI's on it, Will. Just another crank."

"Jim...I don't think you'd be advised to treat this as a crank letter. His postscript should convince us of—"

"What postscript?"

"The additional page where he gives some of the details about—"

"There's no postscript on our letter. I'll have an agent come around to pick it up."

"Dammit, Jim! Will you listen to me? I've been part way down the path this guy describes. He's no amateur. Now, I'm warning you to treat his threat as real. If I were in your shoes, I'd be counseling the President to take at least the first steps toward complying with—"

"Oh, come on, Will! Do you have any idea of the political

implications? He wants a quarantine! Then he wants us to send all Libyans in the U.S. back to Libya, all Irish back to Ireland, all English back to England—everyone, including their diplomats. We can't just—"

"If we don't, he threatens to bring the U.S. into . . ." Ruckerman paused, then read from the letter: ". . . the net of his revenge."

"I read that and I don't give one bit of credence to—"

"You aren't listening, Jim! I'm telling you it's possible to do what this guy threatens."

"Are you serious?"

"I'm deadly serious."

The line went silent and Ruckerman could hear faint crosstalk, the voices too low to make out the words. Saddler came back on: "Will, if it were anyone else telling me this . . . I mean, deadly new diseases for which there are no natural resistances and . . . How the hell could he spread them?"

"I can think of a dozen easy ways without even straining my imagination."

"Dammit! You're beginning to frighten me."

"Good. This letter scares the shit out of me."

"Will, I'll have to see that postscript before—"

"You won't act on my recommendation?"

"How can I be expected to go in to the—"

"Jim . . . time is important. The President should be briefed immediately. The affected diplomats should be alerted. The military, the police in major cities, health officials, Civil Defense . . ."

"That might cause a panic!"

"You have the main body of his letter. He says he's already loosed this thing. That means quarantine. Damn it all, he says it plain enough: *Let it run its course where I have loosed it. Remember that I can introduce malignancy wherever I choose. If you attempt to sterilize the infected areas by atomic means, I shall give my revenge the open run of every land on this globe.* Read that part again, Jim, and in the light of my warning, you tell me what you should be doing right now."

"Will, if you're wrong, do you have any idea what the repercussions—"

"And if *you're* wrong?"

"You're asking me to take a lot on faith."

"Dammit, Jim, you're a scientist! You should know by now that—"

"Then you tell me, Will, how a disease can be made sex-specific."

"Okay. At the present stage of my own project, which I'm convinced is far behind this Madman... Well, I believe diseases can be tailored to many genetic variations—to white skin, for example; to the susceptibility to sickle-cell anemia..."

"But how could one person... I mean, the cost!"

"Peanuts. I've run a calculation on the required equipment—less than three hundred thousand dollars, including the computer. A basement lab somewhere..." Ruckerman fell silent.

Presently, Saddler said: "I'll want that list of equipment. The suppliers should be able to..."

"I'll read it off to you in a minute, but I think it'll be too late even if we locate his lab."

"You really think..."

"I think he's done it. This letter... he lays out the essentials and there's not a mistake in it. I think Ireland, Great Britain and Libya... and probably the rest of us are in for one terrible time. I don't see how we can totally contain such a thing. But for openers, we'd better set about quarantining those areas... for our own safety if not for other reasons."

"What other reasons?"

"This Madman is still running around loose. We don't want him mad at us."

"Will, he says not a human female will survive in those three nations. I mean, really! How can..."

"I'll give you a more complete analysis later. Right now, I'm begging you to take the necessary first steps. The President should be on that hot line to Moscow and to the other major capitals. He should—"

"Will, I believe I'd better send a plane for you. I don't want to take this to the President by myself. If we have to convince him, well, he knows your reputation and if you—"

"Louise already has packed my bag. And Jim, one of the first things to do is to get as many young women as possible into that Denver hideaway the military is so proud of. Women, got that? And only enough men to run the technical end of a survival plan."

Ruckerman let this sink in—many women, few men, just the opposite of what might occur outside such a sanctuary. He continued:

"The Russians and the other world leaders ought to be advised to take similar action. That'll go a long way toward convincing them of our sincerity. We don't want the Russians thinking this is some diabolical capitalist plot. God knows they're paranoid enough as it is."

"I think we should leave high-level diplomatic decisions to the experts, Will. You just get your ass back here with enough evidence to convince me you're right."

Ruckerman replaced the phone in its cradle and looked across the bedroom at his wife.

"He's going to wait for you," she said.

Ruckerman slammed his fist against the dressertop, making the telephone bounce. "Louise, you take the car. Pack only necessities. Buy as much food as you can safely store and get up to our place at Glen Ellen. Take the guns. I'll be in touch."

I obey the Master of Death.

**—Part of an Ulster
secret society oath**

ACHILL ISLAND, south of Blacksod Bay in County Mayo, stood out against a storm-blown Atlantic morning in which the Irish countryfolk already were active, preparing for the first flow of tourists, getting the hay planted, cutting sods and piling them to dry, generally going about the everyday activities of their lives.

The island was a play of many greens interspersed with spots of black rock and flecks of white where the residents had raised their buildings. Achill, split from the main body of Ireland by the retreat of the last glacier, held few trees. The steep slopes of its hills were lined with furze growing along the sod cutters' furrows and the first marsh violets were beginning to show themselves, competing with stone brambles and saxifrage and the omnipresent heather. Here and there, pennywort had begun to poke its way out of the rocks.

A granite ruin lay crumbled into the weeds atop the hill where the road from Mulrany curved around before dropping down to the bridge across to the island. Its lancet arches and crenellated battlements had collapsed into low mounds covered by a few stunted ivy plants and lichen. The scabbed rock sur-

46

faces gave not a hint of the slitted windows where defenders had failed to repel Cromwell.

Two polite young soldiers with Irish Harp insignia at their shoulders stood at the barricade that blocked the bridge to the island. They already had turned back two tourist autos that had entered the road to the island before the barriers had been raised farther back at Mulrany. The soldiers had apologized for the inconvenience and suggested the tourists go instead to Balmullet, "a beautiful place where the old ways may still be seen." To all questions, the soldiers responded: "We're not at liberty to say, but it's sure to be only temporary."

Three goods lorries traveling tandem with supplies for the island's stores were harder to placate.

"We're very sorry, lads, but it's none of our doing. I agree you should've been warned, but it's no use complaining. Orders is orders. This road is closed."

Four armored cars with a major in charge pulled up as the soldiers were arguing with the lorry drivers. The major and a sergeant jumped out, the sergeant with an automatic rifle held at the ready. The major, a thin, stony-eyed man with bushy gray hair under a forage cap, accepted the salutes of the two soldiers, then turned to the lorry drivers.

"Back the way you came, lads. No more arguing."

One of the drivers started to speak, but the major cut him short. "Turn those lorries around and get out of here or one of my men will drive them into the water and we'll take you back under guard!"

Muttering, the drivers climbed into their cabs, backed the lorries into the car park beside the bridge and headed up the road to Mulrany. The major stepped over to his radioman in one of the armored cars and said: "Alert Mulrany to keep those lads moving out."

Returning to the two soldiers at the bridge barricade, he swiveled slowly, studying his surroundings, taking in the high hill above Pullrany and the higher crown of Corraun beyond; there was Alice's Harbour Inn beside the car park, the barricade, the white buildings across the bridge on the island, a group of men standing there, heads close together, talking intently. Presently, the major returned to his radioman and inquired:

"Have the patrol boats taken up position at the Bulls Mouth and Achillbeg?"

The radioman, a pimply young man with nervous manners, bent over his microphone and, in a moment, said: "They're in place, sir, and one's coming down from the Bulls Mouth to pick up the islanders' small boats."

"Good," the major said. "We don't want any boats left over there to tempt them into leaving." He sighed. "Damned stupid mess." He strolled back to the armored cars then and told a sergeant: "Better get the men deployed. No one enters or leaves, except the medics, of course, and they'll be coming by helicopter." The major went into Alice's then and he could be heard inquiring if there was any coffee.

Some two kilometers back up the road toward Mulrany, three squads of soldiers under a lieutenant finished setting up a row of tents in the lee of the hill that commanded the narrow, salty moat separating Achill from Ireland proper. A sandbag emplacement with two machine guns had already been installed on the slope above the tents.

When the tents were up, the lieutenant instructed a corporal: "Take your squad and notify all the locals they're to stay close to home; no wandering about and no going over to the island. Tell them it's a quarantine and nothing more."

On Corraun Hill's 526-meter peak, about four kilometers south of this position, more soldiers had piled sandbags onto a section of an old castle ruin, forming a shelter for two twenty-millimeter cannon and four mortars. It began to rain while they were positioning the mortars. They spread shelter halves over the weapons, then huddled in their waterproofs while a colonel standing slightly below them peered through binoculars at Achill.

"A lot of moving around over there," the colonel said. "I'll be happier when we have their small boats and the water closed to them."

One of the soldiers above him ventured: "Colonel, is it a bad sickness they have over there?"

"So I've been told," the colonel said. He lowered his glasses, scanned the emplacement, fixing his gaze finally on a tall sergeant who stood somewhat apart. "Get some shelters up, Sergeant. And you're to look sharp. Only the medics are to enter that place and no one's to leave."

"We'll not let so much as a fox through, sir."

Turning away, the colonel took long-legged strides down the slope to a jeep waiting on the narrow track below the emplacement.

As one, the soldiers he had left behind looked across at Achill, the island of the eagles, which no longer were there. It was a brooding landscape in the rain, a speckling of white rocks and buildings against the greens. The few roads cut gray ledges around the hills. The ocean was a deeper gray below. Slievemore and Croaghaun thrust almost into the clouds toward Achill Head's outer cliffs. It was a place turned in upon itself and the men looking across at the island could feel the simmering mood of the land. Generations of men and women had brooded passionately there on the wrongs done to Ireland. No Irishman could fail to sense that thing smoldering there, the sullen hopes of all those who had perished for "The Irish Dream."

"It'll be a scurrying-around time for the priests," the sergeant said, then: "Now, men, you heard the colonel. Shouldn't we be raising some shelters?"

Far below this position and at the Achill end of the bridge where the town street became the highroad to the island's interior, Mulvaney's Saloon Bar had begun to collect a crowd of local residents and a few tourists. They hunched against the rain, hurrying from cars and bicycles into the bar's steamy interior with its thick smells of wet wool and beer. Mulvaney's, a two-story whitewashed building with slate roof and three massive chimneys, was one of the island's natural assembly points. It was soon crowded with men talking too loudly, their faces angry, their gestures abrupt and latent with violence.

A small Garda patrol car pulled up outside, bringing a lull in the conversations as the word of it spread through the bar. Denis Flynn, the local Garda, emerged form the car. Flynn, a small blond man with light blue eyes and a boyish face, appeared pale and trembling. Way was made for him as he entered the bar, pressed through the crowd to the western end and climbed onto a chair.

In the expectant silence, Flynn's voice was a thin tenor, which broke in unexpected places. "We've been quarantined," he said. "They're sending medical teams by helicopter. No one is to enter or leave the island except the medical people and officials."

In the sudden babble of shouted questions, Flynn raised his voice to demand silence, then: "We'll just have to be patient. Everything's being done that can be done."

Mulvaney, a soft giant of a man with a bald head as shiny as his polished bar, thrust his way through the crowd to stand below Flynn. Hooking a thumb over his shoulder, Mulvaney said: "It's my Molly sick back there and only the one doctor. I want to know what it is."

"I'm only the Garda," Flynn said. "It's the medical men will have to answer that."

Mulvaney glanced out the windows beyond Flynn, looking toward Knockmore and the village of Droega, which lay hidden beyond the hills in the hollow that protected it from the worst of the Atlantic gales. His brother, Francis, had called from there not ten minutes ago to report another death, his voice full of tears as he spoke.

Turning a hard stare up at Flynn, Mulvaney said: "Your womenfolk are living safe beyond Mulrany. You can take the official view. But it's my sister-in-law, Shaneen, died this morning."

A man back in the press of people shouted: "And my Katie has the sickness! We want answers, Flynn, and we want them now!"

"I've told you what I know," Flynn said. "That's all I can do."

"What's this about officials coming?" Mulvaney demanded.

"From the Health Office in Dublin."

"Why do they have soldiers barring our way?" someone else demanded. "They've even guns up on Corraun!"

"There's no need to create a panic," Flynn said. "But it's a serious matter."

"Then why do we not hear it on the wireless?" Mulvaney asked.

"Haven't I said we don't want a panic?"

"It's the plague, isn't it?" Mulvaney asked.

An abrupt silence settled over the room. A small dark man with pinched features, standing at Flynn's right, cleared his throat.

"There's our own boats," the man said.

"There'll be none of that, Martin!" Flynn snapped, glaring down at the speaker. "The navy'll be here in a few minutes to collect your boats. My orders are to prevent your leaving Achill . . . using what force necessary."

His voice hoarse, Mulvaney asked: "Are all of our women-enfolk to die then? Nineteen dead since yesterday and only the women and girls. Why is that, Denis?"

"The doctors will find the answer," Flynn said. He jumped

down off the chair, steadying himself against Mulvaney, but
not looking the man in the eye. Flynn's own superintendent
had voiced that same fear less than an hour earlier, speaking
with gentle firmness over the telephone.

"If all the women die there it could be very bad, Denis.
And there's talk it was done deliberately. You're not to speak
of that now!"

"Deliberate? By the Ulstermen or the British?"

"I'll not discuss it, Denis. I speak only to impress you with
the gravity of our situation. You there inside the quarantine
will be alone for a bit to represent authority. We depend on
you."

"Will I get no help then?"

"Some soldiers are being asked to volunteer, but they'll not
be along until the afternoon."

"I didn't volunteer, sir."

"But you swore an oath to do your duty and that's what I'm
asking of you now!"

As he pressed his way out of Mulvaney's, ignoring the
questions still being shouted at him, Flynn recalled that telephone conversation. There had been more orders and things he
must do now.

The rain had turned to a light mist as he emerged from the
bar. He got into his car, not looking at the angry faces peering
at him from Mulvaney's. Starting the motor, he turned around
and drove slowly down to the concrete apron overlooking Achill
Sound and the fishboats anchored there. He could see a fast
patrol boat spreading a wide bow wave as it sped down from
the Bulls Mouth. It appeared to be no more than five minutes
away, for which he was thankful. He parked on the concrete
and took his shotgun from its rack, feeling strange with the
weapon in his hands. The superintendent had been firm with
his instructions.

"I want you on armed watch, Denis, until they pick up those
small boats. I want it understood that you'll use your weapon
if necessary."

Flynn stared bleakly across the water at the approaching
patrol boat. Seabirds were wheeling and calling over the strand.
He inhaled the familiar salt odors, the smell of the seaweeds
and the pungency of fish. How many times had he looked on
this scene and never thought it strange? Flynn wondered. Now,
though . . . the differences sent a shuddering through his thin

body. The thing he had wanted to say back at Mulvaney's, the thing that had filled his throat with sourness, stood uppermost in his mind.

But his superintendent had been adamant on the need for secrecy. "A great many women are sure to die, perhaps all on the island. We count on you to keep the peace until help arrives. There must be no panic, no mobs. You must be firm in keeping order."

"I should've told them," Flynn muttered to himself. "They should be bringing in the priests. It's sure nothing else will help them now."

He stared out at the moored fishboats, feeling a deep loneliness and a sense of inadequacy.

"Lord help us now in the hour of our need," he whispered.

Not since the Black Death struck Ireland in the winter of 1348 has there been such a terrible time with disease.

—Fintan Craig Doheny

ON THE day before the Achill Island quarantine, Stephen Browder and Kate O'Gara drove off together to Lough Derg, planning to lunch near Killaloe and then drive on to a cottage on the lake near Cloonoon. It was to be a stolen three days together before examinations and a hectic summer schedule for Stephen, who now planned to specialize in high-pressure medicine.

The cottage, a remodeled farmhouse, belonged to Adrian Peard, who had graduated six years ahead of Stephen and already was recognized as an important researcher in pressure medicine and the ailments of divers. Peard, scion of a wealthy old County Cork family, had established a vacation and weekend base at the cottage on the lake, installing a large steel pressure-decompression tank in the barn behind the cottage. Stephen had been several times to the cottage, earning money as a guinea pig in Peard's experiments.

Since their first *sexual experience* beside the Mallow Road, Kate had rationed them to one or two repeats a month and then only at her least fertile times. She had resisted this outing at first because it coincided with her highest fertility period, but

Stephen had promised to "be careful." Kate, not certain what that meant, had warned:

"We'll not be having any bastards in our family, Stephen Browder!"

They had arranged the outing with care. Kate ostensibly was with her friend, Maggie, on a holiday in Dublin. Stephen supposedly was boating with friends near Kinsale.

Peard, who had guessed the nature of Stephen's involvement with Kate, had volunteered the use of his Lough Derg cottage "when it doesn't interfere with my schedule." He had handed over the keys with a laugh and the admonition: "Leave the place neat and do try to get in a little time for study. I'd like you with me someday, Stephen. You have a talent for solving unusual problems . . . such as this one."

As Peard had expected, Stephen blushed—as much from the praise as from the conspiracy.

The car they took was a tiny green Fiat whose use Stephen had earned tutoring its owner in the niceties of kidney function, a subject that baffled the Fiat's owner until Stephen hit on the stratagem of a large drawing with signposts on pins through which the student was required to maneuver a tiny cardboard automobile labeled "foreign matter." It amused Stephen and Kate to call the Fiat "foreign matter" as they drove north.

A few minutes before noon they crossed the narrow old stone bridge into Killaloe. The castellated tower of St. Flannery's Cathedral stood out like a Norman sentinel against a gathering of clouds on the horizon. The sky overhead was blue, however, and the lake was a blue-and-emerald mirror to the surrounding hills, its surface rippled by a light wind and the passage of a quartet of swans.

Just north of Killaloe, Stephen stopped at a roadside "gypsy stand" for sandwiches, chips and beer, which they ate in the meadow beside the mound where Brian Boru had raised his castle. Their picnic site looked down on Ballyvalle Ford where Patrick Sarsfield and his six hundred troopers had crossed the Shannon on the night of August 10, 1690, during the Siege of Limerick.

Kate, fascinated by her nation's history and a little awed to be "in this very place," began regaling Stephen with the story of Sarsfield's ride when she found him unfamiliar with the details. Watching her color rise as she talked about that "wonderful, futile ride" against the Williamite siege train, Stephen looked longingly at the concealing shade of the trees that hid the circular foundation of Brian Boru's castle, wondering if Kate might agree to walk into that sheltering bower with him for a time. But he could hear children shouting at the lake below the meadow, and the picnic site soon was buzzing with flies attracted by the food. They wolfed their food and ran back to the car, pursued by the flies.

In the shelter of the car, Kate looked back at the meadow and surprised Stephen with a mystical side of her nature that he had not suspected.

"Terrible things were done in that place, Stephen. I can feel it. Could the flies be the souls of the evil men who did those terrible things?"

"Ahhh, now, Kate! What a thing to say."

She did not really cheer up until they turned down the graveled track to the cottage and she saw the old double chimney pot above the trees. When they entered the cottage, she was almost childlike in her admiration.

Stephen, who had come to understand and enjoy most of her moods, took a positive delight in showing her around. The kitchen had been remodeled from its old farmhouse days, a large window added on the lakeside, every piece of equipment not only modern but the best available.

Kate put her hands to her cheeks as she looked at it. "Oh, Stephen, if only we can have a house like this."

"We will, someday, Kate."

She turned and hugged him.

Outside, there was a small orchard and an area set off by stones for a kitchen garden. The barn stood on the far side of the orchard. It was a stone building with a new corrugated metal roof, and was easily half again as big as the house. A tall growth of weeds lapped against the stone sides of the barn but the path from the house through the orchard to a small side door was clear and neatly trimmed at the borders.

Stephen unlocked the padlock and swung the door open for Kate. He flipped the light switch beside the door as she stepped through. Brilliant illumination flooded the one large room, pouring down from banks of reflectors suspended from the rafters by pipes. The big tank dominated the center of the area. It was a full six meters long, two and a quarter meters in diameter. There were two quartz windows on each side, small and set at eye level, plus another even smaller quartz window in the pressure-sealed airlock hatch at the near end.

Kate, who had heard Stephen's descriptions of his stays in the tank, said: "It's so small. Did you really stay in there four days once?"

"It's comfortable enough," he said. "There's a double-seal sanitary exhaust system. It has a telephone. The only uncomfortable part was wearing all the connections for Peard to monitor my vital signs."

Stephen led Kate around to the far side, showing her the long bench of instruments there, the leads into the tank and, at the end, the racks and shelves of scuba gear that they used in the lough, and then at the far end, the two French-made compressors with their elaborate air filters.

Kate peered through one of the quartz windows into the tank. "I'd be bored silly in there all that time," she said.

"I took some of my books. Really, Kate, it was quite peaceful. I studied and slept most of the time."

Kate pushed herself away from the cold metal and brushed her hands against her skirt. "I want to make us a fine dinner in that kitchen," she said. "I've never seen such a grand kitchen. Did you get all the things on my list?"

"They're in the boot."

While Kate busied herself in the kitchen, Stephen brought in their suitcases, the separate packs of their books from school and Peard's blood-saturation tables. He left the suitcases on the bed, made sure Kate did not need anything more from the store at the village, then set himself up to study in the tiny parlor. He could hear Kate humming as she worked, the clatter of pans. It was possible to imagine the two of them safely married, a calm domesticity about their lives. The mood stayed with him all through dinner and right up to the instant in bed when he showed Kate how he intended to be careful. He held up a condom that one of his fellow students had bought in England.

Kate, her face flushed, grabbed it out of his hand and hurled it across the room.

"Stephen! It's sin enough what we do, but I'll not have that on my soul!"

It took him almost an hour to calm her, but then she was especially tender, crying against his shoulder and laughing. They went to sleep with her head cradled against his chest.

Stephen awoke late to the sound of Kate again busy in the

kitchen. He had not expected this domestic side of her nature and it filled him with a warm satisfaction. She had the wireless on and was humming along with the music. Stephen looked at his watch on the bedstand, shocked to find it almost 11:00 A.M., vaguely aware that the music from the wireless had stopped and a man's voice was speaking with controlled excitement.

When he had bathed, dressed and entered the kitchen, he asked: "What was that news broadcast? I couldn't make it out."

"Oh, just some trouble up at Achill," she said. "Will you be having one egg or two?"

"Three," he said, kissing the back of her neck.

"Can we go swimming in the lake?" she asked.

"It'll be cold but we can come back and be warm."

She blushed. Stephen started to turn her around, but the ringing of the telephone interrupted.

He was a time finding the telephone behind a stack of magazines on a stand in the parlor. It was Peard

"Ah, thank God you're there, Stephen. Is your friend with you?"

Stephen hesitated, then: "Yes, but I don't . . ."

"There's no time for niceties! I've been called to a big medical meeting by Fintan Doheny. The subject matter should concern you."

"Doheny? *The* Doheny? What could—"

"I've not much time, Stephen. A madman with knowledge of recombinant DNA has released a new plague up at Achill. They've quarantined the place but no one expects it to be contained there. Now, listen carefully. It seems this plague kills only women. It's one hundred percent fatal so far. Now, it occurred to me that you and your friend are at the cottage and we've that lovely tank in the barn. A woman in that tank with positive pressure in there would be in a pretty effective isolation. Do you understand what I'm saying?"

"Certainly I understand, but I don't see how . . ."

"I've no time to argue. I'm just asking that you do this thing on my request."

Stephen glanced over at Kate, who was standing looking at him.

"I don't know if she'd . . . I mean, you're asking me to . . ."

"I must be going, Stephen. Do whatever you must to get her in that tank. Get in with her if necessary. Connect the telephone. I'll call you there later. Will you do it?"

Stephen took a deep breath. "This plague . . ."

"It's already killed a number of women. We don't know where else the madman may have spread it. Get your friend into that tank!"

Peard broke the connection.

Violence endured too long leads to moral anesthesia. It degrades even religious leaders. Society is separated into sacrificial lambs and those who wield the knives. High-sounding labels mask the bloody reality: phrases with words such as "Freedom" and "Political Autonomy" and the like. Such words have little meaning in a world without morality.

—Father Michael Flannery

ALL BUT twenty of John Roe O'Neill's letters had been mailed before FBI agents entered the Los Angeles drop with a warrant. The drop was a tiny office room in a brick building on Figueroa near downtown LA. It was operated by a Miss Sylvia Trotter, a bony woman in her fifties with hair of a wild henna and heavily rouged cheeks. The two young agents, as alike as clones in their neat blue suits, flipped open their wallets to give her a flashing glance at the identification cards then, like synchronized dancers, returned their wallets to their pockets and demanded to know about the O'Neill letters.

What had been her contact with the author of those letters? Had she seen the contents of any of the letters? Not even one letter? What address had the author of those letters given her?

They examined her records and took away a copy of her ledger, leaving Miss Trotter in damp and nervous confusion.

The agents, trained as both accountants and lawyers, were disgusted with Miss Trotter's laxity. She had not even photocopied the check from the Henry O'Malley who had set up this arrangement! O'Malley, with a false address in Topeka, Kansas, had paid by cashier's checks on a Topeka bank. Even before they investigated, the agents knew Topeka would be a dry well. There was no one at the bank who even remembered this O'Malley's appearance.

The twenty letters they collected with Miss Trotter's ledger included five that suggested the author had anticipated an official visit from investigators. The five were addressed to prominent religious leaders and were headed: "Warning to the authorities!"

They explained that the Madman was hooked to a "deadman switch" that would automatically flood the world with more and different plagues should "anyone interfere with me."

Photocopies of all the letters from the Madman were among the first pieces of evidence studied at the Denver Isolation Center by The Team, as they came to be known. The Team's first meeting came twenty-nine days after the Achill demonstration, a delay caused by political indecision in high places, an indecision which was put aside only after chilling developments worldwide.

O'Neill's disease, now being called *the white plague* because of the pallor of its victims and white blotches that appeared on the extremities, obviously was not being contained in Ireland, Britain and Libya. Looseness of the first quarantine had been largely evaded or ignored by high officials, by the wealthy trying to get their loved ones to safety, by financial messengers, criminals and investigators and others. White Plague outbreaks were being reported all around the world. There was a pocket of it in Brittany. It contaminated a corridor in the United States from Boston almost to Weymouth. The western slopes of the Cascades from well into British Columbia south into California and to the Pacific had to be cordoned off under a brutal quarantine. The World Health Organization's list of "hot spots" included Singapore, Perth (Australia), New Delhi, Santa Barbara, St. Louis, Houston, Miami, Constantinople, Nairobi, Vienna . . . and these were just the most prominent places.

The Team had the current list of "hot spots" and the O'Neill letters when they sat down for their first meeting at the DIC. They met in an underground room, its walls paneled in dark wood. They had a choice of cold, indirect lighting or warmly intimate illumination focused only on the long table around which they gathered. A psychoanalyst probably could have derived deep significance from the fact that they chose the revealing wash of indirect lighting for that first meeting. All six members of The Team knew they were there to study each other as well as the problem.

Selection of The Team's members had cost long hours of searching questions in sound-insulated rooms and by people who raised their voices only for emphasis. The six were divided by nationality—two each from the Soviet Union, from France and from the United States. It had been planned to introduce other nationals later, but circumstances intervened.

William Beckett of the United States pair, who was to become nominal chairman of The Team, came to the first meeting with a particular worry that had been ignited by the devastating plague outbreak on the West Coast of his nation. Had the area been contaminated by disease fractions that had escaped from an insecure laboratory? (It already was suspected that the Madman had set up his laboratory in the Seattle area.) The others were too busy measuring each other, however, and he saved his concern for later.

Ruckerman, who had been Beckett's professor at Harvard, had experienced little difficulty putting his prize pupil on The Team. The selection board had been awed by Beckett's talents and accomplishments: public health consultant on bubonic plague; world-class skipper of racing sailboats; commercial aircraft pilot's license with jet training (a major in the Air Force Reserve); a hobby of creating and solving "brain-twister" puzzles; a consultant on the military code system, "Diascrambler"; a distance swimmer and a generally respected handball player.

"A molecular biologist second to none," Ruckerman had said. "A Renaissance man."

Beckett was a sandy-haired descendant of Scots-English religious refugees. He had the pink skin and pale eyes to go with this ancestry, but features that a college date had described as "latent coarse." Beckett had been a college football linebacker until discovering that the constant jarring collisions of football might scramble his proudest possession—a mind to which most puzzles submitted after a skirmish more exciting than any on the gridiron.

The college date's prediction had proved accurate: Beckett had large, heavy features, but the mind had improved.

Within minutes of meeting Francois Danzas of the French contingent, Beckett had known it would be difficult working with the Frenchman. Danzas was a tall, slender and dark native of Peronne with traces of Celt, Roman, Greek and Viking in his genes. His obviously dyed hair was swept back in two raven's wings over a face that often appeared blank and empty except for the large brown eyes. These stared out in constant incredulity at a world of caprice, now glaring, now withdrawn beneath their heavy black brows. Whenever Danzas closed his eyes, his faced emptied, leaving only that long nose and a narrow, almost lipless mouth. Even the dark brows seemed to fade. As the Brittany expression had it, Danzas was as tough as an old saddle. Seasoned by much use, weathered and shaped, he was now a visible repository of valuable experiences. Danzas relied on Danzas. He knew himself in jeopardy only when traveling or when eating foreign food. Foreigners, especially the English and, by language association, the Americans, were to be distrusted as fundamentally unsound, capable of evil and would cooperate only under duress. The White Plague, for Danzas, merely represented the present duress. In spite of the fact that he looked down his long Gallic nose at Americans, Danzas was recognized in his homeland as an expert on all things Yankee. Had he not endured four interminable years on an exchange-research program in Chicago? Where better to learn Yankee ways than in the Hog Capital of the world?

Danzas could understand the capriciousness of life where this touched on his living arrangements, but not in his laboratory. In the lab, Danzas always expected to be eyewitness to the virgin birth if not the immaculate conception. Certain responsibilities fell upon such an eyewitness. Two observers of the event could not come up with two different stories. Thirty eyewitnesses must produce the same account. It was an infallible rule. A pope could rely on no better.

The joke in France was that Danzas had been put on The Team as contrast to his French companion, Jost Hupp. Hupp's horn-rimmed glasses, the slightly bulging eyes, the youthful insouciance of his features, all conspired to a totality that invited sharing. Those who called Hupp a romantic failed to focus on the underlying strength of his fantasy world. He used romance as Beckett used a concealed anger. Where Beckett's muse led him to a raging intellectual striving, Hupp's muse was endearing and promoted a gregarious sharing of everything—successes, failures, joys, griefs . . . everything. Threaded through this complex personality was an Alsatian tenacity compounded of both French *and* German ancestors. It was in part a hangover from early influence by the Roman Catholic Church. Mephistopheles was real. God was real. The White Knight was real. The grail remained the eternal goal.

There was a pattern in this deeply satisfying to Hupp. Without it, he would have been merely a researcher, a man in a white coat, not white armor.

Beckett thought Hupp was okay. A little weird but okay. Danzas, however, was a scientific prig of the worst sort. What the hell difference did it make where this team assembled just so long as the facilities were acceptable? It angered Beckett that he would have to work with this prig for God alone knew how long. He kept the anger sufficiently under wraps that only Hupp suspected.

Many people had worked with Beckett for years without realizing that he operated on regular anger fixes. He could find something to anger him almost anywhere and, thus charged up, went headlong into the problem confronting him. The White Plague was made to order for Beckett. That son-of-a-bitch! That fucked-up Madman! What right had he to disrupt a world that, admittedly not perfect, was stumbling along in its usual fashion?

Little of this anger escaped an amiable mask. He seldom spoke harshly. If anything, he was even more amiable with Danzas, which brought out the Frenchman's most correct and stiffly proper courtesy. It was a matter of mutual fury that amused Hupp.

The other member of the U.S. contingent, Hupp observed, was the real surprise package, especially to the two from the Soviet Union, Sergei Alexandrovich Lepikov and Dorena Godelinsky. They kept looking speculatively at Beckett's companion, Ariane Foss.

At six feet six inches and 288 pounds, Foss was easily the largest person present. The French dossier on Foss judged her one of the five or six best medical heads in the United States on what her country-doctor grandfather had called "female complaints." Both the French and the Soviets suspected she was with the Central Intelligence Agency. It was noted that she spoke five languages fluently—including French and Russian.

Foss had rather small but even features framed in golden hair kept trimmed to tight, natural curls. Although large, her body was well balanced.

At the moment, Lepikov and Danzas were verbally sparring for dominance, a matter of revealing credentials as though they were card players turning up their cards, each aware that the other reserved powerful aces.

Lepikov, short and stocky with bushy gray hair over a flat face with a touch of Mongol in the eyes, appeared the peasant to Danza's aristocrat, a fact that each noted, thinking it a personal advantage.

Dorena Godelinsky, the other member of the Soviet contingent, showed increasing signs of irritation at the male contest. A slight, graying woman who walked with a limp, she had been cursed, as she often complained to close friends, with an aristocratic face, "a barrier to advancement in the Soviet hierarchy where heavy, peasant features are more favored."

Abruptly, she interrupted the two men with a coarse Russian curse, adding in English: "We are not here to play little boys' games!"

Foss chuckled and translated the curse: "She just called Sergei a country stud. What do we have here—black hat and white hat?"

Lepikov scowled at Foss, then forced a smile. He had done the mandatory tour as an *observer* at the Soviet embassy in Washington, D.C., and understood Foss's jibe.

"It is I who wear the white hat," he said. "Am I not the foremost expert on epidemiology in my nation?"

Foss grinned back at him. The United States dossier on Lepikov had him abnormally concerned with the workings of his liver, a paradox considering the quantities of vodka he was known to consume. These alcoholic indulgences, however, were always followed by bouts of self-loathing, an anguish approaching the pathological during which he dosed himself not only with specifics to which his medical standing gave him access but also with nostrums and massive doses of vitamins carefully concealed in bottles marked for more ordinary contents.

Godelinsky, hearing the boast, muttered: "Peasant!"

She spoke in English, which brought the attention of the others to her.

Beckett cleared his throat and hitched himself closer to the table. Godelinsky, the dossier said, was a renowned code breaker in the Soviet Union as well as being a medical researcher in her country's space program. She was considered a top-ranked diagnostician and her laboratory techniques were rated "superb."

"We have been introduced," Beckett said. "We've all read the secret service dossiers on each other. Perhaps those dossiers contain accurate information. Who knows? I suggest we will learn more important things about each other in the days to come."

"I would like to see your dossier on me," Lepikov said.

"Unfortunately, I was not allowed to keep it," Beckett said.

Godelinsky nodded. Beckett had taken exactly the right tack with Sergei. Spies were everywhere. Admit it and go on. Beckett had intuition, then. Godelinsky knew this was her own strength. She knew her Soviet colleagues considered her unpredictable, but did not understand this. The reasons for her decisions always seemed perfectly clear to her. It was the intermediate steps that the "mud heads" around her failed to understand because their minds could not leap, plodding instead like aged workhorses.

Lepikov shifted his gaze to Foss's large, well-formed breasts. Such a body! He nurtured a secret yen for large women and wondered if . . . perhaps . . .

"I would appreciate it if you would not stare at my chest," Foss said.

Lepikov jerked his attention to Hupp's gentle smile.

Foss was not through with him, however. She patted her curly ringlets. "I'm aware, Doctor Lepikov, that I'm the biggest baby doll in all creation."

Lepikov refused to look at her.

Undeterred, she said: "Don't let that give you any ideas, please. My husband is bigger than I am. That's unimportant, too, because I can take him out any time."

Lepikov was not familiar with this idiom. "Take him out?"

Foss shifted to earthy Russian in which she berated him for his inadequate grasp of English. He might know white hats and black hats, but little else. She then favored him with a colorful description of what she would do to his sexual organs if he ever again stared at her in a boorish fashion.

This brought peals of laughter from Godelinsky.

In Russian, Lepikov admonished: "Act more in keeping with your position!"

Godelinsky shook her head in helpless mirth, then, in Russian, said to Foss: "He's one of the new breed in the Soviet Union. They breed them for fat and unswerving devotion to power and sexual accomplishments."

Beckett intervened: "There are those of us here who do not speak Russian and we do have work."

Still in Russian, Godelinsky said: "He's right. You two behave yourselves. You, Sergei! I know stories about you that you would not want told here. Be warned. And you, Mrs. Foss! That a beautiful woman should know such language!"

Foss grinned and shrugged.

Lepikov tried to appear amused. "It was only a joke."

Beckett began pulling papers out of his briefcase, assembling them on the table in front of him.

Still simmering, Lepikov realized he had been maneuvered into a secondary position here. He wondered if Foss and Godelinsky had done this deliberately? Or perhaps Danzas? And Hupp, he looked so smug! The Soviet dossier on Hupp said he was a prime target for subverting. Was that possible? Hupp had been a student at UCLA, where he often had been mistaken for Latin-American and had even joined a Latino political club. Hupp was a skinny whipcord of a man, the very type Lepikov distrusted most—that dark skin and those soft brown eyes. The eyes of a cow!

"He is a socialist with susceptibilities of the flesh," the Soviet dossier said.

The account said he had been almost irresistible to young blond UCLA coeds imbued with a fanatical drive to fuck for peace. Lepikov glanced at the aging Godelinsky, then at the monumental Foss. Was there more here than met the eye?

Beckett glanced at a page in front of him and, in that moment, took over leadership of The Team. "I have been ordered to tell you," he said, "that we are not the central investigative team."

Godelinsky said: "But we were told . . ."

"Why not?" Foss demanded.

"There are now fifty-eight major research teams working on this problem worldwide," Beckett said. "We are on telefax and closed-circuit TV communications via satellite. By tomorrow afternoon, we'll have a twelve-man clerical and communications team in here plus at least thirty lab technicians. There will, however, be two central clearinghouses for communications: one in East Berlin for all Europe and the other in Washington, D.C."

"Politicians!" Foss barked.

Beckett ignored the outburst. "Our first order of business is to tackle the problem of a psycho-physical profile for our Madman. There is now convincing evidence that it was this John Roe O'Neill."

"What evidence?" Godelinsky demanded.

Hupp raised a hand. "Everything fits: the names of his

children and wife, the particular expertise in molecular biology."

"We haven't pinpointed his lab," Beckett said, "but there's growing evidence that it was somewhere near Seattle."

"Not in Kansas?" Danzas asked.

"That was a first report," Beckett said. "It's been disproved."

"Do you have the new background summary?" Hupp asked.

Beckett distributed duplicate sheets to the others from a stack in front of him. "You'll note that his parents died in a car accident the year he graduated from high school," Beckett said. "He was raised by his maternal grandparents. The grandfather died while O'Neill was in college. The grandmother lived to see O'Neill graduate at the head of his class. She left him a moderate legacy and the McCarthy family business."

"So many deaths," Lepikov muttered, looking at the page in front of him.

"An unlucky clan," Beckett agreed. "Only that aunt in the nursing home in Arizona. Half the time she thinks they're asking about her dead husband."

Hupp said: "We are being asked to determine how far we can move against this Madman without turning him against the rest of the world."

Silence greeted this observation.

"You've read his threats," Beckett said, presently.

"A dead-man switch," Lepikov said. "A device or arrangement that would loose a new plague upon everyone should this Madman be captured or killed."

"Are our hands tied?" Godelinsky asked.

Hupp said: "Surely, O'Neill must know we cannot totally ignore what he has done."

"We have a certain amount of freedom," Beckett said. "This facility—secret, superbly equipped."

"But he warns us not to do exactly what we're doing here," Lepikov said. "We will 'feel his wrath' if we disobey."

Danzas spoke, his tone mild: "That is why we remain hidden here."

Lepikov said: "My associates in the Soviet Union believe this . . . this DIC was chosen because it is not in Europe where the plague is most likely to spread."

Danzas splayed his big hands on the table and addressed himself to Beckett. "I came here in the belief that this was the ideal place for a secret and coordinated assault on this plague.

I was told this would be the central coordinating facility."

"The plans were changed," Beckett said. "I did not change them."

"Goddamned bureaucrats!" Foss said.

Beckett's expression remained bland and amiable. He said: "The DIC may very well become the center of the world's combined medical effort."

"But first we prove ourselves, eh?" Hupp asked.

"First we try to understand our enemy—the man and not the plague," Beckett said.

"Where was this decision made?" Godelinsky asked.

"At the highest levels," Beckett said. "Most of the other groups, so I'm told, are also working in this way as well as on the question of how he spread his plague. That is the highest priority. Can we cut him off and go after him openly on all fronts?"

"Tomorrow, we start the medical work, *hein?*" Danzas demanded. "When the technicians come?"

"That, too," Beckett said.

"Too!" Foss said.

"I have received no such orders," Lepikov said.

"There's a telephone in your room," Beckett said. "You're free to use it."

"And who will listen?" Lepikov demanded.

"Our secret police and yours," Beckett said. "Who cares? Call your boss and get your orders."

"Secrecy is our only hope," Godelinsky said. "If he is insane, we cannot predict him."

"Who doubts he's insane?" Foss asked. "He's driven the whole world nuts. Including the politicians!"

*It must certainly be more danger-
ous to live in ignorance than to live
with knowledge.*

—Phillip Handler

WITHOUT ANY particular pride, John thought his lab in the basement of the Ballard house a marvel of ingenuity. The centrifuge that he had improvised out of tire-balancing equipment had cost less than a thousand dollars. His freezer was stock home bar equipment turned on its back and with a calibrated thermostat added. It was accurate to within one degree Centigrade. He had improvised peristaltic pumps from scuba equipment. His cell disrupter was adapted from a used yachting sonar. The electron microscope, a dual-stage thirty Angstrom resolution ISI model, cost him the most time and considerable money. It was provided as a consignment-theft item by the San Francisco underworld at a cost of twenty-five thousand dollars.

And so it went with the entire lab. He fashioned the negative-pressure research rooms out of plywood and plastic film. The airlock was sealed by two small-boat hatches, which forced him to crawl into and out of the rooms. It was the only major inconvenience.

Before the lab was completed, John was at work with his computer, setting up the full-color graphics of the molecular models upon which he would center his attention. In parallel computer storage circuits, he filed away everything he could ferret out about the ways existing drugs functioned in the body. He paid particular attention to known data on enzymes and specific DNA receptors.

It gratified him to discover that many of the most important requirements for his molecular maps were available in "canned" form—on computer discs or in storage programs that could be bought or stolen. By the time the lab was completed he had his computer loaded with the elemental building blocks of his project.

There was a hypnotic fascination in sitting before the cathode display, watching the double spirals of the primal helix turn and twist at his command. The red, green, purple and yellow lines took on a life of their own. His mind and the display fell into a kind of unified space within which it was difficult to separate which was in his mind and which in the screen. It seemed at times as if his hands on the computer controls created the images in his head, or the image would be in his head and then appear as if miraculously on the screen. There were moments when he thought he was actually speaking in the language of the genetic code, *talking* to specific sites on DNA molecules.

During these periods, the actual flow of time vanished from his consciousness. On one occasion, he crawled from the airlock hatch, staggered to his feet and found it just dawn outside. Investigation revealed that he had been working steadily for thirty-seven hours with only an occasional sip of water. He was achingly hungry and his trembling hands could not even deal with solid food until he drank almost a full quart of milk.

The structure he needed to see and understand was slowly revealing itself, though, both on the screen and in the computer-monitored outputs of his lab. He knew it was only a matter of time until he fitted the proper molecular key into the biological lock. The answers were here in the lab and in his head. They merely had to be opened out into their own reality. The nucleotide sequences of the DNA encoded all of the genetic information for every biological function. It was a code-breaking problem.

Without the computer he would have been lost. At any given moment he might be working with four thousand to twenty thousand genes. The mapped arrangements of these genes and the DNA codes within them could project into more than a million genes. He did not need all of those genes, though—

only the key ones whose coding lay in the particular nucleotide sequences.

By disruption, by enzyme fractionating and temperature-controlled separation with collimators and centrifuge, he sought out the bits and pieces that his mind/computer images told him were there.

Before long, he was fashioning ribosomal RNAs and messenger RNAs from his own DNA templates, selecting and discarding, seeking out the control sites in the genomes. These and the regulatory proteins were his first targets.

Some two months into the project, John realized he would need a special supply of natural DNA for the polymerization cycle. The DNA had to be biologically active and it had to carry the templates he required. There was no escaping the fact that the DNA material transferred in pairs, one of each pair being a mirror of its opposite number.

His head ached with thinking about the problem, but he could not avoid the immediate necessity. It would risk exposure. It was dangerous . . . but he could see no alternative.

A session with his forging kit gave him a passable identification as a John Vicenti, M.D., Public Health Service. He had bought a small hand press early in fitting out the equipment for his project. This now produced some quite adequate letterheads. On these he typed letters of authorization, scrawling big signatures of officials at the bottoms. He bought a dark wig, toned his skin olive and all the while kept watch through the newspapers for a school immunization date. It came within the week, announcement of an immunization program in West Seattle Junior High School for the following Monday.

Wearing a white jacket with stethoscope protruding from a side pocket and a name tag on his lapel identifying him as John Vicenti, M.D., he showed up early at the school. It was a cold winter morning and the halls were crowded with students bundled into heavy jackets. He moved through the shouting, jabbering throng without attracting more than casual notice. In his left hand he carried a carefully arranged wooden kit box containing racks of sterile slides and covers and all of the neatly assembled tools for blood sampling. In his left hand was the briefcase with his authorizations.

He bustled officiously into the school nurse's office, noting her name on the door: "Jeanette Blanquie."

"Hi," he said, all innocence. "I'm Doctor Vicenti. Where do I set up?"

"Set up?" Nurse Blanquie was a slender blond young woman with a permanently harried expression. She stood behind a long table upon which the immunization kits were set out in orderly rows. There was an empty chair at the far end of the table with two stacks of forms in front of it. The wall behind her displayed a calendar and two bowdlerized anatomical charts, one labeled "male," the other "female."

"For the blood samples," he said. He put his wooden box and briefcase on the table and showed her his identification and authorizations. Nurse Blanquie merely glanced at them while her expression became even more harried.

"Blood samples," she muttered.

"We're supposed to get them right along with your immunization program to minimize the upset of school routine," he explained.

"I was supposed to have two clinical technicians here this morning to help me," she said. "One of them just called in sick and the other one has some kind of emergency at Good Samaritan. Now you. This is all I need. What are your samples for?"

"We're doing a genetic typing nationally to see if we can identify correlations with certain diseases and immunities. I'm supposed to use your ID numbers, no names. All I need in addition is whether the sample is from male or female."

Her voice sounded tired. "Doctor Vicenti, nobody's told me a thing." She gestured at the table. "And I'm supposed to process two hundred and sixteen students today, more tomorrow."

He gritted his teeth. "Damn! That's their second slip-up in two weeks! Somebody in that office should be fired."

Nurse Blanquie shook her head in sympathy.

He said: "Well, what can I do to help you? Could we get a student in to handle the paperwork?"

"I've already asked for one," she said. She looked at the table in front of her. "Could you set up here beside me? What kind of samples will you take?"

He opened the kit box, displaying the ranked slides, the swabs and alcohol, lancets, everything neat.

"Oh," she said. "Well, that shouldn't delay us much, Doctor. I guess between the two of us we can handle it."

When he returned to Ballard that evening, "Doctor Vicenti" had two hundred and eleven blood samples, each with a tiny pinch of skin cells deftly included.

There will be specific differences, he told himself as he removed his disguise in the bathroom, which still smelled of stale tobacco. *The genetic information for every biological function—including whether the person is male or female. There is a pattern here into which I can lock a virulent destroyer.*

The positive intermolding effect of the double helix chains, each side able to reproduce its opposite number, his clues lay in there. In the peptide bonds, perhaps, and in the singular tails that trailed out of the helix.

He took the samples down to his lab. The answers had to be in here, he assured himself. It was in the DNA patterns. Had to be. When a bacterial virus infected a bacterium, it was the virus's DNA, not its protein, that entered the bacterial cell. Here was the messenger he needed to make John O'Neill's revenge heard everywhere.

The technique for testing his results already had been worked out. It would be elegant in the extreme. He would require short-lived virus-mediated bacterial forms, bacteria that would induce visible effects in a selected population. The effects would have to be identifiable and visible, not fatal but important enough to cause comment. The test bacilli would have to be self-lethal. They would have to vanish of themselves.

These requirements, which might have daunted a major research center, did not even give him pause. He had a feeling of invincibility. It was only one step in his project. When he had the key to this lock, when he had assured himself of its identity, then he could start shaping the key into its more virulent form.

And *then* the message could be sent.

> This is not my table. *That's the*
> *real, all-inclusive Western mantra.*
> *And look what it got us.*
>
> —Fintan Craig Doheny

THE TEAM reconvened after lunch that first day with its pattern well set—Beckett in charge, Lepikov simmeringly resentful, Godelinsky weaving intuitively through her maze of questions, Danzas reserved and watchful, Hupp darting like a terrier around every new idea, and Foss sitting there like an aloof goddess.

Hupp was amused that they chose the more intimate lighting for the room when they reconvened. It focused only on the long table, leaving the rest of the space in remote shadows.

The Team clustered loosely near one end of the table with their notes and briefcases around them. The sparring between Danzas and Lepikov had become more subtle—a raised eyebrow, a gentle cough at an inappropriate moment. Danzas took to stacking and restacking his papers while Lepikov spoke. Lepikov's animosity toward Foss had resolved itself into calf-like hurt glances that avoided Foss's ample breasts. Godelinsky obviously had made the "sisters under the skin" decision to side with Foss, a thing that galled Lepikov, but he came back to the meeting saying he had orders to follow Beckett's lead.

Preparing himself to speak at length on this, Lepikov pushed himself back in his chair at Beckett's right and stared across

74

the table where Danzas was leafing through notes with a noisy rustling. A glance at Godelinsky beside him showed her looking down the table where Foss had seated herself slightly apart, separated from Hupp by an empty chair. Before he could speak, though, Godelinsky asked Beckett: "Why do they lock the barn door after the horse is slaughtered?" She reached over and tapped a sheet of yellow paper in front of Beckett.

Hupp appeared agitated by the question. "Yes," he said. "Why do they impose the severe quarantine at this time?"

"We must do what the Madman says," Lepikov interrupted.

Beckett nodded. "It's a mess, all right."

"The Madman makes his point," Danzas said.

"I had a brief session with our Security people before coming in here," Beckett said. "We're writing off North Africa from the Atlantic to the Suez. South Africa remains a question mark. Security says it has a report that a Mafia courier contaminated Johannesburg. There are trouble spots in France and an outbreak south of Rome."

"What of Ireland and England?" Danzas asked.

Beckett shook his head. "England's still trying to create safe districts for its women. Ireland has apparently given it up. There's battling in Ireland between the army and the IRA. Belfast . . . they tried to arrange a truce but it's already being called 'the Bloody Amnesty.' I just don't understand the Irish."

"Tell them about Switzerland," Foss said.

"The Swiss have cut themselves off, blown their bridges and tunnels, shut down their airports. They've thrown a military cordon around the country and reportedly are killing and burning with flamethrowers anyone attempting to enter."

"So much murder," Godelinsky murmured.

"I heard about Brittany," Lepikov said. "Is that the trouble you mention in France?"

"There is more," Danzas said. "Certain prefectures are isolating themselves in the Swiss manner. Units of the military have defected from Central Authority to support the . . . uhhhhh . . ."

"Fragmentation," Hupp said.

"Washington, D.C., did the same thing and so did New York," Beckett said. "It's ruthless but it seems to be effective." He looked at Lepikov. "What's happening in the Soviet Union?"

"They do not inform us," Lepikov said. "They ask that we search diligently for the Madman."

"And what do we do if we find him?" Godelinsky asked.

"I'm sure Sergei refers to the search for the Madman's persona," Hupp said, trying to set a new tone of familiarity.

"We must know him as we know ourselves," Lepikov said.

"Oh, better than that, I hope," Foss said. Her bosom quivered as she chuckled.

Lepikov forgot himself and stared at her breasts, fascinated. *A magnificent giantess!*

In Russian, Foss said: "Sergei Alexandrovich, you presume on my maternal instincts."

Godelinsky sneezed to cover a laugh.

Beckett, who sensed a return of open animosity between Foss and Lepikov, said: "Knock it off, Ari. We have work to do. I want us to examine the terrorist references in the Madman's letters. If it's O'Neill, that's where we'll find the most heat."

"My colleague and I have extracted those references," Hupp said. "Bill is right. The passages are significant."

"Let's hear it, Joe," Beckett said.

Hupp smiled. This was exactly the tone he wanted. Bill and Joe. It should become Ari, Sergei and Dorena. He glanced at Godelinsky. *Dorie, perhaps?* No, the Godelinsky was not a Dorie, except, perhaps, in bed.

Danzas slipped a blue folder from the stack in front of him. "This is the gist," he said.

Lepikov raised an eyebrow at the thickness of the folder and murmured: "Gist?"

Danzas ignored him. "We take the original words out of context for the purposes of our analysis." He cleared his throat, adjusted a pair of glasses to his nose and bent forward to read in a clear voice with just a trace of British accent to betray where he had learned his English.

"Their cowardice is masked in lies and guile." Danzas raised his head. "That is from his second letter. We juxtapose a passage from his third letter where he says"—again, Danzas lowered his attention to the page—*"They (the terrorists) seduce the people into belief in violence, then abandon the people to every retaliation that such blind and random action can attract."*

"Accent on cowardice," Hupp said. "Interesting. Does the Madman think his own revenge cowardly? Does he employ guile and tell us lies? Does he even consider himself a terrorist?"

"I recall a number of places where he refers to cowardice,"

Foss said. "Could his own conscience be speaking to us there?"

"Here is another quotation," Danzas said. *"They (the terrorists) commit only crimes that require no true courage. Terrorists are like bomber pilots who need never look upon their tortured victims, never see the faces of people who pay in anguish. Terrorists are kin to the rack-renting landlords who—"*

"What is that?" Godelinsky interrupted. "What is a rack-renting landlord?"

"An interesting bit of Irishness," Hupp said. "It's from the early days of English domination there. The choicest lands were given to English landlords, who appointed overseers to squeeze as much rent out of the peasants as possible. Rack-renting."

"I see," Godelinsky said. "Excuse the interruption."

"But the Madman knows his Irish history," Beckett said.

Danzas bent over once more to his pages: *". . . the rack-renting landlords who never once stared face-to-face into the countenance of a starving peasant."*

"He displays an implicit sympathy for victims of violence," Foss said. "For our purposes, that is a weakness."

"It suggests a kind of schizophrenia," Godelinsky said.

"Either that, or his ideas of an *appropriate revenge* are being fleshed out in his letters," Foss said.

"Exactly!" Hupp said.

Danzas said: "Elsewhere, our Madman describes terrorists as having *the guilt of Pilate.*"

"Isn't that where he calls terrorists *adrenalin addicts?*" Beckett asked.

"You remember correctly," Danzas said. "These are his words: *They create agony, then wash their hands in false patriotism. Their true desire is for personal power and the internal kick of an adrenalin high. They are adrenalin addicts.*"

"Does *he* get this kick?" Hupp asked.

"A diatribe," Foss said. "It's O'Neill raging against the murderers of his family."

"The legitimate uses of violence," Godelinsky murmured.

Lepikov shot a startled look at her. "What?"

"I quote Comrade Lenin," Godelinsky said. "He approved 'the legitimate uses of violence.'"

"We are not here to debate ideology," Lepikov snapped.

"But we are," Hupp said. "The Madman's ideology should occupy our every waking moment."

"Do you suggest Lenin was mad?" Lepikov demanded.

"That's not at issue," Hupp said. "But understanding one madman throws light on others. There are no sacred cows in the laboratory."

"I will not follow the capitalist herring," Lepikov growled.

Hupp grinned. "The original expression, Sergei, was 'red herring.'"

"The color of a fish does not make it less fishy," Lepikov said. "I make myself clear, Joe?" There was no familiarity in Lepikov's tone.

Hupp chose to enjoy the sally, laughing, then: "You are right, Sergei. Absolutely right."

"The issue is how does this Madman think of himself," Beckett said.

Foss agreed: "Does he act with courage and honor? He seems hipped on that."

"There is a passage worthy of note," Danzas said. He leafed through his pages, nodded at something he found, then read:

"Terrorists always assault honor, dignity and self-respect. Their own honor is the first to die. You should recognize that the IRA Provos have abandoned Irish honor. Under Erin's old Brehon Law, you could kill an enemy only in open battle, each equally armed. The better man earned the respect of all. A warrior was generous and fair. Where was the generosity and fairness in the bomb that killed the innocents at Grafton Street?"

"Grafton Street, that is where O'Neill's wife and children were killed by the bomb," Godelinsky said. "This is either O'Neill or an extremely clever disguise."

"Perhaps," Danzas said. Once more, he bent to his notes and read from a letter:

"These Provisional IRA murderers remind me of the boot-licking lackeys who served Dublin Castle in the worst days of Ireland's degradation. Their methods are no different. England ruled with torture and deadly violence. The self-serving Provo cowards learned that lesson well. Having learned it, they refuse to learn any other lesson. So I give them a lesson no one will ever forget!"

"These Provisional IRAs, these Provos, they are the ones who set the bomb at Grafton Street?" Foss asked.

"Our Madman singles them out but he apparently makes little distinction between terrorists," Hupp said. "Regard that he blames Great Britain and Libya equally and he warns the Soviet Union because of alleged complicity with Libya."

"A lie!" Lepikov said.

"Francois," Foss said, leaning forward to stare directly at Danzas. And she thought: *He calls me by my given name. How does he take to the same familiarity?*

Danzas appeared unoffended. "Yes?"

"Do you and Joe see this as more than a schizoid diatribe?"

Hupp answered: "These are words of outrage wrenched from an agonized human being. It is O'Neill, of that I am sure. The question before us is: How does he view himself?"

"Here are his own words," Danzas said, returning to his notes.

"Every tyrant in history is marked by indifference to misery. That is a clear way to identify tyranny. Now, I am the tyrant. You must deal with me. You must answer to me. And I am indifferent to your misery. Out of this indifference, I ask you to consider the consequences of your own violent actions and violent inactions."

"But is he really indifferent?" Beckett asked.

"I think he is," Hupp said. "Otherwise, he could not do this thing. You see the pattern? Real outrage, which comes from an agonized sensitivity and then, on the other hand, the indifference."

"But he calls himself Madman," Godelinsky murmured.

Hupp said: "Ah, Dorena, you have it precisely. This is his defense. 'I am mad,' he says. This is in the dual sense of anger and of insanity. Justification and explanation."

"Bill," Godelinsky said, "what other agencies pursue this O'Neill?"

Beckett shook his head. The question bothered him. There was no room for mistakes. Godelinsky's question went directly to that concern. "I don't know what other agencies."

"But you know others seek him?" she insisted.

"Oh, yes. Depend on it."

"I hope it is being done with the utmost delicacy," she said.

"You begin to see him as I see him," Hupp said.

"How do you see him?" Foss asked.

Hupp leaned back and closed his eyes. This gave him a curiously childlike appearance marred only by the thick glasses. "O'Neill, I am certain. Irish ancestry. Very well educated here in the States. Perhaps I should say *superbly* educated. Intimate knowledge of Irish history. Probably acquired young from his family. Think on it. He carried through a difficult project in molecular biology under what were undoubtedly adverse circumstances. A minimal laboratory, we can be sure."

"Why can we be sure of that?" Foss asked.

"If it's O'Neill," Beckett said, "the FBI estimates he went into hiding with about a half million dollars."

Lepikov sat up straight. "So much? How could an ordinary citizen acquire so much wealth?"

"Not an ordinary citizen," Beckett said.

"That is it precisely," Danzas said, his tone remote and clipped. "Doctor Hupp and I are agreed upon the extraordinary situation of this Madman."

Hupp opened his eyes at mention of his name but appeared unconcerned by Danzas's formality. He said: "Francois has it in a nutshell. Our Madman is an extraordinary human being who has suffered great spiritual anguish, a wrenching of the soul. From this, he achieves a fanatic's motivation to make others share his anguish. Would we not agree that he has been successful in this regard? Not one human female alive on Achill Island and . . . you've all seen the reports from Ireland and Great Britain. The latest reports from North Africa . . ." Hupp let his voice trail off.

Beckett summed up: "With some reservation, we agree that O'Neill is our Madman. He is schizoid in a particular way . . ."

"Not fragmented in the conventional sense," Hupp said. "Split, but aware of the split. Aware, yes. That is it."

"No one answers my question about this man," Lepikov said. "He is extraordinary? How does this acquire for him the five hundred thousand dollars?"

"He inherited part of it with a family business," Beckett said. "And he had a good job and he made good investments."

"Not to mention what he inherited from his wife," Foss said.

Lepikov grunted, then: "He was a capitalist, yes; now, I see. And look what it has brought us. One wrong move on our part and he gives us new diseases, perhaps even worse ones."

"Sergei is right," Hupp said. "Given the ability that O'Neill has demonstrated, he could have a disease that would, say, kill only people with Oriental ancestry." Hupp stared at the slight epicanthic fold in Lepikov's eyes.

"He must be stopped!" Lepikov said.

"And now we understand why the number-one priority is to understand him," Foss said. "We cannot make even one mistake. He is too dangerous an opponent."

"Dear lady," Lepikov said, looking at Foss, "the mind of this Madman may be too subtle for us to understand."

"We have to do it anyway," Beckett said, barely concealing his anger at such defeatist talk.

"This could not have happened in the Soviet Union," Lepikov said.

A short, harsh laugh escaped Godelinsky. "Of course not, Sergei. There is no injustice in the Soviet Union."

Lepikov shook a finger at her. "That is dangerous talk, Dorena." In Russian, he added: "You know well that we do not allow uncontrolled experiments."

"He says they don't allow uncontrolled experiments in Russia," Foss translated.

Godelinsky shook her head. "Sergei is right that there is much internal spying in our homeland, but he is wrong all the same. He is forgetting that one man alone did this thing in the privacy of his own home. Even in the Soviet Union we do not know everything done by one man alone in such privacy."

Beckett ate dinner with Foss and Hupp that first night. The others begged off, saying they preferred dining in their own quarters. Danzas had shuddered at the menu.

"Cauliflower with cheddar cheese? What is this, a new American poison? There is not even wine."

Foss was gloomy all through the meal, staring around the small antiseptic dining room, a white-walled space off the larger DIC kitchen facility where the technical staff, mostly female, ate. Beckett had introduced his party to the staff as they passed through to the smaller room. The technical people had returned looks that mixed awe and a kind of cynical fear.

Perhaps that's what made her gloomy, Beckett thought. *That and that damned Lepikov!*

Once she was seated at the table, Foss confirmed this: "Sergei's right. We have to understand this man perfectly. How can we do that?"

"I do not understand the electron," Hupp said. "But I can use electricity safely."

"Ain't science wonderful!" Foss said.

After dinner, Beckett returned alone to his private quarters, a sterile little room with adjoining bath. The cot was cantilevered from the concrete wall. There was a single straight chair and a desk but the wall beside the desk carried a document safe whose combination was known only to Security and Beckett. His first task each night was to examine the safe and check whatever new material had been left for him.

Beckett sighed as he saw the thick package of papers sitting neatly in the opened safe. He sat down at the desk and began leafing through them, wondering as he did so what system of selection Security was using. Were the priorities determined at a higher level? He thought that probable. The top document carried the presidential seal. The covering page had two red-bordered "overnight transmittal" stamps, one marked "Pentagon Liaison" and unsigned. The other carried the NSC stamp of the National Security Council and was signed with a scrawl that was almost undecipherable, but that Beckett thought might be *something* like Turkwood.

He read the enclosures carefully, more and more puzzled as he went. First was a verbatim transcript of a radio broadcast received at a military listening post, purportedly from someone in Ireland identifying himself as "Brann McCrae." It struck Beckett as the worst kind of religious nonsense, obviously the work of a crank. McCrae asked the world to return to tree worship, naming the rowan as "the most sacred witness of holiness." His broadcast contained an appeal to a nephew, Cranmore McCrae, in the United States, to "take your airplane and fly to me. I shall make you high priest of the rowan."

McCrae's broadcast claimed "the rowan guards my women."

At the bottom of the transcript's last page was an unsigned scribble that Beckett thought might be the writing of the President himself. It read:

"Locate this Cranmore McCrae. Has Brann McCrae isolated a female population in Ireland?"

Next in the package was another transcript, this an official communication to the White House from "The Killaloe Facility" in Ireland. The sender was identified as "Doctor Adrian Peard." The transcript carried a list of "equipment requested for immediate shipment with highest priority."

Beckett scanned the list carefully. It was what would be expected at a good DNA research center. At the bottom of the list, in that same unsigned scribble, was the terse comment: "Ship it." then: "Beckett—anything else they might need?"

Beckett wrote directly below the question: "A reliable source of stereoisomers."

The message from Doctor Peard concluded with the information that a Doctor Fintan Craig Doheny had been appointed chief of the "Plague Research Section."

The scribbler asked, "Who's this Doheny?"

Beckett wrote beneath the scribble: "Unknown to me." He

signed it with his full name and title.

Beneath this page was another page bearing the presidential seal. It was addressed to Beckett and bore only an NSC stamp at the bottom, no name. It read:

"Try to find out from Godelinsky or Lepikov why the Soviet Union has sealed off certain areas beyond the Urals. Satellite confirmation of this but no response from Moscow to our questions."

Beneath this was another similar page with the terse question:

"Where will O'Neill most likely hide?"

So they're convinced it's O'Neill, Beckett thought.

The final page, also stamped with the unsigned NSC cartouche frame, asked merely:

"How on artificial insemination?"

Now what the hell is that supposed to mean? he wondered.

There was no doubt in Beckett's mind that the authorities had hidden away other female populations. He knew of at least one at Carlsbad. Was the government considering repopulation schemes? How many women were really dying out there in the United States?

The more he thought about it, the angrier Beckett became. He scrawled across the final page: "What does this question mean? What's going on out there?"

Only then could he attempt to sleep, knowing it would be short and that he would be up within the hour.

Actually, he slept only twenty-five minutes, bouncing off his cot to write a series of memos to the mysterious NSC questioners. The first memo suggested they ask this Peard to hunt down the religious nut, McCrae, reminding the Irish that they would need women to test whatever their laboratories produced.

On the Doheny question, he said: "Ask the Irish, for God's sake." This was the closest he came to revealing his anger.

On the Soviet question, he said merely: "Will do."

On the question of where O'Neill might hide, Beckett said: "Try Ireland or England. He'll want to watch the effects of his revenge. Doubtful he speaks Arabic. Libya unlikely. Otherwise, he may merge into some city population here, possibly as a bereaved derelict. Will raise this question with full Team."

On the artificial insemination question, he asked: "What is meant by this question? What do you want us to consider?"

Finally, Beckett wrote: "Anything new on how O'Neill spread his disease? If not, intend to raise this question soonest with full Team."

Having finished, Beckett reread his memos, reflecting on the questions that had prompted them. There was a sense of disorganized panic in the questions, a random groping for leads.

We need organization, he thought. *And we need it damn' fast.*

In the way his mind often did, as Beckett's thought focused on this urgent need, he had a sudden flash of insight about Danzas, *the organized man.*

Danzas was a man born, not out of his time, but out of place. By rights he should have been born in northern New Hampshire or in Maine. He was a Down Easter in French disguise—cantankerous, suspicious, close-mouthed, using his accent as a shield more than as a help in communication. Or it could be argued that Danzas had been born in exactly the right place, and similarities to a Down Easter were the product of a social coincidence. Brittany, Beckett had heard, was noted for these selfsame characteristics—an insular place keeping itself to itself, trusting only its own ways, quick to identify and make common cause with its own people—accent, manners, attitudes revealed in regional quips, jokes that often revolved around the confounding of tourists and other strangers.

The insight told Beckett how best to work with Danzas, where the man's strengths would be found and how to employ them.

No small talk. Share his prejudices. Put him in charge of organizing key elements of our project.

I'll have to find out what his food preferences are, Beckett thought.

Without consciously focusing on it, Beckett had begun marshaling his forces, assembling The Team into a working pattern to get the best out of all its members—the whole greater than the sum of its parts.

> *Glory O! Glory O! to the bold
> Fenian Men.*
>
> — Ballad by Peadar Kearney

TWO WEEKS before the Achill demonstration, John was ready to leave his Ballard hideaway. He knew he would have to cover his tracks carefully. The search would be massive and international. The very size of the search meant they probably would find his place quickly. The pressures on anyone who had any contact with him, even his instructor in forgery in St. Louis, guaranteed that no secrets would be kept for long. There were no illusions in his mind about governments obeying his orders not to seek him out.

The new passport was made with extreme care. He made it from Mary's passport, taking the document from her passport case, which contained John O'Neill's passport and the separate ones for the twins. Why he chose Mary's passport he could not say, but he carefully hid the unused passports in the lining of his suitcase.

As he worked on the forgery, he remembered Mary saying that it would make the twins feel important to have their own passports.

The memories were oddly displaced. He felt like an eaves dropper, someone peering into the secret joys of a fellow human, prying without permission into private matters. But he could remember the twins' delight, comparing their pictures, showing off their ability to read and write, signing their own names importantly on the proper lines.

When he had completed the chemical erasure of Mary's passport, he felt that he had removed her even more from the world of the living. He went to the secret compartment in the suitcase and looked at the three blue-bound booklets with their golden embossing. The passports were real. But how much of the real person was contained in them? If he erased all of them, did that actually make the people unreal? He peered closely at the coded perforations on Mary's passport. The laughter and happiness at the arrival of the passports were part of that movie playing in his skull. He could see Mary handing a passport to each of the children, Kevin first and then Mairead.

"They're individuals and now they have the documents to prove it," she said.

How wise she is.

He restored the three unused passports to their hiding place and returned to the forgery. He felt feverish and wondered if he had picked up something from his work down in the laboratory. No. He had been very careful about his own body. That was part of his total purpose.

It was as though only this purpose kept him alive. All else receded into projections and the strange movie-memory. It was only the urgency making him feverish. He could feel time pressing at him. The fateful letters were almost ready to be mailed. He turned on the lights in the narrow stairway off the kitchen and took Mary's erased passport down to the lab. The stairs creaked as he descended and he wondered what time it was. Dark outside. No matter. There was a spiderweb within the exposed studs where the stairs turned.

How many times have I come this way?

He felt that he had always lived here, had always known the creaking stairs. This was the only place where John McCarthy had ever lived, and the basement laboratory restored his sense of being. It had become a basic part of his life—the white-painted bench with its three gas burners, the homemade centrifuge in the corner, the autoclave built out of a pressure-cooker, the oven with its precision thermostat for the controlled environment, the electron microscope, the petri dishes stored sterile in Tupperware boxes . . . He could hear the paint-compressor pump cutting in to prime the vacuum system, which was mediated by the scuba pump.

Carefully, he bent to the forgery, delicate movements, precision in each tiny action. The master forger had been right. He was good at this. And there it was, a new identity. Only the ache in his back told him there had been a significant passage of time. He looked at his wrist, remembering that he had left his watch beside the kitchen sink. It didn't matter. The feverish sense of urgency had gone.

John Garrett O'Day had just been born. There he was on the forged passport—a bald man with a toothbrush mustache, dark eyes that stared directly out of the square photograph.

John stared back at his new self. John Garrett O'Day. He already felt like John Garrett O'Day. There had been O'Days on the O'Neill side of the family. And there he was in the photograph. John felt that he had receded farther back into the ancestry, farther away from John Roe O'Neill, cutting that man off even more sharply.

There would be searchers after O'Neill, and perhaps even more searchers after what John McCarthy had done. But those men were gone. O'Neill and McCarthy. Only O'Day remained and soon O'Day would be far away.

A hunger pang struck him. He turned to the airlock, crawling out and sealing the lab behind him. It was daylight outside. His watch on the drainboard showed 9:36 and he knew it must be morning. It had been dark when he entered the lab. Yes, Saturday morning. In only two weeks, Achill would awaken to its horrible day of reckoning. Then the letters of explanation and warning would start to arrive. His soldiers were on the march. That was how he thought about the things he had sent to Ireland, Britain and Libya.

Soldiers.

The irrevocable thing had been done. There could be no turning back.

He heard children shouting in the alley and thought suddenly of the neighbors around this Ballard hideaway. Would his soldiers come here, too? The question was a matter of indifferent curiosity in his mind, gone as soon as it entered.

Time to leave.

He felt something strange about the house then. Was there something he had forgotten to do downstairs? He strapped on his wristband and hurried back down to the lab, crawled through the airlock hatches, leaving them open. No need for lab security anymore. John McCarthy's meticulous habits could be abandoned.

As he stood up in the first safe room, his gaze fell on the side bench and the kitchen heat-sealer bolted to it. He thought then that the simple kitchen device, a thing made to preserve food, set the style for his entire lab. Investigators might marvel over the inspired adaptations here, the machines and devices put to uses for which they had never been intended.

Now, he remembered what he had forgotten to do, the thing that had sent him hurrying back down the lab. The thermite bombs! Of course. He moved carefully around the lab, setting the timers, then out into the basement where there were more devices.

Back up to the kitchen then and a bowl of dry cereal. The food made him sleepy and he set about brewing coffee, but decided he would rest his head on his arms at the kitchen table for a few minutes first. He had until night to leave.

When he awakened, it was 12:11 and still daylight. He felt rested, but his back was sore from sleeping bent over the table. He could still hear children playing in the alley.

That's right. It's Saturday.

He splashed cold water on his face at the kitchen sink, dried it on a dishtowel, then went into the bedroom and completed his packing. He took his suitcases down to the power wagon and began climbing back up the stairs to the kitchen, intending to brew the coffee he had left unfinished. At the landing, he stopped, frozen in shock at the loud sound of something crashing in the kitchen.

A burglar!

That had been John McCarthy's constant fear during the project.

Rage engulfed him. How dare they? He charged up the final flight into the kitchen and almost tripped over a softball. The sink held a jumble of broken glass. Only a few shreds remained in the frame over the sink.

He could hear a woman's voice shouting in the alley behind his house: "Jimmeeeee! Jimmeeeee! You come here this instant!"

Relief drained him.

"Jimmeeee! I see you there!"

A vague sense of amusement came over him. He picked up the softball and went out onto the back porch. A young woman in a blue housedress came through his gate from the alley and stopped in the backyard. She held the right ear of a boy about ten. The boy, his mouth contorted with pain and fear, his head twisted to accommodate the force holding him, pleaded:

"Ma, please! Please, Ma!"

The woman looked up at John and released the boy's ear. She glanced at the broken window and back to John, then to the softball in his hand. The boy sheltered himself behind her.

"I'm so sorry," she said. "We'll get you a new window, of course. I've warned him time and again, but he forgets. My husband will get the window on his way home. He's good at fixing things."

John forced a smile. "No need, ma'am. I guess I owe for a few windows from my own childhood." He tossed the softball into the yard. "There you go, Jimmy. Why don't you kids play in that empty lot at the end of the block? It's safer than the street or the alley."

Jimmy darted from behind his mother and retrieved the ball. He held it close to his chest, looking up at John as though he could not believe his good fortune.

The woman grinned in relief.

"How very nice of you," she said. "My name's Pachen, Gladys Pachen. We live just across the alley from you on Sixty-fifth. We'll be glad to pay for the window. It shouldn't . . ."

"No need," John said, holding tightly to his good-neighbor pose. The last thing he needed right now was intrusions by neighbors. He spoke easily: "You just make sure Jimmy prepares himself to pay for the window some other youngster breaks when he's my age. We men pass along the cost of broken windows."

Gladys Pachen laughed, then: "I must say you're being so very, very nice about this. I never . . . I mean . . . we didn't . . ." She broke off in confusion.

John maintained his smile with effort. "I guess I must've seemed pretty mysterious all these months. I'm an inventor, Mrs. Pachen. I've been working pretty steadily on . . . well, I guess I can't talk about it just yet. My name's . . ." He hesitated, aware that he almost had spoken of himself as John Garrett O'Day, then, a self-conscious shrug: "John McCarthy. You'll be hearing that name, I think. My friends call me Jack."

That was well done, he thought. Plausible explanation. A smile. No harm in giving out that name.

"George will be delighted," she said. "He fiddles around a

lot in the garage, too. He has a little shop there. I . . . you know, the next time we have a barbecue, you'll have to come over. I won't take no for an answer."

"That sounds wonderful," John said. "I do get tired of my own cooking." He looked at the boy. "You investigate that lot, Jimmy. That looks like a good baseball lot."

Jimmy nodded his head twice, quickly, but didn't speak.

"Well, Gladys, no harm done," John said. "No real harm, anyway. Good way for me to get a clean window over the sink. I have to get back to work now. Got something brewing."

He waved casually and let himself back into the kitchen. An inspired performance, he thought, as he set about putting a temporary sheet of plastic over the sink window. No need to replace the glass. It would all go up in flames tonight anyway.

Gladys Pachen returned to her own kitchen, where she invited her neighbor, Helen Avery, over for coffee.

"I saw you talking to him," Helen Avery said as Gladys poured the coffee. "What's he like? I thought I'd die when I saw Jimmy's ball smash that window."

"He's kind of sweet," Gladys said. "I think he's very shy . . . and lonely." She poured her own coffee. "He's an inventor."

"Is that what he does in that basement! Bill and I have been wondering—the lights on there at all hours."

"He was so nice to Jimmy," Gladys said as she sat down at the kitchen table. "He wouldn't let me pay for the window, said he owed for a few broken windows from when he was Jimmy's age."

"What's he inventing? Did he say?"

"He wouldn't say, but I'll bet it's something important."

> *There was never a greater anti-Irish bigot than Shakespeare. He was the ultimate Elizabethan jackanapes, a perfect reflection of British bigotry. They justified themselves on the grounds of religion. The Reformation! That's where they began their policy of exterminating the Irish. Back then we learned the bitter truth: England's enemy is Ireland's friend.*
>
> **—Joseph Herity**

"WE ARE to concentrate on how he spread the disease," Beckett said. "They still haven't solved it."

It was The Team's third afternoon and they had moved their meeting to the small dining room off the DIC's main cafeteria. It was closer to the lab facilities, had brighter walls and lighting, a smaller table. Coffee or tea could be delivered via a pass-through with a sliding panel from the kitchen. Security had objected and there was a certain amount of crockery clatter to contend with, but it was a more comfortable setting for all of them.

"Is anyone asking does our Madman act alone?" Hupp asked. He moved aside slightly as a white-aproned waiter finished clearing away the dishes from their lunch.

"A conspiracy?" Lepikov asked. He looked at the departing waiter. "Are those waiters in your army, Bill?"

Foss answered: "It's our most carefully guarded secret, Sergei. Two years of this duty and they're guaranteed to be insane killers."

Even Lepikov joined in the wry chuckle at Foss's wit.

Danzas said: "Infected birds. We have the precedent of

91

parrot fever. Could he have modified psittacosis?"

"Somehow that doesn't strike me as his style," Hupp said. "He's not leaving us an easy trail to follow. No." He looked down at a blue folder in front of him, opened it slowly and leafed through the enclosed pages until he found what he was seeking. "There's this from his second letter," Hupp said. *"I know there are links between the IRA and the Fedayeen, links with Japanese terrorists, the Tupamaros and God knows who else. I was tempted to spread my revenge into all the lands that have harbored such cowards. I warn those lands: do not tempt me again for I have released only a small part of my arsenal."*

Hupp closed the folder and looked up at Lepikov across the table from him. "We must assume that this is not an empty threat. I do not think this man bluffs. On that assumption, we must also assume that he has more than one way to spread his *arsenal.* Because if we find the way or ways he did it in the present instance, we could close off that channel."

"Could we?" Beckett asked.

Lepikov nodded to agree that he shared this doubt.

Godelinsky leaned forward, sipped her tea, then: "He infected specific areas. The fact that his plague has spread, this can only mean human carriers are involved in some way."

"Why is that?" Danzas asked.

"The way everything is being sprayed, no insect could be doing it," she said. Godelinsky rubbed her forehead and frowned.

Lepikov said something to her, low-voiced, in Russian. Foss caught only part of it, but turned to peer sharply at the other woman.

"Is something amiss?" Hupp asked.

"Only a headache," Godelinsky said. "I think it is the water change. Perhaps I could have some more tea?"

Beckett turned to the panel behind him, opened it and confronted a face bent close on the other side, a bland, smiling blond man with white teeth. "Anyone else want something from the kitchen?" the man asked.

"Bumpkins!" Lepikov said.

"They just haven't had time to install microphones in this room," Foss said. "It'll be less obtrusive tomorrow. I'll take coffee, black."

Beckett glanced around the table. The others demurred. He returned his attention to the bland face at the pass-through. "You heard?"

"Right-O, Doc."

The covering panel slid closed.

Beckett returned his attention to the table.

Hupp lifted a briefcase from the floor beside his chair, wiped a piece of lettuce from it, and removed a small notepad and pen. "It will be something simple," he said.

The panel behind Beckett slid open. "One tea, one coffee, black." It was Bland Face. He pushed two steaming cups onto the inner ledge, closed the panel.

Without getting up, Beckett took the two cups from the ledge and slid them along the table. As Godelinsky took her cup, Beckett noted a patch of white on the back of her left hand. It was not prominent, but quite noticeable to his trained eye. Before he could comment on it, Lepikov said:

"I think the plague was spread with some devilish American device. A spray can for the hair, possibly."

Hupp wrote on his notepad. "It's on my list, but I doubt it. Again, it's too obvious a thing for our Madman."

Godelinsky sipped noisily at her tea, then: "I agree with Joe. It is not O'Neill's style."

"What is *her* style?" Foss asked.

Hupp smiled at the cautionary change of gender. "As I said, I think it will be something remarkably simple. It will be a thing of which we will say: 'Oh, my God! Of course!'"

"Such as?" Beckett prompted.

Hupp produced a high-shouldered shrug, palms thrust out and upward. "I address only the question of style, not the specific method."

"We don't know the incubation period," Godelinsky said. "This could've been sitting there for months."

"Contaminated gifts?" Foss asked.

"That kind of thing," Hupp said. "A toy that a mother would handle before passing it along to her child. We must not forget that O'Neill's wife and children were slain. He speaks of appropriate revenge."

"Diabolical," Danzas muttered.

"Insane," Lepikov said.

"Indeed," Hupp agreed. "It is the madness in his method that will open the door to him."

Godelinsky drained her teacup, put it down and stared down the table at Foss. "Tell me, Ari, if you are this Mad*woman*, how is it you do this thing?"

"In some common food item, perhaps?" Foss said.

"Potatoes?" Lepikov asked. "That is too droll."

Hupp raised a monitory finger. "Ahhh, but she has touched the essence. It must be a *common* thing. It must be something used in Ireland, Britain and Libya, and it must be a thing that exposes the maximum number of women to contamination."

"Why women?" Beckett asked. "Why can't men be the carriers?"

Danzas, following his usual pattern of not contributing to a Team exchange until it was well along, said: "There is another quality required by the limitations we can assume are imposed on our Madman."

Attention turned toward him.

"How does he gain access to the distribution system?" Danzas asked. "I agree that it must be something simple and common to the three regions, but it also must be available to the Madman, and probably without elaborate preparation or a complicated conspiracy."

"He's a loner," Beckett said.

"A devious intelligence," Lepikov said. "The scientific abilities he demonstrates in the laboratory will, I'm sure, apply to his distribution method."

"Devious, yes," Hupp said, "but not necessarily based in scientific complexity. His style . . . it is more likely to be a very common item he contaminates, perhaps something each of us carries on his person at this very moment."

Silence greeted Hupp's suggestion.

Beckett nodded, more to himself than to Hupp. There was the ring of truth about this suggestion. It was O'Neill's style. Simplicity, that was the keynote.

"Why could it not be a conspiracy?" Lepikov asked.

Godelinsky shook her head.

"Insects?" Foss asked.

"An insect vector of the plague," Lepikov said. "Would that not fit your description, Joe?"

"But how would he distribute them?" Hupp asked.

"The eggs or the larvae?" Foss asked.

"Again, the distribution is the question," Hupp said.

"Air travel makes such a concept the nemesis of our world," Lepikov said.

"What about contamination of the water systems in the target regions?" Danzas asked.

"Insects in the water?" Lepikov asked.

"Or the disease itself," Danzas said.

Hupp pounded a fist gently on the table. "Distribution," he said. "How?"

"Just a minute," Foss said. "Insects in the water—that's not a bad idea. Whaling captains deliberately spread mosquito larvae all through the South Pacific as revenge against native societies that offended them in some way."

"Then perhaps an airline attendant or a pilot," Lepikov said. "Is this O'Neill a pilot?"

"Negative," Beckett said.

"But the involvement of air travel in this thing," Lepikov said. "That idea has its appeal."

Beckett said: "Hawaii gets fifty new insects a year thanks to air travel."

"What is carried universally by such aircraft?" Lepikov asked.

"Luggage, packages," Beckett said. "The tourists themselves, but . . ." He shook his head. "This ignores the fact that he pinpoints his targets—Ireland, Britain and Libya."

"With no guarantee that others escape," Foss said

Godelinsky rubbed at her forehead. "And we cannot be sure that he uses only one method. Incubation period—that is essential to our considerations."

"The mails," Hupp said.

"What are you suggesting?" Beckett asked.

"I don't know, really," Hupp said. "I only try to play O'Neill through his performance. What do we know about him?"

"He was in Ireland," Beckett said.

"Exactly!" Hupp said. "And in Ireland he suffers the great agony that drives him to do this terrible thing. But, at some point he has the other experiences of Ireland. What is it he can learn there?"

"I do not follow this," Lepikov said.

"He learns how people spend their days in Ireland," Hupp said.

"And in Great Britain and Libya as well?" Lepikov asked.

Hupp shook his head. "Perhaps, but let us concentrate first on Ireland and O'Neill there. If his performance there can be made to produce answers, perhaps we can adjust those answers to the other places as well."

"Go ahead," Beckett said. And he experienced the odd feeling that Hupp was sniffing along a hot trail. *Go with it!* he thought

"O'Neill is not a resident of Ireland," Hupp said. "Thus, he must stay someplace there. A hotel? Yes, we know this for a fact. What does he do at this hotel? He sleeps. He uses the various facilities of the hotel and the community."

"I do not see any answers," Lepikov said. "Only more questions. So what if he calls room service?"

"For this he uses a telephone," Hupp said. "He has access to a telephone directory."

"And he has tourist guides," Lepikov said. "So what?"

"Let him go with it," Beckett said.

Lepikov shrugged and turned partly away from Beckett.

"Tours and tourist guides, yes!" Hupp said. "That could be important. The colorful brochures, the stores and the restaurants, the drinking establishments, the public and private means of transportation. Does he rent a car or take taxis?"

"He bought a car first thing," Beckett said. "A cheap Fiat, secondhand. We've just had confirmation. It's there in that sheet I distributed this morning."

"I have not yet read it," Hupp apologized. "But now we know he was mobile."

"What happened to the car?" Lepikov asked.

"It was sold for him by the people who sold it to him," Beckett said.

"But he is mobile," Hupp repeated. "Where does he go? Does he attend a sporting event? A lecture? The theater? I direct your attention to common, everyday activities. He buys a book. He mails a letter. He has the concierge make a booking for him at a restaurant."

Danzas shuddered and muttered: "Irish restaurants."

"But O'Neill was beginning to be an active part of the Irish community before tragedy struck him," Hupp said. "He is there and he thinks with a ... with a *thereness.*"

"How does this get us closer to his distribution methods?" Lepikov asked.

"Before he could employ any distribution means," Hupp said, "he had to know it would work in his target areas."

Lepikov heaved his shoulders. "So?"

"What does he see around him that gives him this knowledge?" Hupp asked. "How does he assure himself his method or methods will work?"

"What if he could contaminate paper?" Foss asked.

Beckett moved his lips soundlessly, an unspoken word. He repeated it aloud: "Money!" He looked up to find himself the focus of five pairs of staring eyes.

Hupp exhaled a long "Ahhhhhhhhhh."

"Through the mails?" Danzas asked.

"Would that not contaminate everyone who handled such mail?" Lepikov asked.

"Not if he sealed it in a sterile package within the envelope," Beckett said.

"In plastic," Hupp said.

"I have a device in my kitchen," Foss said. "It's called a heat-sealer. They sell plastic envelopes for it. You put leftover food in the envelopes, seal them hermetically and they can go in the freezer. Later, you bring them out, thaw and heat them—presto, instant dinner."

"Is this not too simple a thing?" Lepikov objected, but his tone said he was awed by the picture being built here.

"It is precisely the level of simplicity we seek," Hupp said. "It is this man's style."

"He'd send it to charities," Foss said excitedly.

"Or to someone collecting for the IRA," Hupp said. "A poetic madness that would appeal to our Madman."

"An Irish-American," Godelinsky said. "Who better to know where in Ireland to send an IRA contribution?"

"He could send money to almost anyone in Ireland," Beckett said.

They looked at him.

"Well, face it," Beckett said. "You're a store owner. You get an order, money enclosed, to send merchandise to the U.S. Or you're just a private citizen, a name taken at random out of a telephone directory. You get a letter from the States, money in it and a simple letter of explanation. Would you send it back? What if there's no return address?"

"But..." Lepikov shook his head. "The money in plastic within the envelope—does this not arouse the recipient's suspicions?"

"Why?" Hupp asked.

"I do not understand how such a thing is explained to the random recipient," Lepikov said.

"Why bother with an explanation?" Foss asked. "Just send the money, local currency. The recipient thinks God has at last smiled upon him."

Lepikov merely stared at her.

"There could be no need for the inner plastic envelope," Godelinsky said. "A latency period for this plague and there would be no danger to intermediaries. We do not know the incubation period."

"If the opening of the outer envelope broke the seal of the inner package, that would do it," Beckett said.

Lepikov, still looking at Foss, cleared his throat. "Can anyone enter an American store and buy one of these devices to seal plastic envelopes?"

"All you need's money," Foss said.

"It is expensive?"

"The one in my kitchen costs less than thirty dollars. You can get them even cheaper on sale."

"I think we have it," Beckett said.

"And it fits the requirements for the other targets," Hupp said. "All he needs is the currency of the selected nation."

"He walks into any Deke Pereras office and says he needs five hundred dollars in British pounds," Foss said.

"But do they not require him to show a passport or other identification?" Lepikov asked.

Foss merely shrugged.

"I like it but we can't be certain yet," Beckett said.

Danzas said: "We must send word to have this investigated immediately."

"I am not satisfied," Lepikov said. "So he sends money to a charity. That I understand. But with others. . ."

"I hear that Catholic charities in Ireland are never very rich," Foss said. "It'd go into circulation quickly."

"He could send money to a sporting club," Beckett said, his tone thoughtful. "A theater group. There're small theater groups and athletic teams all over Ireland."

"Money, so diabolically simple," Foss said.

"How does he apply this scheme to Libya?" Lepikov asked. "We assume he does not speak the language."

Hupp raised a hand, curiously like a student calling for a teacher's attention. Lepikov looked quizzically at him.

"A visit to a Libyan consul, an embassy," Hupp said. "To the United Nations. What would he need to know? The addresses of charity organizations in Tripoli and Bengasi, perhaps? None of this information is difficult to acquire. There are people anxious to give it to you. It is their job."

"Some charities and relief organizations sell their mailing lists," Beckett said. "Or they'll exchange them—their list for yours."

"When I was at UCLA," Hupp said, "a political activist could get almost any mailing list he wanted. I know of one computer specialist who put himself through school by stealing such lists from computer storage systems and selling them."

Danzas turned and looked down his long nose at Hupp. "You associated with political activists?"

"It is called here a learning experience," Hupp said.

"We describe a world of anarchy and madness," Lepikov said.

"To which the Soviet Union has made significant contributions," Godelinsky said.

In Russian, Lepikov said: "Such remarks do not go without notice."

Godelinsky responded in English: "I don't really care." She pushed her chair away from the table and bent over with her head close to the floor.

"You feel faint?" Beckett asked. He got up and went around to stand beside her chair. He could see the white spot on the back of her hand. It was quite prominent. He had dismissed it earlier as a lab discoloration, spilled makeup or perhaps a daub of toothpaste. Now . . . he felt a chill in his guts.

Godelinsky's voice sounded remote and weak from her bent-over position. "I feel faint, yes." She coughed. "It is a very strange feeling. Both faint and excited."

"I think we'd both better turn ourselves in at the hospital facility," Foss said.

Beckett whirled to stare at her. "You, too?"

"The great granddaddy of all headaches," Foss said.

Godelinsky straightened, looking pale. "I wonder . . ."

"It is not possible!" Lepikov said.

"How could the Madman know about this place and what we do here?" Danzas asked.

Hupp stood up and came around to stand beside Beckett. Both of them looked at Godelinsky. Beckett lifted her left wrist and took her pulse. "One hundred and ten," he said.

"Have our speculations been bootless?" Danzas asked. "Is the Madman someone in our midst?"

Hupp looked startled. "One of us?"

"No, no," Danzas said. "But someone with whom we have commerce."

"Let's get these women to the hospital," Beckett said, and he felt a pang of fear for his own family. He had thought them safely isolated at the family's fishing camp in northern Michigan.

OLD MAN: *What do you know of my grief? You're a stripling lad who's never had a woman!*

YOUTH: *And you're a whining old bastard! It's the likes of you cost me all the hope of my life. You think I can't know the grief of something taken because I'd not yet had it?*

—from *Plague Time,* an Irish play

ON THE flight to Paris, John reflected carefully on the things he had done (and was doing) to cover his tracks. The plane was a Boeing 767 with one of the "facelifts" the airline was promoting—slick leather upholstery in first class, extra cabin attendants there, a fine choice of wines and food. John's seat mate was a chunky Israeli businessman who bragged that he had ordered kosher. John made no response, merely looked out the window beside him at the cloud cover over the Atlantic. The businessman shrugged and brought out a briefcase, from which he took sheafs of papers on which he set to work.

John glanced at his wristwatch, calculating the time difference to Seattle. By now, investigators would be raking through the ashes of the Ballard house. They would suspect arson immediately, of course. An all-consuming blaze—multiple thermite charges, phosphor arranged to spill from its water cover, exploding bottles of ether-ammonium hydroxide.

The investigators naturally would seek human remains, but not even bones could survive the heat of that fire. It would not be surprising to have them conclude that "John McCarthy, the inventor," had perished in the accidental ignition of one of his experiments.

The high heat could be enough.

And the investigators would be scrambling the evidence they would want later. By then it would be too late, the ashes hopelessly disturbed.

John's wrist itched under the watch. He removed the watch and scratched, glancing at the back of the case. The engraving was professionally scrolled there, a Spencerian "J.G.O'D." John Garrett O'Day or John Garrech O'Donnell. The O'Day passport nestled in his coat pocket next to his heart. The O'Donnell passport lay with the spares in the secret compartment of the carry-on bag under the seat in front of him. He restored the watch to his wrist. The engraving was a small touch but he thought a good one.

His wallet contained the proper confirmations for the O'Day identity. The Social Security card had been the easiest forgery of them all. Before becoming a chunk of melted slag in the Ballard basement, the little letterpress had produced an assortment of calling cards and letterheads. His checkbook was a valid one from Seattle First National Bank, the home address one of his drops. Not much money there, but enough to establish the account's validity. The bag next to his feet contained letters from invented friends and business associates, all addressed to the proper drop, stamps canceled. Everything agreed with his passport. John Garrett O'Day would stand up under any casual investigation, not that he expected such an occurrence.

With the spare passports in the bag at his feet was his forger's kit and $238,000 in United States currency. He had $20,000 in traveler's checks, purchased in $5,000 blocks, in a leather pouch around his waist. His wallet held $2,016 U.S. and 2,100 French francs, neat and crisp bills from the Deak-Perera counter at Seatac Airport. He thought of this money as the "ready energy" to complete O'Neill's revenge.

At Charles de Gaulle Airport, he rode up through the rather dated plastic tubes to Baggage Claim, retrieved his other bag and strode out under the "Nothing to Declare" sign into a dark afternoon. The smell of diesel was thick under the concrete canopy covering the taxi and bus pickup lanes. The sounds of engines were loud and jangling. A darkly Romanesque woman with heavy features and thick lips stood directly ahead of him in the taxi queue surrounded by shopping bags and tattered luggage, shouting in harsh Italian at two teenage girls who apparently did not want to wait there. Her voice grated on John. His head felt clogged, thinking slowed. He ascribed this to the swift change of time zones. His circadian rhythms were wrong.

He felt a positive relief when the Italian woman and her children climbed into a taxi and drove off. It was even better to enter his own taxi and lean back against the cool upholstery. The car was a shiny blue Mercedes diesel, the driver a thin, sharp-featured man wearing a black nylon jacket with a rip at the right shoulder from which white lining material protruded.

"Hotel Normandy," John said and closed his eyes.

There was a pain in his stomach and he thought: *I'm hungry.* The hotel would have room service. And a bed. Sleep, that was what he needed.

He did not actually sleep in the taxi, although he kept his eyes closed most of the way. There was a general awareness behind his eyes of the swift movement along the Autoroute. The occasional sound of a heavy truck intruded on his dozing. The driver uttered several low-voiced curses. Once, there was the screech of a high-pitched horn. He was aware when they pulled off the Peripherique onto the streets of Paris, the change of rhythm, more stops and starts.

It was almost dark when they reached the hotel and it was beginning to rain, a light drizzle. He paid off the driver and added a generous tip, which elicited a growled *"Merci, M'sieur."* There was no bellman. John picked up his bags and shouldered his way through the two swinging glass doors, to be met there by a hurrying older man in a red-piped beige uniform, who took the bags and greeted him in English.

"Welcome, sir. Welcome."

The lobby smelled of a pungent insecticide.

When he was in his room, a change of clothing laid out for morning, John put a hand on his stomach. Tender. And it felt hard and distended.

I don't have time to be sick.

The room was oppressive, too warm, and it smelled musty. He closed the shades on the two tall windows, which looked onto the Avenue St. Honoré, turned to survey his quarters: a drab green-and-gray floral pattern in the wallpaper. He could hear the old-fashioned elevator grinding and clanking nearby. The room was not even square: it was a trapezoid with a double bed in the wide end. The door to a tiny bathroom opened off one corner of the narrow end, an entry achieved by skirting a heavy bureau. For a closet, there was a giant monstrosity of dark wood furniture beside the bed—drawers in the center, hanging space on each side behind creaking doors. The bottom drawer came out to reveal a thin space underneath. He put his wallet, passport and traveler's checks there and returned the drawer to its proper place.

I'll call room service for some soup.

He felt his gorge rising at this thought and barely made it to the bathroom, where he vomited into the toilet. He slipped to his knees beside the toilet, one hand clutching the washbasin, his stomach heaving and heaving.

Damn! Damn! Damn!

In the back of his mind lay the fear that he had picked up a "stray" from his lab, a random offshoot of his perfectly tailored plague, something unnoticed in the rush of success.

Presently, he climbed to his feet, bathed his face in the washbasin and flushed the toilet. His legs trembled with weakness. He staggered out of the bathroom and threw himself face down on the bedspread. It smelled of caustic soap and his nose was surrounded by the stink of vomit.

Should I call a doctor? The American Hospital would have a reliable doctor.

But a doctor would be the most likely to remember him. And a doctor would prescribe antibiotics. John reflected on the fact that he had made his plague to feed on antibiotics.

What if it is a stray from the lab?

On will power alone, he climbed to his feet, put his precious carry-on bag on the floor of the clothes cupboard and closed the creaking door. He leaned against the cool wood for a moment to recover his strength. Pushing himself away from the cupboard, he fell back onto the bed and weakly pulled part of the bedspread over him. There was a switch beside the head of the bed. He reached it on the third try. Welcome darkness engulfed the room.

"Not now," he whispered. "Not yet."

He was not aware of falling asleep, but there was daylight around the edges of the window draperies when next he opened his eyes. He tried to sit up and his muscles would not obey. A surge of panic swept over him. His body was cold and drenched in perspiration.

Slowly, by a concentrated focusing of his will, he got one

hand out, groped for and found the telephone. The operator, thinking he wanted Housekeeping, sent a Spanish maid, a buxom elderly woman with dyed gray hair and thick arms, the muscles compressed by tight sleeves.

Using her own key, she swept into the room, wrinkled her nose at the thick smell of vomit, took in John's face pale and weak above the rumpled bedspread and said in thickly accented English: "You wish a doctor, Señor?"

Gasping between each word, John managed: "They... are... too... ex... pensive."

"Everything is expensive!" she agreed, coming to stand beside his head. She put a cool palm on his forehead. "You have the fever, Señor. It is the terrible French sauces. They are bad for the estomach. You should stay away from the rich foods. I will bring you something. We see how you are in a little while, eh?" She patted his shoulder. "And I am not as expensive as the doctors."

He did not sense her departure, but presently she was there beside him again with a steaming cup of something hot in her hand. He smelled chicken soup.

"A little broth for the estomach," she said, helping him to sit up.

The broth burned his tongue but felt soothing in his stomach. He drank most of it before sinking back against the pillows, which the Spanish maid fluffed for him.

"I am Consuela," she said. "I will come back when I have finished the other rooms. You are better then, eh? We get you into bed proper."

Consuela returned with more broth, awakening him and helping him to swing his feet off the bed. She had to steady him there.

"You drink," she said. She held his hand with the cup, forcing him to drink all of the broth.

"You are better," she said, but he did not feel better.

"What time is it?" he asked.

"It is time to make the bed and get you into clothing of the night," she said. She brought a chair from outside, wedged it beside the head of the bed and lifted him into the chair, where he sat while she straightened the bed and folded back the covers.

God, she's strong, he thought.

"You are a modest man," she said, standing in front of him, the thick arms akimbo, hands on hips. "We remove only to the underclothing, eh?" She chuckled. "Do not have the face red, Señor. I have bury two husbands." She crossed herself.

Unable to resist, barely able to comment, John went passive while Consuela undressed him and muscled him into the bed. The sheets felt cool against his flesh.

She left the draperies closed, but he still could see daylight around them.

"What...time...is...it?" he managed.

"It is time for Consuela to do much other work. I come back with more broth. You gotta hungry?"

"No." He shook his head weakly.

A wide grin illuminated her face. "You are lucky man for Consuela, eh? I speak the good English, no?"

He managed a nod.

"It is lucky thing. In Madrid I am the maid for Americans. My firs' husband is Mexican from Chicago in the U.S.A. He is teach me."

"Thank," was all he could say.

"Gracias a Dios," she said and let herself out of the room. John slept.

His sleep was tormented by dreams of Mary and the twins. "Please, no more O'Neill dreams," he muttered. He turned and twisted in the bed, unable to escape the O'Neill memories— the twins playing in the backyard of their home, Mary laughing with joy at a Christmas present.

"She was so happy," he whispered.

"Who has the happy?" It was Consuela standing beside him. Darkness framed the draperies of the windows.

He smelled the chicken broth.

A muscular arm slipped behind him and levered him upright. The other hand held the broth for him to drink. It was only lukewarm and it tasted even better than the first time. He heard the clunk of the cup as she placed it on the stand beside the telephone.

"Escusado," she said and snapped her fingers. "Bathroom! You wish to go to the bathroom?".

He nodded.

She half carried him into the bathroom and left him leaning against the washbasin. "I wait outside," she said. "You call, eh?"

When she had him back in the freshly made bed, he asked: "What...day?"

"This day? It is the day after you arrive, Señor O'Day. It is the day O'Day is better, eh?" She grinned at her own joke.

All he could give her was a twitching of the lips.

"You do not wish the expensive doctor, Señor?"

He shook his head from side to side.

"We see tomorrow," she said. She let herself out, pausing to give him a cheery *"Hasta mañana!"* before closing the door.

Morning was identifiable by the return of Consuela. This time she brought a small bowl with a coddled egg in addition to the broth. She propped him up with pillows and spooned the egg into his mouth, wiping his chin as though he were a baby before giving him the broth.

John thought he felt stronger but his brain remained fuzzy and there was this maddening inability to identify the day or the hour. Consuela frustrated him by responding to his question with quips.

"It is the day O'Day eats two eggs in the morning.

"It is the day O'Day has the bread and meat for dinner.

"It is the day O'Day has ice cream with his *comida*.

". . . day O'Day . . . day O'Day . . ." Consuela's cheerful face became an uncountable daily blur, but John could feel his strength returning. One day he took a bath. He no longer needed help getting to the bathroom.

When Consuela took his breakfast dishes away, he lifted the telephone and asked for the manager. The operator said she would connect him *immediately* with Monsieur Deplais. And Deplais was on the line in almost two minutes, speaking with a pronounced British accent.

"Ah, Mr. O'Day. I have been meaning to call you about your bill. We usually require weekly payment, and it has been nine days . . . but in the circumstances . . ." He cleared his throat.

"If you will send someone, I will sign the necessary traveler's checks," John said.

"Right away, sir. I'll bring the bill myself."

John retrieved a packet of traveler's checks from beneath the cupboard drawer and was waiting in bed with them when Deplais arrived.

"Girard Deplais at your service, sir." The manager was a tall, gray-haired man with pleasant, even features and a wide mouth with large teeth. He presented the bill on a small black tray, a pen placed neatly at one side.

John signed ten checks and asked that the surplus be brought to him. "For Consuela," he explained.

"A jewel among jewels," Deplais said. "Myself, I would

have consulted a doctor, but all's well that ends well. I must say you're looking much fitter, sir."

"Then you looked in on me?" John asked.

"In the circumstances, sir." Deplais picked up the tray and the signed checks. "But Consuela is often correct about the illnesses of guests. She has been with us for a long time."

"If I had my own establishment in France, I would steal her away from you," John said.

Deplais chuckled. "A constant hazard in our business, sir. Is it permitted to inquire of your business in Paris?"

"I'm an investment consultant," John lied. He favored Deplais with a speculative look. "And I'm overdue on an important project. I'm wondering if the hotel could get me a hire car with an English-speaking driver?"

"For what day, sir?"

John consulted his inner reserves—still very weak. But in only four days . . . Achill Island . . . the letters. There were things to be done before he dared take his next step. He could feel time pressing on him. Plans would have to be changed. He took a deep, trembling breath.

"Tomorrow?"

"Is that wise, Mr. O'Day? You do look much better, thanks to Consuela's excellent care, but even so . . ."

"It's necessary," John said.

Deplais lifted his shoulders in a pronounced shrug. "Then may I ask as to your destination, sir?"

"Luxembourg. And then perhaps back to Orly. I am not sure. I'll need the car for several days."

"By car!" Deplais was visibly impressed, then: "Orly? You would fly to some destination?"

"I had thought when I was a bit stronger . . ."

"There is talk of another strike by the air traffic controllers," Deplais said.

"Then I may have the car take me to England."

"So far!" Deplais's tone said he thought his guest profligate. As did the rest of the hotel's staff, especially Consuela.

"These Americans! He will not pay the doctor. Too costly. But he hires a car and English-speaking driver for such a journey. My Americans in Madrid displayed the same species of madness. They scream about *pesetas* and then buy the television so big it cannot be moved except by the technician."

BECKETT LAY stretched out, fully clothed on the spartan cot in his tiny quarters at the DIC. His hands were behind his head and he could feel the lumpy pillow on his knuckles. The only light in the room came from the illuminated clock on the desk near his head: 2:33 A.M. He kept his eyes open, staring upward into the darkness. When he swallowed it was past a lump in his throat.

Thank God my family's still safe, he thought.

That entire area of northern Michigan had been cordoned off by special troops.

We're going the way of France and Switzerland.

Fragmented.

If he closed his eyes he knew his mind would be filled with memory pictures of Ariane Foss as she lay dying.

"I'm freezing!" she'd kept complaining.

Between the complaints, however, she had provided them with a clinical picture of her symptoms as seen from within by a mind finely tuned to medical details.

The room in the hospital facility had light green walls, a hard plastic floor scored by the frequent applications of antiseptic. There were no windows, only an inset picture of peaks in the Cascades, a thing mostly of greens and blues designed to give the illusion of space beyond this sterile room. Lines of gray-clad wire ran from beneath Foss's bedding, out over the head of her bed and into a console that linked them to the ivory box of the electronic system that monitored her vital signs. Only one transparent plastic tube ran down from an IV bottle into her right arm: sterile fluid.

From his chair close beside her bed, Beckett could keep an eye on the monitor and on the patient. Her lips moved. No sound; eyes closed. Lips moved again, then:

"There was that odd sort of disorientation at the onset," she whispered. "You got that?"

"I got it, Ari."

"With Dorena, too? What does she say?"

Beckett moved a swing-arm lamp closer over the notebook in his lap, made a note. "We'll have a report from Joe presently," he said.

"Presently," she whispered. "What's that mean?"

"In an hour or so."

"I may not be here in an hour or so. This thing's fast, Bill. I can feel it."

"I want you to think back," Beckett said. "What's the first thing you experienced that you suspect may have been a symptom?"

"There was a white spot on the instep of my right foot this morning," she said.

"White spots on extremities," Beckett wrote.

"Nothing earlier?" he asked.

She opened her eyes. They looked glazed and the eyelids were swollen. Her skin had the pale, bloodless look of death. Almost the color of the pillow beneath her head. Her babydoll features were bloated, the curly hair tangled and sweaty.

"Think back," he said.

She closed her eyes, then: "Ahhhh, no."

"What?" He bent close to her mouth.

"It couldn't have been," she whispered.

"What?"

"Day before yesterday I woke up horny as hell."

He leaned back and scribbled in his notebook.

"You writing that down, too?" she whispered.

"Anything at all could be important. What else?"

"I took a bath and . . . Jesus! My gut aches."

He made a note, then: "You took a bath."

"It was odd. The water never seemed hot enough. I thought it was the damn conservationists, but there was lots of steam and my skin turned red. Felt cold, though."

"Sensory distortion," he wrote, then: "Did you run any cold water over yourself?"

"No." She moved her head slowly from side to side. "And I was hungry. God, I was hungry. I ate two breakfasts. I thought it was just all this upset and . . . you know."

"Did you check your pulse?"

"I don't think so. I don't remember. God, it bothered me, eating that much. I'm always worried about gaining weight. Where've you got Dorena?"

"Just down the hall. We've rigged a UV gantlet and antiseptic sprays in a passage between the two rooms. We thought it was a good idea . . . just in case . . ."

"In case one of us makes it and the other doesn't. Good thinking. I don't think I'm going to make it, Bill. What's that stuff in the IV?"

"Just fluid. We're going to try some new blood in a few minutes. You need white-cell stimulation."

"So it hits the marrow."

"We're not sure."

"When I saw that spot on my instep, Bill, I think I knew right then. My guts felt like a block of ice. I didn't want to think about it. You notice the spot on Dorena's hand?"

"Yes."

"Do a good autopsy," she said. "Find out everything you can." She closed her eyes, then snapped them open. "Was I unconscious very long?"

"Just now?"

"No! When you brought me in here."

"About an hour."

"It hit like a ton of bricks," she said. "I remember you sitting me on the edge of the bed to help me into the gown, then—whap!"

"Your blood pressure went way down," he said.

"I thought so. What about the other women in the DIC? Is it spreading?"

"I'm afraid so."

"Shit!" She was silent for a moment, then: "Bill, I don't think your antiseptic gantlet will be much use. I think men are the carriers."

"I'm afraid you're right." He cleared his throat.

"How much fever?" she asked.

"First high and now it's low-grade—ninety-nine point seven." He looked up at the monitor. "Heartbeat's one forty."

"You going to try digitalis?"

"I've ordered some lanoxin but we're still debating it. It didn't do much for Dorena."

"The autopsy," she whispered. "Look for fibroblasts."

He nodded.

"Got a hunch," she said. "Liver feels like a used football." Beckett made a note.

"You try interferon... Dorena?" she whispered.

"Yes."

"Well?"

"Might as well have been water."

"Noticed my nurse was male," she said. "How bad is it with the other women?"

"Bad."

"What're you doing?"

"We closed the isolation doors. We're lucky this whole damned complex was designed to resist the spread of radio-active contamination."

"Think any of 'em will make it?"

"Too early to tell."

"Any idea how it got in here?"

"Any of us could have brought it in. Lepikov thinks it was him. He says he can't make any contact with his home in the Soviet Union."

"Danzas is from Brittany," she whispered.

"But he hasn't been there for a long time."

"Lepikov," she said. "He got all kinds of briefings before being sent over here. Godelinsky complained about it. Specialists, envoys..."

"Lepikov believes he had a low-grade infection."

"You have any symptoms?" she asked.

"A small case of the sniffles and a slight fever, but that was five days ago."

"Five days," she whispered. "And already I'm dying."

"We think the incubation period may be as little as three or four days," he said. "Perhaps even shorter. It may take a couple of days for a man to become an active carrier."

"Benign in men, fatal in women," she whispered, then stronger: "That Madman is one sick son-of-a-bitch! They still think it's O'Neill?"

"Nobody doubts it anymore."

"You think he's a carrier, too?"

Beckett shrugged. No sense telling her about Seattle and Tacoma. She had enough on her plate. "I'd like to cover your symptoms one more time."

"One more time may be all we have."

"Don't give up, Ari."

"Easy for you to say." She fell silent for almost a minute, then: "Loose bowels that morning I felt so horny. Then thirst. Dorena have that, too?"

"Identical," he said.

"The headache. Jesus, it was bad for a time. Not so bad now. You giving me any painkiller in that IV?"

"Not yet."

"My nipples ache," she said. "Did I tell you to do the best damn autopsy of your life?"

"You told me."

Danzas tiptoed in and whispered to Beckett: "Dorena just died."

"I heard that," Foss said. "That's another thing, Bill. Acute hearing. Everything's so goddamn loud! Can you get me a rabbi?"

"We're trying," Danzas said.

"A fine time for me to go back to . . . Damn! My fucking stomach's on fire!" She stared past Beckett at Danzas. "That Madman's a dirty sadist. He must know how much agony he's causing."

Beckett considered telling her what they had discovered, that most women lapsed into coma and died without waking. He decided against it. No sense revealing that the efforts to keep Ariane alive were prolonging her pain.

"O'Neill," she whispered. "I wonder if his wife felt any . . ." She closed her eyes and fell silent.

Beckett put a hand to the artery in her neck. He nodded toward the monitor above her bed: Blood pressure sixty over thirty. Pulse dropping.

"Every antibiotic we tried on Dorena only worsened her condition," Danzas said. "But perhaps we could try some chemo—"

"No!" It was Foss, her voice surprisingly loud and shrill. "We agreed . . . shotgun for Dorena, nothing for me." She turned a glazed stare toward Beckett. "Don't tell my husband about the pain."

Beckett swallowed past a lump. "I won't."

"Tell him it was easy . . . very quiet."

"Would you like some morphine?" Beckett asked.

"I can't think with morphine. If I can't think I can't tell you what's happening to me."

A male nurse in army blues with a white jacket entered the room. He was a young man with flat, pinched features. His name tag read "Diggins." He stared fearfully at Foss's still figure.

Beckett looked up at him. "You find a proper blood type with a low-grade infection?"

"Yes, sir. He's a confirmed bladder infection. He's already on bactrim."

"White-cell count?" Beckett asked.

"Doctor Hupp said it was high enough. I don't have the numbers."

"Then get him in here. He just volunteered to give blood."

Diggins remained standing in position. "Is it true, sir, that we're all carriers of this thing? All the men down here?"

"Likely," Beckett said. "That donor, Diggins."

"Sorry, sir, but there're a lot of questions being asked out there . . . the doors being sealed and all."

"We'll just have to sweat it out, Diggins! Are you going to get that blood donor in here?"

Diggins hesitated, then: "I'll see what I can do, sir."

Diggins turned on one heel and hurried from the room.

"Discipline's going to hell," Foss said.

Beckett looked at the monitor: Pulse eighty-three, blood pressure fifty over twenty-five.

"What's my blood pressure?" Foss asked.

Beckett told her.

"Thought so. I'm experiencing some breathing difficulty. I'm cold. Are my feet trembling?"

Beckett put a hand on her right foot. "No."

"Feels like it. You know, Bill, I've figured out something. I'm not afraid of death. It's dying scares the shit out of me."

She fell silent, then weakly: "Don't forget, pal—the best damn' autopsy . . ."

When she did not continue, Beckett looked up at the monitor. He could feel her pulse slowing under his hand. The monitor read ten beats per minute and dropping. Blood pressure was diving. Even as he looked, he felt the pulse under his hand stop. The monitor emitted a shrill and continuous electronic shriek:

Danzas went around the bed and turned off the monitor.

In the sudden silence, Beckett removed his hand from Foss's neck. Tears were running down his cheeks.

"Damn him! Damn him!" Beckett muttered.

"They're arranging for us to do the autopsies in the OR," Danzas said.

"Oh, fuck off, you bloody French prig!" Beckett shouted.

> *I have always felt a certain horror of political economists, since I heard one of them say that he feared the famine of 1848 in Ireland would not kill more than a million people, and that would scarcely be enough to do much good.*
>
> —Benjamin Jowett,
> master of Balliol, Oxford

"SURELY, MISTER PRESIDENT," the secretary-general said, "some way could be found to save what's left of your DIC team. They seem to be so remarkably well met."

The secretary-general, Huls Anders Bergen, was a Norwegian educated in England. He had played a number of golf games with the man on the telephone and, on those occasions; they had been Hab and Adam. But Adam Prescott was firmly seated in his office as President of the United States today. There was no camaraderie in his voice.

What is troubling him besides the obvious? Bergen wondered. It was something that Prescott did not want to say without elaborate preliminaries. The President appeared almost to be rambling. Why should he be talking about the procedures for sterilizing infected areas, and in the same breath as the tragedy at Denver? Those procedures had been worked out and accepted by all parties. Could it be something new in the costs?

"I agree, sir, that the economic realities are a prime consideration," Bergen said.

He listened then while Prescott played out this gambit. The

costs, although now thousands of times greater than for any other disaster in human history, were clearly only a part of the President's immediate concern.

Could he be thinking of sterilizing the Denver complex? Bergen wondered.

The thought set his hand trembling with the telephone against his ear.

Bergen, a man who could talk bluntly when it was required of him, asked the question straight out.

"The facilities, not the people," Prescott said.

Bergen heaved a sigh of relief. There was too much death already. This meant, however, that the rumored Colorado Plague Reservation was a reality. Infected men were to be isolated there. Why couldn't the DIC team be sent there, then?

"Could The Team work effectively without the DIC facilities?" Bergen asked.

Prescott did not think so.

Bergen weighed this factor in his mind. Obviously, Prescott and his advisors needed the Denver military facilities. The DIC complex there could be sterilized and made useful once more for the military. But what of The Team?

"They saved us days in identifying how the plague was spread," Bergen said. "And now that we've confirmed it was O'Neill, surely the four men . . ."

The President interrupted. He did not want to isolate such brilliant minds. But what was to be done with them when the DIC was put to the fire? There was no comparable facility available in the Colorado Reservation.

On a sudden hunch, Bergen asked: "Could they be sent to that new facility in England?"

The President was full of immediate and fulsome praise for this brilliant suggestion. Only a genius could have thought of it.

Bergen took the red phone away from his ear and stared at it, then brought the instrument back to his ear. Praise was still pouring from it. He stared across the office at the paneled wall, the dark wood door. His desk chair was the best the Danes could supply and he leaned back in it, the phone still at his ear. A child could have made the suggestion to send those men to England, but Bergen was beginning to see the President's political problem.

If the four infected men of The Team from the DIC were

on an airplane, they might crash in an uninfected region. The crash site would require the "Panic Fire."

Bergen raised this question with Prescott, listening for subtle hints in the President's response.

Yes, it was too bad the press and public would not accept the official label, "Newfire." The words *panic* and *fire* had particularly noxious connotations when used together that way. More was beginning to emerge, however.

Even if a sealed aircraft did not crash, any new plague outbreak beneath the flight path could arouse powerful suspicions that the occupants had spread the infection, that it had somehow escaped and fallen upon more innocent victims. Demagogues were having a field day and it would not do to provide them and the nut fringe of fanatics with more ammunition.

"I think the French might be willing to supply an escort of fighter planes," Bergen said. He looked at the door to the outer office while Prescott showered him with more praise. The French ambassador was among a group patiently waiting to have lunch with him. *A word or two in quiet, perhaps?*

"Mr. President, you are more than generous," Bergen said, cutting off the new flow of praise. "Can you get volunteers for their flight crew?"

Again, the secretary-general listened. How fortunate that Doctor Beckett of The Team was a pilot—Air Force Reserve of all things! And Prescott had this knowledge at his fingertips. How well informed he was! And a long-range aircraft could be made ready. The four men would drive themselves to the airport. They would take off, pick up their escort—and their car and its surroundings would receive its bath of Panic Fire.

Oh, there was one more thing. Could the secretary-general arrange for the four men to receive positions of "useful importance" at the facility in England?

Useful importance, Bergen mused.

He decided on a small fishing expedition. "Is it the wisest choice to send them to England? That lab at Killaloe in Ireland sounds impressive, especially with all of the new equipment you're providing."

"But you yourself suggested England," Prescott said. "I naturally assumed, since it was your first suggestion, that the British facility was the superior one."

"England it is," Bergen agreed.

It was all very clear now. If anything went wrong, then it

was the idea of the secretary-general of the United Nations. It was Bergen, after all, who made the essential arrangements and pushed this project through.

The red phone at Bergen's ear had still more tidbits to reveal, however. Prescott had things to say about O'Neill. Bergen looked at his wristwatch while he listened. The hunger pangs were intense. Abruptly, he lifted his chin, startled.

"They think O'Neill's in England?" the secretary-general asked. "Why do they think that?"

As Prescott explained, it made a terrible logic. The victims, if they exposed him, might be afraid to retaliate lest the Madman loose an even more terrible disaster upon them. O'Neill had threatened this in one of his letters, after all, and without more certain knowledge, no one could afford the assumption that he was bluffing.

"Why not Ireland?" Bergen asked. .

Ah, yes. O'Neill's features were known to some people in Ireland and even if he disguised himself . . . well, the *psychological people* thought the Irish more prone to heedless revenge. Surely, O'Neill would have considered this. It was logical that he would want to hide in an English-speaking country where he was little known and where he could blend into the background more easily. And there was England, *a certain amount of chaos and disruption.* And England was one of his target areas, a place where he had expressly forbidden those Outside to employ atomic sterilization.

It made terrifying sense, but even more: if accurate, it exposed the workings of a mind that could cut through a problem like the slash of a sword. Bergen had a certain awareness of this quality in himself. Complexities must be reduced to manageable shape and size, even if this involved pulling from a complexity only that which could be managed. Mad, O'Neill might be, but also a genius—a true genius.

"How much certainty do they attach to this idea?" Bergen asked.

Ah, yes: the Profile. This was more of the DIC Team's doing. Prescott and others believed The Team was "getting into the Madman's mind, learning to think the way he does."

Bergen silently agreed. Perhaps they were doing this. Certainly, someone must do it.

"I will make the preliminary arrangements for the flight to England," Bergen said. "Someone from my office will call on your people to work out the details."

Having achieved his object without ever openly expressing it, the President was willing to let the secretary-general go to lunch. There was even a suggestion that they get together soon for a round of golf and, then, finally, a more somber note.

"Terrible times, yes," Bergen agreed. "These are, indeed, terrible times, sir."

> *You'll be noting the Ulstermen no
> longer sing "O God, Our Help in Ages
> Past."*
>
> **—Joseph Herity**

As PRESIDENT PRESCOTT replaced the receiver on his telephone, he reflected on the conversation with Bergen. Quite satisfactory. Yes, quite well done on both sides. Of course, Bergen would be calling in the counter he'd just given. There would be a quid pro quo sometime. Well, that could be an advantage, too. Bergen was too good a politician to ask for something he knew he couldn't get.

Charles Turkwood, the President's personal aide and confidant, stood just across the desk from where Prescott sat. The Oval Office was very quiet, not even the sound of someone typing in one of the outer offices. That was one of the things that had happened—not as much typing. More was being done in direct telephone conversation, as just now with Bergen.

Turkwood was a short, saturnine man with close-cropped black hair. Widely set cold black eyes looked out over a rather short nose. The lips were thick, chin wide and blunt. He knew himself for an ugly man, but power had its compensations. He often thought of himself as a perfect counterpoint to Prescott's tall, gray-haired dignity. Adam Prescott had the look of a kindly and benevolent soap opera grandfather. His voice was a gentle baritone.

"He went for it, eh?" Turkwood asked, deciphering the half of the telephone conversation he had heard.

Prescott did not answer. He bent over the desk reading a copy of one of the Madman's letters. Turkwood, perfectly capable of reading upside down, glanced at what had caught the President's attention. Ah, yes—O'Neill's atomic warning:

"You will think of using atomic sterilization upon the targets of my revenge. Don't do it. I will turn against you if you do. The plague must run its course in Ireland, Great Britain and Libya. I want the men to survive and to know what it was I did to them. You will be permitted to quarantine them, nothing more. Send their nationals home—all of them. Let them stew there. If you fail to expel so much as a babe in arms who belongs in one of those nations by reason of nationality or birth, you will feel my anger."

O'Neill said it plainly enough, Turkwood thought.

The President finished reading, but remained silent, staring out the window toward the Washington Monument.

It was one of the President's more disconcerting habits, maintaining a long silence after a statement or a question by a subordinate. It was assumed during such periods that the President was thinking, which he often was. But a silence unduly prolonged allowed considerable time for an underling to speculate about *what* the President might be thinking. Even unimaginative people can imagine very dark things under such conditions.

Of all his close associates, only Charlie Turkwood guessed that this was a deliberate mannerism, cultivated for precisely the effect it achieved.

"He went for it," Prescott said finally, swiveling to face Turkwood. "We'll have to watch carefully now. It's entirely a United Nations thing and we're just going along for the ride."

"What'll he want in return?" Turkwood asked.

"In due time," Prescott said. "All in due time, Charlie."

"Sir, did the secretary-general try to bring up the question of who has ultimate control over Barrier Command?" Turkwood asked.

"Not a word. Bergen understands that we handle only one hot potato at a time whenever that's possible."

"Barrier Command's a dangerous power base, sir. I can't emphasize enough how . . ."

"Easy does it, Charlie. They have one job right now and only one: Quarantine the infected regions—Ireland, Great Britain and North Africa. If they try to go beyond that mandate, there'll be time enough later to deal with them. We have to hold things together, Charlie. That's our main job: hold it together."

It plows up the wild hair of the sea,
I have no fear that Viking hosts
Will come over the water to me.

—**"The Guardian Storm,"**
    an eighth-century Gaelic poem

A LIGHT cruiser of Barrier Command challenged the little sloop off Courtmacsherry Bay while the small boat was on a reach for the Old Head of Kinsale. The sailboat, driving close-hauled in the dull gray light of early evening, found the blustery wind cut off by the light cruiser's towering metal side. The warship, built on the Clyde for the South Africans in the days before apartheid isolation, flew the United Nations flag from its jack-staff. It had held the small boat on radar for almost an hour while it approached and while signals flashed back and forth between it and the headquarters of Admiral Francis Delacourt, the Canadian who headed Barrier Command from his base in Iceland.

"Warn him off," Barrier Command ordered. "A PT boat is being sent to escort him away."

"Probably the press," one of Delacourt's aides had said. "Stupid bastards."

The cruiser came from upwind, turned and backed all engines. It swung ponderously above the sailboat while a rating with a loud hailer braced himself at the opening of a midships loading port. The electric amplifier carried his voice with clipped mechanical tones to John at the sailboat's helm.

"You are in interdicted waters! Sheer off and set course to the south!"

John stared up at the rust-streaked steel sides of the ship. He could see the United Nations flag snapping sharply in the wind but could not hear the snapping over the surge of waves against the light cruiser's hull. Deprived of its wind, the sloop rocked precariously. He could hear water washing in the bilge under his feet.

Only eight meters long, the sloop had cost him sixty thousands dollars at Brest—forty thousand for the vessel and twenty thousand in bribes. After the placing of one hundred and forty thousand dollars in a numbered Luxembourg account, he had thought his reserves ample for the rest of his plan. But the sloop had taken a large bite out of those reserves and he had been forced also to contend with other complications. Chief among these had been a fifteen-day relapse, endured at a *relais* in the outskirts of Brest, during which he had longed for Consuela's muscular ministrations. By the time he was well enough to move around, the world had entered the first throes of his white plague and the cost of everything had mounted at an astonishing rate. It had not helped that negotiations for the sloop and the port clearance had been protracted by the French awareness of urgency in him. The faster he wanted them to move, the slower the French had been and the higher the price had gone.

It was day forty-nine of the white plague before he reached the fifty-degree latitude mark for his turn northward into the Irish Sea and neither the weather nor his balky little radio direction finder had cooperated. The sloop had been designed for protected waters, not for the open ocean or the Irish Sea. The RDF worked only on some time schedule of its own, which might be an hour or more without malfunction and then again only a minute or so until he had to open it and check the connections and the batteries.

Not until he picked up the light at Fastnet Rock far off aport in the early morning hours had he been sure of his course. Dawn had revealed the hills of Ireland rising out of the coastal mists, not another vessel in sight, and he had thought he might make it to landfall without a confrontation.

But here was the damned Barrier Command guardian trying

to deny him passage. Rage filled John as the rating repeated his command.

"Sheer off or we shall be forced to sink you!"

John lifted the small loud hailer he had readied the moment he had seen the light cruiser. He thumbed the switch and pointed the horn at the rating, who was a doll figure up there in the wide hatch. In his best Irish accent, John demanded: "Would y' have me go back to the mobs?"

That should give them pause. Stories of mobs attacking Irish and British nationals in Europe were prominent on the news broadcasts. Libyans, although fewer, were not faring any better.

The rating turned and spoke to someone behind him, then once more faced John with the loud hailer.

"Identify yourself!"

It was an effort to lift his own loud hailer. John still did not feel fully recovered from whatever disease had stricken him. The long, almost sleepless sail from Brest had left him weak and easily angered. He let the anger come out in his voice.

"I'm John Garrech O'Donnell of County Cork, y' bloody fool! I'm coming home!"

Apparently responding to someone behind him, the rating bellowed: "These waters are prohibited!"

"And so's the rest of the world, y' Limey asshole!" John said. "Where else can an Irishman go but Ireland?"

He lowered his loud hailer and stared upward at the open hatch. The little sloop's erratic bobbing and tipping unsettled his stomach, but he forced himself to ignore this. No time to be sick. And there was something ludicrous about this encounter—Lilliput brought up to date. He could hear the rumbling of the light cruiser's engines as it maintained its position upwind of him. The wave action coming around the ship's bow and stern put the sloop in a nasty cross-chop.

The rating once more turned his back on John and there obviously was a consultation going on up there. Presently, the rating's loud hailer once more presented itself to John like a strange mechanical flower protruding from the man's mouth. "I'm authorized to tell you that we are South Africans, you Irish bog-trotter! You are ordered to lower your sails!"

John lifted his loud hailer. "Me engine's not all that good, y' secondhand Limey!"

He wedged his feet against the opposite side of the cockpit

and kept his attention lifted to the rating far above him. A wind came fretting past the bow of the ship, catching the sloop's mainsail and luffing it. John pulled the tiller into his stomach and sailed once more into the light cruiser's lee. When he could return his attention to the ship's open hatch, the rating was not in view.

They had little choice up there, John felt. His accent was passable and, under these conditions, might even convince an Irishman. Who else but a plague-driven Irishman would be fool enough to venture out here in this cockleshell? Sending him back to Europe would be sending him to certain death at the hands of a mob. Only a pronounced American accent had kept him free to act at Brest. It had worked well enough as long as he had dollars to spend freely, but he had felt his welcome vanishing toward the end, swallowed up by the flood of bad news and mounting suspicions.

He did have an Irish name.

Fair play had never been a French strong point, he thought, but fair play might still exist among English-speaking seafarers. Some of that ancient camaraderie of the sea should hold, especially under present circumstances: the steel-ship sailor's romantic admiration for the wind sailor. The angry words he had blared at them could be ascribed to his Irishness and the personal tragedy they must believe he had suffered.

As far as these Barrier Command people were concerned, his condition was simply stated: *To hell or to Ireland.* And they would not be able to avoid the fact. The unwritten law of the sea would be in their thoughts, at least unconsciously.

Any port in a storm.

And when had there been such a *storm* as the plague shaking their world at this very moment?

The rating reappeared at the hatch, his loud hailer directed at John.

"What was your port of departure?"

The question told John he was winning. "Jersey," he lied.

"Have you had contact with the plague?"

"How the hell would I know?"

John lowered his loud hailer and waited. The rating could be seen bending his head to listen to someone behind him, then: "Stand by one! We are putting over a small boat to tow you into Kinsale."

John allowed himself a deep sigh. He felt drained. He restored the loud hailer to its cradle under his seat.

Presently, a derrick boom tracked out of the hatch where the rating had stood. It carried a motor launch in the same dull gray as the unrusted parts of the ship's side. The launch swayed crazily, then was steadied by boat hooks. The boom extended to its limit. John heard the faint rumble and whine of the winch as the launch slid downward to stop just above the wave tops. Men appeared on the launch's deck. They moved purposefully to the cable hooks. Suddenly, the launch plunged into a wave trough. Water splashed around it and the launching tackle swung clear. The small boat surged away from the light cruiser's side in a widely curved white wake. John watched the coxswain at the tiller. The man shaded his eyes against the spray as he swung his boat into position about thirty meters upwind and dropped the power.

The launch was a low craft with a trunk cabin. Its sides gleamed with brass-bound ports. A lieutenant came out of the trunk cabin and pointed a loud hailer at John. Men on the bow readied a small rocket launcher with a line.

"We will shoot a line aboard you," the lieutenant called. "Keep your distance. Does your engine work at all?"

John lifted his own loud hailer. "Sometimes."

"We will cast you free within the bay," the lieutenant shouted. "If your engine starts, proceed to the yacht pier in the south arm. Tie up at the pier and leave your boat immediately. We will sink it before returning. If your engine does not work, you'll have to swim for it."

John retrieved his loud hailer and directed it at the lieutenant. "Aye, aye!"

"When you are under way in tow, drop your sails," the lieutenant called. "If you fall overboard we will not pick you up. Signify that you understand."

"Affirmative."

A sailor crouched in the lee of the launch's cabin steadied himself, raised the launcher, aimed and shot the line neatly under John's boom. John lashed his tiller and carried the line forward where he made it fast to the bitt. He waited for the towline to pull his boat around, then lowered his sails and lashed them loosely before returning to the cockpit.

The cold breeze hit him as they swept out of the light cruiser's protection. In spite of the chill, John felt sweaty. The wind set him to shivering. The surge and pull of the towline had his stomach upset within a mile. He coughed in the stink of the launch's exhaust. Only the coxswain was visible there standing in the stern, the tiller held in his left hand.

It began to grow dark as they cleared the Old Head of Kinsale. John noted that there were no lights of habitation along the shore. The light cruiser keeping pace with them farther out was ablaze with light, though, and John could see the radar antenna sweeping around and around.

John wedged himself into a corner of the cockpit, wondering now how he would be greeted onshore. He had only the O'Donnell identification. It lay in a small shoulder bag just inside the sloop's cabin, nestling there with a Belgian automatic he had bought in Brest, a spartan supply of dried food, a change of clothing and an emergency medical kit he had bought on the Brest black market.

To the north, John could begin to see the glow of other ships, their lights bright against the lowering gray darkness. The six-second blinker at Bulman came into view as they rounded the Old Head. A spotlight on the launch's cabin came on and John could see the signal flashing of it in the glow that bathed the boat's bow. An answering light came blinking from Hangman's Point. The launch held to the left directly into the mouth of Kinsale Harbour, picking up speed now as it went with the incoming tide.

John saw the marker light below the ruins of Charles's Fort off to starboard, one of the landmarks he had memorized. It was full dark now but a sliver of moon gave enough light to show the dark shoreline sweeping past. He felt the turn as they rounded into the south arm of the bay and there was the light at the Customs quay and the town pier. John stood up, steadying himself against the boom. The tow slackened, almost spilling him. The lights of the launch swept past him on the left and it took up station behind. Abruptly, a long row of brilliant lights came on along the pier.

The launch's loud hailer blared: "Clear away the towline before starting your engine."

John scrambled forward, hauled in the wet line and left it tangled on the foredeck. Wet and cold, he crawled back to the cockpit and uncovered the engine, working in the dim glow of the single six-volt bulb in the compartment. He could see the tide race sweeping him toward the pier. The former owner of the sloop had demonstrated the engine once. John primed it, set the throttle and choke, then pulled the starter line.

Nothing.

He pulled again. The engine balked, backfired, then caught. Exhaust fumes drifted across the cockpit.

The loud hailer behind him bawled: "Dock at the float below the pier. Make it quick."

John eased in the clutch and the little engine began to labor, bringing the bow around. It was slow going after the launch but the float was close dead ahead. He realized there were armed men standing along the pier above the float and more armed men on the float. Men caught the sloop as it grated against the landing.

"Leave your engine running," one of them ordered.

"Right."

John took his knapsack from the cabin and leaped onto the float. One of the men there grabbed his arm to steady him, but John felt no friendliness in the gesture.

As though they had done this many times before, the men made fast a line to the sloop's stern, swung the bow around until it pointed out into the bay. One of the men jumped aboard, lashed the tiller and engaged the clutch. White water surged, washing across the float in a shallow wave, as the man on the sloop returned. As he jumped, another man cut the shoreline with an axe. The sloop surged out toward the waiting navy launch.

An arc of flame leaped suddenly from the launch to the sloop. With a roar, the sailboat's bow vanished. Its mast fell backward as the stern tipped up. The propeller could still be seen turning in the lights from the pier. The engine went abruptly silent then and the sailboat slid under the black water.

The launch made a tight turn over the place where it had gone down, a spotlight aimed into the water, then the launch backed and turned with its stern toward the float. Once more the loud hailer blared:

"There's one of your own come home to you, boys. We'll see you next week."

"So it's one of our own, is it?" The voice was a reedy tenor with undertones that sent a chill along John's spine.

John turned toward the pier to confront the speaker and found a machine pistol pointed at his chest. The weapon was held by a tall, skinny man in whipcord trousers, a bulky green jacket and a wide-brimmed hat with the left side of the brim turned up Aussie style. He stood at the foot of the ramp leading up to the pier, his figure outlined by the bright lights from above. The shadow of the hat against the glare concealed his features from John.

"My name's John Garrech O'Donnell," John said, not trying for an Irish accent in this company.

"Sounds like a Yank, Kevin," a man behind John said. "Even though his name's O'Donnell, shouldn't we be feeding him to the fishes?"

"I'll do the deciding, Muiris," Aussie-Hat said. He kept his attention fixed on John. "And what brings you to fair Ireland, John Garrech O'Donnell?"

"I've a talent needed here now," John said, and he wondered at the menace he could feel all around him.

"So you've come back to the land of your ancestors," Aussie-Hat said. "From what place in Yankeeland do you come now?"

"Boston," John lied.

Aussie-Hat nodded. "Ohhh, now, and they're sayin' on the wireless that the plague is bad in Boston. How did you leave the place?"

"I was in Europe," John said. "There's no going back to Boston now. They've put it to the fire."

"That's what they say," Aussie-Hat agreed. "You've family in Boston?"

John shrugged.

"In Ireland then?" Aussie-Hat asked.

"I don't know," John said.

"Is Ireland the only place you could go, then?"

"You've heard about the mobs in France and Spain," John said.

"To hell or to Ireland," Aussie-Hat said. "Was that your thinking?"

John swallowed past a lump in his throat. This man in the Aussie hat—Kevin—his voice cut like a knife. There was life or death here at the man's whim.

"I've a talent Ireland needs right now," John repeated.

"And what might that be?" Aussie-Hat asked. There was no softening of his manner. The machine pistol's muzzle remained pointed at John's chest.

"I'm a molecular biologist," John said. He stared at the shadowy face, looking for a sign that this had registered.

Nothing.

"You're a molecular biowhatsist?" someone behind John asked.

"If we're to find a cure for the plague, my specialty is needed," John said.

"Aw, now, Kevin," the man behind John said, "he's come to cure us of the plague! Isn't that a wonderful thing?"

Several of the men behind John on the float laughed. There was no humor in the sound.

Abruptly, a violent push from behind sent John stumbling toward the machine pistol. Hands grabbed him on both sides, holding him in a painful grip.

"See what's in his pack," Aussie-Hat said.

The bag was jerked from John's grasp and removed to somewhere behind him.

"Who are you people?" John asked.

"We're the Finn Sadal," Aussie-Hat said. "They call us the Beach Boys."

"Look at this, will you, Kevin!" One of the men came from behind John carrying the small case containing his money and the Belgian automatic.

Aussie-Hat took the case and looked into it, holding the machine pistol steady with one hand. "So much money," he said. "You *were* a wealthy man, John Garrech O'Donnell. What did you intend with such wealth?"

"To help Ireland," John lied. His mouth felt dry. There was a feeling of rage all around him, something held poorly in check and that might be unleashed against him at any moment.

"And the little pistol?" Aussie-Hat asked. "What of that?"

"If the mob came for me I was going to make them pay," John said.

Aussie-Hat slipped the case with the automatic and money into a side pocket of his jacket. "Is there any identification on him?"

Hands groped in John's pockets. He felt his pocketknife removed. The wristwatch was slipped off. His wallet and the forged identification was passed to Aussie-Hat, who cradled the machine pistol in one arm while he examined it. He removed the money from the wallet, stuffed it into his jacket pocket and flipped the wallet into the bay.

The forged passport was handed to him next.

He examined it and flipped it casually after the wallet, saying: "O'Donnell, right enough." He leaned close to John, cutting out the glare from the lights above him. John could make out the shadowy features now—a narrow face, two pits of eyes, a sharp chin. Rage threatened to send John struggling against the men who held him. Aussie-Hat seemed to see this and a flash of madness passed between them, rage upon rage, insanity upon insanity. It came and was gone so quickly that John wondered if it had actually happened. He felt that something had touched all of him, the visible and the hidden. And he had glimpsed in the other man, as though in a dark mirror, the other half of himself.

Both men drew back from it.

John stood once more in the glare of the lights from the pier. Aussie-Hat's face lay in the shadows of the hat brim.

Presently, Aussie-Hat said: "I'm inclined to stretch the rule a bit, boys."

Someone behind John demanded: "Because he's an O'Donnell like yourself?"

"You've a better reason, Muiris?" The machine pistol came up and pointed past John at the man who had asked this question.

John realized then that this man in the Aussie hat was capable of killing his companion, that Aussie-Hat ruled by a killing rage, that he had probably killed more than once to win and hold his position of authority.

Was that what we saw in each other?

"Aw, now, Kevin," Muiris said, a whine in his voice.

"I'll kill the next man who questions my authority, or my name's not Kevin O'Donnell," Aussie-Hat said.

"Sure, Kevin," Muiris said, and there was relief in his tone.

"He's to be stripped bare and taken in the lorry to the usual place," Kevin O'Donnell said. "Maybe he'll make it and maybe he won't. That's my decision. Does anyone question it?"

Not a sound came from the men around them.

Kevin O'Donnell returned his attention to John. "The coast belongs to the Finn Sadal. Don't come back to the coast or you'll be killed on sight. You're in Ireland now and here you'll stay, dead or alive."

> *Since it was contaminated money O'Neill used to spread his plague, the Swiss escape is remarkable. It demonstrates that the Swiss are essentially turtles. At the first sign of danger, they pull in all vulnerable parts and expose only the hard shell, and I'd wager everything I own that they burned out some pockets of infection within their borders. It's a thing to remember for later. If people believe the Swiss remained virtually untouched, there'll be a great deal of useful jealousy scattered around.*
>
> **—President Adam Prescott**

ENOS LUDLOW, chairman of the Tactical Advisory Committee, placed the thin folder gently on President Prescott's desk and stepped back one pace. He lifted his attention to the windows behind the President, where a team of gardeners could be seen removing exhausted bedding plants to racked trays for transportation to the White House holding gardens in Bethesda. It was a regular afternoon project these days, this frantic attempt to keep their surroundings alive and beautiful in the midst of death.

The President stared with distaste at the folder, a plain light yellow thing marked Barrier Command. He glanced up at Ludlow, a fat, florid-faced man with cold blue eyes and thinning blond hair.

"Do the Russians agree?" Prescott asked.

"Yes, sir." Ludlow had a soft, almost creamy voice, which Prescott did not like. "The Russians are pragmatists, if nothing else. Satellites confirm that they've lost Kostroma and . . ."

"Kostroma?" The President looked startled, although he had

133

been briefed earlier on this as "a possibility." "Isn't that pretty damned close to Moscow?"

"Yes, sir. And they've lost a whole corridor from Magnitogorsk to Tyumen. It may include Sverdlovsk."

"Any signs of fire?"

"Still smoking."

"The damned media are still calling it Panic Fire," Prescott said.

"Appropriate but deplorable," Ludlow said.

The President glanced at the unopened folder, then once more up at his TAC chairman. "You had family in Boston, didn't you?"

"A brother, sir—his wife and three children." Ludlow's voice lost its creamy tones and sounded strained.

"There was no other choice. We did what the Swiss . . ." Prescott glanced at the folder. ". . . and the Russians did."

"I know."

The President swiveled his chair and looked out at the departing gardeners. He nodded toward them. "Usually, I hear them working. They were very quiet today."

"Everyone feels guilty, sir."

"Jim tells me television is still showing the fires only from a distance," Prescott said.

"That may be a mistake, sir. It leaves the imagination free to create its own pictures of what's happened in Boston and the other places."

The President addressed the window: "Nothing could be worse than the reality, Enos. Nothing." He swiveled his chair back to the desk. "We've decontaminated and replaced the money to the point where we can start lifting the quarantine on the banks."

"Are we sure he only contaminated money, sir?"

"For the time being. He was diabolical. He sent the contaminated money to charities, to individuals, to committees, to stores and shops. Harrods in London confirms that it filled almost eighty orders from him for 'gift packages' to people in Ireland. And the contaminated money was all back in circulation quickly."

"There'll be resistance to using paper money, sir."

"I know. I plan to make a broadcast on the subject. We don't have enough coins to conduct necessary commerce."

"Everyone's waiting for the other shoe to drop, sir."

"And they'll continue to wait as long as O'Neill remains at

large. You're right to be cautious, Enos. We only know *one* way he did it. Our teams have come up with a list of almost two hundred other ways the plague could be spread."

Ludlow's lips shaped the figure soundlessly.

"Two hundred?"

"Contaminated birds, for instance," Prescott said. "And birds don't check in at the border for decontamination. Then there are weather balloons, proprietary medicines.... This O'Neill was also a pharmacist, for Christ's sake!"

The President opened the folder on his desk and looked at the first page. Presently, he lifted his chin and said: "Such a fragile repository of human life, this planet. All our eggs in one basket."

"Sir?"

The President straightened his shoulders and fixed the TAC chairman with a steady glare. "Enos, you make damned sure this is a completely joint mission. I want Chinese, Japanese, French, Soviet and German crewmen on every one of our planes, an exact match for the exchange crews we send to them. When the bombs begin to fall on Rome there'll be hell to pay!"

"Responsibility will be shared equally and completely, sir. They didn't argue that. Pyotr was almost hysterical. 'We waste time!' he kept shouting. 'This thing spreads even as we talk! Do not waste time!'"

"Was there argument?"

"The French wanted to be left out. Catholicism's still a factor there. We didn't even dare approach the Spanish."

"Has the pope been informed?"

"Yes, sir. Vatican Radio's broadcasting a general remission of all sins, the pope's own voice. And they're asking listeners to stand by for an important announcement."

"Do we have enough volunteers for the mop-up?"

"Yes, sir. They'll be isolated on Cyprus afterward. No women alive there at all."

"Fire's the only thing that's sure," Prescott said. "Flamethrowers..." A fit of trembling shook his body, then: "The Joint Chiefs say atomic bombs will leave a ring of *questionable* areas, especially the Russian bombs." Abruptly, he pounded a fist on the desk. "God! I curse the day I ever ran for this office!"

"Someone has to make these decisions, sir. No one questions that."

Prescott grated his teeth at this platitude, then: "What about India?"

"No word yet, sir. But we sent the joint communiqué. If they haven't responded by nineteen hundred hours, they know what to expect."

"There's no such thing as exclusive sovereignty anymore, Enos. If they have hot spots and fail to report them, we'll sterilize the whole fucking subcontinent!"

"After Rome, sir, I'm sure they'll understand."

"They had better! Isn't there any good news?"

"Sri Lanka is clean, sir. Quite a number of the Polynesian islands escaped. Even Kauai in the Hawaiian chain—that's confirmed now. And Alaska—only Anchorage got it and the decontamination is complete there."

"Decontamination," Prescott said. "Every outrage has its own euphemism, Enos."

"Yes, sir."

Prescott closed the folder on his desk.

Ludlow pointed at it. "Sir, there's something you should know before the Joint Chiefs come in. The Chinese are threatening to hit India on their own. Apparently, there's been an exchange of notes—not friendly."

"Do the Russians know?"

"They're the ones who informed us. They advised hands off, but say they'll understand if we interfere."

"Understand? What the hell does that mean?"

"They'd like us to get our hands dirty, sir."

"And how the hell could we interfere?"

"Perhaps a diplomatic delegation to . . ."

"Delegation, shit!"

"I thought you should know, sir."

Prescott sighed. "Yes, of course. You did the right thing."

"There's something else, sir."

"Won't it wait?"

"I'm afraid not, sir. The Saudis have closed their borders."

"Oil?"

"The pipelines remain open, but the pilgrims to Mecca . . ."

"Oh, Christ!"

"It's pretty certain they're contaminated, sir. Big contingents from North Africa and . . ."

"I thought we quarantined . . ."

"Not in time, sir. The Saudis want help."

"What're the Israelis doing?"

"Their borders are still closed and heavily patrolled. They say they're doing fine."

"Do you believe them?"

"No."

"Do they know about this Saudi thing?"

"We assume so."

"Give the Saudis whatever help they need."

"Sir, it's not quite that—"

"I know the complexity of it! But we'll lose Japan if they don't get oil and our own needs..." Again, he shook his head.

"There's one other thing, sir."

"Haven't you done enough?"

"Sir, you'd better know this. The cardinals have voted by telephone conference. James Cardinal MacIntyre will be the new pope when...I mean, when Rome..."

"MacIntyre? That asshole! That's all I need!"

"He was a compromise, sir. My informants..."

"You know what they call MacIntyre in Philadelphia? The Baptist!"

"I've heard that, sir."

"He's a disaster! The Church may not survive him." Prescott sighed. "Get out, Enos. On your way, tell Sam to wait two minutes before sending in the Joint Chiefs."

"Sir, someone has to bring you the bad news."

"You've brought me enough for today, Enos. Get out! And two minutes, mind you."

"Yes, sir."

As the TAC chairman let himself out, Prescott opened the folder once more and looked at the first page.

"So fragile," the President muttered.

> *Though you bring back the sons of Morna and the Seven Armies of the Fianna you will not lift this sadness.*
>
> **—Father Michael Flannery**

THE DIC Team's takeoff had been scheduled for 10:00 A.M. Denver time, but there was a half-hour delay while the flamethrower tanks were redeployed because of a wind shift. Beckett and his three companions waited it out in the plane, conscious of the tanks rumbling as they moved around the airport's perimeter. The plane smelled of jet fuel.

An Air Force colonel had set up the flight necessities, briefing Beckett by radio and telephone. "Expect some changes and ambiguities," he had warned.

The colonel had pointedly referred to Beckett as "Major." Lepikov, overhearing one of these conversations, had asked: "Tell me, Bill, how is it a doctor is also a pilot in your Air Force?"

Beckett's answer: "I wanted a second career in case my knife ever slipped."

This had aroused no smile from Lepikov, who said: "I think you are more than you appear."

"Aren't we all?"

The plane was a modified Lear with tip tanks and extra tanks

138

inside, which made the cabin a cramped area bound in by new fiberglass walls behind which the extra fuel could be heard sloshing when the aircraft moved.

Choice of the Lear had been motivated by Beckett's experience: he had twenty-one hours in Lears. His jet ratings also were current for three different fighters, including the old Phantoms, which he admired the way a teenager would admire a hot automobile. Beckett had also once flown an Egyptian Air Force Mirage and said he was looking forward to a proficiency demonstration by the French escort, which would be using relays of the Mirage III.

The extra half hour gave Beckett time to make a careful cockpit check. He went through it methodically, a pattern any of his nurses would have recognized from his operating-room behavior.

Sectional charts all in order.

Notams provided.

Weather information current

He noted that the initial altitude would be 35,500 feet and muttered under his breath. He had asked for clearance to fifty.

The flight plan had been extended where possible to take them over less populated areas, but it swung past Cleveland and south of Buffalo, then out over Boston. From there it passed south of Greenland and Iceland, then down into the United Kingdom. Barrier Command escorts would take over at Iceland.

Beckett had been warned that escort instructions were to shoot down the Lear if it deviated from a five-mile-wide corridor.

The fuel-conserving flight time had been estimated at about thirteen hours, putting them at Manchester, England, about 6:30 A.M. local. Barrier Command rockets were scheduled to smash into the Lear six minutes after Beckett parked it at the end of the Manchester strip. Before landing, Beckett's instructions were to dump any excess fuel, using a switch system that automatically transmitted a confirmation signal to Barrier Command.

"Otherwise you will be strafed while ground personnel are still in and around the aircraft," the briefing colonel had warned.

They were taking no chances that someone on the ground would attempt to hijack the Lear and leave England.

As Beckett was finishing the cockpit check, Hupp moved

forward and slipped into the right-hand seat. "Do you mind, Bill?"

"Just don't touch anything."

Beckett scanned the instruments. He was glad to see the latest satellite-relay navigation screen on the panel. There was a note from the installers giving him a list of the critical deviations. There had been no time to fine-tune the thing.

As the booster truck moved into position, its operator wearing a spacesuit and breathing through tanks on the truck, Beckett went through the procedures automatically while his mind read him the flight numbers: four hours fifty-seven minutes Colorado Springs to Boston; thirteen hours thirty-three minutes elapsed time to Manchester—twenty-nine minutes behind the original schedule. Headwinds over the Atlantic. They should be over Boston about 5:30 P.M. And they should have two pilots in this cockpit! He glanced speculatively at Hupp beside him and decided against delegating some of the takeoff routine. Hupp was obviously nervous.

Beckett turned back to his instruments and controls, reminding himself that this plane had to be flown Lear-fashion. This was a demanding aircraft susceptible to pilot-induced lateral oscillation. He had to be on his toes at every minute during takeoff and landing to avoid a Dutch roll, a half snap that could whip them into the ground. He had to fly it by the numbers.

His earphones told him: "Taxi to runway thirty-five, Mister Beckett. Your gross weight figures at 12,439 pounds."

Beckett made a note of this and responded: "Goodbye, Peterson Field."

"Good flight, Major."

Beckett recognized the voice of the briefing colonel up there in the tower. Strange that the man had never provided a name. Lots of odd things in this new world.

"Activate your special transmitter," the colonel ordered.

Beckett flipped a red switch on his panel.

"What's that?" Hupp asked.

"Our leper's bell." Beckett glanced left and right. "Now, shut up until I get us straight and level topside."

As the Lear gathered speed down the runway, Beckett saw the flamethrower tanks already speeding in to the parking position. Their car, which had been left at the taxi ramp, would get it first, then the entire area would be washed in flame. Fire carried a sense of cleansing finality, Beckett thought. Burned things tended not to reproduce.

The Mirage III escort, four aircraft, was with him before he reached the Thurman Intersection outside Denver. He waved at the flanking pilots rather than tip his wings. The pilots gave him a thumbs-up before dropping back. One took up station directly behind. Beckett nodded to himself. He had seen the armed rockets under the swept wings. Those rockets were an important reality on this flight. They required some tight navigation from Bill Beckett.

The radio interrupted his thoughts with a weather check. Headwinds eased back slightly over the Atlantic but nothing to cheer about.

Beckett heard it out, then thumbed his mike for intercom and said: "Keep your seatbelts fastened when you're not in the toilet. No unnecessary moving around. We have uncertain weather off the coast and I'll have to nurse this bird all the way. We need every ounce of fuel."

At thirty-five thousand feet, he leveled off and trimmed, announced his position, then turned to Hupp. "We may not have a pisscup of fuel left when we get there."

"I have confidence in you, Bill. Tell me, what is the leper's bell?"

"We transmit a constant special ID. If it goes silent, whammo!" He glanced out at a Mirage III that had taken up position on the right. "Your buddies out there mean business."

"I see the rockets. They would use them."

"You better believe it, Joe."

"You don't mind if I ride up here with you?"

"Glad of the company when I'm not busy. Just keep your feet off those pedals and don't touch the wheel."

"I hear and obey, Mon Capitaine."

"Very good," Beckett said, grinning and relaxing for the first time since he had climbed into the plane. "Just keep the Foreign Legion in mind and remember how a *capitaine* punishes disobedience."

"Stretched out in the hot sun for the Berbers," Hupp said. "The vultures waiting. Yes, I have seen that movie."

Beckett thumbed his microphone for a position check from ground stations, then: "Have you thought what this little trip is costing? This plane with modifications and all, I'd guess close to ten million. One trip and bam! This may be the costliest trans-Atlantic flight in history."

"But first class," Hupp said. "Except in the back. You can hear the fuel moving in those tanks."

"That bothers you?"

"I do not like fire."

"You'd never feel it. Someone once said an airplane is one of the better ways to go. It may kill you but it won't hurt you."

Hupp shuddered. "I once steered the airplane of a friend near Lyon. I did not like the feeling."

"Some do; some don't. What were you and Sergei and Francois buzzing about back there before we took off?"

For answer, Hupp said: "You have children, Bill?"

"Huh? Yeah. Marge and I have two daughters." He crossed his fingers. "And they're still safe, thank God. What's that have to do with..."

"I have two boys. They are with my family near Bergerac in the Dordogne."

"Are you changing the subject, Joe?"

"Not at all. I like the Bergerac region."

"Cyrano's hometown," Beckett said, deciding to go along with this strange turn in the conversation. "How come you don't have a big nose?"

"I was never asked to hunt truffles as a child."

Beckett emitted a barking laugh, feeling it relieve his tensions. Was that Hupp's motive, ease things?

"We are a good team, Bill," Hupp said.

"One helluva team! Even old Sergei back there."

"Ahhh, poor Sergei. He has convinced himself that he and Ariane would have experienced the grand passion. Death has thwarted the great love story of the age."

"Was that what you were talking about?"

"Only in passing. It is a strange thing about our group. We are fitted to each other in a most remarkable fashion—almost as though fate had designed us to work together on this thing."

"We're going to lick it, Joe."

"I agree. Those two tragic deaths have motivated us in a very powerful way. And the information from the autopsies— my head is buzzing with it. If the liver..."

"What's it like in the Dordogne?" Beckett interrupted.

Hupp glanced at him, remembering the other Beckett under the hot lights of the OR, the deft and certain movements of his scalpel. Yes, this Beckett here in the aircraft was the one who had cursed Francois.

"Every fall in the Dordogne, we hunt the *cèpe* mushroom, the *boletus edulis*," Hupp said. He touched his fingertips to his lips and blew a kiss. "Bill, when we have triumphed over this plague, you must bring your family. We will have a party—*cèpe* and strawberries—the little *fraises des bois.*"

"That's a deal."

Beckett paused to make a course correction. The land below him was a patchwork of rectangular farms glimpsed through a partial cloud cover. The Lear felt smooth and steady.

"We are very old-fashioned in the Dordogne," Hupp said. "In France we are thought of much the way your people think of hillbillies. My marriage to Yvonne was arranged. We had known each other since childhood, of course."

"No hanky-panky beforehand?"

"In spite of all the stories, we French do not kiss and tell. My lips are sealed."

"An arranged marriage? I thought that went out with tin pants and matching jacket."

Hupp looked puzzled. "Tin pants and...Oh, you mean armor." He shrugged. "How old are your daughters, Bill?"

"Eight and eleven. Why? You thinking of arranging marriages for them?"

"My sons are fourteen and twelve. Not a bad difference in the ages."

Beckett stared at him. "You serious?"

"Bill, have you thought of the kind of world we will enter when we have beaten this plague?"

"A little, yeah."

"It is not good that our team must communicate with the other investigators through the political leaders of our nations."

"They're all looking for an advantage."

"The very thing Sergei said. But things are changing. I am serious about our children, Bill. Why shouldn't the intelligent marry their children to children of the intelligent?"

"You know it doesn't work that way, Joe. The offspring wouldn't necessarily..."

"I know the genetic rule, Bill. Deviation to the center. Our grandchildren would tend to be not quite as smart as their parents...perhaps."

"What's on your mind, Joe?"

"The very different world our children will inherit. The pattern is already making itself evident. Small local governments with strong borders. Switzerlands everywhere. Suspicion of strangers."

"With good reason!"

"Granted, but consider the consequences if the big governments vanish."

"You really think they're on the way out?"

"It's obvious. Of what use is a big government when a single individual can destroy it? Governments will have to be small enough that you know every one of your neighbors."

"Good God!" Beckett took a deep, trembling breath.

"We may achieve a single worldwide currency," Hupp said. "Perhaps an electronic currency. There will still be some trade, I think. But who would dare attack his neighbor when one survivor could exterminate the attackers?"

"Yes, but if we can cure . . ."

"The variations on this plague are infinite, Bill. That's already plain."

"There'll still be armies," Beckett said, his tone cynical.

"Who would dare maintain a military force when the possession of such a force is an invitation to disaster, keeping your populace in constant peril?"

"What do you mean?"

"Your military force cannot practice its arts upon its neighbors. The old weapons are outmoded."

Beckett took his attention off the Lear's course and stared at Hupp. "Jesus Christ!" he whispered.

"We have opened Pandora's Box," Hupp said. "This plague is just the first, I fear. Think about it a moment, Bill—the variations on this plague . . ."

"One man alone did it," Beckett said, nodding.

He glanced out at the Mirage III beyond his left wingtip, then back to Hupp. "A police state could . . ."

"Sergei thinks not. He has been thinking very hard about this matter. He even suspects his masters have a plan to kill off some scientists once they have . . ."

"What if they miss the wrong one?"

"Yes. What if there is another plague, a mutation? And they have no resources with which to meet this threat? Or what are your neighbors doing with *their* scientists? Oh, no! This tiger has a long tail."

Beckett put the Lear on autopilot and announced this to their escort. He leaned back and clasped his hands behind his head.

"The airplane flies itself?" Hupp asked, a touch of fear in his voice.

"It flies itself."

"English has this valuable reflexive form," Hupp said. "My thought is expressed better in English—that we ourselves created this Madman. We have done this thing to ourselves. We are both action and object."

"You've been thinking about this for some time," Beckett said.

"I think I know what kind of world our children will inherit."

"I only hope they'll inherit any kind of world."

"That is the first order of business, yes."

Beckett glanced sideways at Hupp. "You were serious about marrying your sons to my daughters."

"I am serious. We will find a need to arrange marriages across the new borders. Exogamy is not a new device, Bill."

"Yeah, we'll have to keep expanding the gene pool."

"Or suffer genetic deterioration."

Beckett lowered his hands and scanned the instruments. He made a course correction. Presently, he said: "We not only need a cure for the plague, we need a medical technique for dealing with the general problem."

"Medical?" Hupp asked. "Only medical?"

"I see what you mean, Joe. Public medicine has always had its political hurdles, but this one . . ."

"We think there should be strategically placed centers around the world, tight communications links, a complete computer interchange without regard to national boundaries, voice and video, no censorship. Scientists should join hands with no regard to nationality."

"You're dreaming, Joe."

"Perhaps."

"Our families are hostage to our good behavior, dammit!"

"And the rest of our world is hostage to its good behavior."

"What if some research establishment in the Soviet Union solves it before we do?"

"It makes little difference as long as many of us know the solution."

"Christ! You're talking about a conspiracy of scientists!"

"Exactly. And any researcher who thinks this thing through will come to our conclusions."

"You really think so? Why?"

"Because there's enormous power in it . . . and anything else is chaos."

"Sergei goes along with this?"

"Sergei has a fine appreciation for personal power. And he

has friends in strategic places within the Soviet Union."

"He agrees to plot against his bosses?"

"He suggests we call it among ourselves the 'Foss-Gode-linsky Cabal.'" Hupp cleared his throat. "Your friend Ruck-erman..."

"He's in Washington and I'm here."

"But if the opportunity arose?"

"I'll have to think about it."

"Think long and hard, Bill. Think about all the good things that could be done with this knowledge. Think of the value in such knowledge."

Beckett stared at him. "You surprise me, Joe."

"I surprise myself, but I think this is a logical answer to giving our children a world they will want to inherit."

"Francois, what does he say about it?"

"You value his opinion?"

"On this sort of thing, yes."

"In a way, you're alike, you and Francois. You are con-servatives. It is that which convinced Francois. He wishes to conserve certain values in our world."

"Well, the politicians have sure as hell made a mess of it."

"Francois said something similar, but then he has not ad-mired a politician since de Gaulle."

"Another general," Beckett said.

"Like Eisenhower?"

"Touché."

"Then you will think about this?"

"Yeah."

"Good. Where is the autopsy summation? I saw you with it before we left the DIC."

"It's in my flight bag right behind me." Beckett gestured with his elbow. "Right on top. It's open."

Hupp leaned across the console and slipped a sheaf of papers from the bag behind Beckett's seat. As he did so, he glanced back into the aircraft.

"Sergei and Francois are asleep," he said. Hupp straightened and flattened the papers on his lap.

"Best thing they could do," Beckett said. He pulled up a sectional chart and took an RDF bearing for his position.

"Where are we?" Hupp asked. He looked down, seeing cloud cover bright in the sunlight.

"We'll be crossing Mansfield, Ohio, pretty soon. We have to head north there to miss Pittsburgh."

Hupp looked at the autopsy report in his lap. "Is it true, Bill," he asked, "that you cried when Ariane died?"

"Is that what Francois said?"

"He said you cursed him and you cried, and he said it was an admirable thing in you. The passing of a friend should not go unremarked."

"That lady had balls," Beckett muttered.

> *If I am not for myself, who is for me? But if I am for myself alone, who am I?*
>
> —**Hillel**

HULS ANDERS BERGEN turned off all of his office lights and strode to the window, knowing the way even in darkness. New York street lights from the United Nations Plaza far below filled the foggy night with a faint glow, an underlighted silvery movement, vaporous and mysterious. Although he knew the temperature had not changed in the office, he felt suddenly cold.

For more than an hour he had been going over and over in his mind that afternoon's press conference. The well-known Kissinger admonition was much in his thoughts:

"It is a mistake to assume everything said in a press conference is fully considered."

But all of his staff had agreed that something had to be said to the reporters. He had chosen to make it a background briefing, something they could credit to "a high official of the United Nations."

Too many delicate unknowns complicated the world scene. There was too much secrecy. He had chosen to part the veils slightly.

There had been the preliminary report of the archaeologists

148

who had been called in to sift the ashes of the burned-out house in Seattle. There was a touch of brilliance in that decision, he thought. Archaeologists! Brave men. They had known they could not return to their families.

The foggy curtain outside his window thinned somewhat in a drift of wind, giving him a glimpse of a convoy far below moving out toward the end of the island. That would be their military guardians changing shifts. With its tunnels blocked and the bridges down, Manhattan was now considered a fairly secure bastion. There were still some burned-out pockets within the city and only official traffic moved on the streets at night, but it had shaken down into a new pattern that some were calling "secure."

It was a false security, Bergen thought.

The military cordon drew a jagged line around the city, extending into New Jersey from near Red Bank west to Bound Brook, swinging northward there along the Watchung Mountains to Paterson; then, growing increasingly erratic, it meandered over the New York–New Jersey boundary through White Plains and out to Long Island Sound north of Port Chester.

"The Flame Wall," people called it, taking their sense of security from the image of the wide blackened barrier beyond this land, a place where ashes drifted across mounds of ruins and the unburied bodies of those who had perished on that ground.

Bergen did not like to think of the human deaths represented by the Flame Wall, the ones killed in its creation and the ones who had died trying to cross it into the sanctuary of New York.

Barriers, he thought.

Everything was barriers in this new world. Identity cards and barriers. You could be summarily shot for not possessing a valid identity card.

Barrier Command had set the pattern.

Within the reassurance of that label there lay a nasty sound to Bergen's ears. He pictured the naval blockade around Ireland and Great Britain, the combined naval and land blockade around North Africa. *Massive* was the only word for it.

The glowing face of Bergen's wristwatch told him it was only 8:53 P.M., less than three hours since he had measured his press-conference performance against the evening's television reports. The anchorman had parroted the words of the "high official."

"Essentially, we ignored a crucial thing happening in technology and scientific research. We failed to see the central bearing of this factor on all international affairs. To my knowledge, not a single high official in any government seriously considered that one individual alone could create such devastating chaos as this man, O'Neill, has done."

The next question had been anticipated and the answer carefully prepared.

"The evidence is overwhelming that it was this John Roe O'Neill and that he acted alone."

They had not expected him to be open and candid about the findings in Seattle.

"There is virtually conclusive evidence that the Ballard basement is where he concocted his devilish brew."

"Sir! Brew? Singular?"

That had been a balding reporter from the *Post*.

"We cannot be certain," Bergen had admitted.

The conference had moved then into the area that had prompted Bergen to call it, defying the President of the United States and a half-dozen prime ministers.

North Africa and, now, the Saudis.

"Led by the Soviet delegation," he had told the reporters, "there is pressure for a drastic change of tactics in North Africa and surrounding regions."

After all of the years of carefully censoring his words, it had felt good to Bergen just to say this, speaking out truthfully and with no diplomatic embroidery.

Let them vote me out, he thought.

The Rommel campaign had been a clear demonstration that desert patrols could be penetrated. The British had moved in and out of Rommel's lines. And now, the Saudi problem had to be confronted in the light of that knowledge.

How bad was the contamination?

Israel was threatening atomic sterilization of its "borders," a clear Talmudic fist being shaken in the direction of Saudi Arabia.

The only thing holding them back was the Madman's threat. Would this atomic sterilization be considered an act against the targets of O'Neill's revenge? There had been an untallied number of Libyans among the Mecca pilgrims.

And what about the source of the contamination—North Africa?

The Russians wanted a "ring of fire," another Flame Barrier.

It was their euphemism for a plan to put a linked series of outposts around the land perimeter: flamethrowers, radar, day and night air patrols, barbed wire . . .

"Damn the cost!" they said. "We're talking about survival!"

The real question, though, was where would their perimeter be drawn? The Saudi problem threw this issue into high relief. Israel had its own suspicions about where the Soviet Union wanted to install its "ring of fire."

Hysteria is infectious, Bergen thought.

The United States wanted a "ribbon track" of cobalt dust around the area, a radioactive moat that no life could cross and survive. This told Bergen, among other things, that the United States had squirreled away a large stockpile of such dust. He had argued that radioactive contamination of the entire Mediterranean basin would be an inevitable consequence. Israel had been outraged.

What choice did they have? the United States had asked. What other decisions made sense now that Turkey, Lebanon, Syria and southern Italy were being written off? Only Israel remained as a fragile island of plague-free land within that contaminated region.

And how plague-free were they? No outside observers were being permitted to investigate.

As the French ambassador had said at their morning meeting: "Losses are inevitable. The sooner we accept them the better."

He had cited Brittany, Cyprus and Greece as his supporting arguments.

All of this Bergen had told the press, speaking plainly and without the usual euphemisms. He had held back only on the heated argument between the French and the Israelis. Name-calling was not a new thing within the United Nations' walls, but this had transcended past performances.

"You are anti-Semitic animals!" the Israeli had shouted.

Oddly, the Frenchman had responded only: "France, too, is a Mediterranean nation. Whatever we do there will have its effect upon us."

The Israeli would not accept this: "Don't think you fool us! France has a long history of anti-Semitism!"

It was understandable that tempers were short, Bergen thought. Somehow, diplomacy had to survive despite this atmosphere. They did not dare go their separate ways.

Could Israel be relocated in the Brazilian heartland, as had been suggested?

A new Diaspora?

It might come to that, Bergen thought, even though Brazil said it could take no more than half of Israel's population, and there were a multitude of strings attached to the offer. Brazil, of course, was looking at Israel's *atomic capability*.

Bergen thought of the Israelis sitting there in their desert oasis, their atom bombs wrapped in the Talmud. An excitable people, he thought. There was no telling how they might respond to such an international decision. And Brazil—had it really considered what it might be letting within its borders? It was Bergen's opinion that Brazil would become the new Israel, that there would be no way to confine such resourceful people.

And there were so many unknowns. What was really going on within Israel's borders? They would have to permit outside inspection and soon.

He put aside the Brazilian suggestion, although it had excited the media. An interesting distraction, perhaps, but the magnitude of such a move made Bergen shudder.

As he had been expecting, the red telephone's light came on and its chime sounded. Bergen returned to his chair and lifted the phone from its cradle.

Prescott surprised him immediately.

"That was a damn smart move going public that way, Hab!"

Familiarity! Something was cooking, as the Americans were fond of saying.

"I'm glad you think so, Adam. I must confess I was a bit uncertain of your reaction."

The President produced a mild chuckle. "My old mother used to say that when things start to stick to the bottom of the pot, you give it a brisk stir."

Cooking, indeed, Bergen thought. He said: "I had something on that order in my mind."

"Knew you did. I told Charlie that was what you were doing. Tell me, Hab, what's your reading on this Admiral Francis Delacourt?"

Bergen recognized the tone. Prescott was getting right to the point. Barrier Command's chief was an obvious question mark. A lot of power sitting out there on its own in Iceland. The secretary-general did not envy Delacourt, especially now with Prescott probably gunning for him.

"He seems to be doing a pretty good job, Adam."

"Pretty good?"

"Something bothering you, Adam?" That was an advantage of the familiar, Bergen thought. You could ask the loaded question without any resort to diplomatic niceties.

"He's French back there somewhere, isn't he?" Prescott asked.

"His family came from Quebec, yes."

"I hear he's a historian."

Bergen recalled Delacourt's statement accepting the Barrier Command post. There had been a pedantic tone in it: *"It's the same problem the Romans had but with modern tools."*

My sources say he's quite a respectable historian, Adam," Bergen agreed.

"Patton was a historian," Prescott said.

Patton? Oh, yes, the World War II tank commander. And there had been something at the time about Patton admiring the Romans.

"Quite a few military leaders have had that hobby," Bergen said.

"Bothers me," Prescott said. "Is he going to have delusions of grandeur, too?"

Too? Bergen wondered. Was that how Prescott thought of Patton?

"I've seen no signs of that," Bergen said.

"I think we should keep an eye on him," Prescott said, and then the kicker: "The Russians have just been talking to us about him. He worries them, too. And by the way, Hab, I had the devil's own time smoothing them down. They were really upset by your off-the-record briefing today."

"It's good to have you on my side, Adam."

"Depend on it, Hab. Well, 'nuff said. Why don't you get out the admiral's general orders and have another look at them?"

"I'll do that, Adam. Anything special I should look for?"

"Damn! You talk just like an American sometimes," Prescott said. "I've nothing special there, nothing in mind at the moment. I just think we should start making sure he has to second-guess us, not the other way around."

"I'll make it a point to give his performance my special attention," Bergen said.

"You do that, Hab. And while you're at it, you might look into the rumor that Delacourt's boys have sunk a few coffin ships with all their occupants aboard."

"Ahhh, I hadn't heard that rumor, Adam. New?"

"It just surfaced. Well, good talking to you, Hab. Long as

we stay clean we may get in that golf game yet."

They broke the connection.

Bergen got out his copy of Delacourt's general orders and read them over twice. They were pretty direct.

"If you make physical contact with any person from the Proscribed Areas, your own people will kill you or drive you onto the shore, where the inhabitants likely will do the job for us."

That paragraph, for instance. There was no mistaking its meaning.

Bergen sat back and thought about Delacourt. It was pretty clear that the admiral thought of his problem as deer-stalking in the coves and inlets of those rocky coasts.

A game?

If so, death was the price of failure.

". . . the same problem the Romans had but with modern tools."

Tools? Was that how Delacourt thought of battleships and all the rest of it? Tools? All of that firepower. Then again, perhaps he was right. Caesar had probably thought in a similar way.

And what did the coffin ships have to do with Prescott's concerns?

Bergen did not want to think about the coffin ships, but there was no avoiding it now. Did it matter in the larger sense if Delacourt's people sank some of those ships with occupants aboard? Morally, yes, it mattered, but . . . the ships themselves were a necessity. God alone knew what the Madman might learn. He had to be obeyed. The Irish must all go back to Ireland, the Libyans back to Libya and the British back to their little island.

It was utter madness.

The reports made Bergen sick. Mobs hunting the poor refugees—French mobs, Spanish mobs, German mobs, Canadian mobs, American mobs, Mexican mobs, Japanese mobs . . . Even in China and Australia and probably everywhere else. The anguish and terror were so awful that blame had to be lodged somewhere.

Television coverage of the wrenching embarcations had brought tears to Bergen's eyes. He knew there were instances of brave defiance around the world, babies, women and children being hidden . . . but the hysteria and savagery—suicides, murders, lynchings—those were the dominant pattern.

And we thought we were civilized.

Coffin ships—every female aboard being sent home to certain death. And there were stories—rapes, torture . . . The floating prisons were forced to anchor offshore at their destinations; passengers driven ashore in small boats by gunfire.

The secretary-general shuddered.

The many suicides were understandable.

Perhaps sinking the ships was a mercy.

Sighing, Bergen turned on the single low swinglamp at the side of his desk and centered it over his blotter. Methodically, he took a notepad and wrote a brief order to an aide. Delacourt's behavior would have to be scrutinized.

When he had finished the order, he put both palms flat on the blotter and forced himself to think about the priorities. The Saudis and Israel—number one. Ring of fire or a cobalt moat? He feared there would be no pulling of rabbits out of hats here. Whatever they did, it would be a monumental mess. Another Kissinger comment came unbidden to Bergen's mind:

"The difficulties in the Middle East occurred not because the parties don't understand each other, but in some respects, because they understand each other only too well."

Cobalt radioactivity would be sure to spread. The American experts admitted it. If it destroyed the usefulness of Saudi oil, would the Soviets pick up the slack as they had hinted?

Bergen was tempted to laugh hysterically and say: "Tune in tomorrow at this same time!"

No vapid American soap opera had ever contemplated such monumental disaster.

A trembling anger overcame him then. Why should the secretary-general have sole responsibility for such terrible decisions? It was too much! He had to admit then that, in all honesty, he did not have sole responsibility. Decision-making worked on a different system nowadays.

Abruptly, he turned to the red phone and lifted it out of the open drawer onto the desk, keying the sophisticated scrambler equipment as he did this.

A United States Navy communications officer answered on the first ring. He identified himself as Lieutenant Commander Avery.

"May I speak to the President?" Bergen asked.

"One moment, sir. He's at Camp David."

The President's voice sounded alert and curious. "Something new come up, Hab?"

Still familiarity. Good.

"Adam, I forgot to ask whether the Russians discussed your cobalt suggestion when they called."

"Oh, glad you brought that up." Prescott did not sound at all glad. "There's a big argument between them and the Chinese over it. The Chinese favor our suggestion."

"If we decide on the cobalt, Adam, could we announce at the same time that air transport from all over the world is standing by to remove the Israelis to Brazil in an orderly manner?"

"That's quite a mouthful, Hab."

"But could we do it?"

"You could say it but it might not be true."

"We must do our best. The Jews have suffered too much. We can't abandon them."

"The way we did with the Greeks, the Cypriots and some others."

"Those others did not have atomic weapons."

"That sounds rather cold-blooded," Prescott said.

"I don't mean it that way. We have to address these emergencies by a priority system, which we both understand very well. Will you do your part in this, Adam?"

"Shared responsibility," Prescott said.

"That's what I had in mind, Adam."

"I'll do my best, Hab."

As the President returned his phone to the cradle in the lounge of the main lodge at Camp David, he looked at Charlie Turkwood, who stood at the fireplace, back to the flames.

"That son-of-a-bitch Bergen just called in his counter," Prescott said. "And it's a doozy."

The past is dead.

—Arab proverb

THE METAL bed of the lorry was chilling beneath John's bare skin. He curled himself into a tight ball, his arms hugged around his chest, but the lorry's movement jostled him and a cold wind blew through the canvas cover over the bed. They had stripped him bare on the float at Kinsale, parceling out his clothes and the contents of his pack, arguing over who would get the six French chocolate bars.

Kevin O'Donnell had appeared uninterested in all of this, but he had kept the money and the Belgian pistol.

"Why're you doing this?" John had demanded.

"Because we're kindly men," Kevin O'Donnell had said. "We kill anyone we catch within five hundred meters of the shore."

"Even if we come in from the sea?"

"Well, me and the boys were disappointed in you, Yank. We were expecting some folks from another coffin ship, maybe a pretty woman or two."

One of the men stripping John said: "Not many women surviving the trip anymore."

They finished with him, removing even his shoes and socks.

He stood, hugging himself, bare and shivering on the cold float.

"Just be happy we're sparing you, Yank," Kevin O'Donnell had said. "Up y' go, Yank. Into the lorry with him, boys. And this time, bring some of the good stuff back wi' you."

Three guards had entered the back of the lorry with John. He caught the name of only one, Muiris Cohn, a small man with a face that appeared compressed from top to bottom, the closely set eyes too near the nose, the nose to close to the mouth and the chin almost touching his lower lip.

While the three guards occupied a bench on one side, John was forced to stay on the chilled bed. When he complained of the cold, Cohn nudged him roughly with a heavy boot and said: "Now, y' heard Kevin! You're alive and it's more than you deserve."

To John, the trip drew itself out into an interminable frigid torture, which he endured by promising himself he would live and, if his story was believed, he would work his way into whatever the Irish were doing to solve the plague problem. There, he would sabotage that effort.

The lorry went first up a steep hill, rolling John toward the back. His captors dragged him forward again, wedging him near their feet.

"Which way we going?" one of them asked the others.

"I heard them say the road through Belgooly is safest," Cohn said.

"That means they've restored Fivemilebridge," the questioner said. He was silent for a moment, then: "How long'll we be stopping in Cork?"

"Now, Gilly," Cohn said, "the times you've made this trip and you still asking such a question!"

"I've a thirst the River Lee itself and it running full in the spring could not wet," the questioner said.

"And you'll have to wait until we rid ourselves of this lout," Cohn said. He kicked John in the shoulder. "We'll get as wet as the seas themselves on the way back. It's either that or answer to Kevin himself, which I'll not be doing, him in the mad mood as you could see."

John, sensing a faint warmth from his captors' feet, wriggled closer, but Cohn felt the movement in the darkness and thrust him away with one foot, sneering: "Keep your stinking self away from us, Yank. I'll be bathing for a week just to get the smell of you off me feet."

John found himself wedged against a metal support post for the bench on his side of the lorry's bed. The sharp edge of the post cut into his back, but it was a different pain from the cold. He focused on this new pain, clinging to it. The darkness, the cold, the pain began to work on him. He had thought O'Neill safely buried deep within, obscured and hidden away forever. But his nakedness, the dark and cold bed of the lorry, these were not a place he had ever imagined. He could feel a terrible inner warfare waiting to occur. And he began to hear the lunatic sound of that inner voice—John Roe O'Neill clamoring for his revenge.

"You'll have it," he muttered.

The sound of his voice was almost covered by the grinding rumble of the lorry as it climbed a hill. Cohn heard him, though, and asked:

"Did y' say something, Yank?"

When John did not answer, Cohn kicked him. "I'll have an answer from you, damn your evil soul!"

"It's cold," John said.

"Ahhh, that's fine now," Cohn said. "We wouldn't want you to enter our world comfortable like."

Cohn's companions laughed.

"It's the way we all enter Ireland, y' know," Cohn said. "Naked as plucked chickens and them ready for the pot. You've no mind for the pot you're in now, you Yankee devil."

They fell silent then and John lapsed back into the arena of his inner war. He could feel the presence of O'Neill. It was a single eye like a beam of light glaring from within his head. No warmth in it. Cold . . . cold . . . as cold as the metal upon which his body lay.

The lorry rumbled across a wooden bridge and the sound of the tires against the planks was a drumbeat in John's head. He could sense O'Neill trying to emerge and this terrified him. O'Neill did not belong here! O'Neill would scream. The three guards would enjoy that.

Lights!

He sensed lights out the open rear of the lorry and this restored him somewhat. He realized that his eyes were tightly closed and, slowly, he opened them. O'Neill sank back into obscurity.

The lights were on both sides of the lorry—a well-lighted city street. He could hear people shouting. It was a drunken sound. There was a gunshot, then high-pitched laughter. He tried to sit up, but Cohn pushed him back with a foot.

"Painted like hussies," one of the other guards said.

John felt a crouching sensation. Had some of the women survived? That high-pitched laughter. Had his plague failed?

"Would they were hussies," Cohn said. "I'd even welcome old Bella Cohen and the Monto, the saucy darlin's beckoning us with their skirts lifted."

"It'd be better than this," the other guard said. "Men with men! It's against the Commandments, Muiris!"

"It's all they have, Gilly," Cohn said. "They haven't our opportunities to get a warm woman into bed."

"It's the buryin' of 'em afterwards I don't like," the other guard said. "Why didn't the sanctuaries save 'em, Muiris?"

"Ohhhh, it's a terrible, virulent thing, this plague. A short life. Better it be merry, as the poet said."

"I'll never lay with a man!" Gilly said.

"Save that for the time when the coffin ships come no more, Gilly." Cohn slid back along the bench past John and peered out the rear of the lorry. "Isn't it a shame, the fine city of Cork come to this!" He returned to the others.

"Did you hear that the English queen died?" Gilly asked.

"Good riddance! Best see an end to the House of Windsor!"

The lorry made a slow, tight turn to the left and the driver shifted down for a hill. The guards lapsed into silence.

John kept his eyes open, watching the shadows on the canvas overhead. The lorry picked up speed along smooth paving.

"The N-Twenty-five's mostly clean now," Cohn said. "We'll be in Youghal soon enough. Then it's back to the bright lights, eh, Gilly?"

"I think it was the devil kissed your mother," Gilly said.

Cohn laughed. "And maybe he did a bit more, eh?"

"Have you the cloven hoof, Muiris?"

"I know how to survive in these times, Gilly. You just be remembering that. Kevin and me, we know the ways that're needed now."

Gilly did not answer.

In spite of the pain and the cold, John felt himself dozing. It had been a long, tiring time at the sailboat's tiller and then the shock of his reception. His eyes closed. He opened them quickly, willing them to stay open despite fatigue. He did not want O'Neill to return.

They passed an occasional vehicle going the other way and the lights through the canvas cover showed the guards with their eyes closed. Once, a car overtook them moving very fast, its lights flashing into the lorry's rear, then darkness. The car's motor whined in very high revolutions.

"From Dublin," Cohn said. "I saw the flag on its fender."

"He was doing at least two hundred," Gilly said.

"All of that," Cohn said. "They move very fast, do our superiors."

Three times the lorry slowed to a lurching crawl over rough ground before returning to the smooth pavement. The fourth time it slowed, Cohn said the one word: "Youghal."

"I'll be glad to load and turn around," Gilly said.

"And be shut of this baggage," Cohn said, nudging John with a foot.

John felt them making a sweeping turn to the left, then low gears for about five minutes. They came to a jerking stop and someone up front shouted: "Get him out!"

Cohn leaped over the tailgate and there was the sound of his feet on gravel. Presently, Cohn said: "All right. Let's have him."

The two guards remaining with John had to help him to his feet. His voice not unkind, Gilly said: "Out you go, Yank. Mind the gravel on your feet."

John let himself down over the tailgate, moving stiffly, his muscles cramped with the cold and inactivity. Cohn took his left arm above the elbow and led him fast around the lorry into its headlights. Limping and stumbling on gravel and broken blacktop, John was glad to stop. The lorry's lights carved out two tunnels of insect-populated brilliance, glimpses of bush-overgrown embankments on both sides of the road. He could hear a river somewhere off to the right.

Cohn pointed to the direction revealed by the lights. "There's the direction you go, Yank. Don't come back this way. That's the Blackwater below you there. Keep it on your right until you cross the bridge. There's a stone hut about a kilometer up. The priests keep a store of clothing there for them as gets that far. There maybe something to fit your ugly flesh. And one thing more, Yank. If anyone should ask, it was Kevin O'Donnell of the Clogheen O'Donnells who spared your stupid life. If I know Kevin, he didn't want the wasting of a good bullet on his conscience. Me, I expect to see your dead body floating down the Blackwater."

Trembling with the cold, John muttered: "Wh . . . where d . . . do I g . . . go?"

"To hell for all of me! Move smartly now."

Stumbling painfully on the broken surface, John set off up
the road. He heard the lorry turn around behind him, its lights
gone quickly, the sound of it lasting only a bit longer. He was
alone in darkness on a road sparsely illuminated by a broken
cup of moon revealed occasionally when clouds were swept
clear of it. Tall trees in heavy leaf bowered the road for most
of the way. The road angled to his left slowly, then right. He
felt ridiculous, angry and powerless.

What did I expect? he wondered. *Not this.*

The road began to climb steadily and, the clouds passing,
he emerged from the covering trees to find the way a thin
ribbon through gorse, a bridge directly ahead across the river
and a Y-branching just beyond. The left-hand way was blocked
by a jumble of fallen trees and there was the heavy smell of
something rotten.

John made his way cautiously across the river bridge and,
as he neared the blockaded road, saw a naked body hanging
in the tangle of trees. It was bloated and the flesh falling away.
He hurried past, coming on a steeper climb, hills rising sharply
on both sides of the road. The cold moonlight revealed leafless
trees sheathed in ivy, a witch barrier on the heights.

Both feet were bleeding by now but he forced himself to
ignore the pain, trying to move as silently as he could.

What had killed that man back there? He felt that the body
had been left there as a warning.

They don't expect me to survive very long.

At the top of the hill he came out into an open area where
the grass had been burned away all around a stone hut that
stood in a depression off to his right. The moonlight revealed
a flat stone-and-mortar construction with a lean-to shelter at
the rear. There was the burned ruin of a house directly across
the road from it.

What should I do?

He thought that if he entered the hut he might encounter an
occupant who would kill him the minute he entered. But Cohn
had said something about priests.

"Hello the hut," John called.

There was no response.

Stone paving marked a narrow path between burned bushes
down to the hut.

I must have clothing and shoes.

Cautiously, he limped down the stone path to the black

oblong of a doorway. He put a hand out to the latch but before he could lift it, the door creaked open. A candle flared and he discerned a brown-faced man in a black cassock. The candle held high, the man stared back at John without a word.

John found his voice. "They said . . . I . . . some clothing?"

The cassocked man stood aside, nodding John into the hut. The dark figure closed the creaking door, put the candle on a wall-bracket shelf and went through a low opening into the shed at the rear of the hut. He returned presently with a mound of clothing in his arms. John accepted the clothing, noting then the empty look in his benefactor's eyes.

Blind?

No, the cassocked figure moved with too much purpose and he had known where to put the clothes in John's hands. John looked around him, found a low chair on his left beneath the candle. He put the clothing there and began dressing. The underwear was a full suit of long johns, white and soft. He felt better the minute he had pulled this garment over his chilled body. There was a pair of black-and-gray tweed trousers, a rough woolen shirt of dark green, a yellow woolen pullover.

John stared at his companion while he dressed.

"Are you a priest?" John asked.

Without speaking, the man inclined his head in agreement.

"Have you taken a vow of silence?" John asked.

Again, the head inclined.

John looked down at his bruised and bleeding feet. The priest also looked down.

"Do you have shoes?" John asked.

Once more, the cassocked man went into the shed at the rear, merging with the shadows there. Spooky, the silent way he moved, John thought. There was a thud, then a creaking sound from the shed. Presently, the priest emerged carrying a pair of worn brogans and a pair of thick socks in green wool. John accepted them gratefully. He sat on the low chair to ease the socks over his sore feet. The brogans felt long enough but too wide. It helped when he tightened the shoelaces.

All this time, the priest waited silently above him.

John stood.

"I've come from the States to help where I can," he said. "I'm a molecular biologist. Is there a research establishment of some kind where . . ."

The priest held up a hand for silence. One hand went under the cassock and emerged with a small notepad and a pencil attached to it by a short length of string. The priest scribbled on the pad and passed it to John.

Taking it to the candle, John read: "Take the Cappoquin road. There are signs. Go on to Cahir. Ask there."

The priest removed the pad from John's hands, tore off the used page and held it to the candle flame. He let it burn in the candle holder. When the paper had been consumed, he went to the door and opened it. Leading John outside, he pointed to the road leading off beyond the hilltop. John could see the way entering a stretch of high hedges there, the growth black in the moon shadows.

"Cappoquin," John said.

The priest nodded and, once more, a hand went under the cassock.

Expecting the notepad, John almost missed the long knife when it came slashing out at him from beneath the cassock. John jerked backward, the knife narrowly missing his throat. His assailant merely stood there, the knife held motionless at the end of its swing.

Never taking his attention from the man, John stumbled backward up the stone path to the road.

All that time, the cassocked figure stood there, a lethal statue.

At the road, John turned and ran toward the hedge-bordered stretch. The road dipped and then rose. John ran, panting and glancing backward whenever he could, stopping only when he came out of the hedges onto another hilltop where the road curved left along a ridge. He sat down on a stone wall to catch his breath and keep watch back along the way he had come. There was no sound of pursuit.

Was that really a priest back there? An insane priest, perhaps? Then:

Cohn knew! He expected me to be killed.

It was quiet on the hilltop, only a faint soughing of wind in the gorse. He was thankful for the warm clothing. The attack at the hut left him unsettled. Things were not what they appeared here.

When he had recovered his breath, John set off more slowly.

But I'm here, he thought.

The clothing on his body smelled of fresh laundering and sun-drying. It felt warm but unfamiliar. And he suddenly realized there wasn't a scrap of identification on his person. Cohn had been right about that. John was freshly born in Ireland.

The best hiding place in all the world. John Roe O'Neill could watch the workings of his revenge here and no one the wiser.

O'Neill within made no response and, for this, John was thankful.

Daylight found him in another river valley. He stopped at a rusted gate that once had been painted white. Brick pedestals stood on each side, their mortar falling away in irregular patches. On the far side of the gate, an overgrown single track with grass on the crown led away into thick stands of maple and pine. Nettles and mallow bordered the edges of the track. John glimpsed stone shapes rising from the growth off to his left and realized he was looking at a cemetery. He felt weak with hunger and his throat was dry.

Cappoquin? he wondered. Would it be safe to go where the cassocked man had directed him?

Who do I dare ask?

Anyone he met here could be dangerous. That was the lesson of the cassocked man's knife. Perhaps that had been the intention.

The river below the road beckoned him. It would have cold water to allay his thirst.

I'll get a drink of water, he thought. *Then I can decide what to do.*

> *There's nothing so passionate as
> a vested interest disguised as an in-
> tellectual conviction.*
>
> **—Sean O'Casey**

JOSEPH HERITY stood in front of the long table, arms hanging loosely at his sides, his eyes not really focused on the three important men who sat facing him on the other side of the table. It was too early in the morning to focus, barely dawn, and Kevin O'Donnell, the man seated to the middle, directly in front of Herity, had a reputation for crazy blather that he already had confirmed here.

Listening carefully, Herity sought for the thing that had raised his hackles on entering the room. There was fear in this place. To Herity, that was like the smell of warm blood to a predator. Who was fearful here and what did he fear? Could it be all three of them? They did seem a bit on the nervous side.

Except for the table and three chairs, the room was unfurnished. It was not a large space, only about four meters long and three wide. One high window, narrow and without shade, stood open on Herity's right, framing a faint rose color in the clouds as the sun lifted over the horizon somewhere behind him. Light came from two double-sconce lamps behind the seated men. The lamps gave a yellow cast to the fawn cream walls.

"We've been saving you for a moment such as this," O'Donnell said. "You must appreciate this, Joseph. 'Tis a fine thing for a man of your talents, well recognized as they are in this company."

O'Donnell glanced left and right at his companions and once more Herity sensed that flare of near panic. Who was it? What was it? He studied O'Donnell's companions behind the table.

Alex Coleman, seated on O'Donnell's left, would not have been recognized by many of his old newspaper contemporaries in the preplague Dublin. Since the deaths of his wife and children at the hands of a Spanish mob, Coleman had devolved into a simmering container of rage. His hands often trembled with it or with the aftermath of drink, which he had taken to as a man comes back to the Church driven by the whip of his sins. Coleman's thin features, still as dark as an Armada castaway's, had acquired a questing, thrusting look, something almost furtive, as though he were a hunting animal stalking its prey. The most dramatic change was the removal of the hair from his head. Once thick and black with a deep wave across the crown, it now was kept shaved to no more than a shadowy stubble.

There was rage in Coleman and perhaps something else, Herity thought, as he shifted his attention to O'Donnell's other side. Now Herity focused because this was the most important member of the trio—Fintan Craig Doheny. None of the three would admit that importance, Coleman because he did not care, O'Donnell out of pride, and Doheny because it was not his nature to lift his head out of the pack.

Herity had made it a point to learn something about Doheny when the man had been made secretary for plague research in the new Government of All Ireland. Doheny had been born to an Athlone family that had produced many priests and nuns but no medical doctors "until Fin came along." Right now, he had the look of a beardless but still jolly Father Christmas in mufti. His face was round and benign, framed in a curly fuzz of light blond hair. Widely set blue eyes stared out of this face at a world that he appeared to find amusing.

It was a mask, Herity decided. Doheny had flat lips with smile creases at the corners and a rather short, narrow nose with flaring nostrils that two generations of medical and nursing students at Dublin College had learned to read for their own survival. Jolly as he might appear, Fin Doheny was notoriously savage to "slackers" and the flaring of his nostrils was an infallible signal of the wrath near eruption.

The fear came from Doheny, Herity realized. And from O'Donnell as well. What was it?

These three constituted the Regional Committee for the Southeast Coast, originally an ad hoc emergency group that had become formalized by use and recognition that they held the power and knew how to use it. Kevin O'Donnell had assumed the chairmanship early in their association, on the presumption that he "had the guns"—which indeed he did because the power in the new government was divided between the Beach Boys and the Regular Army. Herity knew this suited Doheny. It allowed him to sit back and "maneuver the pieces."

Alex Coleman did not care who directed the committee as long as actions were being taken that might eventually destroy the murderers of his family. There were some who claimed Coleman might try to escape Ireland and "infect every last unholy bastard still living in Spain."

It was all three of them afraid of something, Herity sensed— but was it the same thing they all feared?

Kevin O'Donnell, having looked to his companions for agreement with what he was saying, and taking their silence for that agreement, now favored Herity with a predator's grin, a pouncing look of sadistic pleasure.

Herity recognized the look, having suffered from it on previous occasions. Since setting off the bomb at the Grafton Street corner, Herity had lived a rabbit's life, blamed by those who knew of his hand in the bombing for "bringing down the wrath of God upon us all." Since the plague, he had lived in constant fear that his role might become general knowledge.

To anyone he trusted to listen, Herity protested: "How was I to know?" O'Donnell, who had been area commander of Herity's group, had refused to accept this excuse. Singling out Herity as a special target, O'Donnell had seized on any opportunity for bedevilment. Herity suspected that something worse than any previous punishment was about to come. He tried to draw into himself, preserving his energies for an opportunity to escape. This made him appear more solid, more tightly coiled. Herity was one of those people many called "well knit," as though God had sat there with a pair of long needles doing up the substance of Herity in a workmanlike fashion until the whole persona was finished.

Misinterpreting Herity's posture, Kevin O'Donnell thought: *That Herity! He acts like he owns every place he's in!*

"This is no Easter Week Rising!" Kevin O'Donnell said. He passed a look of scorn down the length of Herity's body and back up to his face.

"Some of us will come through it," Alex Coleman said, as though he had been holding a private conversation within himself and only now felt that this much of it should be made public.

Kevin O'Donnell looked at Coleman. "What's that you're saying, Alex?"

"If only one of us gets through," Coleman said, "he can spread the plague among 'em, give them a taste of this White Death!" He spat on the floor beside him and looked around, hoping there might be a bottle somewhere near to soothe his sudden thirst.

"Ah, yes," Kevin O'Donnell said, thinking that sometimes Coleman sounded a bit around the twist. Returning his attention to Herity, O'Donnell said: "I'm still looking to your past mistakes, Joseph." His voice low and sad, O'Donnell added: "They should be erased, completely gone, as though they were no more."

"We have no past, none of us," Coleman said.

"Alex speaks the truth," Kevin O'Donnell said. "There's only the four of us here and we're still Irishmen."

Fin Doheny cleared his throat. "God knows where that man might have got to by now, Kevin."

Herity came full alert. Ahhh, there was the fear. It had something to do with all of that material on John Roe O'Neill they had required him to memorize before this meeting—that profile from America, the history, and then the Finn Sadal report on someone called John Garrech O'Donnell.

"Joseph, you've studied all of that material we gave you?" Kevin O'Donnell asked.

There's the fear, right enough! Herity thought. *Something in this terrifies them.*

Herity nodded.

"That Yank who calls himself O'Donnell has been many days in our land since we passed him through at Kinsale," Kevin O'Donnell said. "Until we're certain of him, no harm can come to the man."

His nostrils flaring but his voice even, Doheny leaned forward. "You've seen the description of him. It's verrry suggestive in light of the American profile on O'Neill."

"It's a shame it is that you didn't share that description with the Finn Sadal," Kevin O'Donnell said, and there was a bitter spite in his tone.

"We asked you to keep a special eye out for anyone claiming to be a molecular biologist," Doheny said. There was a sharpness in his voice that any of his students would have recognized.

"We thought it was only the Yank making his brag," Kevin O'Donnell said. "He's come to Ireland out of goodness!"

"And where is he right now?" Coleman demanded.

"Wandering the hills above Youghal," Kevin O'Donnell said. "Him being an O'Donnell like myself, so he says, I thought he should have his own chance. He'll not be hard to find."

"But is he alive?" Coleman asked.

"As to that, perhaps Joseph can discover."

"But you claim he's been seen," Doheny said.

Herity, homing in on the committee's fear, said: "You really think this John O'Donnell is . . ."

"It's not for you to question what we think!" Kevin O'Donnell snapped. "You're here to follow orders!"

"As I've followed your orders in the past," Herity said.

"Exceeding them on occasion, as well!" Kevin O'Donnell's tone said he was not about to share blame for that Grafton Street bomb fiasco.

"But you're suggesting this Yank could be the Madman," Herity insisted.

"And him wandering around where he could be killed," Doheny said.

"That's not my doing," Herity protested. And he saw it now: the fear . . . yes, the panic. The Madman here in Ireland. And what was he doing here? Had he brought an even more terrible plague to exterminate the survivors? They did not have to spell it out for Joseph Herity! If that wandering Yank was the Madman, he could have wired himself for something more devastating than his plague.

"I didn't pass him through like a visiting tourist," Herity said.

"Keep a civil tongue in your head!" Kevin O'Donnell flared. "You're only a soldier!" A wolfish smile spread across his features.

Herity glowered at the smiling O'Donnell, then looked out the window at the cloudy sky: full daylight now. It was going to rain. *That dirty bastard, Kevin O'Donnell! All the O'Donnells are bastards!*

Doheny filled the tense quiet with a low, calming voice. "Joseph, we want you to go out there and find him. See that no harm comes to the man. You're not to let him know what we suspect. Only watch him and report. Is he O'Neill?"

"And how am I to know that?" Herity stared back at that fearful light in Doheny's eyes.

"Get him to give himself away."

"He cannot be interrogated, more's the pity," Coleman said. He trembled and looked away, wondering if they would object should he leave for a moment to find a drink.

"God knows what other nastiness he may have in his kit," Doheny said.

"He has no kit at all," Kevin O'Donnell said. "We stripped him bare."

"And threw away his papers!" Doheny said, nostrils flaring.

"Are we to save every scrap brought in by the folk of the coffin ships?" Kevin O'Donnell asked.

"You shared out his food and kept his money, I'm sure of that," Doheny said. "It's God's own luck you haven't spread another plague among us."

"I'll wager he's just another vagabond Yank," O'Donnell said, but there was fearful defensiveness in him now.

"Paaaah!" Doheny waved a hand as though clearing the air of smoke. "If it's O'Neill, it's the style of the man to set a fuse burning. He's the kind to have a dead-man switch ready. Do we annoy him, the switch closes and we're in the boiling oil for sure."

"Mind that, Joseph," Kevin O'Donnell said. "A most dangerous man. We're sending you to shepherd a cobra."

Doheny shook his head. "But if he's O'Neill, he's the most valuable man in our world—simply because of what's in his head."

"And what if he isn't the Madman?" Herity asked.

Kevin O'Donnell shrugged. "Then you'll have a fine tramp across the hills and vales of our lovely land. And mayhap there'll be evenings of grand conversation around a fire. You're to make friends with him, you understand?"

"And how long do I carry on this little journey?"

"All winter if need be," Kevin O'Donnell said. "The decision has been made at the highest levels not to tip over this applecart."

"Perhaps the Americans can get us O'Neill's dental charts or his fingerprints," Doheny said. "But you're to keep him out there *and alive* until we've positive identification."

"So we don't dare turn him loose and we don't dare bring him in until we know," Herity said. "But is it wise to let the Yanks know we may have O'Neill here? What might they do if they learn that?"

"We think they'll fear O'Neill more than we do," Doheny said.

"And himself maybe having set a nasty dead-man trap in his homeland," Kevin O'Donnell said. "Another plague to be let loose on everyone, men as well as women."

Alex Coleman glared at Herity. "You're not to make any more mistakes, you hear?"

"You're to be his leech," Kevin O'Donnell said. "Not a word he speaks, not a shit he shits, must go without your notice. And all of it must come back to us."

"We've arranged for you to be met along the way," Doheny said. "Couriers and written reports."

Herity grimaced. There were no secrets in this company. All of them knew he had set the Grafton Street bomb. "You're handing me this dirty sack because of that bomb," he said.

"You're the one blew away O'Neill's wife and wains," Kevin O'Donnell said. "There's a kind of poetry in it, you going out there to see if it's really him. You've a special motivation."

"I'm told you know that country above Youghal," Doheny said.

"It's dangerous there," Herity said. "Your report says that mad priest almost put a knife in him."

Kevin O'Donnell smiled. "Two of my boys camped in the ruin across the way for the night. They heard the Yank call out. They thought it amusing."

"It gives me palpitations just to think about it," Doheny said.

"And it may not be the Madman," Kevin O'Donnell said. "There's other suspects wandering around. The Brits are watching two of them this very instant. The heathens in Libya aren't saying, but that's hardly a likely place for the man to hide. This John Garrech O'Donnell, he could be the prize."

Alex Coleman focused on Herity, his look anxious. "You be careful of him, Herity! O'Neill dead and they learn of it Outside, they may just give us a quick dose of atomic sterilization." Coleman grimaced, a brittle movement of his lips.

Herity's mouth went suddenly dry.

"The possibilities have been discussed at some length, Joseph," Kevin O'Donnell said. "It has been suggested that certain powers outside our land, finding a cure for this devil's plague, may keep that fact to themselves. Then, learning the whereabouts of the Madman, they give us a touch of the atom, killing all the birds in one blow, as Alex so kindly reminds us."

Herity could only blink at the problem they had dumped on him.

"Who do we suspect out there?" Herity asked. "Would it be the Yanks or the Russians doing this thing if they could?"

Doheny shook his head. "Does the ant care whose foot squashes it?"

> *When all the tourists had gone for the day, we used to piss on the Blarney Stone. It gave us a strange feeling of superiority when we saw tourists kissing that place where we had seen our own piss, and it splashing off so pretty and yellow.*
>
> **—Stephen Browder**

IT WAS a picture out of prehistory, a lake absolutely untouched by wind, black and flat under a layer of morning fog that hovered about a meter off the surface. A green mountain, only its top gilded by sunlight, anchored the background of lake and fog layer.

John huddled in a copse of Scots pines near the western shore, listening. He could hear a faint splashing, rhythmic and ominous, from somewhere off in the mist. Shivering in the cold, he rubbed the arms of the rough yellow sweater. He had been six weeks without seeing another human, although he thought he could feel people watching him from every shadow, from the distances and, at night, pressing close to kill him.

What was that rhythmic splashing?

He had spent three weeks in a tiny cottage of neatly fitted stones, huddled there indecisively until the stored food in the place ran out. The cottage nestled in a hollow west of the lake, not another habitation in view from it. There had been a notice board on the door.

"These premises which once knew life and love have been

*abandoned. There is food in the larder, bedding on the bed,
linen in the cupboard and utensils in the kitchen. I have left it
clean and neat. Please do the same. Perhaps there will be love
here again someday."*

No signature.

John had found the cottage at the end of a narrow, grass-
clogged lane. Its thatched roof had been shielded by a thick
stand of conifers. He had been startled to see it sitting there
untouched after all the distance punctuated by ashes and ruins.
The thatch had been recently patched and the cottage was a
picture of tranquility sitting neatly in a field of ferns and weeds
colored by tiny pink flowers. There had been blackberries beside the lane, fruit ripe on the vines. Hungry and thirsty, he
had picked and eaten berries until his fingers and lips were
stained with the juice.

Approaching the entrance of the cottage, he had stopped at
the notice board, neatly burned letters in a pale plank. He had
read the words over several times, alarmed in some way he
could not define. A stirring from O'Neill-Within upset him and
anger threatened to engulf him. A desire to rip the board off
the door swept over him. He even reached for the board but
his fingers stopped short of it, groping instead for the latch. It
clicked beneath his hand and the door creaked open.

Inside was the smell of mildew, old ashes and tobacco mixed
with old cooking. The mixed odors permeated a small sitting
room with an oval hooked rug on the tiled floor between two
rocking chairs that sat facing a small fireplace. Bricks of peat
were stacked with a dish of matches to one side on the hearth.
He noted the afghans on the chair backs: crochet work. A
knitting basket sat beside one of the chairs, a green mound of
knitted fabric, apparently unfinished, protruding from it and
two long red knitting needles sticking up out of the work like
markers on a place where someone would return to the clicking
progress of the yarn.

John closed the door. Was there anyone here? Surely they
would come to investigate the creaking of the door.

He skirted the rockers and went through a narrow doorway
into a tiny kitchen with a water-stained drainboard around a
diminutive sink. It was like a doll house: clean dishes neatly
stacked beside the sink. Flies buzzed somewhere. Canned goods
lay in neat rows behind one of the cupboard doors. He found
the mildew in an open bin of flour.

It felt damp in the cottage. Did he dare make a fire? Would someone come to investigate the smoke?

The bedroom on the other side of the sitting room contained a bed, the covers neatly laid back, inviting someone to enter them and sleep. The sheets were clammy to his touch. He dragged the blankets off the bed and draped them over the rocking chairs in the sitting room before stooping to build a fire. He would chance it, he decided. This place was made to order for a confused wayfarer. Ireland was not at all what he had expected.

What did I expect?

He knew it was a question he would return to many times and he doubted he would be able to answer it. It was not something he had explored in detail.

When he left the cottage three weeks later, he took the last four tins of fish and closed the door, the notice board still on it, the place neat behind him.

On the lake, the rhythmic splashing had grown louder.

He stared in the direction of the sound. Something dark within the mists there.

Out of the fog layer came a boat, a long double-oared craft with only one rower leaning back into the sweeps. The vessel glided through the oddly motionless mist, oars creaking faintly, a light plashing rhythm to match the strokes. Concentric ripples formed under the bow, spreading out at a sharp angle as the boat approached the reedy shore below John's copse of Scots pines.

John stood entranced by the timeless feeling of the scene. The boat was a black thing with a hull that rippled against the water's fabric as though it had always been there.

He could make out three shapes in the craft—something huddled in the bow and another mound in the stern. The rower wore black clothing. Even his hat was black.

John debated whether to break from his cover and run. What danger lay in that dark boat? He studied the oarsman. The hands on the oars were pale against all of that black. The motions of the shoulders held his attention for a moment: muscular contractions of the shoulder blades as the man swept the oars back for each new stroke.

As the boat neared John's side of the lake, it came to him that the blue object in the stern and the lumpy green darkness in the bow were other human forms. There were gray-clad legs poking from beneath the blue, a hand clutching a jacket hood over the head for protection from the cold mist. The pale blond head of a youth appeared suddenly from beneath the blue hood. Eyes of pale fawn-gold looked directly at John in the pine copse.

Should I run? John wondered. He did not know what held him here. The youth in the stern of that boat obviously had seen him, but the youth said nothing.

The boat slithered into the deep stretch of reeds at the shore. The green mound at the bow lifted, becoming a hatless man, long and shaggy blond hair, a narrow, almost effeminate face with pug nose and a sharp chin, a face dominated by light brown eyes. The brown eyes, when they focused on John, were like a physical impact. John stood frozen in his position within the pines. Not taking his attention from John, the man lifted a green cap into sight and pulled it over his hair. He then brought up a worn green packsack, which he slipped over his left shoulder by a single strap.

The oarsman had stood up and lifted an oar from its lock, using this as a pole to push against the bottom and thrust the boat through the reeds. The man in the bow said something over his shoulder to the oarsman, but the words were obscured by the noisy passage through the reeds. The boat rasped to a halt, on bottom almost half a length from the boggy turf that formed a strip between the pines and the reeds. At a motion from the man in the bow, the youth in the stern stood and stepped over the side, wading and pulling the boat to the turf shingle.

Now, the oarsman turned. John confronted a cadaverous face pale under a black felt hat. Wisps of black hair touched by gray poked from beneath the hat. The eyes were electric blue above a ship's prow of a nose, a thin, almost lipless mouth and a stabbing thrust of chin with only the faintest of clefts above a reversed collar.

A priest! John thought, and he remembered the man with the knife at the clothing hut.

The priest steadied himself against a thwart, looked at John and asked: "And who might you be?"

The priest's tone was sane, but so had been the manner of the cowled, monkish figure at the clothing hut.

"My name's John O'Donnell," John said.

The man in the bow nodded as though this conveyed important information. The priest merely pursed his thin lips. He said: "You've the sound of a Yank."

John let this pass.

The youth waded to the bow and gave the boat an ineffectual tug.

"Leave be, boy," the priest said.

"Who are you people?" John asked.

The priest glanced at his companion in the boat. "This is Joseph Herity, a wanderer like myself. The boy there . . . I don't know if he has a name. He'll not speak. The ones who gave him to me said he had vowed to remain silent until he rejoined his mother."

Once more, the priest looked at John. "As for myself, I'm Father Michael Flannery of the Maynooth Fathers."

Herity said: "Take off your hat, Father Michael, and show him the proof."

"Be still," Father Flannery said. He sounded frightened.

"Do it!" Herity ordered.

Slowly, the priest removed his hat, exposing the partly healed scar of an encircled cross on his forehead.

"Some blame the Church for our troubles," Herity said. "They brand the ministers they allow to live—cross in a circle for the Catholics and a plain cross for the Prods. To tell 'em apart, you understand?"

"These are savage times," Father Flannery said. "But our Savior suffered worse." He replaced his hat, lifted a bulky blue knapsack from the bottom of the boat and stepped out into the reeds. Taking the boy's hand, he waded ashore, sloshed through the boggy ground and stopped the two of them only a few paces from John.

Without turning, the priest asked: "Will you be coming with us, Mister Herity?"

"And why shouldn't I be along with you?" Herity asked. "Such fine company." He stepped out of the boat, splashed through the boggy ground and strode past the priest and boy. Stopping directly in front of John within the pine shadows, Herity studied John from shoes to headtop. Focusing at last on John's eyes, he asked:

"What would a Yank be doing here?"

"I came to help," John said.

"You've a cure for the plague, then?" Herity asked.

"No, but I'm a molecular biologist. There must be somewhere in Ireland where I can use my talents to help."

"That'll be the Lab at Killaloe," Herity said.

"Is that far away?" John asked.

"You're a long ways from the Lab now," Herity said.

Father Flannery came up beside Herity. "Have done, Mister Herity! This man has exiled himself here out of goodness. Have you no appreciation for that?"

"Appreciation, he asks!" Herity chuckled.

John thought it was not a pleasant sound. This Herity had all the look and sound of a devious, dangerous man.

The priest turned almost away from John. Pointing a black-sleeved arm northward along the lake, one bony hand with all the fingers together in the old Irish fashion, he said: "The Lab is off there quite a ways, Mister O'Donnell."

"Why don't we tramp a ways with him to show our good hearts and our appreciation?" Herity asked. "Sure and he needs our help or he'll go astray." Herity shook his head mournfully. "We should be certain he's not under a faery spell."

Father Flannery glanced into the pines, then up to the road bordering the lake beyond the trees, back to the lake.

"It's higher powers than ourselves ordering things now," Herity said, a mock seriousness in his voice. "You said it yourself, Father Michael, last night when we found the curragh." He looked at the boat. "Perhaps it's a faery curragh brought here to help us to the Yank."

John heard the McCarthy grandfather's accent in Herity, but there was an undercurrent of spitefulness in it.

"Don't trouble yourselves," John said. "I'll find my own way."

"Ahhh, but it's dangerous, a man alone out there," Herity said. "Four together is safer. What say, Father Michael? Shouldn't we be Christian gentlemen and see this fine Yank safely to the Lab?"

"He should know it'll be no easy journey," Father Michael said. "Months likely. All of it on foot, or I miss my guess."

"But sure, Father, and the man who made time made plenty of it. We can be Sweeneys together, tramping over the land, seeing the sorry sights of our poor Ireland. Ohh, and the Yank needs friendly native guides now."

John sensed an argument between the two men, an undercurrent of vindictive humor in Herity. The boy stood head down through it all, apparently not caring.

When Father Michael did not respond, Herity said: "Well, then, I'll guide the Yank myself, the good priest not being up to his Christian duty." Herity turned slightly left toward the trace of trail that led out of the trees and up to the narrow road along the lake. "Let's be going along, Yank."

"The name is O'Donnell, John Garrech O'Donnell," John said.

With elaborate courtesy, Herity said: "Ahhh, now, I meant no offense, Mister O'Donnell. Sure and O'Donnell is a grand name. I've known many an O'Donnell, and some as would never slit me throat in the dark of a night. Yank, now, that's just a way of speaking."

"Will y' have done, Mister Herity?" Father Michael asked.

"But I'm just explaining to Mister O'Donnell," Herity said. "We'd not want to offend him, now would we?" He turned back to John. "We've some other Yanks, so I'm told; some Frenchies and Canucks, a Brit or two, and even a Mexican contingent, they being caught when the warships came. But none, I think, so foolish as to come here afterwards. How did y' get through the warships, Mister O'Donnell?"

"What else could they do, except kill me?" John asked.

"There's that now," Herity said. "It was a great risk you took."

"There's some in America want to help," John said. And he wondered at this Herity. What was the man doing? There was too much being left unspoken here.

"To help," Herity said. "To bring all the fair damsels back to life. Ahhh, now."

"If only we could," John said. "And all the women and children killed by the terrorist bombs, too."

A look of black rage pressed over Herity's face and was gone. He spoke pleasantly: "And what would you be knowing of such bombs, Mister O'Donnell?"

"What I read in the news," John lied.

"The news!" Herity said. "That's not the same as being in the presence of a real bomb."

"This is not getting Mister O'Donnell to the Lab," Father Michael said. "Shall we be on our way?"

"We!" Herity said. "The good Father is coming with us! How grand it'll be, Mister O'Donnell, to tramp along in the safe keeping of God's grace!"

Without replying, Father Michael strode around John and up the thin trail toward the road. The boy, clutching his blue jacket close in front, ran quickly to catch up, falling into step behind the priest.

"Come along, Mister O'Donnell," Father Michael called without turning.

John turned his back on Herity and followed. He heard

Herity striding along behind, closer than felt comfortable. But that priest would go to the Lab. John felt confident of this. He was going to be led right into the heart of the Irish effort to combat the plague!

For his part, Herity felt an immense dissatisfaction with the exchange between himself and this *O'Donnell*. The man could be just what he said he was. And what then? A bald-headed gawk who didn't fit the O'Neill descriptions at all.

Herity cursed under his breath.

This assignment galled, and the worst of that was his knowledge that Kevin had intended it to gall. And saddling him with Father Michael at the last minute! And then the priest refusing to abandon that weak-faced boy! Useless little shagger! Everything about this mission was odious. Well, sooner started, sooner finished.

Herity, setting off after O'Donnell, pressed close behind, watching the man's movements, the bunching of his shoulders under the thick woolen sweater.

He's my onion, Herity thought. *If he's really O'Neill . . .* Herity contemplated the project with a bit more good humor—verbally stripping away O'Donnell's layers of concealment, getting the dry skin off the onion to find the sweet, tearful meat underneath.

Father Michael reached the road and helped the boy over the stone fence there. They paused to watch O'Donnell and Herity climb toward them.

That Herity was a bad one, Father Michael thought. On the edge of blasphemy every second. Always probing for weaknesses in everyone around him. Something vicious in Herity enjoyed pain. The Yank would not be safe alone with Herity. The powers in Dublin had been wise to fill out their party this way.

O'Donnell reached the road, breathing hard from the climb. Herity, right behind him, hesitated on the far side of the stone fence, looking back the way they had come.

Always watching his back trail, that Herity! Father Michael thought. *Bad things back there.*

Father Michael turned slightly and met O'Donnell's gaze, a veiled and measuring look in the Yankee's eyes. Could that truly be the Madman? He had a strange look about him, that for sure. Well, the powers in Dublin had made it plain that this was a question to be answered by Herity. They had said Father Michael was only to see that Herity gave no harm to

O'Donnell. Father Michael did not ask: "Why me?" He knew.

Because Herity saved my life. We're bound together, Herity and me, by the bond of shame. The powers in Dublin know what happened at Maynooth.

Slinging his pack over his shoulders, Father Michael set off northward along the road. He could hear Herity and O'Donnell coming along behind. The boy hurried up beside Father Michael and walked close to the Priest, as though seeking protection there.

It's your life, lad, Father Michael thought. *And I wish you joy of it. But I do wish you'd speak.*

Presently, Herity began singing "The Wearing of the Green." The words echoed in the lake valley.

Herity had a fine voice, Father Michael thought, but his choice of song for this occasion . . . Father Michael shook his head in dismay.

> *There is no truth on earth that I*
> *fear to be known.*
>
> —Thomas Jefferson

FINTAN CRAIG DOHENY was more than five minutes into the private conversation with Kevin O'Donnell before realizing that his own life was on the line. Doheny had always known Kevin was a killer, but had thought the need for the Doheny medical expertise was protection enough.

Apparently not.

They had come together into one of the new cell-offices in Kilmainham Jail at Kevin's request. Doheny did not like Kilmainham. Its choice as a central control point for Dublin Command had been a Finn Sadal move "for historic reasons." The place repelled Doheny. Every time he walked across the inner court with its wire-guarded walkway all around, the giant curved skylight overhead, he thought of the men who had lived—or died—in the minuscule cells that ringed the area: Robert Emmet, Patrick McCann, Charles Parnell . . .

But Kilmainham Castle and the Royal Hospital were less than a block away and Doheny was forced to admit that the hospital facilities were excellent.

The meeting had begun calmly enough when they entered the cell-office shortly after breakfast. Kevin had received a

183

"general circulation" report about the Killaloe Lab. When both of them were seated, a tiny desk and one light on it between them, Kevin said:

"Themselves say our only hope is the Lab."

"If we ourselves are first to find the cure, the whole world must come to us," Doheny said.

"The Lab, that's not much hope after all this time," Kevin said.

"We have as much chance at it as anyone."

It was as though Kevin had not heard. "But we're used to disappointments in Ireland. We've come to expect them." He leaned back and stared at Doheny. "Anything else is the true unexpected."

"That's defeatist talk, Kevin. I tell you Adrian Peard is as fine a mind as I've ever met."

Kevin opened a drawer of his desk, brought out a small Belgian automatic pistol and placed it on the desk near his right hand.

"I think often of that young medical student and his woman in that tank," Kevin said. "Them holding each other in the night while the rest of us go lonely to our beds."

Doheny looked at the pistol, feeling a chill in his stomach. What was happening here? And what was this hypocritical talk about young Browder and Kate? It was common knowledge how the Beach Boys treated any surviving woman off the coffin ships. And the way Kevin's people often killed outsiders driven ashore because of plague contamination. Hunting these "shore birds" was considered sport by the Finn Sadal. Then burning the poor fellows in the old Celtic way—confined in wicker baskets over flames! This Kevin O'Donnell was a cruel man and that pistol on the desk could not be an idle gesture.

"What's on your mind, Kevin?" Doheny asked.

"I wonder who'll be the last man in Ireland?" Kevin asked. "Some think it'll be that wee wain in Athlone, the one taken alive from his dead mother. Where should I place my money, Fin?"

"I haven't the slightest idea. If I were you, I'd not bet. There's still a few women around."

"There's those think it'll be that boy being trained by the priests in Bantree," Kevin said. "And then there's 'the Gypsy boy of Moern'—himself already eight, but from a family where many lived past one hundred. Do you fancy him, Fin?"

"I've no concern except the plague," Doheny said. "We've

nothing before us but a desperate search for the cure. And Adrian Peard's people are..."

"Then you don't think it's O'Neill himself out there with Herity and the priests?"

"I've doubts. And even if it is, how do we make him help us to a solution?"

"Oh, there's ways, Fin. There's ways."

"O'Neill was in that Seattle-Tacoma area," Doheny said. "And after the searchers left his house, they put the whole region to the Panic Fire. Not even a count of the bodies and no way to identify the dead."

"Fin, I tell you all of this lovely island is one great coffin ship. And I've seen the proof of it."

Such an anger as he had never before felt filled Doheny. He barely managed to ask: "What proof?"

"In due time, Fin. In due time."

Doheny made to rise, but Kevin put a hand on the pistol.

"All those deaths," Doheny said. "No true Irishman would wish them to have been in vain!"

"Which deaths?" Kevin asked, not taking his hand from the pistol. "The ones killed by the Brits and the Ulstermen?"

"Them, too." Doheny stared at the hand on the pistol, realizing: *He means to kill me. Why?*

"Them, too?" Kevin asked in a tone of incredulity. A mad light in his eyes, he stared across the desk at Doheny.

He's insane, Doheny thought. *He's truly insane.*

"No death in the name of Ireland can be abandoned by us," Doheny said. "That's why Peard and I and all of our people are working so hard to..."

"Such blather explains nothing, Fin! I know why this curse was laid upon us. It was because we wouldn't forgive Dermot and the woman he stole from Ternan O'Ruarc."

"Good God, man!" Doheny shook his head. "That was more than eight hundred years ago!"

"And they're wandering Ireland yet, Fin. The Brefney curse. They're never to find peace, never be together until one Irishman forgives them. It's those two in the tank at Killaloe, Dermot and Dervogilla come alive! We must forgive them, Fin."

Doheny took two shallow breaths. "If you say so, Kevin."

"And didn't I just say it?" Kevin brought the pistol into his lap, caressing it with one hand. "Every brother killed by the Brits must be avenged, but Dermot and his woman must be laid to rest at last."

"Without the work Peard and I are doing, there'll be no future for Ireland," Doheny said.

"Have you heard, Fin, about the throng of headless women in the Vale of Avoca? There's some say they hear their cries at night."

"You believe that?" Doheny asked.

"Foolishness! Without heads, how can they cry?"

I must humor him, Doheny thought. *There's no reasoning with a madman.*

When Doheny did not respond, Kevin said: "There's a new kind of American Wake for those being sent back to die in Ireland. Have you heard, Fin?"

Once more the pistol was placed on the desk, but Kevin's hand remained on it.

"I hadn't heard."

"They distribute poison to them as don't want to get on the ships."

Doheny could only shake his head.

"We've been listening in on your telephone calls to England, Fin," Kevin said. He lifted the pistol and pointed it at Doheny's chest.

Doheny's throat and mouth went dry.

Kevin said: "You've forgotten, Fin, that we cannot trust the Gall. Never."

"The Huddersfield Establishment is helping us," Doheny said, a note of desperation in his voice.

"Is it now? And this fine fellow, this Doctor Dudley Wycombe-Finch, is not a Brit after all?"

"You know he is, but he's got one of the finest research establishments in the world. And they've just received a new lot of help from America."

"Oh, that's grand it is," Kevin said. "We've tapes of your telephone calls, Fin. Would you deny you've committed treason?"

Kevin's finger began to tighten on the pistol's trigger.

Desperately, Doheny said: "You'd forgive Dermot and his woman but you'd not listen to my explanation?"

"I'm listening," Kevin said.

"Everything Wycombe-Finch has told us has been tested in our Lab. Every bit of it has proven out. He hasn't lied to us."

"Many an hour I've spent listening to those tapes," Kevin said. "That British public school accent, many's the time I've heard that before from the likes of your Brit friend."

"But never under these conditions," Doheny said. "Their fat's as much in the fire as ours!"

"The carefully cultivated sound of sweet reason in their voices," Kevin said, "even when they're making the most unreasonable demands."

"You don't have to take my word for what he's given us," Doheny said. "Ask Peard."

"Oh, I have. The problem with that accent, Fin, is that they tend to believe the accent itself and not give too much thought to the words spoken in it."

"What did Peard say?"

"The same as you, Fin. And he was very sorry if he'd offended us. No harm intended."

"You . . . you haven't harmed him?"

"Oh, no! He's still there at Killaloe, working away at his little test tubes. It's all harmless enough." Kevin shook his head sadly. "But you, Fin. You're the one consorted with the Gall. It wasn't Peard." Kevin lifted the pistol until Doheny was staring into the barrel.

"After you've killed me, what do you intend with Peard and the people at the Lab?" Doheny asked.

"I'll keep them alive and comfortable until the day I want that woman in the tank," Kevin said.

Doheny nodded, deciding on a desperate lie. "We thought as much," he said. "That's why we prepared to spread the word of it all over Ireland."

"Word of what?" Kevin demanded.

"Word of that woman and your designs on her," Doheny said. "You'll find mobs marching on you to tear out your heart with their hands. You'll not have bullets enough to stop them."

"You haven't!" But the pistol lowered slightly.

"But we have, Kevin. And there's not a way in this world you could stop it."

Kevin returned the pistol to his lap. He studied Doheny for a moment. "Ah, that's a fine kettle of fish!"

"Go ahead and shoot me if you've a mind to," Doheny said. "And once you've done it, put the next bullet in your own head."

"You'd like that, wouldn't you, Fin?"

"You'll die slow or fast, one way or the other."

"There'll be no more calls to the Brits, Fin."

Angered beyond his ability to measure the consequences, Doheny said: "There will be, damn you! And I'll call the Yanks or the Russkies or the Chinamen! Anyone who can help us, I'll call him!" Doheny passed a hand across his lips. "And you can listen to every word I say!"

Kevin lifted the pistol, then lowered it.

"What you don't understand, Kevin O'Donnell, you stay out of!" Doheny said. "Unless you don't want us to find a cure for the plague!"

"What a thing to say, Fin!" Kevin sounded hurt. "Find the cure then if you can. It's your work and I wish you joy of it. But when you find the cure, it'll be mine as much as yours. You understand?" Kevin put the pistol back in his side pocket.

Doheny stared at him, realizing that Kevin saw the plague as just another weapon. With a cure, he would want to use it against everyone outside Ireland. He'd play at Madman and the whole world his target!

"You'd spread this madness?" Doheny whispered.

"There'll be kings once more in Ireland," Doheny said. "Now, be gone to your Lab and thank Kevin O'Donnell for the sparing of your life."

Doheny lurched to his feet and left the cell, staggering at the threshold, expecting a bullet in the back at every step. Not until he was in the outer court, Kevin's guards opening the gate, did he believe he had been spared. Inchicore Road looked insanely ordinary, even a flow of auto traffic along it. Doheny turned right and, once out of sight of the gate, leaned against the old Kilmainham wall. His legs felt as though the muscles had been stripped from them, only the bones and weak flesh left behind.

What could be done about Kevin O'Donnell? The man was as mad as poor O'Neill. Doheny felt mostly pity for Kevin, but something had to be done. There was no escaping the neccessity. Doheny looked up past a full-leaved tree at a sky with patches of blue in it.

"Ireland, Ireland," he whispered. "What your sons have come to!"

He understood Kevin well—all the fighting and the living with death at your elbow. It banked a fire in every Irishman. It had gone on for so long, for so many generations, that the brooding, unquenchable flame had become a full partner in the Irish psyche. It was fixed there by the adhesive of oppression and starvation, kept alive in each new generation by the hearth-side stories in the night—of tyrant cruelties and the agonies of ancestors. The shuddering realities of Ireland's travail were never farther from any Irishman than the words of his own family.

Doheny looked left where a group of armed Finn Sadal were emerging from Kilmainham. They paid no attention to the man leaning against the wall.

There goes the fire to be renewed, Doheny thought.

The Irish past was a sullen ember, always ready to erupt. Melancholy could become in an instant the berserker's abandon. It was hatred of the English; that was the hub of their lives. Each new Irishman pledged that a thousand years of cruelty would be avenged. It was ground into the Irish soul.

It is the source of our passion, the grim aspect behind every jest. And the object of our hatred was never more than sixty miles away across the Irish sea.

Oh, Kevin was easy to understand, but he would be harder to stop.

Doheny pushed himself away from the cold wall of Kilmainham Jail. Sweat was chilly against his skin. He turned and headed for the Royal Hospital.

I must call Adrian immediately.

Original sin? Ahh, Father Michael, what a fine question for me as knows it so well! Original sin is the being born Irish. And that's sin enough for any god!

—Joseph Herity

KATE O'GARA sat at the little wall desk in their new quarters writing in her diary the things she could not say to Stephen. She knew it was a bit after 10:30 A.M. because she had just heard Moone Colum and Hugh Stiles come on guard duty outside there in the castle courtyard, which, she thought, must be almost completely bricked in and covered over by now. The daylight was much dimmer than when they had been moved here.

She wrote in the diary:

"I do not like Adrian Peard. He enjoys his authority too much."

In all fairness, she knew why Stephen admired the man so much. No denying Peard's brilliance, but he demanded this recognition at every turn. There was something lacking in him, she thought. Peard did not project Stephen's solid reliability.

I'm being ungrateful.

Everything done here was part of a design to hold the plague at bay for one lone woman—herself. Nothing was being spared, so they assured her, to keep her happy in this protracted isolation. Only eleven days after Stephen had almost physically forced her into the pressure tank, a great mob of men had come with a lorry and cranes and big machines. By nightfall they had been ready to move the tank entire with Stephen and herself in it like two beans rattling in a pot. There had been soldiers all around, armored vehicles and motorcycles and guns. The air pumps and great diesel generator had been carried on the lorry with the tank. The noise of them so close had alarmed her and she had clung to Stephen.

"What if the tank breaks?"

"It's steel and very strong, love." Her ear against his chest, she could hear his voice rumbling there and the strong steady beat of his heart. That, more than the words, had calmed her.

She had peered through the ports once and seen the lights of a city burning in the night far off across the fields. There had been fires on a distant hill as they drove down into a valley and, once, protracted gunfire stopped the convoy beside a bridge with dark water flowing nearby in the starlight. She had huddled against Stephen until the lorry once more began to move.

They had arrived finally at this courtyard, it illuminated by brilliant lights up high on the inner walls. Through the ports, Kate had glimpsed stones and bricks piled all around, stacks of cement in sacks. There had been the crackling blue of welders and men working over large sheets of steel.

"They're building us bigger quarters, love," Stephen had explained. "The airlock end of this tank will be fitted into the other quarters."

"Will it be safe?"

No mistaking the source of her anxiety. The stories of women dying—on the radio and relayed by the men outside—had filled her with terror.

"Adrian will sterilize the place and everything in it," Stephen had reassured her.

Still, she had been reluctant to crawl out the airlock into the other rooms when the workmen had finished there. Stephen had pointed out that the new chamber contained a television and a private room for the toilet, and it even had a bath.

To Kate, the toilet facilities had been the ugliest part of living in the smaller tank. Never mind her training as a nurse and all the understanding of bodily functions. The little tank had only this pressure-operated bowl for a toilet and it right out in the open opposite a port. Wastes went out through a pipe into a sterile container designed originally to capture specimens for medical examination. She had forced Stephen to turn his back while she used the *convenience,* but anyone could look in from outside . . . although she had to admit she had never seen a face at the port while she was on the damned toilet.

And there was the smell. Within a day, the confined quarters had taken on the stench of a latrine.

Canned food was her other complaint.

"Cold canned food!"

Those three words uttered with revulsion had grated on Stephen. She had known this but could not stop herself from saying them.

And the water in sterile bottles! No taste to it at all.

The new quarters had vertical walls and a flat ceiling of steel. There was even brown-and-white lino on the floor and two electric burners on a bench beside a small pressure sink. Nothing near as grand as the kitchen in Peard's cottage, but the food could be heated. It all continued to come from cans, though. And the water, the tasteless water in sterile bottles! Although now they could get an occasional bottle of Guinness if it had been made before the plague.

They still slept in the original tank, but now it was on a big mattress left sterile in the new chamber. It sagged a bit toward the middle because of the tank's curvature, this in spite of resting on a big sheet of plywood supported at the middle by wooden blocks. The blocks had a disturbing tendency to bounce and drum when she and Stephen made love.

"We're animals in a zoo!" she complained, thinking about the men outside hearing that noise.

"But you're alive, Kate!"

She could not explain why this terrified her. It should have been reassuring.

I'm alive.

But the terrible news relayed from outside, and even some of it now seen on the telly, only made her continued existence more alarming. She felt fragile and subject to the awful whims of a malignant fate.

In her diary, she had drawn a crude map and plotted on it the plague's inexorable spread—Brittany, North Africa, Sicily, the toe of Italy, then Rome itself, the citadel of her faith. On her map, she blotted out each new plague place with ink and felt as she did this that she removed these regions from her world. The plague spots were like the places marked on antique maps—Terra Incognita. They would have to be rediscovered . . . if anyone survived.

She knew she was not the only woman left alive in Ireland. There was talk outside that she could overhear and they answered her questions when she asked. There were women isolated in the old mines near Mountmellick and near Castleblayney. Another group of women was said to be in a great house on its own land near Clonmel with a madman named Brann McCrae. Rumors and reports spoke of tiny groups here and there throughout the land, each protected by desperate men.

Her own position, though, was unique.

In his own cold-blooded way, Peard had let her know this as an eavesdropper while he discussed the situation with Stephen.

"Most of the other women are sure to go as their men are contaminated in the search for food."

She had stood at a port, looking out at Peard while he spoke to Stephen by telephone. Peard was a bitter-faced little dynamo, no more than a meter and a half tall, with frigid blue eyes and a thin-lipped mouth that Kate had never seen smile. He had straw-colored hair, which he kept close-cropped or shaved off entirely, as did many of the men she saw through the ports. Peard's skin was tanned and the brow heavily creased by frown wrinkles.

"Can't we do anything for those women?" Stephen had asked.

"We're providing sterilized food, but the men are all suspicious and won't accept our medical advice nor anything else. We thought of taking some of them by force, but that would be fatal for the women. Best leave things as they are and hope."

"What about the women being sent back from overseas?" Stephen had asked.

"Not many of them getting here alive. Those who do . . ." Peard's features had grown glowering and thoughtful " . . . well, we tried isolating some of them, to no avail. And the Beach Boys control all the coast. They aren't cooperating. We've had to go along or risk a civil war . . . which we may do yet, although Fin says . . ." Peard had shook his head silently, not revealing what Fin had said.

Fin, she knew, would be Fintan Doheny, a man of power in the high councils.

"What about England?" Stephen's voice had sounded beaten down, hopeless.

"Worse than here, so we're told. It spread faster there for some reason. The Welsh say they have some women in a coal mine, but the problem of food is terrible. And the water . . . Some Scots have thirty-two women isolated in Stirling Castle, but there's violence in Edinburgh and mobs. Last we heard, the people at the castle were starving and some religious madman with a mob at their gates."

"Surely, we'll have an answer to the plague before all the women die," Stephen had protested.

"We're working on it. Rest assured of that."

Peard's words, uttered as they were in his coldly impersonal way, had given her no reassurance at all.

She had begun to cry, deep racking sobs. Her poor mother dead! And not even a funeral nor a priest to pray over her. All the women of Cork gone excepting herself. And what was she here in this room of steel? A guinea pig! She could hear it in Peard's voice, see it in his manner. He thought of her as an easily available *test subject!*

She longed for Maggie to talk to, a woman friend to understand and speak the common language of their concerns. But Maggie was gone with the rest.

Hearing her sobs, Stephen had broken off the conversation with Peard. His arms around her helped some, but the sobs died off only when she grew too tired and lost in her misery to continue them.

"I want us to be married," she whispered finally.

"I know, love. I've asked them to bring a priest. They're trying."

Seated at the little desk against the cold steel wall, Kate wrote in her diary: "When will they bring a priest? It's been fifteen days since Stephen asked."

She could hear Moone Colum and Hugh Stiles arguing outside her wall. A trick of the acoustics made the desk a focal point for overhearing the words of the two men out there. She often sat here listening to them. She liked old Moone in spite of his blasphemous attitude toward the Church. But he and Hugh kept up an argument about religion that had begun to bore her. They were at it again, she noted.

"The system of birth and death has been broken, that it has," Moone said.

From behind her, she heard the page of a book turn and Stephen's whisper: "Moone's off again."

So he could hear them, too. She folded her arms on the

desk and lowered her head to her arms, wishing the two men would take their argument someplace else.

But Moone was ranting in that peculiar rasping whine of his, which Kate had come to identify as his angry sound: "This completes the process begun by the Catholic Church!"

"Aw, you're daft," Hugh said. "Birth, death—how can such a thing be broken?"

"Would y' grant me, Hugh, that the work of bearin' children was once part of a circle, part of an endless return?"

"You sound like one of them heathen Indians," Hugh protested. "Next thing you'll be tellin' me you're the spirit of Moses himself come back to . . ."

"I'm just talkin' about the circle of birth and death, y' old idiot!"

Stephen came up behind Kate and put a hand on her shoulder. "They know out there that you're pregnant."

Without lifting her head, she said: "Make them bring a priest."

"I'll ask again." He stroked her hair. "Don't cut your hair, Kate. It's beautiful when it's long this way."

Hearing a bustle of movement outside, Kate lifted her head against his hand. She heard Peard's voice commanding someone to ready the small airlock.

Stephen went to the speaker phone and keyed it. "What is it, Adrian?"

"I'm sending in a pistol, Stephen. We're sterilizing it right now."

"A pistol? In the name of heaven, why?"

"Fin told me to do it, in case someone tries to break in there."

"Who would do that?"

"We'd not let them!" That was Moone Colum.

"It's just a precaution, Stephen," Peard said. "But keep it handy."

He's lying, Stephen thought. But he knew if he continued to question, it would upset Kate. She was looking up at him now, fear in her eyes.

"Well, if Fin says it, I'll do it," Stephen said, "but I think it's a damned foolishness with men like Moone and Hugh out there guarding us."

Kate's mouth formed a silent question.

Stephen nodded. "When're you going to bring us that priest?" he asked.

"We're doing our best. There were so many of them killed at Maynooth and now, well, we must find one willing to come here and one we can trust, to boot."

"What do you mean *trust?*" Kate demanded.

"There're some strange goings-on in our world, Katie," Peard said. "Don't you worry your pretty head, though. We'll find you a priest."

She hated it when Peard called her Katie. So damned condescending! But she felt so helpless in here, so dependent upon the good will of everyone out there. And such terrible things were happening.

"Thank you," she said.

Stephen and Peard began talking about her as a patient, then. Peard said he was bringing an obstetrician to brief Stephen. Kate tuned them out. She did not like being discussed as though she were a piece of meat. She knew Stephen had wanted this briefing, though. It was his loving concern about her and she was thankful for that, at least.

When they were finished, Peard went away, but he left his phone key open and she could hear Hugh and Moone through the speaker. They were talking about the efforts to maintain a semblance of normalcy in the land.

"There's talk of restoring the canals," Hugh said. "Why? What would they carry? From where and to where?"

Moone agreed with him. "There's no future in it, Hugh."

Kate put her hands over her ears.

No future in it!

Hardly a day went by without someone outside there using those awful words in just that way. *No future in it.*

She lowered her hands to her abdomen, feeling for it to begin swelling with the new life, trying to feel the actual living presence there.

"We must have a future," she whispered.

But Stephen had gone back to his medical books and did not hear her.

She's the most distressful country
that ever yet was seen,
They are hanging men and women
for the wearing of the green.
Then since the color we must wear
is England's cruel red,
Sure Ireland's sons will ne'er forget
the blood that they have shed.

—**Dion Boucicault,**
"The Wearing of the Green"

WITHIN AN hour of the meeting at the lake, the road along which John walked with his new companions began to climb toward a notch at the top of the valley. It was still and hot on the macadam, the sunlight glinting off the leaves beside the road, reflecting glitter dazzles from minerals in the rock walls on both sides.

Herity looked at the three backs ahead of him, thinking how easy it would be to eliminate them there—one short burst from the machine pistol in his pack. Someone would hear, though. And there'd be the bodies for Kevin's people to find. Dirty son of a witch-whore, that Kevin. Of all the types in Ireland now, Kevin's was probably the most dangerous: Creepies. No telling what they might do next. Those three up ahead, now: They were natural wanderers—even the Yank. No place could hold them for long. They weren't like the coffin-sleepers waiting just to die. That Yank might be a hater, as well, though.

There was steel in his eyes. And the priest could easily become a death-drinker, a Slobber. Lucky the boy didn't talk. He'd be a wee whiner for sure. God save us from the moaners and the psalm singers and the professional patriots!

John, glancing back at Herity, thought what an oddly silent lot they were: the boy who would not speak, the priest who made decisions without discussing them, and Herity back there— a dangerous man sunk in a sullen remoteness from which only his dark eyes probed occasionally at the passing landscape. Something about Herity disturbed O'Neill-Within, vexing John with unwanted flickers of other-memories, things better not recalled lest they awaken the screams. He looked at the priest for distraction and found a wild look there in eyes that did not flinch away. John was the first to break their locked gazes, putting down a surge of rage at this priest, this Flannery. It was easy to recognize the priest's type—a man who early in his life discovered the violence and power in an absolutely arrogant belief. Oh, yes, that was this Flannery. He'd wrapped this belief around himself, put it on like armor . . . and now . . . now, his armor had been penetrated.

Once more, John glanced at the priest and found the man looking back at Herity.

No help there, Priest!

Easy to see what Flannery was doing: he was desperately engaged in repairing the wreck of his armor. His life was pouring out through the holes and he was grasping at the old arrogance, trying to fit the broken pieces in place, trying to restore the armor behind which he could stand untouched by his world while he made others dance to his whims. He was like a virgin compromised and there was something furtively dirty about him.

John looked down at the boy. Where was the mother? Probably dead. Just as dead as Mary and the twins.

Father Michael, seeing John look at the boy, asked: "How did you come to Ireland, Mister O'Donnell?"

It was as though the name restored him to himself, setting up the genial pose that he knew would work best there. "Call me John."

"It's a good name, John," Father Michael said.

John heard Herity quickening his pace to catch up.

"I came to Ireland . . ." John said, "well, it's a long story."

"We've all the time there is," Herity said from John's right. They were walking four abreast now up the steepening road.

John thought a moment, then picked up his story where the warship's launch left him in the bay at Kinsale.

"They stripped you naked and left you to die on the road?" Father Michael asked. "Ahhh, those Beach Boys—violent men and full of rage. No appreciation of man's goodness."

"They let him live," Herity said.

"They trade on our sorrows," Father Michael said.

The remotely unctuous tone grated on John. He asked: "Do the men of the warships come in to Kinsale regularly?"

"They send in supplies and armaments on unmanned boats, which they sink afterwards. The Beach Boys repay this by guarding our shores, preventing anyone from trying to leave."

"And what else would you have them do?" Herity asked. "Would you send this madness into other lands? And you a man of the cloth!"

"That's not what I mean, Joseph Herity, and you know it!"

"Then you don't think our shores need guarding?"

"That they do, but I'd take no pleasure in it. And I'd greet such as Mister O'Donnell with a more kindly reception than the one he describes." Father Michael shook his head sadly. "The IRA come to this."

"What's that you say?" John asked. He felt his heartbeat quickening. His face felt warm and flushed.

Father Michael said: "The Finn Sadal, our Beach Boys, is mostly the IRA. They fell so easy into this, I wonder did they not always trade on our sorrow?"

"There's some would kill you for saying less," Herity said.

"And you among them, Mister Herity?" Father Michael asked. He sent a probing stare at Herity.

"Aw now, Father," Herity said, his tone smooth and placating. "I was only giving you the caution. Watch your tongue, man."

The boy, who had been looking from one speaker to the other during this exchange, his face expressionless, suddenly darted off to the edge of the road. He picked up a rock there and hurled it down into the trees at the head of the lake. A cloud of rooks lifted from the trees as the rock disappeared into the greenery. The birds' harsh cries filled the air as they whirled in a black spiral that threaded out into a line winging southward across the lake.

"There's Ireland for you," Father Michael said. "Shouts and cries when we're disturbed, then off we go someplace else to wait for another disturbance."

"Is there no government then?" John asked.

"Oh, there's all the trappings," Father Michael said. "But the real power's with the army and that means the rule of guns."

The boy returned to Father Michael's side where he took up his position, walking along as though he had never left there. His face was placid. John wondered if the boy might be deaf . . . but, no. He obeyed spoken orders.

"It's always been the rule of guns, I fear," Father Michael said. "Nothing's changed."

"Are the Beach Boys part of the government?" John asked. He felt O'Neill-Within waiting for the answer.

"They've guns," Father Michael said. "And they've men in the high councils."

Herity said: "Oh, some things has changed, Priest. Some things has changed very much."

" 'Tis a fact, I agree," Father Michael said. "We've gone back to the feudal times. Futile, too, if you take my meaning."

"Ah, the priest's a poet!" Herity said.

John looked up as the light around them darkened abruptly. He saw that clouds had come in from the west, a dark scudding line of them carrying the hint of rain.

"There's no democracy," Father Michael said. "Perhaps there never was, it being a precious jewel men steal when it's left unguarded."

"But we've one government in Dublin for all of Ireland," Herity said. "Tell me, Father Michael, isn't that something we've always wanted?" He turned a sly grin toward the priest.

"It's the same old bickering and jealousies," Father Michael said. "We're still divided."

"Don't listen to him, Mister O'Donnell," Herity said. "He's just a crazy old priest."

The boy scowled at Herity but only John noticed.

"It's a very ancient way with us," Father Michael said, "part of the original Gaelic madness. We divide ourselves so others can conquer us. The Vikings found us easy because we were too busy fighting each other. If we'd once united aginst the Norsemen—be they white or black—we would've driven them in to the sea." He looked at Herity. "And there'd've been no blond Irishmen at all!"

Herity glared at him, understanding the dig at his own ancestry.

"The Norsemen mixed their blood with ours," Father Michael said, looking at the tufts of blond hair poking from beneath Herity's green cap. "One of the great calamities of history, the mix of the berserkers and the Irish! We became great self-slaughterers—ready to throw ourselves to death for any cause."

John glanced at Herity and was startled by the wild rage in the man's face. Herity's hands were clenching and unclenching as though he longed to choke the priest.

Father Michael appeared not to notice.

"It was a bad mix all around," he said. "Rotting out the communal roots of the Irish, degrading as well what was best in the Norsemen—their sense of camaraderie."

"Be still, you mad priest!" Herity grated.

Father Michael only smiled. "You will note, Mister O'Donnell, that the mixed breed was left only with a greedy loyalty to self and the swagger to take advantage of anything for personal glory."

"Are you quite through, Priest?" Herity demanded, his voice barely controlled.

"No, I'm not. I was about to observe that there were ancient ties between us and the Northumbrians, and them right in the heart of the bloody Brits over the water there. The Vikings cut those ties, as well. And when you come back to it, Mister Herity, we did it to ourselves by refusing to be united, by letting the Vikings take us!"

Herity no longer could contain himself. He jumped ahead, whirled and smashed a fist into the side of Father Michael's head. The priest fell against the boy and both tumbled onto the roadway.

The boy, fists clenched, tried to leap up, and it was apparent he would have attacked Herity, but Father Michael held him down.

"Easy, lad, easy. Violence does us no good."

Slowly, the boy's anger subsided.

Father Michael climbed painfully to his feet, dusted the dirt of the road off his black clothing and smiled at John, ignoring Herity, who stood with fists clenched, but a blank and questioning look on his face, as though he listened for attack to come from any side.

"An object lesson in what I was saying, Mister O'Donnell," Father Michael said. He turned and helped the boy to stand, then looked at Herity. "Now that you've shown us all your power, Mister Herity, should we be going along?"

Leading the boy by one hand, Father Michael stepped around Herity and set off up the road, which was now curving left through low conifers and growing steeper.

John and Herity fell into step behind them, Herity glaring at the priest's back. John had the feeling that Herity felt he had been beaten back there.

"Now, as to the English," Father Michael said, as though there had been no interruption, "the wireless tells us, Mister O'Donnell, that they've the two parliaments there—one at Dundee for the Scots and one at Leeds for the Gall of the south."

"Knowing the Brits have the plague, too," Herity muttered, "and *them* divided north and south—that's one of the few joys we have left us."

"What's the word from London?" John asked.

"Bless me!" Herity said, brightening. "It's still mob rule in London, so they say. As it'd be in Belfast and Dublin if the army let it happen."

"There's no English army, then?"

"As to that," Herity said, "they say the mob's allowed in London because no one cares to go in and clean it up. Isn't that like the Brits, now?"

"No word yet from Libya?" John asked. He found himself enjoying the sense of spiteful jockeying for dominance between the priest and Herity.

"Who cares about the heathen?" Herity asked.

"God cares," Father Michael said.

"God cares!" Herity sneered. "Y' know, Mister O'Donnell, the furst things that went in Ireland was the Restriction Laws— licensed premises, consenting adults, speed limits, dress codes, the Sunday bans and all of it. The new law's a simple one: If it feels good, do it."

Father Michael glanced back at Herity and spoke in outrage: "Men still have their immortal souls to preserve, and don't you forget that, Joseph Herity!"

"Mister Joseph Herity to you, Priest! And would y' show me your immortal soul now? Show it me, you Papist pig! Show it!"

"I'll hear no more of such blasphemy," Father Michael said, but his voice was low and stricken.

"Father Michael did his priestly juties at Maynooth in County Kildare," Herity said, glee in his voice. "Tell Mister O'Donnell what's happened to Maynooth, Priest."

John looked at Father Michael, but the priest had turned away and walked now, head down, praying in a low, mumbling voice from which only a few words could be understood: "Father ... pray ... give ..." Then, louder: "God help us find our brotherhood!"

"The brotherhood of despair," Herity said. "That's the only brotherhood we have now. Some do it in the drink, Mister O'Donnell, and some in other ways. It's all the same."

They were almost into the notch at the head of the valley now, the rock walls covered with blackberries, spittle bugs on the leaves. There was low gorse to the left beyond the walls, the burned-out ruin of a farmhouse down there, equipment in the yard rusty and smashed, a power pole leaning at a crazy angle over the crumpled metal roof of an outbuilding. Everything pointed to the frenzy of destruction he had seen from his first day here.

John stopped and looked back the way they had come. He glimpsed the lake through the low conifers and the shelf line of another road on the far side of the water. Looking at Herity, who also was studying the road behind them, John had the feeling that Herity and the priest were contending for him, that he, John Garrech O'Donnell, was a prize that each of those two men sought.

The priest and the boy had not stopped. Herity touched John's arm. "Let's be hurrying along." He sounded fearful.

John fell into quick step with Herity, looking up once at the scudding clouds. There was a damp smell of ashes in the air. The road turned down to the right, cooler here, the trees much taller on this side of the notch. Herity did not slacken the pace until they were beside Father Michael and the boy, walking once more four abreast.

The road curved left along a rock outcropping, then up a slight rise and once more down. There were gateways here, two on each side of the road, the whitewash weathered away, the gates themselves barricaded by high piles of fallen trees. Beyond the second barricade on the right, John could see an overgrown cart track cutting through a field of rye where tall weeds poked. There was a battered sign board dangling from the gatepost, some of its letters still visible. John tried to read them as he passed:

"JF————PA————blessed officially————Rev. M— ————PO————ER."

"What's that place?" John asked, nodding.

"Who cares?" Herity asked. "It's the dead and gone."

Deciduous trees bowered the road here and the four walkers

emerged from the shadows of them to find a house on each side crowded up to the road. The one on the right was a smashed and burned ruin, but the one on the left appeared intact, only a bit of moss on its slate roof, no smoke from its two chimneys. There was even a door standing open with a coat hanging inside as though the owner had just come in from the fields.

John, sensing the nearness of rain, asked: "Shouldn't we take shelter in there?" He stopped and the others stopped with him.

"Are y' daft?" Father Michael asked, his voice low. "Can't you smell it? That's a death house."

John sniffed, smelling a faint carrion odor. He looked at Herity.

"But it is shelter, Priest, and the rain's coming," Herity said. He acted as though he would not enter without Father Michael's approval.

"There's unburied dead around," Father Michael said. "Perhaps . . . suicides." He looked up the road ahead of them, then down at a patch of yellow pimpernel against the house wall. "There'll be a town ahead and shelter there."

"Towns is not so safe these days," Herity said. "I had it in mind to take the upper road and miss the town."

John heard the short sharp calls of rooks beyond the trees and now that they had stopped walking, the air felt chilled.

"Best be going along," Father Michael said. "I don't like the feel of this place."

"The faeries have been at it for sure," Herity said. He headed past the priest, adjusting the straps of his pack. Father Michael and the boy hurried to catch up. John joined them, wondering at the strangeness of that exchange. Another hidden conversation between the two men. One minute they were fighting, the next they found some secret agreement.

At the crest of the next hill, there was a cleared space on the right, another burned ruin in it and an intact sign at the drive curving in and out of the cleared space.

"Shamrock Inn."

Herity trotted up the drive and peered behind the ruin. "Back buildings are still intact," he called. He brought a pistol from beneath his jacket and went around the wreckage, returning in a moment to announce: "No one at home. Smells of piss, though, if you don't mind, Father Michael."

It began to rain as John, the priest and boy came up to Herity. He led the way around the ruin on a muddy path, waving proudly at a low, windowless building that came into view on the other side.

"The bath house and toilets remain!" Herity said. "The emblems of our civilization survive. You smell it, Father Michael. There's the piss, but more."

Father Michael entered the open door of the weathered building, the others right behind. It was raining hard now, the drumming loud on the metal roof over them. Father Michael sniffed the air.

"He smells it!" Herity said, watching Father Michael with a look of glee. "He's like his precious Vikings, is my priest, following the smell of hay to a settlement they could despoil. See how he sniffs the air! He had the brewery smell in his nose and he's thinking how fine it'd be to have that savor on his tongue."

Father Michael aimed a hurt and pleading look at Herity, who only chuckled.

John sniffed. He could smell the latrine odors from the toilets next door, but Herity was right: there was the smell of beer in this room, as though it had been spilled on the floor and allowed to soak in for years. John glanced around. It apparently had been a bath house and laundry, but only the sinks remained and someone had ripped them almost completely out of the wall. A disordered clutter of broken green glass and paper had been kicked into a corner. Otherwise, the floor appeared swept, only a few windblown leaves scattered across it.

Herity dropped his pack onto the concrete floor by the door and ducked outside. He returned presently, his hands caked with wet black dirt, five bottles of Guinness clutched in his arms.

"Buried, b'gawd!" he said. "But I know the ways of them as tries to hide. And there's plenty more in the hole, enough to lose all our sorrows. Here, Father Michael!" Herity thrust a dark-brown bottle at the priest, who took it with a trembling hand. "And one for Mister O'Donnell!"

John took the bottle, feeling the coldness of it. He shook away the dirt around the cap.

"Here now!" Herity said, taking a bottle opener from his pack. "Don't disturb the precious brew."

As Herity opened John's bottle and returned it, John heard O'Neill Within screaming: "Don't! Don't!"

One sip, he thought, *Enough to clear my throat.*

He met Herity's gaze over the upturned bottle. There was

a measuring, waiting look in the man's eyes and he was not drinking, although Father Michael already had drained his own bottle.

John lowered the bottle and met Herity's gaze again, grinning. "You're not drinking, Mister Herity."

John wiped his lips on a sleeve of the yellow sweater.

"I was enjoying the sight of you and you so pleasured with the pride of Ireland," Herity said. He passed an opened bottle to Father Michael. "I'll bring more." He made three trips, leaving a row of bottles along the wall—twenty of them with glass shining between the patches of brown dirt. "And there's more," Herity said, wiping a bottle and opening it for himself.

John sipped at his drink. It was bitter and thirst-quenching. He could feel the glow of it and thought about the cans of fish in his pocket. He brought them out.

"Should we be making a meal here?"

"I was wondering at the bulge of those," Herity said. He drank deeply of his brew. "We can eat later. This is a rare moment for serious drinking."

He wants to get me drunk, John thought. Putting aside a half-full bottle, he stared out the doorway, sensing the roiling mutter of O'Neill-Within, screams hanging at the edge of awareness. *Why do I move to the demands of O'Neill-Within?* he wondered. O'Neill was always there, always watching, always aware of what was said and done around him, always with a special alertness to the pain of those he observed. John felt then that O'Neill-Within ran the O'Donnell persona as though O'Neill were a puppetmaster playing the other persona on a special stage. *And wouldn't Herity like to find that puppetmaster!*

"You drink like a nandy," Herity said, opening another bottle. "There must be a hundred bottles out there in the hole." He passed the open bottle to Father Michael, who took it firmly and drained it without stopping for breath. The boy crawled into the corner near the ruined sink and sat there staring at the three men with a sullen expression.

"I'll go to sleep if I drink on an empty stomach," John said. He looked at the boy. "And the boy's hungry. Wouldn't you agree, Father Michael?"

"Leave the priest out of it!" Herity bawled. "He's a drinkin' man, is our Father Michael."

Father Michael accepted another open bottle from Herity. There was a glazed look in the priest's eyes. He shuddered as though from the cold, holding the bottle indecisively. He looked from the bottle to the boy, obviously trying to make a choice. Abruptly, he opened his hand. The bottle smashed on the floor.

"Now look what you've went and done," Herity accused.

"No more," Father Michael muttered.

"That's not the Father Michael I know!"

"Bring the can opener, boy," Father Michael said.

The boy stood and produced a small, razor-tip can opener from his pocket. He took it to Father Michael, who accepted a can of fish from John and opened it with elaborate steadiness before passing it to the boy with the opener.

His voice hoarse, Father Michael asked: "You've more of these?" He pointed at the can of fish in the boy's hands.

"One for each of us."

"None for me," Herity said. "There's one drinking man in this lot at least." He sat down beside the unopened bottles and rested an arm across his green pack. "I'm the only man among us can appreciate the honor of the occasion." He started to drink one bottle after another.

John found a wall to sit against where he could watch his companions. The boy took two more cans of fish from John and opened them, passing one to Father Michael and the other to John before returning to his corner. Rain continued to drum on the metal roof. It grew darker and cold.

There was something fermenting in the boy, John thought. There was a depth charge in him, pressure waiting to reach that limit which would explode it. For the first time since he had seen the boy in the boat, John sensed a personality in him, a dim thing made of resentments and fears.

The boy glanced once at the priest. John, following his gaze, saw that Father Michael had curled into a corner and gone to sleep. A gentle wheezing sound could be heard from him.

"Would y' look at the little shagger there?" Herity asked, his voice low.

John jerked his gaze around, realizing that Herity had been studying him and had noticed his attention on the boy.

"Now, what would his name be?" Herity asked. "Does he have a name?" Herity drained a bottle and opened a fresh one. "Could it be the little shagger had no parents? Is he something turned out by the faeries?"

The boy glared at Herity, unmoving, chin resting on his knees.

Herity appeared unaffected by the drink. He drained the

new bottle and opened yet another, keeping his attention on the boy.

"Should we be wearing our coats inside out?" Herity asked. "The faeries cannot follow you when you wear your coat that way. I've a mind to shake the name out of him. What right does he have to keep himself to himself that way?"

Herity's voice had taken on a slight thickness, John noted. But the man appeared steady where he sat, head firm on the neck, no shakiness in his hands.

"I could get the speech of him soon enough," Herity said. He drained the bottle and placed it neatly with the empties on his left. Leaning an arm on his pack, his head on his arm, he continued to stare at the boy.

What was all this talk of faeries? John wondered. Herity appeared to have his own sense of reality, his own saints and devils. Herity sober was a man whose judgments had been made long ago and never changed. But Herity drunk, and he must be touched by the liquor now, could be another matter. He had sounded argumentative and bitter, but now silent . . . and John could feel the deep internal angers of him. Were there memories? Herity could be one of those who could not hide in the drink. The Guinness could have brought acid memories and even feelings of guilt. For what would Herity feel guilty? For striking the priest?

Herity closed his eyes. Presently, a deep snore shook him.

The boy stood up and cat-footed across the room to stand over Herity. There was something in the boy's right hand but John could not make it out in the gathering gloom.

Without any warning, the boy fell on Herity, striking out with the thing in his hand which, John saw now, was the razor-tip can opener. He was trying to slit Herity's throat, but the jacket collar prevented it.

Herity, awakened in shock, grabbed for the arm with the opener and caught it. They fought silently, the wild strength of the young body revealed in a flailing, unrestrained violence, terrifying in its silent intensity.

"All right! I'll leave you be!" Herity's voice carried a high-pitched hysteria. He caught the other arm and held both arms while the boy strained against him.

"Leave be, lad! I won't bother you more."

Father Michael sat up and asked: "What's wrong?"

The boy appeared to react to the priest's voice. He subsided slowly, his eyes still blazing at Herity, but the weapon dropped from the boy's hand and Herity thrust him away, releasing the arms. The boy stood and backed away.

A strangely chastened Herity picked up the weapon. He looked at it as though he had never seen such a thing before, and felt at his collar where the thing had struck. He looked up at the boy then and, in a voice of contrition, said: "I'm sorry, lad. I'd no right to intrude on your grief."

"What's happening?" Father Michael asked.

Herity hurled the opener at him and Father Michael groped for it, lifting it to where he could see it.

"You be the keeper of that, Priest," Herity said. "Your little shagger tried to use it on me throat." Herity began to laugh. "He's more of a man than you, Priest, and him no more than a chin above your belt buckle. But if he tries that again I'll break him like a piece of kindlin' wood."

The boy went to Father Michael and sat down beside him, still watchful of Herity.

"Didn't I tell you violence serves no purpose?" Father Michael asked. "Look at Joseph there, a man of violence, and ask do you want to become like him?"

The boy curled his knees up and buried his face in them. His shoulders shook but no sound emerged.

Watching them, John felt a surge of unexplainable anger. These people were so ineffectual! The boy couldn't even carry out a proper killing. He'd had every opportunity and he'd failed.

Father Michael put an arm over the boy's shoulder. "It's bitter cold," he said. "Should we have a fire?"

"Don't try to be more of a fool than you are," Herity said. "Cuddle up to your little shagger there and keep him from harm. We're here for the night."

The Irish, that harmless nation which has always been so friendly to the English.

—The Venerable Bede

ADRIAN PEARD stood at the window of Doheny's office in the Royal Hospital. It was early evening of a cold and cloudy day, a sky to match the gray battlements of Kilmainham off to the right. His view out the window was down across Inchicore Road toward Camac Creek and the burned ruins of a petrol station. He could hear Doheny stirring in his chair at the desk but did not turn.

"Why did they send you?" Doheny asked. His voice sounded strained.

"Because they knew you'd listen to me."

"He meant to kill me, I tell you! He had the gun right out on the desk and was fingering it the way he does. You've seen it."

"None of us doubt your word, Fin. That isn't the point."

"Then what is the point?"

"There's no one else can control the Beach Boys as well as Kevin."

"So we just sit idly by and let him threaten our researchers, kill off anyone he . . ."

"No, Fin! That's not the way of it at all."

Peard turned his back to the window. It was a depressing scene out there, the petrol station ruins a reminder of the mob violence that had swept through here before the army and the Finn Sadal had brought back a semblance of order.

Doheny sat with his elbows on his desk, fists clenched and his chin resting on the fists. He looked ready to explode.

"You're to stop threatening Kevin O'Donnell," Peard said. "That's the message I was told to convey. The army wants no internal battles. As for Kevin, they've taken him aside and warned him to leave the Lab alone. It's off limits to him."

"Unless he takes it into his mad head to kill us all in our sleep!"

"He's been told the army will execute him if he doesn't obey."

"And the same for me?"

"I'm sorry, Fin."

"He'll not try to stop our exchanges with the Huddersfield people?"

"He's been warned off, Fin."

"They'll continue to listen in on us, of course."

"Of course."

"And pass it along to Kevin?"

"He has his friends in the army."

"So it would appear."

"Well, that's the lot, Fin. You'll not disobey?"

"I'm not a foolhardy young idiot!"

"Good."

Doheny lowered his hands and unclenched his fists. "How're Kate and Browder doing?"

"As well as could be expected. She's still crying she wants a priest to marry them."

"Then get her one."

"That's not as easy as it sounds, Fin."

"Yes . . . yes, I know." Doheny shook his head. "That was a bad thing, Maynooth."

"One man I know for certain is a priest, he denied it to my face," Peard said. "Two of them still wearing the collar refused when I told them what we wanted. They don't trust anyone in authority, Fin."

"We've been consigned to hell, so they say."

"I've been trying to find a Father Michael Flannery," Peard said. "I was told he might . . ."

"Flannery's busy and can't be reached."

"You know where he is?"

"In a manner of speaking."

"Could you get word to him and ask if he . . ."

"I'll do what I can, but you keep looking."

Peard sighed. "I'd best be getting down to the corner. The convoy to Killaloe is supposed to leave on time."

"They never do."

"I'll not fault them for a delay right now. The darker the night the better, I say."

"I was told the N-Seven is safe," Doheny said.

Peard shrugged. "I still think we should move the pressure tank and those two here to Dublin."

"Not with Kevin O'Donnell right around the corner!"

"Well, there's something in what you say, Fin."

"Did you send a pistol in to Browder like I told you?"

"Yes, but he didn't like it and I thought Kate would make a scene about it."

"It's little enough."

"The army's warned him off, Fin. Depend on it."

"Where a madman's concerned, depend on nothing except the unexpected." Doheny pushed his chair back and stood. "Myself, I'm going everywhere armed and guarded. I'd advise you to do the same, Adrian."

"He'll not come to Killaloe. They promised."

"Sure, and they also promised they could find all the other uncontaminated women and protect them! You've heard, haven't you? Everyone in the Mountmellick mines is dead!"

"What happened?"

"One contaminated man. They killed him, of course, but it was too late."

"I'll be getting back to the Lab," Peard said. "How're things going here?"

"Not a glimmer yet, but that's to be expected. You'll have the readouts on our latest findings when you get back to Killaloe. Let me know what you make of them."

"I'll do that. Damn! I wish we could go back and forth to Huddersfield!"

"Barrier Command won't allow it. I asked."

"I know, but it seems criminal. Who could we contaminate? They're as full of the plague as we are."

"More."

"Open research is the only hope the world has," Peard said.

"The only hope Ireland has," Doheny said. "Don't you forget it. But if the Yankees or the Russkies find the answer first, they're as likely as not to just wipe us out. All in the sweet name of sterilization, you understand?"

"Do they accept this at Huddersfield?"

"Why do y' think we're being so open with each other, Adrian? They're still the British, you know."

"And we're still Irish," Peard said.

His slight body was shaken immediately by a high-pitched laugh. Doheny thought it a particularly nasty laugh.

DOCTOR DUDLEY WYCOMBE-FINCH knew what his people thought of this working office he had chosen—much too small for the director of the all-important English Research Establishment, too cluttered and too remote form the center of things here at Huddersfield.

In the days when Huddersfield had been devoted to the physical sciences, this had been the basement office of a research assistant. The building above it stood on the perimeter of the fence-enclosed grounds. It was a three-story concrete structure with no ivy and little character. Wycombe-Finch did maintain another office "for state occasions" back in the Administration Building. That was a spacious oaken suite with thick rugs and barriers of administrative assistants in the outer rooms, but this little cubicle and its adjoining lab was where he was to be found most of the time—here in an enclosure of windowless walls covered by bookshelves, its one door leading into the small laboratory. The desk was small enough that he could reach the farthest corner easily with either hand. The one chair was comfortable, high-backed and swiveled. And here he kept his radio and the listening devices and the electronic tools.

He leaned back in the chair and puffed on his long, thin-stemmed pipe while waiting for the morning call from Doheny. He and Doheny had met on several occasions at international conferences and Wycombe-Finch could picture his Irish counterpart when they spoke on the telephone—a short, rather stout man with a blustery manner. Wycombe-Finch was a contrasting tall, thin, gray-mantled figure. An American colleague once, seeing him with Doheny, had called them Mutt and Jeff, labels that Wycombe-Finch had found offensive.

A dottle of bitter nicotine burbled out of his pipe stem, burning his tongue. Wycombe-Finch wiped away the offending particles with a white linen handkerchief, which he realized belatedly was one from the bottom of the drawer, one of those his wife, Helen, had laundered before . . . He veered his mind away from that channel.

Outside the small office, he knew, the morning was a cold and misty grayness, all distances lost in the drifting diffusion. A Lakes Country morning, they called it locally.

The telephone in front of him weighted a scattering of papers—reports, summations. He stared at them while he smoked and waited. The telephone link between Ireland and England was none too satisfactory at best and he had learned to be patient in dealing with these regular exchanges between himself and Doheny.

The telephone buzzed.

He put the instrument to his ear, laying aside the pipe in an ashtray. "Wycombe-Finch here."

Doheny's distinct tenor was identifiable despite a poor connection that provided static and distinct clicks. *Lots of listeners,* Wycombe-Finch thought.

"Ahhh, there you are, Wye. The damnable phone service is at its worst this morning."

Wycombe-Finch smiled. He had last met Doheny at a London conference on interdisciplinary cooperation. Jolly fellow and with a first-class scientific mind behind those wide blue eyes. It was only during these regular telephone exchanges, though, that they had formed what Wycombe-Finch thought of as a working friendship.

Doe and Wye.

They had fallen into this first-name familiar relationship by the third call

"I'm convinced the telephone was created to teach us patience, Doe," Wycombe-Finch said.

"Stiff upper lip and all that, eh?" Doheny said. "Well, what's new, Wye?"

"We've a new government boffin coming down this morning for an assessment of our progress," Wycombe-Finch said. "I know the chap—Rupert Stonar. No head for science but very alert to wool over the eyes."

"Stonar," Doheny said. "I've heard of him. Political."

"Oh, very."

"What do you have to tell him?"

"Bloody nothing. Plodding, that's what we're doing. Good plodding, the kind that'll produce in time but no big break-through, which is what Stonar and his people want."

"What about those four new people you've added? The American, Beckett—I hear he's the one figured out how the Madman spread this thing."

"Brilliant fellow, no doubt of it. I've kept the four of them together as a team. There's something about the way they work together. I hesitate to call it electric, but they are one of those happy associations that often produce great things."

"Tell that to Stonar."

"He already knows it. I was hoping you might produce a little tidbit we could share with him, Doe."

After a moment's silence, Doheny said: "We don't hide very much from you, do we, Wye?"

Wycombe-Finch recognized this approach, part of a subtle code he and Doheny had worked out between the lines. Doheny had something to reveal, something hot that his masters might resent his telling, but that wouldn't matter now because Wy-combe-Finch obviously already knew it.

"I hope you don't even try," Wycombe-Finch said, picking up on his side. "God knows I resent the use of spies, and I assure you, Doe, that we're being completely candid with you."

Doheny's laughter rattled in the phone. Wycombe-Finch smiled gently. What in the devil had Doheny come up with?

"Well," Doheny said, "it's true. We may have O'Neill him-self."

Wycombe-Finch took advantage of a long burst of static to ask sharply: "What? I didn't hear that."

"The Madman. We may have him here."

"You have the fellow in durance, interrogators and all that?"

"God in heaven, no! I'm sending him the long way to our

facility at Killaloe. He's using the name John Garrech O'Donnell. Claims to be a molecular biologist."

"How sure are you?" Wycombe-Finch could feel his heart beating rapidly. No telling who might be listening to this conversation. Very dangerous. Doheny had to answer that question correctly.

"We're not positive, Wye. But I tell you, he tickles my neck hairs. We've one of our best men clinging to him like a leech, a priest ready at hand should he wish to confess, and a poor bereaved young boy in the party so he can see constantly what he's done."

Wycombe-Finch shook his head slowly from side to side. "Doe, you are a bloody awful man. You set this up."

"I took advantage of a situation that was handed to us."

"You're still bloody clever, Doe. Conscience, that'll be the key to the fellow, that is if we're to believe that profile the Americans produced. My God! This does take a little thinking. I confess I doubted it when our cloak-and-dagger boys told me."

"We're not getting our hopes up too high, but it is something to tell your man Stonar."

"He probably already knows. I suggest you be very careful, Doe. O'Neill may have some new nastiness up his sleeve . . . that is, if it's the Madman."

"Kid gloves, that's the way we're doing it."

"Terribly muddy waters, Doe."

This referred to a joke they had exchanged at a conference, muddy waters being the most fertile for new growth.

Doheny picked up on it immediately. "Very roiled, indeed. I'll let you know if they get muddier."

"Quite. Are the Americans helping?"

"We haven't said anything to them for the obvious reasons, Wye. Earlier, they did send us some material . . . just in case, but it's very scanty. No fingerprints, no dental records. They blame the Panic Fire, which may be the actual case."

"And if this . . . O'Donnell, you say? If he's just what he says he is?"

"We're going to give him the mental thumbscrews: a triple approach, all adding up to one thing—he must come up with a brilliant new approach to our researches."

"Triple approach? Ahh, you mean in case he's actually O'Neill and you're unable to prove it."

"Damned right. He could give us a real clue, or try artful concealment or a diversion."

"Or actual sabotage."

"As good as a confession, that." A burst of static, painfully loud, intruded on the line. When it passed, Doheny could be heard saying ". . . Beckett's group is doing."

Wycombe-Finch took it as a question. "I think the fellow to watch there is the little frog, Hupp. Got a devious mind. He feeds things to Beckett, almost as though he were playing Beckett, using the man as a personal computer."

"Blimey! As you Brits say."

"We say nothing of the kind, you Irish potato-eater."

Both chuckled. It was a weak enough chiggering, Wycombe-Finch thought, not enough to fool the listeners, but it had become almost ritual between them now, signaling that they were near the end of the conversation.

"If we ever meet face to face again, I'll whip your ears with my shillelagh—if I can find one of the blasted things," Doheny said.

A tear slid down Wycombe-Finch's left cheek. The stereotypes had been laid out to be chuckled at, but could they be discarded? Perhaps they played this game to keep the mistakes of the past fresh in their minds—brolly against shillelagh, the ridiculous against the ridiculous. A sigh shook Wycombe-Finch and he thought he heard its echo from Doheny.

"I'll fill Stonar with visions of sugarplum faeries from Ireland," Wycombe-Finch said, "but your man O'Donnell is probably just what he says."

"A molecular biologist is a molecular biologist," Doheny said. "We'd use Jesus, Mary and Joseph themselves if they showed up."

"Didn't O'Donnell carry any identification?" Wycombe-Finch asked, speaking as the thought hit him.

"A thick-head in command of the party that met him threw away the man's passport."

"Threw it away?"

"Over his shoulder into the sea. No chance to scrutinize it now and determine if it was a forgery."

"Doe, I think sometimes we are the victims of a deliberately malign fate."

"Let's pray there is a balancing benevolent fate. Perhaps it's Beckett's team."

"By the by, Doe, Beckett and his people think the zipper

theory may be confusing us, leading us down the garden path, so to speak."

"Interesting. I'll pass it along."

"Sorry I've nothing more substantial for you."

"Wye, a thought just occurs to me. Why don't you put Stonar together with Beckett? Brilliant Yank explaining the intricacies of marvelous scientific research to uninformed politician."

"Might be interesting," Wycombe-Finch agreed.

"It could even spark some new ideas in Beckett," Doheny said. "Explaining things to the uninitiated sometimes does that."

"I'll give it a think. Beckett, when he gets going, can be quite fluent."

"I'd like to talk to Beckett myself. Could he join us for one of these confabs?"

"I'll arrange it. Hupp, too?"

"No . . . just Beckett. Perhaps Hupp later. And please prime Beckett for heavy interrogation, would you, Wye."

"As I say, he is quite fluent, Doe."

There was silence filled with static for a moment, then Wycombe-Finch said: "I'll put together a report on their ideas about the zipper theory. We'll fax it to you first thing. Might be something in it, although I'm not giving ground."

"Beckett needs resistance, eh?"

"It primes him well. Keep that in mind when you talk."

"Does he get angry?"

"Never shows it, but it's there."

"Fine! Fine! I'll be at my Yankee-baiting best. And as far as this possible Madman is concerned, I'll let you know if the waters get muddier."

Wycombe-Finch nodded to himself. Totally muddy, of course, would mean they had confirmed the man as O'Neill. He said: "There is one thing more, Doe. Stonar may be coming here to dismiss me."

"Tell him to cut the phone lines to us if he does."

"Now, Doe, don't burn any bridges."

"I mean it! We Irish don't take naturally to you Brits. I'll not waste my time breaking in another contact at Huddersfield. You tell him."

"It only took us a week to get on a solid footing."

"Nowadays, a week is forever. The politicians haven't figured that out yet. They need us, we don't need them."

"Oh, I think we do, Doe."

"We stand together, Wye, or the whole bloody edifice comes crashing down. You tell that Stonar I said so. Until next time, then?"

"As you say, Doe."

Wycombe-Finch heard the click of the connection being broken. The static stopped. He replaced his telephone in its cradle and stared at his cold pipe beside it. Well, the listeners had been told.

Doheny was right in his own way, of course. Scientists had created this awful mess. Contributed to it, anyway, and no denying that. Bad communication, bad liaison with governments, failure to exercise what power we had or even to recognize the real nature of power. When we did move, we played the same old political games.

He glanced up at the wall of books on his left without really seeing them. What if it was Madman O'Neill over there in Ireland? Should there prove to be a way of using him, Doheny was sly enough to find it. But God help us all if the wrong people learned about it on the Outside.

Wycombe-Finch shook his head. Good thing the man was in Doheny's hands. He picked up his pipe and relighted it, thinking about this. Not until this moment had he realized how much faith he had developed in Doheny's crafty ways.

> *If there is one principle clearer than any other it is this: that in any business, whether of government or mere merchandising, somebody must be trusted.*
>
> —Woodrow Wilson

All this time with the damned Yank and not a clue! Herity thought.

It was midafternoon and they were plodding upward out of another shallow valley, the boy and the priest walking a bit ahead. The boy had been even more withdrawn since the fight in the bath house, his silence a deeper thing. Father Michael was accusatory. It was all Herity's fault.

It's all that damned Yank's fault!

And the priest isn't helping.

A Yank did it to us—made a ghetto of Ireland.

Herity had never thought of himself as a super-patriot—only a typical Irishman, bitter over the centuries of British oppression. He felt a tribal loyalty to his people and the land, a kinship of the rath. There was a pulling force in the Irish earth, he thought. It was a memory that lived in the soil itself. It remembered and always had. Even if there were no more people, there would be something here, an essence that would tell how the Gaels had passed this way once.

Father Michael was talking to the Yank, not probing, not doing what he should to see if it was a mask the man wore and the Madman himself underneath. Black thoughts in his mind, Herity listened.

"There are more ruins now," Father Michael said. "You noticed that?"

"Destruction, it seems," John said. "But plenty of food."

"More that's falling down. We've lost the look of the picaresque that really great ruins sometimes have. Now . . . it's just tumbledown."

They fell silent, passing another burned cottage whose walls butted up against the road. The blank windows exposed ashed tatters of curtains like wounded eyelids.

Someone will answer for that, Herity thought.

He felt the long Irish memory barbed like a spear. Offend it and someday you would feel the thrust and see your life welling from the wound.

They crested the top of the hill then and paused for breath, looking ahead to the long curve of another valley stretched out into mists at the upper end where a stream cascaded off black rocks, making its mark on the air with a moist screen that hid the farther hills. A hen cackled nearby.

Herity cocked an ear, hearing the gurgle of water; a brook or a spring.

"I hear water," John said.

"We could do with a bit of rest and some food," Father Michael said.

He crossed to the lower side of the road where tall grass covered a long slope into trees. Finding a spot in the stone wall where he could swing himself across, he went a few paces out into the tall grass. The boy leaped the wall and joined the priest.

John looked up at the sky. Clouds were coming in, filling the western horizon. He glanced at Herity, who waved for him to join the priest and boy. John climbed onto the wall and stood there looking across the open land before jumping down. The landscape had been defined by gray rock walls into green rectangles with a few cottages, all black and roofless, sprinkled among them. He heard Herity cross the wall and come up beside him.

"There's a beauty to it yet," Herity said.

John glanced at him, then returned his attention to the view. The thin mist reduced the middle distances to muted pastels, a rolling meadowland with a river winding through it, tall trees and darker greens on the far side.

"Are you thirsty, Mister O'Donnell?" Herity asked. But he looked at Father Michael as he spoke.

"I could do with a cool drink of spring water," John agreed.

"I'm thinking you have no knowledge of thirst," Herity said. "A cool glass of Guinness with foam as white as a virgin's panties flowing over the edges. Now there's a vision to raise a man's thirst!"

Father Michael and the boy began walking toward the trees below the meadow.

"I heard you and the priest talking about the ruins," Herity said. "It's not ruins. Decay! That's the word. Hope destroyed finally."

The priest and the boy stopped short of the trees near a granite outcropping. Looking after them, Herity said, "A fine man, the priest. Wouldn't you agree, Mister O'Donnell?"

At the jibing question, John felt O'Neill-Within begin to rise. Panic threatened him, then rage. "Others have suffered as much as you, Herity! You're not alone!"

A flush of blood darkened Herity's face. His lips tightened into a thin line and his right hand went toward the pistol under his jacket but hesitated and lifted instead to scratch the beard stubble on his chin.

"Would you listen to us now?" he asked. "We're like a couple of wains in..."

He broke off, stopped by the loud report of a shot from down in the trees below them. In one motion, Herity knocked John off his feet into the grass, rolled away with one hand in his pack, and before he stopped rolling had a small machine gun in his hands and was scrambling down to the shelter of the granite outcropping. He stopped there, peering down into the trees. John was right behind him, leaning up against the cold stone.

John peered around his edge of the rock, looking for the priest and the boy. Were they hurt? Who had shot and where had it been aimed? A limb cracked below him and Father Michael's pale and hatless head poked out of covering bushes under the trees. He was a wide-eyed blob of white against the green-and-brown background, the scar on his forehead very plain against the pale skin. He was staring directly up at John.

"Get your face back in here!" Herity said. He yanked John back into the rock's cover.

"I saw Father Michael. He seems to be all right."

"And the boy?"

"I didn't see him."

"We'll be patient a bit," Herity said. "That was a rifle shot." He cradled the machine gun against his chest and leaned back, scanning the rock wall bordering the road above them.

John looked at the weapon in Herity's hands.

Seeing John's attention, Herity said: "The Jews make fine guns, now don't they?" He whirled at the sound of swishing grass below them.

John looked up to see Father Michael peering down at them. The black felt hat once more covered the brand-scarred forehead.

Herity scrambled to his feet and peered past the priest toward the trees. "Where's the boy?"

"Safe behind some more boulders down there in the trees."

"Only the one rifle shot," Herity said.

"Likely someone shooting a cow or a pig."

"Or himself, that being the more common thing nowadays."

"You're a man full of evil," Father Michael said. He pointed at the machine gun. "Where did you get that terrible weapon?"

"This fine Uzi made by the clever Jews, I took it off a dead man, Father Michael. Isn't that where we get most things nowadays?"

"What do you intend with it?" Father Michael asked.

"To use it if need be. Exactly where did you leave the boy?"

Father Michael turned and pointed at the gray gleam of more rocks just within the trees, the granite partly hidden by invading gorse.

"We will go down there one at a time," Herity said. "I will go first, Mister O'Donnell next, then you, Priest. Stay here until I call."

Crouching low, Herity darted from behind the rocks and ran zig-zagging down the slope into the trees. They saw him duck behind the other rocks, then his voice called:

"Just the way I did it!"

John darted from behind the boulder, feeling exposed and vulnerable as he ran down the slope—left, right, left and into a pocket between the rocks where he saw the boy crouched, huddled into the blue coat. There was no sign of Herity. The boy stared at John with a blank expression.

There came the sound of running and Father Michael joined them, putting a protective arm around the boy.

Herity reappeared then, trotting up from deeper in the trees.

He joined them in the rock shelter, breathing heavily, the machine gun held at the ready across his chest.

"The three of you will stay here until I've looked over the land below us," Herity said. "That was a foolish thing you did, Priest, sauntering up there through the open after such a shot."

"If God means me to go now, He will take me now," Father Michael said.

"Or so you hoped," Herity said. "It's a sin, Father. Remember that. When you court death, how is that different from deliberate suicide?"

Father Michael cringed.

Herity started to leave but John detained him with a hand on his arm. "Joseph."

Herity turned a surprised look at John.

"I'm grateful for your concern," John said. "And I'd like you to call me John, but I'll not change one word of what I said up there." He gestured with his chin up the hill toward where Herity had knocked him down to protect him. "I meant every word of it."

Herity grinned. "Of course you did, Yank!"

With that, Herity ducked from behind the sheltering rocks and ran down into the trees. They heard a limb crack, then silence.

"A strange man, that," Father Michael said.

The boy pulled away from the priest and peered over the sheltering rocks.

"Here! Stay down!" Father Michael said. He pulled the boy back.

"Herity acts like a soldier," John said.

"That he does."

"Where did you encounter him?"

Father Michael looked away, hiding his face from John, but not before John saw a look of near panic there. What was it between those two—the priest and the violent man of action?

Father Michael spoke in a choked voice: "You might say God threw Joseph and me together. The reason for it, I cannot say." He returned his gaze to John, the features composed.

"What about the boy?" John asked. "Why is he with you?"

"A band of tinkers gave him to me," Father Michael said. "You'd call them Gypsies, but they're not really, 'y' know. They treated him well. They were the ones told me of his vow of silence."

"Then he can talk?"

"I've heard him cry out in his sleep."

The boy closed his eyes and bowed his head into the blue jacket.

"Has he a name?" John asked.

"Only he can say and he won't."

"Have you made any attempt to find his . . ."

"Hush now!" Father Michael glared at John. "Some pains are best not poked at, man."

John turned his head away abruptly, trying to control a rictus grin. There was a pain in his breast. He could feel O'Neill-Within moving closer and closer to the surface. John put both hands over his face, trying to quell the dangerous Other. A sound of tumbling pebbles brought his face jerking up out of his hands.

Herity ducked into their shelter. Perspiration ran down his face. Burrs and catchseeds tangled the lower part of his green trousers. The Israeli machine gun was still cradled against his breast. He took a moment to catch his breath, then: "There's two cottages just over the next ridge and smoke from the both of them. There's a radio and them listening to the news, talking about it."

Father Michael cleared his throat. "Any . . . any sign of . . ."

"Nary a sign of a female," Herity said. "Only men's clothing on the washline. Neat, though, both cottages neat and well tended. I'm thinking it's only men who've been well trained by their womenfolk."

"Graves?" Father Michael asked.

"Four of 'em in the meadow below the cottages."

"Then perhaps the people there would shelter us," Father Michael said.

"Not so quick!" Herity said. He looked at John. "Do you think you could use this weapon, John?"

John looked at the machine gun, sensing the power in it. He flexed his fingers. "Use it for what?"

"I've a mind to walk up to those cottages open and friendly like," Herity said. "With yourself covering me from above. There's rocks and a fine vantage on the ridge."

John glanced at the priest.

"I'll not bless this," Father Michael said. "The Church has sinned enough, calling on God to bless murder."

"We've no mind to murder anyone," Herity said.

"You're going soldiering," Father Michael said.

"Ohhh, that," Herity said. "I'm just not ready to commit suicide, Father." He looked at John. "What about it, John?"

John held out his hands for the machine gun. "Show me how it works."

"Very simple," Herity said. He stepped up beside John with the gun. "This here's the safety. When it's like this..." he clicked it, "...all you need to do is point it and pull the trigger. Steady as the Rock of Cashel it is." Herity restored the gun to safety and passed it to John.

John hefted the weapon. It felt warm from Herity's touch. A thing much more direct than the plague. Would O'Neill-Within rise up now and kill with noisy violence? John looked up to see Herity studying him.

"Can you do it?" Herity asked.

John nodded.

"Then follow me, silent as a mouse in a featherbed. Priest, you and the boy stay where you are until we call."

"God willing," Father Michael said.

"There now!" Herity pounced, grinning. "He's blessed us after all!"

Herity led the way then at a bent-over trot. They went down into the trees, following a scuffed track in the needle duff, crossing over a thin runnel of water splashing across black rocks.

John stopped, thirsty, looking first at the water and then at Herity.

"I'd not drink it," Herity whispered. "There's a dead man upwind." He pointed up the stream's course. "Dead a week at least and fouling the water." Herity smiled. "Pigs has been at him."

John shuddered.

Herity turned away. John followed him up the opposite slope, moving slowly through scrub conifers. The duff underfoot muffled their steps. At the ridgetop, Herity motioned John to stay low, then pointed along the ridge to the left where a gray rock buttress could be glimpsed through the brown trunks.

"From up there," Herity whispered, "you've a grand view down into their dooryard. I'll wait until I see you in place, then go along whistling, friendly and open without a weapon in sight. You understand?"

John nodded. He bent low and scrambled upward through the trees, approaching the rocks from below the ridgetop. Creeping over the top, he found he could slide out onto the rocks. They smelled flinty and were still warm from the earlier sunlight. He glanced upward. It would be dark soon and the clouds had rain in them. Slowly, he crept out onto a shallow cup within the rocks until his eyes could peer over the end.

He found himself looking down a steep slope no more than a hundred meters into a fenced yard behind a neat cottage—whitewashed walls there, two chimneys and smoke from both of them . . . chickens scratching in the yard. The roof of another cottage poked up against the valley backdrop beyond the first one, smoke from only one of its chimneys. A cow byre had been built into the hillside off to the left. There was a smell of cow manure from it. The valley beyond contained a scattering of burned-out cottages and wrecked outbuildings, not a sign of smoke there. He returned his attention to the near cottage. A clothesline had been strung from a corner of the building to a post in the stone-enclosed yard. Clothing waved in the wind there—trousers, shirts, long underwear . . . There was the faint sound of a radio, someone talking, Everything looked so bucolic . . . except for the stillness and something lacking behind the sound of the radio and the clucking of the chickens.

Abruptly, John froze at the sound of voices almost directly below him under the rock outcropping where he could not see.

"They'll not see us in here." It was the voice of a young boy.

"How much in the bottle?" Another young voice.

"Almost a cup." That was the first one.

"Do you really think this caused it?" There was the sound of something scraping, a gurgling followed by a fit of coughing. "Gahhh! That's awful!"

"She said it was the drink, Burgh, and now she's gone."

"It's all stupid grownup stuff!"

Something brushed against the rocks below John. He held his breath.

"Grownups never know what they want!"

There came a long silence below John in which he thought he could hear his own heart beating too loudly. He dared not move. He might scrape against the rock, alerting the boys, and they could call a warning to the people in the cottages. He moved only his eyes, trying to glimpse Herity, wondering where the man might be.

"I'm glad you and your da came to live in the other cottage, Burgh." That was the first child.

"It was bad in the city."

"Lots of shooting?"

"Yes."

"Here, too. We hid in a cave."

Again, they were silent.

Why was Herity delaying? John wondered. His chest felt painful when he breathed.

"Do you remember what happened to your ma?"

That was the first child.

"Yes."

"I miss mine. Sometimes I think I'd best go to heaven and be with her. My da's no fun anymore."

"Mine drinks this stuff."

"I know."

"What's the drink do to you?"

"I think it's going to make me sick."

"Naw, you didn't have enough of it."

"Hist!"

There was silence beneath John's hiding place.

He heard it then: Herity singing of his Dark Rosaleen, a fine tenor voice approaching the cottages from below.

"Someone coming!" That was the first child, a hoarse whisper.

"A stranger. I see him."

A man's voice called from the near cottage: "Burgh! Terry!"

"Should we answer?" That was the second child.

"No! Stay here. If it's trouble we'll be safer in here."

"The stranger's alone."

Herity called out loudly from below: "Hello, the cottages! Anybody home?"

A man's voice responded: "Who is it asking?"

"It's Joseph Herity of Dublin town. I've a priest and a young boy with me and a Yank who fancies himself the savior of Ireland. Would you be giving food and shelter to weary travelers?"

The man in the house shouted: "Step up close and let's have a look at you."

Herity strode to within a few meters of the near cottage's rear door. He raised his arms and turned to show he was unarmed. John saw movement of a gun barrel behind an open window of the cottage, but no shot came.

"You've a priest with you, did you say?" the man in the house asked.

"I did that. It's Father Michael Flannery of Maynooth, himself as fine a priest as ever wore the black. And I see a cross over your door that tells me you're not priest-haters in this house."

"We've graves that need blessing," the man in the house said, his voice lower.

"Sure and Father Michael would be happy to do that," Herity said. "Shall I be calling him to join us?"

"Yes . . . and welcome."

Herity turned and cupped his hands to his mouth: "Father Michael! You can all come in now. Pass the word to the Yank."

John started to rise, but at the last words, hesitated. Something wrong down there? Herity would know John could hear him.

A wide smile on his face, Herity strode up to the cottage door as it was opened from inside. He thrust out a hand. "It's Joseph Herity would like the name of you, sir."

"Terrence Gannon," said the man in the house. A thick hand was extended toward Herity.

Herity took the hand and jerked Gannon out of the house, deflecting a shotgun's muzzle while he spilled the man and removed the weapon from him. Gannon lay sprawled in the yard, Herity's pistol at his head.

"All right in there!" Herity called through the open door. "One move out of you and I blow the head off poor Terry Gannon here. My Yank friend is up there on the ridge with a machine gun if you've a mind to make the sacrifice."

A thin, older man with gray hair and a pinched face, wearing green suspenders over underwear tops to hold up his brown woolen trousers, came out of the cottage with his hands over his head.

"Well now," Herity said. "The two of you will be lying here on your faces, if you please?" He picked up the shotgun and threw it over the wall of the yard.

When both men were stretched out on the ground in front of the door, Herity lifted his head toward John's vantage place. "You heard him call, Yank! There's more of 'em here."

"Only two little boys," Gannon said, his voice muffled against the ground.

"They're in the rock right below me," John shouted, "and that's where they'll stay."

"That's grand!" Herity called. Turning with his pistol at the ready, Herity entered the house. He emerged presently and strode around the side toward the other cottage. There was the sound of a door being slammed open and, in a moment, Herity reappeared herding a teenage boy whose round face was a pale mask of terror framed in loose black hair.

"That's the lot of 'em!" Herity called. "This one was in there playing with hisself! For shame!" Herity laughed loudly.

John stood, seeing Father Michael and the boy emerge from the trees along a narrow farm track off to the right. Father Michael waved a cheery hand, then stopped as he saw Herity recovering the shotgun from the ground, the two men still stretched out near the door.

"Now, what've you done, Joseph Herity?" Father Michael demanded.

"I've just made certain sure we were not walking into the hornet's nest, Father." He glanced at the two men on the ground. "You and your friend can be standing now, Mister Gannon. And I pray you'll forgive me cautious ways."

Gannon climbed to his feet and dusted himself off before helping the other man to stand. Gannon was a heavyset man with long black hair. He had a broad chin and wide, thick-lipped mouth. His eyes, when he looked up at John, appeared withdrawn into hopeless defeat.

John peered over the edge of the rock into the declivity beneath him. "You boys down there—come out. No one's going to hurt you."

That was true, John thought. O'Neill-Within had withdrawn to some silent place, content to watch and enjoy the fruit of his revenge.

Two tow-headed boys—one about ten and the other slightly younger—emerged from beneath John and peered up at him.

"Which of you is Burgh?" John asked.

The younger one raised a hand.

"Well, Burgh," John said, "if there's any more in that bottle I'd be grateful if you'd bring it down to the cottage."

> *Human societies have seldom been accustomed to long-range planning, reluctant to think of the generations. The unborn, the unconceived do not vote on current affairs. We conform our researches to immediate conviction, our projects to immediate desires. Where is the voice of the yet-to-be? Without a voice, they will never be.*
>
> **—Fintan Craig Doheny**

IT WAS half past lunch and too long to dinner. Stephen Browder prowled the steel-walled quarters that confined him with Kate, aware of her sitting in the corner there reading, aware that she knew of his restlessness.

There was a visible mounding of her abdomen—evidence of the child forming there. And Peard had yet to produce a priest!

Browder knew what had happened at Maynooth, but surely there must be a trustworthy priest available in all of Ireland. A *real* priest. There were enough fakes around, he knew, that Peard and his people had to be cautious, but somewhere there *must* be a priest to marry the two plague prisoners.

He stopped at the tiny table where he had laid out some of his books and a stack of reports on the progress of plague research. Should he begin clearing away this mess in preparation for the table's use at dinner? No. Too early.

Peard and his associates, thinking it would relieve tensions in the isolation chamber, had sent in a small fax machine. It produced regular copies on what the various research centers were reporting. From these reports, Browder achieved a fragmented picture of work all over the world. He could picture countless white-coated figures carefully distributing loops of culture, the incubation chambers meticulously adjusted to thirty-seven degrees centigrade, the impatient waiting through the mandatory two days of incubation for each test.

And I'm confined here. No facilities. Only these damned books and these stupid, frustrating reports. What can I do to help?

Was Peard deliberately withholding a priest, as Kate accused?

Idly, Browder picked up the top report on his table—a double-folded sheet off the fax printer. It was a copy of recent material from Huddersfield. And what use was it? So some people over there in England thought the zipper theory was faulty!

He let his mind play with the theory, knowing that the Japanese were convinced of it—two strands of the helix chained together by chemical bonds, replicationg each other like the closing of a zipper. What was wrong with that idea? The Russians liked it. Doheny himself said it was "a useful concept." Why would some people at Huddersfield begin to doubt it?

He let the fax sheet drop back to the table.

The plague intervenes in the body's enzyme systems. That was one fact emerging clearly all over the world. Very little ammonia in the bacterial cultures. The amino acids were being used for both structure and energy . . . but the energy was being bound up in structures that inhibited enzyme systems. Without enzymes, death intervened. But which systems? Structural function was being virtually stopped somewhere. Inhibited. Agglutinins were not forming in the presence of antibiotics.

The structure! They had to know the structure!

The plague inhibited the oxygen–carbon-dioxide cycle.

By simple deduction, they knew that the DNA pattern for women had to be somewhere distinctly different from that for men. The deaths and severe illnesses of hermaphroditic individuals only confirmed this fact.

Was the clue in the hormone systems, as the Canadians asserted?

There had to be an interlocking virus-to-bacteria line of transmission in the plague. Had to be. Then what was the shape of the bacteriophage vector? Here was a pathogen that had been shaped to resist antibiotics. And the Americans were convinced that O'Neill had created a form of free DNA that searched for a place in the helix and locked itself there.

"Grows rapidly in culture medium," the Americans said.

If they actually were looking at the plague pathogen, the rapid growth in itself was alarming. Other man-made recombinants did not do this.

The shape . . . the structure . . . what was it?

He thought about the double molecule, one chain twined around the other in helical form, one chain fitted to the other in an elegant fashion, the adenine, guanine, cytosine and thymine each determining a link on the oppposite chain.

It was like an elegant Maypole, Browder thought. A Maypole without the central pole, the ribbons held together by their interlocking placement in the . . .

Browder froze, seeing this shape in his mind.

"Is something wrong, dear?" Kate asked.

He looked at her wild-eyed.

"They're right," he said. "It's not a zipper."

He could visualize the helix itself winding upon itself, ribbon upon ribbon—a chain of chains, locked into shape by the way it twisted.

Browder began scrambling in the papers on his table, looking for a particular page. He found it and spread it flat, studying it.

"The thing is like a spiral staircase with only four structural parts."

Those were the words of someone at Huddersfield named Hupp, a man obviously trying to simplify the picture of the DNA helix, allowing him an entry point in visualizing what O'Neill had done.

"The RNA transmitter and the DNA result may have another relationship. Could this be what the Madman means when he refers to superimposition? One set off against the other could reveal that relationship."

Browder looked up, thinking, aware that Kate was watching him with worry on her face.

Maypole, he thought. *A twisted, convoluted Maypole!*

Explicitly coded instructions with only four letters in the code, but the four together in any combination represented another codon series . . . and then another . . . another . . .

The Maypole! The combinations!

Kate put her book aside and stood up.

"Stephen! What's wrong?"

"I must talk to the people at Huddersfield," he said. "Where is Adrian?"

"He's gone to Dublin again. Don't you remember?"

"Oh . . . yes. Well, could they patch me through with our telephone? Who's outside there?"

"Only Moone, I think. There's influenza going around and they're shorthanded."

"Moone could do it! He's clever with electronics. Have you heard how he bugged the Paras' HQ?"

Browder strode to the phone on its stand beside the little wall desk. "Moone! Hey, out there! I've got a job for you, Moone, and you the only man in all of Ireland who could do it!"

"A PERFESSER of philosophies!" Herity said in an exaggerated country accent.

Terrence Gannon had just reaffirmed over after-dinner tea of wild herbs that he had been a faculty member at Dublin's Trinity College.

They sat on stiff furniture in the formal front parlor of the upper cottage. It was coming on to full dark outside, cloudy and hesitating on the edge of rain, and three candles had been lighted on saucers. They gave a spectral appearance to the traditional parlor with its framed photographs and heavy wooden furniture. A peat fire hissed in the narrow fireplace, giving little heat but emitting puffs of pungent smoke when the wind backed on the chimney.

Herity was showing some signs of unsteadiness from Gannon's poteen, but they had left the jug at the kitchen table when they went outside to collect the household's hidden weapons and had not brought the liquor into the parlor. The guns, a rifle and a pistol, lay unloaded on the floor at Herity's feet.

Gannon's voice had taken on the stillness of a man speaking in a haunted place the minute he entered the parlor, although

236

he moved with old formality to make sure his guests were comfortable.

"We fled here to my family's old place when it was no longer possible to stay in Dublin," he explained. "My brother-in-law there, he came up from Cork, it being no time to keep children in a city."

The brother-in-law, Wick Murphey, had brought his two surviving sons, Terry and Kenneth. Two daughters and a housekeeper had died before they left. His wife, Gannon's older sister, had died at the birth of Terry. Family history had come pouring out of Murphey's narrow mouth in relief at the discovery that Herity's party was merely being cautious and was not "some of those terrible mean ones roaming about."

John had taken a low stool and placed himself with his back against one side of the fireplace. The peat smell was stronger there but the tiles at his back were warm.

Father Michael and the children had taken a lantern and gone down to visit the graves in their little stone enclosure below the cottages.

Murphey, somewhat drunker than Herity, sat on a rocking chair that creaked at his every move. He had the contented look of a man who had eaten and drunk well and whose life was no worse than it had been the day before.

Herity sat alone on the parlor settee, the machine gun suspended at his chest by a thin leather strap around his neck. He appeared amused by this all-male domesticity and had been full of praise for Gannon's cooking.

Gannon appeared to bear no resentment of Herity's rough treatment, but he had that look in his eyes of a man who could never again play in a game he was sure to lose. His shotgun had even been on safety when Herity took it from him.

He is a man waiting only to die, John thought.

Supper had been fresh pork and greens with marrows from the kitchen garden cooked in eggs. Herity and John prowled the area around the cottages and had inspected the byre while Gannon cooked.

"That look in Gannon's eyes, we call that the suicide look," Herity had said.

"How did these cottages escape?" John asked. He looked at the yellow light in the window of Gannon's kitchen. The burning and destruction appeared to have stopped at least a mile away. In the gloom of a cloud-covered evening, there was not a light to be seen in the entire valley.

"In the tumult of these times 'tis a miracle," Herity said, his voice low. "But I do *not* think it was a Church miracle. It may be that nothing was ever broken in Gannon's house. The faeries are liking that. There are strange things in this land, let them say what they will."

"I don't like that brother-in-law," John said. He watched for Herity's reaction to this.

"Murphey, oh! He's a survivor. Many's the time I've seen his kind. They'll sell their souls for ten more minutes of the breathing. They'll sell their friends and steal from the starving. Oh, you're right, John. That Murphey bears watching."

John nodded.

Herity tapped the Israeli machine gun on its strap around his neck. "He'd like me gun, Murphey would." Herity looked back at the byre where he had hidden the shotgun up in the attic straw without its ammunition.

"Did they say who's buried down there?" John asked, looking down at the graves' enclosure.

"That little Burgh's mother, two neighbor women who took shelter with Gannon, and then there was the daughter of one of them. Gannon's been here awhile. You noticed the garden? That's been planted for a spell."

John glanced back at the ridge, thinking of the watercourse beyond it where Herity had found a body. "Do they know who it was died up there?"

"A stranger, so they say. But he was killed with a shotgun."

"And they can't explain that rifle shot we heard," John said.

"Now isn't that a mystery!" Herity said. "Their pig was killed with a rifle and not a rifle to be found."

"You're sure it was a rifle killed the pig?"

"I looked at it careful when I was in the byre. Ahhh, you know, John, we Irish learned many a clever way to hide weapons during the English Ascendancy. I'm looking forward to the discovery of this one."

"Could it be in one of the cottages?"

"I assure you it's not and me being the cleverest searcher me father ever raised. No, John, it's under the byre, wrapped in oilskins and all safe in the grease. You saw how Murphey watched us from the window when we went out here? And there'll be a pistol with it. Murphey's a man who would favor a pistol. Gannon? Now, he was a hunter once or I miss my guess."

Herity rocked back on his heels, sniffing the air—the good smells of cooking coming from the open door of the cottage.

John looked at the machine gun at Herity's chest, remembering the feeling of it, the power there.

"I have a curiosity about how you came by that gun," John said.

"Curiosity! Aw, that's what killed the cat."

"From a dead man, you said."

"This fine weapon was the possession of a political officer with the Paras in Ulster," Herity said. "What a fine gentleman he was with his little mustache and the blue eyes like silk. We knew all about him, we did. He was one of the English public school quares what caused their fine government so much lovely troubles. This one was left behind when the plague came. I found him hiding in an old barn near Rosslea. He made the mistake of leaving his weapon behind when he went out to get water at the pump. And I slipped into the barn before he saw me."

"You told Father Michael he was dead."

"That I did. And him coming at me with a billhook! What could I do?" Herity grinned at him and patted the machine gun. "He had a whole bag of ammo for it, as well."

At supper, John watched Murphey and Gannon, observing the accuracy of Herity's assessment.

How does Herity judge me? John wondered.

It was an unsettling thought. He looked at Herity seated across from him, busily spooning the marrow into his mouth.

He trusted me with the machine gun.

It had been a test, John decided. From Herity's reactions, John guessed the test had been passed. But it did not do to let your guard down with this man.

They ate at the long table in the kitchen—a checkered red cloth on it, heavy dishes, water in tall glasses with ridged sides. The pork had been boiled with some wild leafy green that gave it a tart, rather pleasant flavor and cut the greasiness. Gannon had the kitchen manner of someone who had cooked for pleasure and not lost the touch.

"You'd make somebody a lovely wife," Herity joked.

Gannon did not rise to the barb. Murphey had glowered at Gannon, pinched face drawn into a tight scowl, which changed to a smile when Herity looked at him.

"Have you noticed, John," Herity asked, gesturing with his table knife, "how the passions are burnt out of the Irish? I do believe the Madman himself could walk into our midst without harm, and him covered with the blood of all those millions. We'd only make room for him at table and ask did he want a drink?"

"It's not apathy," Gannon said. It was his first remark since bringing the food to the table.

Father Michael looked down the table at Gannon, caught by the sharpness in the man's voice.

"Mister Gannon is about to favor us with his grand opinion," Herity said.

"You listen when the professor talks!" Murphey bridled.

It was then that Gannon first revealed his Trinity College background.

"I knew I'd seen you someplace," Father Michael said.

"We're beyond apathy," Gannon said.

Herity sat back, smiling. "Then would you tell us, Perfesser, what's beyond apathy?"

"The women are gone forever," Gannon said, his voice heavy. "The women are gone and nothing . . . nothing! will bring them back. The Irish Diaspora is ended. We have all come home to die."

"There must be women somewhere." That was the older boy, Kenneth, who sat beside his father.

"And wise men like Mister O'Donnell here will find a cure for the plague," Murphey said. "Things will come back to an even keel, Professor. Depend on it."

"While we was still in Cork," Kenneth said, "I heard there was women in the old Lucan castle—all safe and protected there by guns."

Through this exchange, Gannon merely stared down at his plate.

"Lots of those stories going around," Herity agreed. "I believe what I see."

"You're a wise man, Mister Herity," Gannon said, looking up at him. "You see the truth and accept it."

"And what might that truth be?" Herity asked.

"That we are moving inexorably toward an edge where we'll drop off into nothing. What's beyond apathy? This thing some of you think of as life—this is already death."

"Welcome to Ireland, Yank!" Herity said. "There's this Ireland the perfesser has just described for us. Then there's the Ireland of the literary fancies. Was it one of those you thought you'd find, Mister O'Donnell?"

John felt turmoil in his breast. He fell back on the pretense that had shielded him thus far: "I came only to help."

"I keep forgetting," Herity said. "Well, this is Ireland, Mister O'Donnell, what you see around us right now. It may be the only Ireland there ever was, and it suffering from a thousand years of agony. I welcome you to it."

Herity bent once more to his eating.

Gannon got up, went to a cupboard and returned with a full jug of clear poteen. The acrid alcohol smell wafted over the table when he pulled the cork. John already had tasted this brew from the bit left in the bottle the boys had brought down from the ridge. He waved a hand to deflect Gannon from pouring him a glass.

"Now, John," Herity said. "Would you be turning down the poteen the way you did the Guinness? You'll not be wanting us to drink alone!"

"There's plenty to drink with you," Father Michael said.

"And you among them?" Herity asked.

Father Michael looked across the table where the silent boy was regarding him with alarm. Stiffly, the priest shook his head. "No . . . I'll not be having any, thank you, Mister Herity."

"Is it a temperance priest you've become?" Herity asked. "Faith! What a terrible thing to happen." He accepted a glass of the poteen from Gannon and sipped at it, smacking his lips in elaborate appreciation. "Ahhh, it's the milk of the little people, it is."

Gannon slid the bottle down the table toward Murphey, who took it greedily, pouring himself a large glass of it.

Seating himself once more at the table, Gannon looked at Father Michael. "Do you have family in these parts, Father?"

Father Michael shook his head from side to side.

Herity took a long swallow of the poteen, put down the glass and wiped his lips on the back of his hand. "Family? Our Father Michael? Don't you know that all priests come from great huge families?"

Father Michael cast a stricken look at Gannon. "I've two brothers living."

"Living!" Herity said. "Now, didn't you hear the perfesser? This is not living." He lifted his glass. "A toast. Give Mister O'Donnell a glass. He'll drink the toast with us."

Gannon splashed some poteen into a glass and slid it across to John.

"To bloody Ireland!" Herity said, raising his glass high.

"May she rise up from the dead and smite down the devil who injured us! And may he suffer a thousand deaths for every one he caused."

Herity downed his glass and thrust it out for a refill.

"I'll drink to that!" Murphey said and emptied his own glass, taking the jug from the table and refilling his own and Herity's.

Kenneth, whose age John estimated at fourteen, glowered at his father. The boy pushed his chair back with a harsh scraping and stood. "I'm going outside."

"You'll sit there in your chair," Herity said. He gestured at the chair with his glass.

Kenneth looked at his father, who shook his head.

Sullen, Kenneth sank back onto his chair but did not pull it up to the table.

"Where was y' going, Kenneth?" Herity asked.

"Outside."

"Out to the byre, it being full of soft straw? Out there to dream of rolling in the straw with a young woman of your choice?"

"Leave him alone," Murphey said, his voice mild.

Herity glanced at him. "That I will, Mister Murphey. But it being almost night outside and us not having found the per-fesser's rifle nor your pistol, I like to see everyone gathered around me." Herity drank deeply of his poteen, looking over the rim of his glass at Murphey and then at Gannon.

Father Michael said: "Joseph! You're a bad guest. These good people mean us no harm."

"Nor do I mean them harm," Herity said. "But sure and it's a caution how much harm you miss when you're careful about weapons."

Again, he drank deeply of his poteen.

Murphey tried to smile at him but managed only a twitch of the lips, his gaze fixed on the machine gun at Herity's chest. Gannon merely looked at his plate.

"Mister Gannon?" Herity asked.

Not looking up, Gannon said: "We will collect the other guns after the news."

"After the news?"

"It's time," Gannon said. "I'll get the wireless. It's just behind me in that cupboard by the sink." He stood.

Herity turned in his chair, watching as Gannon went to the cupboard and returned with a battery-operated radio, which he placed in the middle of the table.

"We've a store of batteries," Murphy said. "Terrence planned well when he came here."

Gannon turned a knob. The click was loud in the suddenly silent kitchen. Everyone was looking at the radio.

It emitted a *blat*, then a soft humming followed by a man's voice: "Good evening. This is Continental BBC with our special edition for Great Britain, Ireland, and Libya." The announcer's voice had the tones of Eton.

"As is our custom, we are beginning with a silent prayer," the announcer said. "We pray for a quick solution to this disaster that the world may find new strength and a lasting peace."

The humming of the radio seemed loud to John, filling the space around them with its reminder of other people and other places, many minds focused on prayer. He tasted a sourness in his throat and glanced around the table. All heads were bowed except his own and Herity's. The latter winked when he met John's gaze.

"Did y' take notice of the order?" Herity asked. Great Britain, Ireland and Libya. They may speak it first, but Britain's not great anymore."

"It is the BBC," Gannon said.

"And from France now," Herity said. "Not an Englishman in the lot, though I grant they all sound like Oxford dons. Americans, Frenchies and Pakistanis, so I'm told."

"What does it matter?" Gannon asked.

"It matters because it's a fact that no man of reason can deny! Those Yanks and Pakkies and Frenchies has been brainwashed. England's first, *then* Ireland and then the heathens."

"May our prayers be answered quickly," the announcer said. "Amen." His voice went on briskly. "And now to the news."

John listened raptly. Istanbul was being put to the Panic Fire. New "hot spots" were identified. Thirty-one cities, villages and towns in Africa were named, Nairobi and Kinshasa among the confirmed. Johannesburg remained a radioactive ruin. In France, the loss of Nîmes was confirmed. A mob in Dijon had lynched two priests suspected of being Irish. In the United States, they were still trying to save "most of New Orleans." The Swiss had retreated behind something they called "the Lausanne Barrier," announcing that the rest of their country remained free of contamination.

"What a grand and glorious thing!" Herity exulted. "The whole world becomes Swiss! An antiseptic world with featherbeds and them soft as a young breast, eh, Kenneth?" Herity stared at the boy, whose face became deep red.

John felt only wonderment at the extent of what had been set in motion. It went far beyond expectations, although he could not say what those expectations had been and, when he thought about this, he felt the stirring of O'Neill-Within. Still, he felt no remorse, only a sense of awe that Nemesis could enter the ranks of national disasters.

The announcer's list of places where the plague had struck seemed interminable. John realized then that this must be the most important part of the news—places to avoid. *How close is it coming?* He was aware of the restrictions on travel—special passes validated by the United Nations Barrier Command being required to cross most borders . . . and those borders no longer merely national ones.

The Soviet Union announced no new hot spots, but satellite observation released by the United States reported evidence of new Panic Fires in the region southeastward from Omsk almost to Semipalatinsk—"many towns and villages visibly burning, but Omsk appears as yet intact."

The announcer interrupted this section with a late bulletin on the destruction of Istanbul, which he said had been "successfully purified in a closed circle of attrition."

"So many new euphemisms for violence," Gannon muttered. He swept his gaze around the table, as though seeking something or someone not there. "Did the Madman think he was bringing peace and an end to violence?"

John looked down at his hands. Peace had never been part of it, he thought. There had only been O'Neill's need to strike back. Who could deny the bereaved man that? John felt somehow like O'Neill's psychiatrist, understanding the man, neither condemning nor absolving.

In the little notebook where Herity jotted the notes for his reports to Dublin, Herity would write that night: "If O'Donnell is the Madman, he seems thunderstruck by the extent of disaster. Did he know how far his plague would range? Did he care? No signs of remorse. No indications of guilty conscience. How could he not react if he is O'Neill?"

Mid-broadcast, there was a telephone interview with Doctor Dudley Wycombe-Finch, director of the Huddersfield Research Establishment in England. Wycombe-Finch could report "no significant advances in the search for a cure," although there were "promising lines of endeavor upon which I hope to report later."

Asked by the announcer to compare this plague with "similar historical disasters," Wycombe-Finch said he thought it served no useful purpose to make such comparisons, adding:

"Such mass destruction of people has not been seen for a very long time. This is destruction on a new scale, whose influence upon our descendants—if we are fortunate enough to have any—cannot be fully measured. In simple financial terms, there is no precedent, nothing with which to make valid comparison. In human terms . . ."

Here, he fell into obvious sobbing.

The BBC let it continue for a time, obviously milking it for effect, then: "Thank you, Doctor. We quite understand your reaction. We pray that your deep and obvious emotion will only strengthen your determination at the Huddersfield Establishment."

"Strengthen your determination!" Herity sneered, his voice thick with poteen. "The English tears could end a drought, I think."

"How can they even think of the financial cost?" Gannon demanded.

It was the first spark of near-anger John had seen in the man.

"The game between God and Mammon having been called on account of half the players leaving," Herity said.

John looked at Father Michael, noting tears running down his cheeks. The branded forehead was a red smear in the lamplight.

The BBC announcer was concluding his broadcast with another prayer: "That we may find it in our hearts to forgive all past injustices, setting the stage for a world in which mankind will find that true brotherhood and mercy which every religion exhorts from us."

This prayer was provided by courtesy of the Buddhist Overseas Mission Church of San Rafael, California.

Gannon turned the knob. The radio went silent with a snap.

"We should save the batteries," he said.

"For what?" his brother-in-law asked, his words slurred from the drink. "To hear the fucking news? Why? There's no future in it!"

*The stranger came and tried to
teach us their ways.
They scorned us for being what we
are.*

— "Galway Bay," an Irish ballad

IN LESS than an hour there was to be a working dinner in the
small private dining room off the White House Mess, and
President Adam Prescott knew he had not the slightest handle
on a new approach to their problems. He knew, though, that
he would have to appear confident and full of purpose. Leaders
were supposed to lead.

He sat alone in the Oval Office, the history of the place
thick around him. Momentous decisions had been made here
and something of that seemed to cling to the walls. The desk
in front of him had been given to Rutherford B. Hayes by
Queen Victoria. The painting over the mantel across from him,
by Dominic Serres, showed the battle between the *Bonhomme
Richard* and the *Serapis*. John F. Kennedy had admired it from
this very position. The pier table behind him had been ordered
and used by James Monroe. The chair beneath Prescott had
been part of the same order.

The chair felt like a prison to Prescott. And his back ached
despite the chair's fine design by Pierre-Antoine Bellange.

A stack of reports lay on the leather-bound green blotter in
front of him, their tabs fanned out for him to read and extract

what suited him. He had read them all and they had succeeded only in amplifying his dismay.

Information, he thought. *What good is it?*

Prescott thought it all carried a grandiose power of inflation, automatic importance. If it was for the President's eyes, it must be not only important but *very* important. Presidents must never be bothered with trivia.

Information. Not facts, not data, not truth. It was accumulated out of human observations. People had seen the thing or heard it or felt it and a digested version found its way to this desk that Rutherford B. Hayes had admired.

Prescott glanced at the tabs protruding from the report folders. *Breakouts.* New plague pockets were being called "Hot Spots" by the media. There no longer was any question of evacuating people. Where could they go? Strangers were dangerous. People who had been away from home were dangerous. Good friends returning from far places no longer were good friends. Railroad lines were being torn up. Airports were strewn with wreckage to block the landing strips. Roads were blockaded and guarded by armed men. Bridges were blown down.

A report in front of Prescott said every curve of spaghetti overpass and rerouting on the A-11 from Paris had been dumped onto the highway by expertly placed charges of explosives and the lack of transport was creating starvation pockets. The Maquis had remembered what they learned for another war but they had forgotten that food traveled the highways, too.

It was no better at many places in the United States. Men dared not go foraging and food was a serious problem in cities and even in the countryside. New York was getting by on what it grew along the fire barrier, thankful for a reduced population and warehouses stocked with canned goods. Washington, D.C., had an estimated two years before the belt tightened. It was getting by on emergency reserves stockpiled against atomic attack plus gardens planted on its lawns and open spaces.

Washington and its ring of bedroom communities remained plague-free largely because General William D. Caffron had acted on his own to spread a flamethrower cordon around the city, backed by tanks and infantry with orders to shoot and burn intruders. He had sent suicide squads then against every contaminated pocket his ruthless methods could ferret out. Quarantine stations had been installed at all entry points, all served by women volunteers flown in from regional prisons and constantly observed by remote TV.

Prescott slid the report tabbed "Tribute" from the pile on his desk and opened it.

Weird, that was the only word for it.

No doubt this was an outgrowth of the Barrier Command's "free boats" policy, sending in supplies to the Irish Finn Sadal and the English Border Beaters. The free boats had seemed a good idea at the time—small, self-propelled, radio-guided craft dispatched into Kinsale, Howth, Liverpool and the other port stations by the Barrier Command, carrying newspapers, food, liquor, small arms, ammunition, clothing. . . . A simple radio signal destroyed the boats when they had completed their mission.

Finn Sadal.

Border Beaters.

Prescott shuddered at some of the things he had heard about Finn Sadal behavior. But . . . tribute?

Dublin was threatening to remove the Finn Sadal from its guardian posts along the beaches and to mount an active attempt to infect other regions *outside* their borders if their demands were not met.

Prescott scanned the page in front of him. Ireland wanted the Viking plunder returned. All of that priceless accumulation from the museums of Denmark, Norway and Sweden was to be brought back and sent in on the free boats.

"All of the wealth stolen from us by the barbarians will be interred at Armagh," the Irish said.

Interred?

They spoke of plans for a great ceremony full of pagan overtones.

Norway and Sweden had signaled immediate agreement but the Danes were showing reluctance.

"If they ask this now, what might they demand next?"

Damned greedy Danes!

Prescott scribbled a note on the margin of the page: "Tell the Danes they've been outvoted. They comply or we'll do it the hard way." He signed it.

The order would have to be expressed more diplomatically, of course, but the Danes were good at sensing the iron intentions behind diplomatic doubletalk. Small nations learned that sensitivity very early.

England's demands were even stranger at first glance. Although coming after the Irish broadcast and couched in more urbane terms, they were backed by a similar threat.

Libraries.

"When this time is only bitter memory, we wish to be the nation of published treasures—books, manuscripts, charts and religious documents, artists' sketches and paintings. We want the originals from wherever they may now be. You will be allowed to make suitable copies."

His security analysts called this "canny." Civilized nations would think long and hard before incinerating such treasures . . . should it come to that. The trouble was, this was no longer a civilized world.

Prescott turned to the tribute section of England and at the top wrote a single word: "Comply." He initialed it.

Libya had not joined this new game, but there remained a question whether Libya had any sort of central government at all. Satellite observation said the country lay in ruins and the population might have been reduced to a scant fraction of its former numbers . . . and what had that been? Three million? All of North Africa was a shambles. Sterilization squads, "the new SS" they were being called, had put the torch to every population center bordering Libya and across the land from the Suez to Cap Blanc, moving in ahead of the cobalt barrier that now ringed the doomed land.

And what about Israel?

Prescott pushed the folder tabbed "Brazil" aside, deciding to take it with him to the dinner session. North Africa remained a primary concern. Survivors were massing in Chad and Sudan, their intentions obvious. There was a new jihad about to begin.

Neutron bombs! Prescott thought. *The only answer.*

The area was outside that proscribed by O'Neill. And what difference did it make now whether O'Neill prohibited atomics in Libya? That nation no longer existed.

The anchorman on the previous night's "final news" had not been privy to Prescott's satellite information, but he had obviously heard.

"We have only a terrible silence from that land."

Prescott put the tribute folder aside and stared sourly at the spread of tabs—words on paper. Could any of it really touch the core of this disaster?

China appeared to have the India problem in hand but there remained that bitter schism between China and the Soviets. That had to be a key subject at this working session. He glanced at his watch: a half hour yet. A war in the Far East could be the final disaster—refugees, loss of central control, no way to impose a tight system of observation and quarantine on the movements of large groups.

The fragility of the human condition felt overwhelming to the President. He experienced a tightness in his chest, his breathing short and quick. The tabs on the reports took on a life of their own, the letters large and burning, each one conjuring new potentials of extinction.

"Denver . . . Ulan Bator . . . Peronne . . . Omsk . . . Tsiempo . . . Luanda . . ."

Slowly, the tight feeling subsided. He considered calling in his doctor but another glance at his watch told him there wasn't time before the dinner session. Blood sugar problem, probably.

His eyes focused on a folder: "Success question."

Yes, that was one of the more serious concerns. What assurance did they have that Ireland or England would share any discovery? What if they found a cure and blackmailed the rest of the world? And if that Madman O'Neill were really hiding in England or Ireland . . .

The question would have to be raised at this dinner. And the agents they had managed to place in both countries were not enough. Some other means of on-sight surveillance had to be found.

The buzzer beneath the desk sounded: two peremptory calls. They would be standing out there, waiting.

Putting both hands on the desk, he heaved himself to his feet. As he stood, a band of agony encircled his chest. The room wavered like a scene underwater, whirling and whirling around him. He heard a distant hissing ring that filled his awareness. There was no sensation of falling, only the blessed rise of unconsciousness that took away the terror, the agony and the view under the side table beside his desk, a brass-footed and fluted wood pillar deeply scratched where one of Andrew Johnson's spurs had gouged the rosewood.

FEELING ODDLY displaced, John went to sleep that night in an upper bedroom of Gannon's cottage, clean sheets and a lumpy mattress. He had one short stub of a candle to light him to the room, which smelled of soap and some flowery perfume. There was a single wooden chair, a low dresser and a standing wardrobe that reminded him of the one in the Hotel Normandy.

O'Neill-Within had become quiescent, moving deeper, more remote and ... John felt it: satisfied.

He had seen what he had seen.

While preparing for bed, John thought about the drinking session at the supper table. It had resumed in the kitchen after the herb tea in the parlor—Herity and Murphey seated across from each other, drinking glass for glass, staring at each other with strange intensity.

Father Michael had sent the silent boy to bed and had taken a position at the end of the long table as far as he could get from the drinkers, but his eyes were on the glasses of poteen, not on the men. Gannon had sent the other children off to their beds and had busied himself cleaning up at the sink.

John, bringing his cup from the parlor, had handed it to

Gannon and seated himself near the priest. Looking at the branded forehead, he thought about the question of the priest's family.

"Where are your brothers, Father Michael?"

Father Michael turned a hunted look toward John.

"You said you have two brothers."

"I've not heard of Matthew since the plague, but he lived in Cloone and that's a ways off. Timothy . . . Little Tim has built a hut beside his wife's grave at Glasnevin and that's where he sleeps now."

Murphey cleared his throat, his attention on the empty jug that Gannon was removing to the sink. "We'll solve it, by God! I know we will!" He cast a bleary glance around the table. "Where's my Kenneth?"

"Gone to bed," Gannon said.

"I'll yet dandle me grandson on me knee," Murphey said.

"Everyone clings to a dream such as that," Gannon said, leaning against the drainboard. "Until something overwhelms them. It's the dream of personal survival—a victory over Time. Some submit to religion or make a daring assault on 'the secrets of the universe,' or live in hope of genie-chance. It's all the same thing."

John could visualize Gannon standing in front of a classroom delivering those portentous phrases, and in that same pedantic tone. Gannon had said that same thing many times and in those same words.

Murphey looked admiringly at his brother-in-law. "The wisdom in that man!"

Herity chuckled. "You know what the Yanks call your perfesser's 'genie-chance'? They call it . . . they call it the blond in the Cadillac automobile!" Laughter set his hand trembling, spilling some of the poteen from his glass.

"It has other variations," Gannon said. "The magic number, the winning ticket on the Sweeps, the treasure that you stumble upon in your own backyard."

"Such things happen," Murphey said.

Gannon smiled sadly. "I think I'll go down to the graves. Where did you leave the lantern, Wick?"

"On the back stoop."

"Would you care to accompany me, Father Michael?" Gannon asked.

"I'll wait for morning and bless them then," Father Michael said.

"He's no mind to visit graves in the night, Father Michael hasn't," Herity said. "The ghosts now! And them ranging across the whole land in these parlous times."

"There's no such thing as ghosts," Father Michael said. "There's spirits . . ."

"And sure and we all know there's witches, don't we, Father Michael?" Herity peered at the priest with owlish glee. "And the faeries, now! What about them?"

"Dream of anything you like," Father Michael said. "I'm going to bed."

"The first room to the right at the top of the stairs, Father," Gannon said. "Sleep with the angels, God willing."

Gannon turned and let himself out the kitchen door.

On impulse, John followed, finding Gannon there lighting a slender lantern with a kitchen match. Clouds covered the sky and there was a feeling of mist in the air.

"Tell me, Mister O'Donnell, are you accompanying me because you fear I have other weapons hidden out here?"

"Not me," John said. "And don't mind Herity. He lives by his suspicions."

"A soldier, that one," Gannon said. "A Provo or I miss my guess. I know the type."

John felt an abrupt emptiness in his stomach. Herity . . . one of the Provisional IRA. There was the sound of truth in Gannon's words. Herity was one of those who made the terrorist bombs and slaughtered innocents such as Kevin and Mairead and Mary O'Neill.

"I will open my heart and pray as never before that you shall reach Killaloe safely and there find a cure for the plague," Gannon said.

In the morning when he awakened in the cold upstairs room, John went to the window and looked down on the stone enclosure around the graves. He could just see it past the corner of the other cottage.

The night before, the stone enclosure had been a ghostly rath in the yellow light of Gannon's lantern, the silence weighted. An owl had floated past and Gannon had not even looked up from his silent praying.

Only Herity had been at the table when they returned to the house. He sat there still nursing a half glass of the poteen. It had occurred to John then that Herity was one of those Irish prodigies who could imbibe ruinous amounts of alcohol with only minimal evidence of it. That was a good thing to know.

John realized he was seeing Herity in a new light since Gannon's assessment—a Provo, no doubt of it.

"It's glad I am you've returned safely from the ghostly night," Herity said. "There's wild animals about, you know."

"A few pigs running loose," Gannon said.

"I was speaking of the two-legged kind," Herity said. He drained his glass. Standing slowly, deliberately, Herity said: "To bed, to bed, the sleep of the dead. I'll give you the dawn for an evening's yawn and one small bullet of lead." He patted the machine gun at his chest.

As he stood at the upstairs window in the dawn, John became aware of someone walking up through the lower meadows and stopping at the graves. John was a moment recognizing Herity, and then by the machine gun, which became visible when he rounded the stone walls and peered up at the cottages. Herity was wearing a green poncho.

Something from his pack, John thought.

He hurried to dress, hearing the sounds of people moving downstairs, smelling lard heating in a pan. The odor of the tea herb mingled with peat smoke.

Breakfast was a silent time—boiled eggs and soda bread. Murphey appeared bright-eyed, showing no effects of the night's drinking. His eyes winked with delight at the food Gannon placed in front of him.

After breakfast, they followed Father Michael down to the graves for the promised blessing. The air was still cold and misty, gray light through heavy cloud cover. John brought up the rear, the silent boy just ahead, clutching the blue anorak close around his neck.

John found himself interested in the silent boy's reaction to this ritual. These were women buried here. Had the boy attended the funeral of his mother? John felt no emotion as he wondered these things. There had been a coldness in him the previous night as he felt O'Neill receding. O'Neill had struck the ones who injured him; he had done it through his successors.

Through me, John thought.

Had O'Neill imagined such a scene as this?

There was no memory of such a thing, no inner movie to recount it. *Cold I was when I did the thing. Cold and murderous—not caring who I hurt.*

Nothing had mattered except the striking out.

Father Michael finished his office of the dead. Looking at Gannon, he said: "I shall pray for you and for your loved ones."

Gannon lifted his right hand limply, dropped it.

He turned and plodded toward the cottages, moving as though each step were painful.

"Go along, Father Michael," Herity said. "Mister Gannon has promised us provisions for the road. We must be getting Mister O'Donnell to Killaloe and it's a long tramp over the hills."

Father Michael put a hand over the silent boy's shoulders and followed Gannon. Murphey and the three other boys fell in behind.

"Mister Murphey, how about a bit of that pig to take on the way with us?" Herity said.

As Murphey stopped and turned, Herity took off at a trot up the hill. The two men headed at an angle for the byre.

John followed the others into the cottage. What was Herity doing? He had not given in to a sudden urge for pork. It was something else.

Gannon was already busy in the kitchen, Father Michael helping him, when John entered. It felt warm in the cottage after the outside chill. There was a pair of tall, military binoculars on the kitchen table.

"I've given my binoculars to Father Michael," Gannon said. "Wick brought his when he came from Cork and there's no need for us to have two pairs."

Father Michael sighed. "It's a sad truth, John, but the farther ahead we see, the safer we are in our going."

Gannon had found a small blue-and-yellow hiker's pack with one patched shoulder strap. He put several chunks of soda bread around the outside and packed fresh eggs in the nest thus formed. "There's a jar of sweet jelly and a bit of lard," he said. "I've left room in the top for the pork when Wick brings it."

"You're a kind man, Mister Gannon," Father Michael said.

Gannon nodded his head at this and turned to look at John. "Mister O'Donnell, I shall pray again that you gain safely to Killaloe and that your hand helps us there. You have come across the water in our time of need. I'll not have you misunderstanding the way of us nor how much we appreciate your coming here."

Father Michael busied himself arranging the food in the pack, not looking at Gannon or John.

"I've talked to Mister Herity this morning," Gannon said, "and I've a better understanding of your party. He's told me the sorry way you were treated by the Beach Boys. I think there's a dispute among the soldiery about the way you were greeted, Ireland needing wisdom such as yours these days. I'm thinking Herity has come along to see you safely to Killaloe. He's a rough man but there's times such men are needed."

John rubbed at the stubble on his chin, wondering how he should respond to this pedantic outburst.

Herity and Murphey entered then, Herity with his pack already slung over his left shoulder, the machine gun riding in the cradle of his right arm.

"The pig's already turning bad," Murphey said.

"It needs ice this time of year," Herity said.

John looked at the two men, sensing a subtle change in their behavior toward each other. There was some kind of an understanding between them.

"It's a long tramp," Herity said. "Best be on our way." He glanced at Father Michael, who was stuffing the blue-and-yellow pack into his larger pack, preparing to shoulder it. "Call the boy, Father, and we'll be on our way."

"He's welcome to stay here," Gannon said. "If you . . ."

Father Michael shook his head. "No, he'd best come along with us."

"The Father has formed a special attachment for the lad," Herity said. He made it sound insinuatingly evil, grinning as he spoke.

Scowling, Father Michael took up his pack and brushed past Herity out the door. They heard him calling the boy. John followed, feeling oddly put out by Herity's manner.

What do I care how he treats the priest? John wondered.

He puzzled over this as they said their goodbyes and walked up the hill toward the farm track that led to the valley road.

When they rounded a screen of trees and no longer could see the cottages, Herity called a halt. The sky was already brighter, even a few patches of blue overhead. John looked back the way they had come, then at Herity rummaging in his green pack. Herity pulled out a small, short-barreled revolver and a box of ammunition. The gun glistened with oil.

"This is a gift from Mr. Murphey," Herity said. "It's only a Smith & Wesson five-shooter, but it'll fit in your pocket, John. Best go armed these days."

John accepted the revolver, feeling the cold oiliness of it.

"Into your hip pocket and pull the sweater over it," Herity said. "There, that's the way."

"Murphey gave this to you?" John asked.

Herity handed him the box of ammunition. "Yes. Stuff this in your side pocket. There was two of 'em Gannon didn't know about. T'other's a big Colt monster y' wouldn't want to be carrying, it being heavy as a tub of lead and not as useful." Herity returned his pack to his shoulder and started to turn but stopped as a shot sounded behind them.

Father Michael whirled and would have run back to the cottages had Herity not stopped him with a firm grip on the arm. The priest tried to pry Herity's fingers away. "They may need our help, Joseph!"

"You haven't thought it through, Father. What are the possibilities?"

"What do you . . ."

"Another pig?" Herity asked. "I've returned all their weapons and the ammunition. If it's a pig, fine! They'll be eating a grand meal tonight and Mister Gannon cooking it. If it's intruders, our friends are well armed. And that was a pistol shot, I remind you."

Father Michael looked around him warily, listening. The woods around them were silent, not even a bird call, and the valley below, still shrouded in morning mist, was immersed in primal silence.

"If it was Gannon ending his miseries, you'd not be praying over him, anyway," Herity said.

"You're a cruel man, Joseph."

"That's been observed by better men than you." Herity turned away and headed up the track toward the road. "Come along now."

The silent boy edged close to Father Michael, tugged his arm and looked after Herity.

Fascinated, John watched the indecision in Father Michael become resignation. The priest allowed the boy to lead him up the track in Herity's wake.

John fell in step behind them, feeling the pistol heavy in his rear pocket. Why had Herity given him this weapon? Was it trust? Had Gannon assessed it correctly? Was Herity assigned to escort John to the lab at Killaloe? Then why hadn't he said so? And why were the priest and the boy tagging along?

Herity stopped at the road, waiting for them. He looked to the left where the road edged the valley floor, curving toward another tree-bordered notch at the upper end.

John stopped beside Herity and found himself caught by the

diffused vista, the design of this landscape to control his eyes'
movements—patchwork earth and groves in the middle distance, a willow-bordered stream there, then more distant fields
and up to the thin gray sliver of road into the other notch. The
clouds in the eastern sky presented a rose-tinted border to the
scene.

Herity said: "This land holds our history in its palm." He
pointed. "That notch over there—O'Sullivan Beare and his
pitiful leavings of an army went through there."

Something in Herity's tone held John, forcing him to see
this land as Herity did—a place where armies marched back
and forth and where, not long ago, men who were hunted by
the Black-and-Tans had fled through darkness to be hidden in
the cottages of the poor. Grampa Jack McCarthy had told the
story many a time, always ending: "'Tis the fate of the Irish
always to be driven from pillar to post."

Father Michael stepped around Herity and set off briskly
on the valley road. The boy trotted occasionally, sometimes
jumping to catch a leaf from an overhanging bough.

Herity waited until they were almost a hundred meters ahead
before nodding to John and setting off after them.

"Safer to keep some distance between us," he said. He
gestured with the machine gun at the two ahead. "Look at that
mad priest, would you now? He wants to make another sheguts
out of that lad. And the lad, he wants only his dead mother
back to him like Lazarus out of the grave."

Out of the corners of his eyes, Herity watched John, looking
for some effect from these words. There was nothing. Well,
the gloves would have to come off sometime soon. He thought
of the message he had left with Wick Murphey to pass along
to the Finn Sadal horse-post for transmittal to Dublin.

*"I've convinced him he's fully trusted. We'll be taking him
now past McCrae's place and see how that works on him. Will
he try to spread the plague? Send word to Liam and warn him
to be on watch when he passes us along."*

Let Kevin O'Donnell think of the cleverness in this plan!

"Why do you keep calling Father Michael mad?" John asked,
thinking of the cowled figure at the clothing hut. Were all
priests mad now?

"Because he's mad as the hatter!" Herity said. "I've a friend,
Liam Cullen, calls them all 'Lucans of the Liturgy,' him being
a man who likes to turn a curious phrase."

"Lucans of the Liturgy?" John asked. "What's that supposed

to . . ." He broke off, stumbling on a rock, then caught his balance.

"You've not heard of Lucan the Monster? Him as ordered the Charge of the Light Brigade? Not to be confused with Patrick Sarsfield, the Earl of Lucan, who defended Limerick after the Boyne. When he took his Irish Brigade to King Louis in France, they routed the Coldstream Guards at the battle of Fountenoy."

"The Wild Geese," John said.

"Ahhh, y' know of the Brigade, then. But it's the other Lucan Liam means, him as drove forty thousand Irish farmers from their land—most of 'em to their deaths. And what does English history memorialize? Six hundred English bastards and them stupid enough to follow the orders of such a monstrous man!"

"What does that have to do with priests?"

"Don't you hear 'em quoting scripture to our despair and destruction? Obedience! Into the valley of death, he says. In we go! 'Leave your land,' the hell beast says. Off we go! They move us all to suicide and they won't even pray over us. Like docile lambs, we say, 'Give us a place to dig our graves.' Liam's right: Lucans of the Liturgy."

John looked away to the low scrub on his left, the rock wall covered with lichen patches here. How carefully Herity watched him. What was Herity seeking?

"Only the ones with a will to fight back are deserving of our tears," Herity said. "Have you the will to fight back, John?"

John tried to swallow past a lump in his throat, then: "You see me here. I didn't have to come."

But I did have to come, he thought.

Herity appeared curiously moved by John's response. He patted John on the shoulder. "That you are. You're here with the rest of us."

And why are you here?

Herity shook his head, knowing he had to assume this was O'Neill, the Madman himself. And if he was O'Neill . . . Herity forced himself to face it.

The bomb we made killed his wife and wains. He fought back, damn his soul to hell!

Presently, Herity began humming a tune, then he sang:

> "O my Dark Rosaleen!
> Do not sigh, do not weep!

> *The priests are on the ocean green,*
> *They march along the deep."*

He broke off and cast a probing stare at John beside him, that bald head outlined against the valley mist, the lean, bearded face without a change of expression in it.

With a sigh, Herity marched in silence for a time, then he picked up his pace, forcing John to quick step for a moment to keep up.

"There's priests marching everywhere," Herity said, nodding at the black-suited figure ahead of them. "And more than wine from a Royal Pope in their bags. Though I wish I had some Spanish ale this moment to give me hope and glad me heart."

> *By now you know what earned my anger. Don't question it! Remind yourselves often of the impenetrable ignorance of the Irish and the English, their mass perpetuation of mutual misery. Remember the bloody hand of Libya with its training camps for terrorists and the free weapons. How could I suffer such fools to live?*
>
> —John Roe O'Neill, Letter Two

MOST OF the Huddersfield's top staff and researchers were being gathered in the Administration Building's Executive Lounge for the morning meeting with Rupert Stonar. People trooped along the walks, their umbrellas pointed dangerously ahead, keeping to the covered passages where they could to avoid the light rain that had set in about daylight.

Stonar had arrived forty minutes early, requiring Wycombe-Finch to phone ahead to his assistants and to Beckett, then to dash back on foot from his working office. He arrived out of breath, his tweed jacket dark from the rain that had swept past his umbrella. Luckily, his assistants had laid on coffee and sweet rolls and there was a brief interlude with Stonar, both of them recalling old times in public school: Wye and Stoney.

Wycombe-Finch thought Stonar had not changed for the better since their upperclassman days when they were preparing to be the privileged carriers of civilization's burdens. Stonar had been a chunky ruddy-complexioned youth with unruly hair that tended toward dark-sandy. He'd had a rather blocky face with pale blue and coldly observant eyes. Stonar remained ruddy-faced, the sandy hair still unruly, although this now had

261

more the look of a calculated effect. The eyes were even more chilly. Stonar's childhood nickname fitted him even better now: the blockiness had hardened.

"We're gathering people in the lounge, Stoney," Wycombe-Finch said. "Should be there by now. I've spoken briefly to Bill Beckett and he should be along, too."

"The American chap?" Stonar's voice was a deep baritone, which showed the marks of special training.

"Quite a remarkable fellow really," Wycombe-Finch said. "Good at making our work understandable to others."

"Does he have anything definite to report?"

There it is! Wycombe-Finch thought.

He sensed the sudden stillness of his assistants at the table with the coffee and sweet rolls. He said: "I'll leave that to him."

"Expected to find you here in your office when I arrived," Stonar said.

"I've a working office in one of the lab buildings," Wycombe-Finch said. "Morning's a good time to get in my own contributions."

"And what might your contribution be?" Stonar asked.

"I'm afraid this morning was rather taken up by a telephone conference with my opposite number in Ireland."

"Doheny? Don't trust the bastard!"

"Well, he did provide some interesting information this morning." Wycombe-Finch proceeded to recount Doheny's revelation about the suspected John Roe O'Neill.

"You give credence to that story?" Stonar demanded.

"The scientist always waits for the evidence," Wycombe-Finch said. "Speaking of which, I think my people are all gathered now. Shall we go into the lounge?"

Wycombe-Finch nodded to an assistant, who led the way, opening the double doors ahead of the executives.

The lounge was a softly unobtrusive space modeled after the smoking room of a London club, but larger. Dark wainscoting with a maroon print on black cloth above it circled the room, broken only by four windows, now closed by matching draperies, and a large marble fireplace in which a real fire flickered. There were deep leather chairs of glowing red-brown, a long refectory table of glossy mahogany to one side of the fireplace, and stand ashtrays on heavy brass pedestals. Light came from four chandeliers, which staff joked had been modeled after the spaceship in *Close Encounters,* and from a perimeter of wall-sconce spotlights focused on the table where Beckett had seated himself behind three neatly stacked report folders. Most of the other staff already was seated in chairs away from the table, obviously choosing not to be at the center of action.

Word does get around, Wycombe-Finch thought.

Beckett lifted himself easily from the chair as the party from the Executive Suite entered. There was some soft bustling around the room. A few throats were cleared.

Beckett looked like a pink-faced schoolboy this morning, Wycombe-Finch thought. Very deceptive appearance. There had been little time to brief him, but Wycombe-Finch thought Beckett understood the delicacy of the situation.

Wycombe-Finch performed the introduction. Stonar and Beckett shook hands briefly across the table. Chairs for Stonar and the director were brought unobtrusively by assistants, who retired into the farther reaches of the room.

Thirty-one others had been assembled here, Wycombe-Finch noted, counting silently. He made no move toward introductions. Later, perhaps. The curious were not gathering about this morning to meet with the powerful. He busied himself lighting the long-stemmed pipe while he took the chair beside Stonar. An ashtray appeared as though by magic, thrust forward by a hand from behind. Wycombe-Finch waved the assistant back, leaned his gold pipe lighter against the ashtray with grave deliberation, then:

"Well, Stoney, I don't know how much you understand about our—"

"Wye, let's not try the scientific-mystery approach, eh?" Stonar said.

Beckett leaned forward, his voice deceptively calm. "The director's words were polite and to the point."

Ahhhh, Wycombe-Finch thought. *Beckett has an object for his anger. This should be interesting, to say the least.*

"Really?" Stonar's voice dripped ice chips.

"I would not have said it were it not real," Beckett said. "Without knowing how much you understand about our work, we cannot begin to brief you. I will say at the outset that there's nothing wrong with being ignorant about our work. Guilt should attach only to anyone who remains ignorant in the presence of an opportunity to learn."

Well said, old boy! Wycombe-Finch thought

Stonar leaned back in his chair, his face blank, only a slight throbbing at the neck to reveal his emotion. "I've always heard Yankees were a cheeky and impetuous lot," he said. "Do proceed to remove my ignorance."

Beckett straightened. The pontifical approach was what this bastard needed, he thought. Get him off balance and keep him there. Wycombe-Finch had said the man was weak in science, only fair in math. Stonar would have feelings of inadequacy. Beckett took his time opening the folders and spreading papers before him.

"We're currently focusing on the enzyme-inhibiting characteristics of the disease," Beckett said. "You've no doubt heard about the Canadian team's work. We're particularly interested because the absence of an enzyme can lead to the absence of a particular amino acid, and a change in one amino acid out of some three hundred of them can result in a fatal condition. We're certain O'Neill blocked certain amino acids by tying up the structures that make them."

"I've read the Canadian report," Stonar said.

But did you understand it? Beckett wondered. He said: "Good. Then you'll follow that we believe this plague causes a kind of premature aging, very swift, no time for many of the usual side manifestations. I call your attention to the white blotches on the extremities. Very suggestive."

"Genes to control aging?" Stonar asked, a sudden intense curiosity in his voice.

"Action of a gene is concerned with formation of a particular enzyme, which is a protein," Beckett said. "Genes control the amino acid makeup of specific proteins. Rendering certain DNA combinations incapable of producing particular amino acids can be a deadly disease."

"I hear mention of RNA as well," Stonar said.

"RNA and DNA relate to each other like a template and the finished product," Beckett said. "Like a mold and the casting that comes from it. The infected host manufactures protein dictated by the RNA. When bacterial viruses infect bacteria, RNA is formed that resembles the virus DNA and not that of the host. The sequence of the nucleotides in the new RNA molecule is complementary to that of the RNA of the virus."

"He transmitted this thing with a virus?" Stonar asked.

"He shaped new bacteria with a new virus. Very fine determinations in very fine structures. It was a superb accomplishment."

"I don't enjoy hearing praise for the man," Stonar said, his voice flat.

Beckett shrugged. If the man didn't understand, he didn't understand. Beckett said: "O'Neill created subcellular organisms, plasmids, for their bonding characteristics, attaching them at key places in the recombinant process. Had it not taken such a twisted turn, his work would have qualified him for a Nobel. Pure genius but driven by the dark side of human motivations."

Stonar let this pass. He said, "You mention nucleotides."

"Nucleic acids are the molecules upon which the coding is written. They direct the manufacture of proteins and hold the keys to heredity. Like proteins, nucleic acids are heavy polymers."

"I hear it rumored that you're finding fault with something called 'the zipper theory,'" Stonar said.

Wycombe-Finch shot a hard glance at Stonar. So the man did have his spies in the Huddersfield Establishment! Or on the telephone.

"DNA is a double molecule with one chain twined around the other in helical form," Beckett said. "It is a flexed compound that turns and twists upon itself in a peculiar fashion. We think these flexings are extremely significant."

"How is that?"

"Things that lock together do so according to their intrinsic shape. The twistings are a clue to that shape."

"Clever," Stonar said.

"We think the thing may lock together more like your winter waterproof," Beckett said. "First one set of connections and then a second, overlapping set."

"What kills this plague?" Stonar asked. "Besides fire, that is."

"Intense concentrations of ozone seem to inhibit it. But the growth is explosive in both men and women. To say it is biologically active is to understate the case."

Stonar pulled at his lower lip. "What necessary thing does it lock up?"

"We think it blocks vasopressin, among other things."

"Essential to life, eh?"

Beckett nodded.

"Is it true the plague kills hermaphrodites?" Stonar said "hermaphrodite" as though it were a particularly foul thing.

"True hermaphrodites, yes," Beckett said. "That's very suggestive, isn't it?"

"I was thinking that the resultant society could be very male and very female, the hermaphrodites mostly weeded out." He cleared his throat. "This is all very interesting, but I hear nothing new really, nothing indicating a dramatic insight."

"We're still gathering data," Beckett said. "For instance, we're running a parallel line of inquiry into some plague symptoms that are similar to those in neutropenia."

"Neutro . . . what?" Stonar asked.

Wycombe-Finch stared at Beckett. This was new!

"Neutropenia," Beckett said, noting how Stonar's eyelids lowered in a speculative squint. "Neutrophils are granular leukocytes having a nucleus of three to five lobes connected by chromatin and a cytoplasm containing very fine granules. They're part of the body's first line of defense against bacterial invasion. It's a disease that can have a genetic origin."

He's being too technical for Stoney, Wycombe-Finch thought, but the revelation was fascinating. He said: "You got that from the Foss autopsy?"

Beckett was silent for a moment, looking down at the papers in front of him but not seeing them, then: "Ariane provided us with quite a number of clues before she died."

"This was Doctor Ariane Foss, who worked with Bill and the others before the plague killed her," Wycombe-Finch explained to Stonar.

Stonar nodded, noting the pain in Beckett's expression.

"Before she died, she gave us her own internal view of her symptoms," Beckett said. "This plague kills with central nervous system breakdown and enzyme blockage. There is general degradation of functions and a final lapse into unconsciousness with death following quickly."

"I've seen plague victims die," Stonar said. His tone was brittle.

"The disease process does not extend long enough," Beckett said, "for many symptoms to manifest. We're forced to interpret from only the beginning traumata, but Ariane gave us a finely tuned assessment of those."

Stonar spoke nervously. "Very interesting."

Wycombe-Finch took a deep puff on his pipe and pointed the stem at Stonar. "Let's not forget, Stoney, that the plague was tailored for a specific effect—to kill only women and to kill them quickly despite medical efforts to the contrary."

Stonar's tone was dry: "I'm aware of the selectivity."

"Remarkable achievement," Wycombe-Finch said.

"If we can leave this meeting of the Madman Admiration Society for a moment," Stonar said, "I must say my ignorance has not been removed."

"We're dealing with a remarkable code," Beckett said. "Equivalent to a highly complex combination on an extremely sophisticated safe. O'Neill solved it, so we know it can be done."

"It seems you've taken all this time to tell me you're faced with an extremely difficult project," Stonar said. "Nobody questions that. What we're asking is: How close are you to a solution?"

"Perhaps closer than many suspect," Beckett said.

Wycombe-Finch sat up sharply.

Beckett glanced out into the lounge where Hupp sat placidly behind his thick glasses, his chair slightly ahead of those occupied by Danzas and Lepikov. All three were watching Beckett carefully and, with this last utterance, attention of the entire staff was centered on Beckett.

That wild call from Browder to Hupp, Beckett thought. He could imagine the young man in the isolation chamber with his pregnant lady—then the idea! How had he come by it? Both accurate and inaccurate—but the insight it ignited!

Wycombe-Finch favored Beckett with a reserved stare.

Stonar leaned forward: "Closer than we suspect?"

"O'Neill demonstrated several things," Beckett said. "The cell is not inviolate. He has shown that the cell's chemical fragments can be refitted, reshaped to carry out extraordinary processes. The living organization in the cell, that system which mediates the cell's operations, has been solved! We no longer can doubt whether this is achievable. The important thing, though, is that we also know now that genetically directed alterations in cell function need not stop with maturity. The neutropenia clue assures us that we can contract a new genetic disease as adults."

Stonar blinked.

Wycombe-Finch continued to stare silently at Beckett. Was this what the Americans called a "snow job"?

"If some of the thousands upon thousands of chemical processes taking place continuously in each of our living cells are blocked, slowed or otherwise removed, development of the organism is specifically altered," Beckett said. "O'Neill has demonstrated that this is just as true after the development of complex, higher organisms as it is of the simpler forms. Massive alterations can be achieved. And he has shown that the system is subject to fine tuning."

"My word!" someone out in the lounge said.

Wycombe-Finch took his pipe out of his mouth, suddenly aware of what Beckett was implying. It was a two-way process! It was obvious, once stated. Did Stonar have the slightest idea of what he had just heard?

"I was briefed by a Home Office M. D.," Stonar said. He sounded irritated and the chill had returned to his eyes. "It's like a paper chase where not one scrap may be overlooked."

Stonar did not understand the implications, Wycombe-Finch realized. It had gone over his head.

"You've implied that you're close to the end of the chase," Stonar said. "Is that what I tell the prime minister? He will ask me: 'How close are we?'"

"We cannot tell yet," Beckett said. "But we see the trail more clearly now. What O'Neill developed was a viral strain that carried a donor DNA message to the living human cell via an infected bacterial agent."

"This spirochete thing the Canadians say they've detected," Stonar said. "Is that the disease?"

"My guess is that it's not. We think they're seeing a remnant, a breakdown product of O'Neill's plague. A mutation, perhaps."

"Locked in the cell," Stonar muttered.

"Like the overlappings of a Maypole," Beckett said.

"Maypole!" Stonar said. He nodded, obviously liking the concept. It would make an impression at the Home Office.

"There's obviously a genetic series that dictates that a fetus will be female," Beckett said. "The plague locks into that sex-differentiated pattern and stays there long enough to create swift and general chaos."

"Takes the old ball and carries it off the field," Stonar said.

Forgot he was a soccer fan, Wycombe-Finch thought.

"Well put," he said.

Beckett's tone was puzzled. "The block, once formed, is remarkably strong. It must be associated with more powerful chemical bonds. O'Neill identified repetitive satellite-DNA processes in sufficient detail he could pick and choose among them."

"You really think you're close on his heels?" Stonar asked.

"I say what I believe," Beckett said and he saw Hupp across the room nodding agreement.

Wycombe-Finch, his teeth firmly clamped on the stem of the pipe, which had gone out, managed to look sage and wished he felt as confident as Beckett sounded.

Stonar looked at the director, and there was suspicion in the look. "What do you say to all this, Wye?"

Wycombe-Finch removed the pipe from his mouth. He put it into the ashtray, bowl down, looking at it as he spoke. "We are convinced that O'Neill mated the two halves of specific portions within the DNA/RNA helix of the human genetic system. He did this in a binding way." Here, Wycombe-Finch nodded at Beckett. "The two halves dovetail into an extremely powerful bond. Bill's team believes there may be independently replicating systems within that helical chain to form this bond."

"And what do you believe?" Stonar asked.

Wycombe-Finch looked at Stonar. "They may have produced the most promising insight yet achieved."

"May have," Stonar said. "You're not convinced."

"I'm a scientist!" Wycombe-Finch protested. "I must see the proof."

"Then why do you think their approach is promising?"

"It indicts the viral DNA, for one thing. We all know that has to be part of it, but it also sketches clear steps into the cellular system."

"I fail to see those steps," Stonar said.

"The paper in this paper chase is the blocked enzymes," Beckett said.

Stonar flicked a glance at him, then back to Wycombe-Finch. He had noted this comment, though, and it was obvious this would be replayed for the prime minister.

"Viral DNA can be associated with bacterial DNA in a quite straightforward process," Wycombe-Finch said. "All progeny of the bacteria will contain the viral DNA and any messages written into that viral DNA."

"Message," Stonar said, his voice blank.

"It encounters that portion of the human DNA chain which dictates that the host be female," Wycombe-Finch said. "The viral DNA, we believe, then locks into that cellular substratum and dissociates from its bacterial carrier."

"Message delivered," Beckett said.

"But do you know how it does this?" Stonar asked.

"We can follow its trail now," Beckett said. "We will begin

to see the shape of it up ahead very soon."

"How soon, dammit?" Stonar glared at Beckett.

Beckett only shrugged. "We're working on it as fast as we're able."

"We're fairly certain of the conditions under which it reproduces," Wycombe-Finch said. "Not to forget that it proliferates in the presence of antibiotics."

"We're getting impatient," Stonar said.

"Right now, your impatience is keeping us from our work," Beckett said.

Stonar pushed his chair back and lifted himself to his feet. "Would someone tell my driver I'm ready to go?"

Wycombe-Finch lifted a hand and saw an assistant get up hastily and leave the room.

Stonar turned and focused on Wycombe-Finch. "You turn my blood to water, Wye. If I had my way we'd come in here and absolutely burn out all of you. We'd sterilize the ground you walk on and then we'd try to start over."

"Making the same mistakes all over again," Beckett said, coming around the end of the table.

Stonar turned his coldly observant stare on Beckett. "Perhaps not. We might make scientific research a lethal offense." Turning away, he strode out of the room, not even glancing at the assistant who swung the door wide for him.

Beckett stood beside Wycombe-Finch, watching until the door closed behind Stonar.

"What do you suppose he'll tell the prime minister?" Wycombe-Finch asked.

"He'll say we have a new theory that may pan out, but the government must wait and see."

"You really think that?" The director stared hard at Beckett, then bent to the table and retrieved the pipe.

"Very scientific," Beckett said. "Wait to see the proof."

Wycombe-Finch looked at his pipe while he spoke: "Tell me, Bill, was that what you chaps call a snow job?"

"Not a bit of it."

The director looked up and met Beckett's gaze. "Then I do wish you'd briefed me before dumping it out like that. Especially the two-way implications."

"Surely you don't question . . ."

"Of course not! I'm just not sure I would've shared it with Stoney."

"It went right over his head."

"Yes, I'm sure you're right about that." Wycombe-Finch glanced at the staff members, who were slowly filing out of the room, none of them meeting the director's gaze. "But he'll have his spies here and one of them's sure to explain it."

"Then he'll know about the carrot as well as the stick."

"Politicians don't like sticks in other people's hands. Carrots either, for that matter."

"We're quite excited by the implications," Beckett said.

Wycombe-Finch glanced at Hupp, still seated in the big chair. The room was almost empty.

"I do believe," the director said, "that Doctor Hupp is not as excited as you are, Bill. Doctor Hupp appears to be asleep."

"Well, what the hell!" Beckett said. "We did work all night."

Out of Ireland have we come,
Great hatred, little room,
Maimed us at the start.
I carry from my mother's womb
A fanatic heart.

—**William Butler Yeats**

As THEY came down onto the central floor of the valley just before noon, John found it not as flat as it had appeared from the heights. Low hillocks lifted and fell beneath the road, some with cottages nestled into them. A few of the cottages had not been burned, but most of the windows were gone. Doors stood open. Not a sign of human life still here. The occasional barking of a dog fox could be heard back in the trees and, once, as they rounded a granite-girt corner, there was the frightened cackling of a hen, a glimpse of brown feathers darting into the roadside bushes. Jackdaws nested in many of the chimneys. One giant maple standing alone in a field was decorated with a flock of collared doves, soft fawn-gray speckled throughout the green. Vernal grass had taken over in many of the fields.

Herity, walking beside John, sniffed the air and said: "There's a certain smell to human occupation that's gone from this valley."

John stared at the backs of the boy and the priest walking about twenty paces ahead. They were separated by the width of the road, the priest on the left, his head bowed, the knapsack riding high on his shoulders. The boy sometimes darted to the middle of the road, glancing all around and occasionally bending his head to listen. The sound of their feet on the blacktop echoed between the road's rock-fenced boundaries. He began to look more closely at the empty valley around them, the blacktop winding through it, over the hillocks and around them. There was a penetrating loneliness to this region, more empty by far than any wilderness. He sensed that it came from the fact people had lived here. The people had been and now they were gone. It was that kind of loneliness.

"What happened to this valley?" John asked.

"Who knows? A simple rumor can empty a village. Maybe there was a mob. Maybe they burned it and left. You hear stories now: a cure and women living in the next valley. Maybe men came here and found the rumor false."

"Are we taking the shortest way to the Lab?"

"The safest."

Ahhh! John thought. *The safest! Then Herity has knowledge of such things. Where does he come by it?*

The road wound its way around another hillock and the way was opened to a view of the trees along the river about a half mile ahead. Patchy cloud cover had let the sun shine through. A meadow glistened in the golden light on their left. Beyond it, elder trees stood thick along the riverbank, a tall hedge of them feeding on the flow of water. The elders swayed and beckoned in a soft breeze.

"Parnell came to hunt in this valley," Herity said. "He had English manners, he did. His middle name, y' know, was Stuart with the Frenchies' spelling. Charles Stuart Parnell . . . the same as Jim Dung. James Dung Stuart!"

John marveled at the way history was preserved here. It was not just the broad sweep of historical events and the dates of battles, but the intimate details. Parnell had hunted in this valley! And when James Stuart abandoned the Irish to their foes, the Irish had renamed him "Jim Dung." That was four hundred years ago and there was still venom in Herity's voice when he uttered the name. And what of Parnell, whose dream of reform had been killed by English exposure that a mistress had borne his children? Parnell was reduced to "English ways!"

"Joyce wrote a poem about those hills ahead of us," Herity said.

John turned a sly look on Herity. "He wrote about Parnell, too."

"Ahhh, you're a literary man!" Herity said. "You'd a grandfather who dreamed Irish dreams, or I miss my guess."

John felt a hollowness in his breast. He heard Mary's voice saying: "I still miss Grampa Jack." There was confusion in his thoughts. *Whatever I say, Herity hears and interprets.*

"Wherever the Irish go, they take Ireland with 'em," Herity said.

They walked in silence for a time. The river was audible now and they could see a stone bridge through a gap in the elders. Framed by the gap, a mansard roof and bits of stone walls could be glimpsed far up ahead at the top of the valley.

Herity, seeing the green-framed mansion, thought: *There's Brann McCrae's little dovecote! We'll soon see what this John O'Donnell's made of!*

The priest and the boy stopped at the near abutment of the bridge and turned to watch their companions approach.

John walked out onto the bridge and looked downstream where water rippled over green rocks. The meadow visible through the trees sloped down to a narrow stretch of boggy ground beside the river. Valerian and yellow flags could be glimpsed in the marsh. Bees were working the meadow, but the river sounds masked their humming. The sun, the warmth, the river—a sense of relaxation settled over John. He accepted a slab of soda bread from the boy, a thin slice of white cheese on it. The boy put his elbows on the bridge's stone rail and watched the water while he ate. John could smell the perspiration of the boy, a sweet odor. The young cheeks moved evenly with the chewing.

What a strange child, John thought. A personality attempting to be transparent. Not here! But he *was* here. He ate the food Father Michael gave him. He called attention to things by looking sharply at them. He nestled against the priest at times, a hurt animal seeking such comfort as he could find. And the attention he called to himself by his silence—discordant! A protest louder than any scream.

"I do not speak!"

It was a thing repeated every time John looked at him. As a protest, it was remarkably irritating—especially to Herity.

John looked at Herity and Father Michael standing there beside their packs at the end of the bridge, eating silently, not looking at each other. Herity occasionally glanced at John and the boy. Herity, slowly eating his soda bread and cheese, keeping an eye on the road they had traversed, studying the land around them, looking for anything that moved, anything with a threat in it. Wary, that was the word for Herity. He was as isolated as the silent boy, but the wariness was different. There! He had his pocketknife out again! Always manicuring his fingernails with that knife—meticulous and purposeful, an action like a habit. Cleanliness by rote. He had handsome fingers, too—long and slender but with power in them. John had seen them flex like claws, the tendons standing out along the knuckles.

The priest beside him: tall and haggard. Very tall. A Hamlet in a dark suit, the black hat pulled low over his eyes. The features put John in mind of "horse face"—that protruding jaw, the forward thrust at the neck, the strong nose and the dark eyes beneath those heavy brows, those thick and powerful teeth slightly protruding. Not a handsome man but it was a face not easily forgotten.

The boy beside John coughed and spat into the river. John tried to imagine the boy happy, playing merrily, some fat on him. He had been a toddler once, animated with joy of life, running to his mother. Such things were back there somewhere. A sturdy lad. The flesh appeared healthy in spite of its emptiness. Dead but not dead.

Why did the boy irritate Herity so? Time and again, John had seen Herity try to make the boy break that vow of silence. "What good is such a vow? It won't bring back the dead!"

There was never an answer. The boy withdrew farther into his silent armor. The way he pulled his head into the blue anorak begged comparison with a turtle, but the comparison failed. The turtle might withdraw its vulnerable parts, staring out fearfully until danger passed. This boy cowered in some far deeper place than the hood of his anorak. So deep it was that the eyes sometimes had not a glimmer of life in them. Everything the boy did at such times was transformed into a sullen patience far more stilled than mere silence. It was suspended animation, as though the life processes were put on hold while the flesh plodded along. The flesh remained merely the carrier of an inert spirit, a mass without internal direction.

Except when he threw rocks at the rooks.

Why did this boy hate the black birds so? Had he seen them settle onto beloved flesh? Perhaps that was the explanation. There could be bleached bones somewhere, cleansed by the birds, bones that once had carried someone this boy loved.

John finished his soda bread and cheese, dusted his hand and crossed the bridge to where worn, irregular stone steps led down to the water. Beside the stream, he knelt and scooped the cold water into his palms, drinking it noisily, enjoying the coldness on his cheeks. The water tasted sweet and faintly of granite. John turned his head at a sound beside him. The boy had joined him on the ledge beside the flow and was drinking with his face plunged into the current.

Face dripping water, the boy looked up at John, a solemn, studying expression. *Who are you? Should I be like you?*

In a sudden feeling of confusion, John stood, shook the water from his hands and climbed back to the bridge. How could the boy speak so plainly without words?

John stood at the bridge rail above the boy, not looking at him. There were low willows along the boggy ground beneath the elders. A cloud came over the sun then, throwing the world between the trees into a sudden chill gray. The river sounds were only river sounds, John told himself. Not people talking. Once this land might have been enchanted, but now the spirits were gone. It possessed only this emptiness, an absolute vitiation at one with the gnarled willows beneath the elders and the dank bog at the river's edge. The river spoke to him, a blasphemous echo: "My spirits are gone. I am wasted."

The cloud passed and once more the sun beat down between the trees, sparkling on the water, but it was different.

The boy joined John on the bridge. The priest came to them, carrying his pack in one hand, leaving Herity at the end of the bridge, staring off across the meadows.

"This is desecration," Father Michael said.

The boy looked up at Father Michael, a question plain on the silent young face: *What does that mean?*

The priest met the boy's gaze. "It's a terrible place."

The boy turned and looked all around, his expression clearly puzzled, saying that he thought this a pretty place—the trees, the river, a full stomach.

He's healing, John thought. Would he speak when he was fully healed?

Herity, coming up to them, said: "Ahhh, the priest's in one of his black moods. His faith is wavering in his mouth and it like a faucet that lets everything run out."

Father Michael whirled on him. "Would you destroy faith, Herity?"

"Och! It's not me destroys the faith, Priest." Herity smiled at John. "This great tragedy is what kills the faith."

"For once, you're right," Father Michael said.

Herity pretended surprise. "Am I now?"

Father Michael inhaled a deep breath. "All the doubts that ever were are growing like weeds in the untended garden that was Ireland."

"What a poet you are, Father!" Herity turned and met the gaze of the silent boy. "It's Shaw's stony land you've inherited, poor lad, and you've not mind nor senses to see it."

A deep shuddering sigh shook Father Michael. "I think sometimes this must be a terrible nightmare, the white horse of all horrors. And we'll wake soon enough, laughing at the night's terrors, going on about our ways as before. Please, God!"

The boy clutched his anorak around his throat and turned away from them, plodding off the bridge. Father Michael slung his pack onto his shoulders and followed.

Herity glanced at John. "Shall we be going along now?"

Almost imperceptibly at first, the road began to climb out of the valley. Herity, with John beside him, stayed closer to the priest and boy, no more than five paces behind.

Was it safer here? John wondered. Herity was not keeping them spread out. Or was it the sharp turns in the road around which nothing could be seen? Did Herity want to be closer to the priest and see with him what next the road revealed?

"D' y' know what happened to our Father Michael there?" Herity asked. "I can see he'll not be telling you and him the best witness to it all."

The priest did not turn, but his shoulders stiffened.

Herity addressed the stiff back, his voice loud. "In the first days of the plague's terrible scything, a great maddened mob of men burned Maynooth in County Kildare—the whole place, even St. Patrick's College where Fitzgerald Castle once stood and it a shrine to the old ways. The new block burned like a torch, it did. And the old block came tumbling down to the big machines pushing it and the explosives. It was a sight to see!"

"Why did they do it?"

"The terrible anger in them. God had abandoned them. They couldn't get at God so they got at the Church." Herity lifted his chin and called out: "Isn't that what you told me, Father Michael?"

The priest remained as silent as the boy walking beside him.

"The smoke rose to heaven for three days," Herity said, "and longer if you count the smoldering. Ahh, the flames so high and the mob capering about it and hunting priests to burn the while."

"They burned priests?"

"Right into the fire with 'em!"

"And Father Michael was there?"

"Oh, yes. Our Father Michael was there to see all that capering. The priests had a fine store of drink in their cellars, they did."

John thought of the brand on Father Michael's forehead. "Was that when they branded him?"

"Oh, no! That was later. His own folk did that because they knew he'd been at Maynooth and him still alive. Ahh, no, it was death for a priest to be seen there during the whole time of the burning."

Herity fell silent. Only the sound of their footsteps echoed between the road's rock boundaries and there was a faint, murmurous praying from Father Michael.

"Listen to him pray!" Herity said. "Remember how it was, Priest? Ahhh, John, the burning of Maynooth could be seen for miles. The smoke of it went straight up, it did. I know a priest was there and I heard him say it was a signal to God."

Only the low droning of prayer came from Father Michael.

"We saw the message to God, didn't we, Father Michael?" Herity called. "And what did we say? God can lie! That's what we said. God can lie to us."

John pictured the scene in Herity's vivid words. O'Neill-Within could be sensed there, listening, but not attempting to come out. The fire, the shrieks . . . he could almost hear them.

"You were there with Father Michael," John said.

"Lucky for him! Saved his mangy skin, I did." Laughter bubbled from Herity. "Oh, he doesn't like that, him owing his life to the likes of me. So many priests dying and him alive. It was a sight, I tell you! They kept no count but it was over two hundred of 'em burned, I'm sure. Into the fire and straight to hell!"

Father Michael raised his fists to heaven, but did not turn. His voice continued its murmurous prayer.

Herity said: "It was a fiery martyrdom the likes of which has not been seen in this land for many a century. But our Father Michael doesn't have the stuff of martyrs."

The priest fell silent. His movements looked weary. The

pack on his back dragged at his shoulders.

"Some say only twelve priests escaped," Herity said. "In mufti, hidden by the few of us who kept our senses. I sometimes wonder why I helped, but then it was a terrible stench and the drink running out. No reason to stay."

Herity smiled secretly to himself, then turned and winked at John. "But the Madman would've loved the sight of it! Of that I'm sure."

John's step faltered. He could sense O'Neill-Within, hysterical giggling.

Why had Herity said that? *Why tell me?*

Herity had lowered his attention to the road at his feet, though, and his expression was unreadable. It was steeper here, the road climbing around hills that, when they opened to a view ahead, showed the way rising toward the tree-framed notch at the top of the valley.

There was a damp, almost tropical heat in the afternoon air. John's senses wanted jungle and palms, not these green hills and this black, narrow roadway cutting like a sheep terrace into the land. The bracket of trees ahead was mostly European poplars, scrawny from fighting the winter storms that used the notch as their pathway into the forests and boglands to the east.

The memory of Herity's words in his ears, John was taken suddenly by the oddity of the Irish relationship with this landscape. Why had Herity saved the priest? Because Father Michael had been born of the same soil. Something happened in this marriage of people and land. The Celts had got under the skin of Ireland. They did not move just across the surface of the land like nomads. Even this tramp was more through Ireland than across it. Herity's people had made themselves part of the very soil. There was never any question of them owning Ireland. Quite the contrary. Ireland owned them.

John lifted his gaze to the path ahead. Behind the poplars could be glimpsed the deeper stain of evergreens clinging closely to the hillsides in neatly planted rows. There, within the deeper trees, lay the great house with its mansard roof: a French château appearing untouched above the ruins in the valley. Smoke lifted from its chimneys. The house nestled into the trees; it had been adopted by Ireland. No longer French. It was an Irish house. The smoke smelled of peat.

> *And finally I tell the Irish to re-*
> *member the Banshee of Dalcais Ai-*
> *bell, the Banshee warning Brian Boru*
> *that he would die at Clontarf. Listen*
> *for the Banshee, Ireland, for I will have*
> *my revenge upon all of you. No more*
> *can you evade personal responsibility*
> *for what you did to me and mine. I*
> *am the ultimate gombeen man come*
> *to make you pay — not just during the*
> *hard months but forevermore.*

> **—John Roe O'Neill, Letter Three**

SAMUEL BENJAMIN VELCOURT had come up through the ranks in the United States Consular Service and the U.S. Agency for International Development. Maverick tendencies had restricted his advancement but he had managed to make many military friends during his USAID days, a fact which helped him now. There were, also, his reports, often praised for their insights.

At age sixty-one, seeing the way ahead finally blocked, he had quit USAID, where he had only been on loan from the Consular Service anyway, and he ran for the Senate from Ohio. His assets were formidable—

An ability to make himself understood in almost any company and in four languages.

A rich family willing to back his campaign.

A wife, May, who appealed to both young and old feminists for her outspoken wit. (Older women liked her because she looked what she was, a feisty, independent grandmother.)

The back-room support of the Ohio Democratic Machine plus that maverick record gave him immediate appeal to Independents and Liberal Republicans.

Finally, there were the crowning facts: a rich, compelling

baritone voice coupled to a dignified appearance. He looked like a senator and he talked like one.

On the platform, Samuel Benjamin Velcourt was a *presence* and he knew how to project himself on TV.

The effect had been devastating—a landslide victory in a year when Republicans were making new gains everywhere except in the presidency.

In an Akron columnist's words: "Voters were saying they liked this guy's style and they wanted him in the Senate to keep an eye on the bastards."

A British observer of the election had commented: "The wonder is he sat so long on the back benches."

Within two months of entering the Senate, Sam Velcourt pulled out of the ruck, proving that all those years in the ranks had really taught him how the system worked.

He worked it with the hand of an impresario drawing the most from the talent available to him.

It surprised very few to see him tapped for the vice-presidency in Prescott's second campaign. They needed Ohio, someone with Republican appeal, an energetic campaigner with an attractive wife, who also was willing to campaign, a man with his own power base—all of those things which really determine how candidates are chosen. Only Velcourt's maverick tendencies bothered the national organization.

Adam Prescott had tipped the scales. "Let's park him there and see how he works. Anyway, another term in the Senate and there'll be no stopping him. We might as well get him in close where we can keep an eye on him."

"He scares the hell out of the State Department," a presidential aide had said.

This had amused Prescott. "It's good for State to be scared. But he doesn't strike me as one to use an axe. A little surgery here and there, maybe, but no big pools of blood."

Prescott's assessment had proven correct on all counts and, when the plague struck late in that second term, they had worked like two halves of the same machine. Velcourt's military friends had proved most invaluable then, an essential part of Prescott's own authority.

Velcourt thought of these things as he stood at the window of the Blue Room looking out toward the light traffic on Executive Avenue South. It was early evening and he had been sworn in as President less than three hours before, a quiet ceremony at the edge of the Rose Garden, minimal fuss and only pool coverage by the media—two reporters, one TV camera, two still cameras and one of those from the White House itself.

Velcourt knew he was going to miss the pragmatic decisiveness of his predecessor. Adam had been a tough and experienced political in-fighter, a man who kept personal doubts carefully concealed.

I tend to show my doubts, Velcourt thought. *I'll have to watch that.*

A Harvard professor had once told the younger Velcourt: "The uses of power require a certain measure of inhumanity. Imagination is a piece of baggage you often can't afford to carry. If you begin thinking about people in general as individuals, that gets in your way. They are clay to be shaped. That's the real truth of the democratic process."

In spite of such thoughts, or perhaps in contrast to them, Velcourt found the view in front of him pleasant. May was safe upstairs. One of their daughters had survived up in the Michigan Reserve and they had only grandsons.

It was an evening made for love songs, he decided. One of those soft evenings after a cold spell and with the promise of more warmth to come. Pastoral, Velcourt labeled it—quietly pastoral: the cattle munching away at the tall pasture that had been the White House lawn. Guitar music, that was what it needed. Everything muted, not a hint of violence. Nothing to remind him of those ranked bodies burning at the capital's eastern perimeter. He could see the orange glow when he looked in that direction.

The fire's pungent cleansing would end soon and enfolding darkness would erase the scene from sight—but not from memory.

Clay, Velcourt reminded himself.

No miracles kept Washington plague-free. It was simply that the area was occupied by people capable of brutal decisions. Manhattan was no different and it had the added advantage of a water perimeter no longer spanned by bridges, the tunnels blocked, and that outer buffer zone with its black fire lanes.

All the "safe" places waiting out the plague had at least this thing in common and one other common characteristic as well: There were no mobs inside.

The mob that had assaulted Washington's perimeter less than an hour after Adam's death had thought a few pieces of armor and some automatic weapons might win them through the Washington Barrier. The attackers had been incapable of imagining the inferno effect from flaming splashes of Newfire, the hell temperatures and immunity to ordinary retardants. Although it provided no feelings of absolute security, Newfire was making a big difference in the landscape. Melted concrete tended to sober those who saw it. Velcourt did not try to fool himself, though: Individuals would still try to penetrate the barriers. All it took was one infected individual and the plague could feed on new victims. A very tenuous way to survive, Velcourt thought.

He turned toward the darkening room and the open door to the lighted hallway. Secret Service agents could be heard in low-voiced conversation out there. The sound reminded Velcourt that there were things to do, decisions to be made.

There was a stirring in the lighted hallway, hurrying footsteps. A Secret Service agent leaned in and said: "Mister President?"

"I'll be out soon," Velcourt said. "The East Room."

The Cabinet and the heads of the special committees had arrived with their reports for the new President. They would meet just down the hall where all the impedimenta of audiovisual presentation had been laid out. It promised to be a long session. There would be special emphasis on one particular problem—the new Jewish Diaspora. Only a handful of diehards had remained in Israel. The ones in Brazil would have to be fed and housed. It must be a madhouse down there in Brazil, Velcourt thought. God! When will the Jews ever find a home? The ones who had stayed behind had promised to fight their way across the desert and restore the flow of Saudi oil. Foolishness! The plague had driven energy requirements to a fraction of their former level. Who traveled anymore? A lot of the survivors lived communal lives. Only the Barrier Command needed great quantities of oil, and the Soviet Union was carrying most of that load.

Velcourt could hear another voice in the hallway now, the voice for which he had been delaying, Shiloh Broderick. The aging Broderick had come over from his Washington town house with a request that he be allowed to "brief the President." Along with the full-protocol request there had been a "Dear

Sam" note recalling their past association. Without ever stating it openly, the note made clear who had sent Shiloh Broderick to "brief the President."

On a whim (*After all, I am the President!*), Velcourt said: "Send Broderick in. Tell the others to get started without us. They can hash out some of their differences before I go in."

Velcourt bent and turned on a single floor lamp over a comfortable chair and seated himself opposite it in the shadows. Broderick, when he entered, saw the setup and understood.

"Don't get up, sir."

Shiloh had aged greatly since they had last met, Velcourt noted. He walked with an old man's limping gait, favoring the left leg. There were new and deeper wrinkles in his lean face, the wavy hair gone completely gray. The corners of his eyes looked moist. The narrow mouth was even more severe.

They shook hands while Broderick stood and Velcourt remained seated. Broderick took the chair under the light, its downward-pointing reflector bathing him in an unkind glare.

"Thank you, Mister President, for seeing me ahead of the others."

"I didn't move you ahead, Shiloh. I moved the others back."

This brought an appreciative chuckle.

Velcourt could see Shiloh debating whether to address the President as Sam. All of that diplomatic training won out.

"Mister President, I don't know if you appreciate the opportunity that has been presented to us of settling the Communist Question once and for all."

Oh, shit! Velcourt thought. *And I thought his people might come up with something new.*

"Get it off your chest, Shiloh."

"You realize, of course, that they still have some agents in place even here in Washington."

"Immunity is a word without its old meanings nowadays," Velcourt said.

Broderick sniffed, then: "You're saying that we have our people over there, too. However, I was addressing a different situation. The Soviets and the United States are now confined to leopard spots of plague-free communities. A comparison of the relative vulnerability of these population centers shows us clearly at the advantage."

"Is that so?"

"It certainly is, sir. We have more scattered communities

of smaller population. Have you focused on that?"

Jesus Christ! Was he going to bring up old First Strike?

"My predecessor and I talked about this at some length."
Velcourt's tone was dry. "But surely you're not..."

"Not atomics, sir. Bacteriological!"

"And we blame it on O'Neill, of course." Velcourt's tone
was even drier.

"Exactly!"

"What do Soviet agents have to do with this?"

"We give them a trail to follow, a trail that proves we are
blameless."

"How would you propose to infect the Soviets?"

"Birds."

Velcourt suppressed a grin, shaking his head.

"Migratory birds, Mister President," Broderick said. "It's
just the kind of thing this Madman..."

Velcourt no longer could suppress his laughter. His whole
body shook with it.

"What is it, Mister President?"

"Right after I was sworn in, Shiloh, I called the premier
and we had about a half hour of discussion—the commitments
already made are still standing, what new options there may
be—that sort of thing."

"Good move," Broderick said. "Allay their suspicions. Who
was your translator?" He coughed, realizing his faux pas. "Sorry,
sir."

"Yes, we spoke in Russian. The premier thinks I have a
Georgian accent. He finds it very helpful that I speak his language. Minimizes misunderstanding."

"Then why did you laugh just now?"

"The premier was at great pains to tell me about a recent
proposal of his military. I leave it for you to guess the content
of that proposal."

"Infected birds?"

Another chuckle shook Velcourt.

Broderick leaned forward, his manner intense. "Sir, you
know you can't trust them to keep their word on a damned
thing! And if they're already—"

"Shiloh! The Soviet Union will follow its own best interests.
As will we. The premier is a pragmatist."

"He's a lying son-of-a-bitch who—"

"All of that! And he knows, of course, that I have not always been fully candid with him. Didn't you say one time, Shiloh, that this was the essence of diplomacy—creating acceptable solutions out of lies?"

"You have a good memory, sir, but the Communists mean to do us in. We can't afford to relax for a . . ."

"Shiloh, please! I don't need lectures on the dangers of communism. We all have a more immediate danger in front of us and, thus far, we're cooperating well in the search for some way of preventing human extinction."

"And what if they're first to find a cure?"

"Some of our people are working in their labs, Shiloh, and some of their people are with us. We even have Lepikov and Beckett together in England. Communication is open. I talked to Beckett myself last week before. . . . Well, we're communicating. Of course, each of us listens to these communications. I don't suppose this will lead to the millennium but it is one hopeful sign in a world beset by the threat of extinction. And if there's an advantage to be gained, Shiloh, from this cooperation, an advantage gained without compromising our mutual efforts, I will take that advantage."

"With all due respect, sir, are you assuming they don't have research facilities that are kept completely secret from us?"

"With all due respect, Shiloh, are you assuming we don't have similar establishments?"

Broderick sat back, steepled his fingers and put them against his lips.

Velcourt knew who Broderick represented—certain very powerful and very wealthy people, a large contingent in the bureaucracy and retired from it, people whose careers had been predicated on "being right even when they were wrong." In a bureaucracy, Velcourt had learned early, the simple fact of being right did not win popularity contests, especially if someone higher up in the hierarchy was thus proven wrong. People who gained power in a bureaucracy, Velcourt had noted, tended to be media-minded. They wanted headline items, the more dramatic the better. Simple answers, no matter how wrong they might be proven later. Drama, that was the thing—a most powerful advantage in a conference room, especially when presented in the driest and most analytical terms. Broderick had made a career on this one fact.

Velcourt said: "You've been out of government for a long time, Shiloh. I know you have important contacts, but they may not be telling you everything they know."

"And you are?" There was anger in the old diplomat's voice.

"I have adopted a policy of increasing candor—not complete, but trending that way."

Shiloh Broderick absorbed this in silence.

The plague had produced a new kind of consciousness in most powerful people, Velcourt had noted. It was not just adapting to a sequence of new political situations but a different level of awareness, more penetrating. It put survival first and political games second. Politics had been reduced to its most personal level: *Who do I trust?* Whenever that question was asked at a life-and-death level, there could be only one answer: *I trust the people I know.*

I know you, Shiloh Broderick, and I don't trust you.

"Mister President," Broderick said, "why did you invite me in here?"

"I've had some experience of trying to get through the political barricades, Shiloh, trying to reach the ear of someone who could 'do something.' I have some sense of your present situation."

Broderick again leaned forward. "Sir, out there . . ." he pointed at the windows ". . . are people who know things you need to know. I represent some of the finest—"

"Shiloh, you've put your finger precisely on my problem. How do I find them? And having found them, how do I wade through and weed through what they bring?"

"You trust your friends!"

Velcourt sighed. "But, Shiloh, things presented to me . . . well, things excluded are often more important than things presented. I'm the President, now, Shiloh. My first resolution is to weed out the advisors who produce only drama. I'll listen once in case they bring something new, but I don't have time for old nonsense."

Broderick heard dismissal in the President's words and tone but refused to move.

"Mister President, I presume on past association. We go a long way back where—"

"Where I was often right and you were wrong."

Broderick's mouth drew into a tight line.

Velcourt spoke first: "Don't assume that I hold grudges. We've no time for such nonsense. What I'm telling you is that I intend to rely on my own judgment. That's the nature of this office. And the record shows that my judgment has been better than yours. You have one value to me, Shiloh—information."

And Velcourt thought: *Does Shiloh suspect the real nature of the information he brought me today?* Broderick represented people who might act independently to endanger an extremely delicate balance. An upset in these times could lead to a planet empty of humans. Broderick's people clearly were acting out of a context whose time had passed. Operation Backfire would have to be alerted.

Broderick's lips moved against each other but did not part, then, he spoke in a tightly controlled voice: "We always said you weren't a very good team player."

"I'm glad to know you held such a high opinion of me. You'd do me a favor, Shiloh, if you went back to your people and told them that my opinion of our bureaucracy has not changed much."

"I've never heard that opinion."

"They made a fatal error, Shiloh. They tried to copy the Soviet model." He raised a hand for silence as Broderick started to respond. "Oh, I know the reasons. But you take a better look at the Soviet example, Shiloh. They've created a bureaucratic aristocracy, recreated, I should say, because it's patterned on the czarist model. You always did want to be an aristocrat, Shiloh. You just chose the wrong country in which to make the attempt."

Broderick gripped the arms of his chair, knuckles white. His voice came out in barely controlled fury: "Sir, the intelligent ones must lead!"

"Who's to be the judge of what's intelligent, Shiloh? Was it intelligence got us into this mess? You see, aristocrats can bury their mistakes only so long as the mistakes are small enough."

Velcourt lifted himself from the chair and spoke to the seated Broderick from the deeper shadows above the lamplight. "If you'll excuse me, Shiloh, I have to go next door and see if I can detect what other mistakes we're about to make."

"And I'm no longer invited?"

"I've heard your argument, Shiloh."

"So you're not going to take advantage of . . ."

"I'll take any and every advantage that I judge to be a real one! And that I judge does not endanger the primary concern—finding a cure for this plague. That's why my door remains open to you, Shiloh, whenever time permits. Maybe you'll bring me something useful."

Velcourt turned and strode out of the room, unconsciously

copying the purposeful stride he'd seen so many times in Adam Prescott. In the main hall, seeing one of his aides, Velcourt dictated a memo as they hurried toward the East Room.

The alternative to the Brodericks was not to bury himself in information, he thought. No, the alternative was to surround himself with people who used their powers of observation the way he did. He knew a few such. They might know of more. This memo was a first step. The aware people would have to be found . . . the bright ones who were not afraid to report unpopular things.

Analysis in depth was a thing that had to happen outside the President's presence. Perhaps that had been the need for a long time. It had taken the plague's immediacy to suppress all the drama-pushers and make this approach so obvious.

Broderick had been right on one thing, though: Find the right people. But when he found them, when he had digested their information and acted upon it, he had to make sure his orders were carried out. It was clear that the power of the people Broderick represented often transcended that of the transients who occupied the Oval Office. It even transcended the power of people in other offices, in the corner offices or in the large spaces at the ends of long halls lined with portraits of past transients. Bureaucrats came to recognize early a simple truth about their powers: "We will be here after the transients have been replaced by the electorate."

Time was on their side.

Velcourt paused at the door to the East Room. Well, the plague had changed that, too. Time had only one use now—find the path to survival.

'Tis I that outraged Jesus of old;
'Tis I that robbed my children of
heaven!
By rights 'tis I that should have gone
upon the cross.
There would be no hell, there would
be no sorrow,
There would be no fear if it were not
for me.

—**"Eve's Lament,"**
an old Irish poem

THE ROAD beneath John's feet crested the ridge at the top of the valley much farther to the right of the slate-roofed mansion than he had expected. He could see a shallow swale on his right close with young pines, which thickened into taller pines at a higher crest beyond. At his left, a steep slope descended some fifty meters before gentling into a deep bowl perhaps a thousand meters across. The château, three stories high and with four levels to its roofline, nestled into a black rock elbow at the far side of the bowl. Sheep cropped the meadow grass in front of the building. A double line of poplars led in at an angle from far to the right, an overgrown lane between them. The poplars and a tall stand of evergreens partly concealed a deeper lawn beyond.

A wind from the west swayed the poplars and bent the tall grass growing up through the rock fence along the road beside John. He turned to look at his companions. Herity had put one foot on the rock fence and leaned forward on the upraised knee, listening. Father Michael and the boy stood near him, staring at the pastoral scene below them.

"Would you look at that now," Herity said, his voice hushed. Father Michael cupped a hand behind his left ear. "Listen!"

John heard it then: the sounds of children playing—thin cries, excitement in the shouts. A game, he thought. He clambered onto the rock wall near Herity and stared off across the bowl toward the building. The sound came from beyond the poplars and the screening evergreens.

Herity removed his foot from the wall and trotted down the road until he was past the screening trees. John and the others hurried to follow.

Father Michael pulled Gannon's gift binoculars out of his pack as he ran. He stopped and aimed them at the flat expanse of lawn revealed from this new position. The others stopped beside him.

John saw them now—children played on the lawn, kicking a ball. They wore white blouses and matching stockings, black shoes and . . . skirts! Dark skirts!

Herity reached a hand toward Father Michael. "Give me those binoculars!"

Father Michael passed them to Herity, who focused them on the players. His lips worked soundlessly as he looked, then: "Ahhh, the little beauties. The little beauties." Slowly, Herity lowered the binoculars, then thrust them at John. "See what the Madman missed?"

With trembling hands, John focused the binoculars and aimed them at the lawn. The players were girls of about twelve to sixteen years of age. Their hair had been done into twin braids, which swung wide as they ran and twisted after the ball shouting, calling out to other players. Some of the girls, John noted, wore yellow armbands, some green. Two teams.

"A girls' school?" John asked, his voice husky. He could sense the faint and distant stirring of O'Neill-Within, querulous movement that he knew had to be stilled.

"That's Brann McCrae's little dovecote," Herity said. "Him as made this little place off limits to the Finn Sadal and others and, it being common knowledge that McCrae has at least five rocket launchers plus other assorted instruments of violence, the Military Council does not question his decree."

The silent boy crowded close to Father Michael, his gaze intent on the lawn.

John lowered the binoculars and returned them to the priest, who proffered them to the boy, but the boy only shook his head.

"Is it really girls or is it boys dressed up as girls?" John asked.

"Girls and young women they are," Herity said, "all preserved in Mister McCrae's transplanted French château. Would you say that's a French château, John?"

"It could be." John was only conscious of his reply after he had spoken. He looked toward the building's roof, visible over the treetops. Smoke trailed from four of the building's chimneys. He could smell turf fires.

"Joseph, why have we come this way?" Father Michael asked, his voice trembling. "We must not go near that place. It's certain sure we're contaminated with the plague."

"As are the soldiers guarding them," Herity said. "But it's isolation they have and we'll see them through this patch alive. All the women of Ireland are not dead."

"Who is this Brann McCrae?" John asked.

"The Croesus of imported farm machinery," Herity said. "A rich man, himself as has big houses such as this and guns and, so I'm told, tough women to use them." He turned away and, as he moved, a rifle shot sounded from the direction of the mansion. A bullet slammed into the rock wall beside him and went keening off in ricochet. Father Michael tumbled the boy to the road behind the wall. John ducked and found his arm gripped, Herity dragging him across the road. They rolled across the opposite wall as another bullet hit behind them. Father Michael and the boy squirmed across the road, crossed the wall and joined Herity and John. They lay in heavy grass above the shallow, pine-filled swale John had noted earlier.

John listened. The sounds of girls at play were gone. A masculine voice barked a one-word command in the distance, the ringing sound of a bullhorn amplifier in it:

"Inside!"

"They're only warning us off," Father Michael said.

"Not Brann McCrae," Herity said. He peered into the swale and the ridge beyond it. "Follow me." Keeping his head low, Herity ran down the shallow hill into the pines, crashing through branches, turning to present his shoulder to the worst of the obstructions.

John and the others followed. John's arms and shoulders were slapped and buffeted by springing limbs.

"In here!" Herity called.

They burst through a screen of limbs to a small clearing with cottage-size outcroppings of granite in its center. Herity dove behind the rocks, the others with him. They lay panting on grass that smelled of dust and flint. Father Michael crossed himself. The boy cowered against the priest.

"Why are we running?" John asked.

"Because I know Mister McCrae," Herity said.

Silence settled over the clearing, then a hissing roar sounded from the mansion's valley. A deafening explosion erupted at the road they had just quit. Black shards of road surface and rock showered the area.

Herity looked at Father Michael. "He doesn't cooperate, that Brann McCrae."

John's ears were ringing from the explosion. He put his hands over them and shook his head. O'Neill-Within had stirred to something near wakefulness. Explosions were only bombs to him, not rockets. Bombs killed your loved ones.

"You have no loved ones left," John muttered.

"What was that?" Herity asked.

John lowered his hands. "Nothing." He could feel O'Neill-Within returning to quiescence but there was no solace in this respite. What if O'Neill-Within should come out fully in Herity's presence? That would be disaster.

"We must get away from here," Father Michael said.

Herity raised a hand for silence. He stared off into the pines to the north. A limb cracked there and something large could be heard moving through the branches. Herity pointed at John's pocket and mouthed the word: "Pistol." Placing a finger to his lips, his machine gun cradled close to his chest, Herity crept off toward the sound, wriggling along under the branches. He was lost from view within only a few heartbeats.

John slipped the pistol from his pocket and stared after Herity. He felt foolish. What good was this little peashooter against a rocket launcher? There was no more sound of the large something moving through the pines.

Father Michael had found a rosary and fingered the beads, his lips moving. The boy had pulled his head almost completely into his anorak.

The silence dragged out—oppressive, weighted. John crept forward past the priest and turned until he could sit up with his back against the warm rock of the outcropping. The low pines were directly in front of him only a few paces away, tall brown grass in the foreground, thick green limbs beyond. It was an almost perfect screen to conceal anything outside the clearing.

A masculine voice shouted from up toward the ridge on his right. John could detect no word in the sound. He felt exposed here, set out as a target for anyone in the concealment of the trees. John lifted the revolver and cocked it. Sounds of movement in the pines—Herity?

"Yank!" It was Herity's voice. "It's friends. We're coming in."

John lowered the pistol, uncocked it and returned it to his pocket.

Herity emerged from the trees followed by two tall men— scarecrows in green uniforms, dark green berets, the harp insignia of Eire at the shoulders and on the berets. Both carried automatic rifles. Herity held his machine gun casually cradled in his right arm.

John studied the two men with Herity. They were enough alike to be twins, although the one in the lead appeared older, more lines around the eyes, skin somewhat more weathered. Wisps of sandy hair poked from beneath their berets. Their pale blue eyes stared out warily over flat cheeks and short noses. They had softly rounded chins and full lips.

The three men strode up to the rock shelter as John and Father Michael arose. The boy remained seated, peering up from the hood of his anorak.

The men stopped in front of John.

Herity said, "This is John Garrech O'Donnell, Liam. Father Michael you'll be knowing. And this down here . . ." he glanced at the boy on the ground ". . . is the boy."

The older of the two newcomers nodded.

For John's benefit, Herity said, "This is Liam," indicating the older man, "and his cousin, Jock. They're Cullens, the both of them. Liam and Jock are with the eight full squads of regulars to keep watch on Mister McCrae's fine establishment there, it being a tempting morsel for unsavory types."

"God be praised," Father Michael said. "Nothing must harm those young women."

Liam glanced at Father Michael, a heavy-lidded stare full of animosity. Seeing it, John wondered at this show of anger. There were undercurrents here that troubled John. Herity knew these two men. They knew Father Michael. The priest's early question was appropriate. Why *had* they come this way?

"The Arrrmy be praised," Jock said, a heavy burr in his voice.

He doesn't sound Irish, John thought.

As though he read John's mind, Herity said: "Doesn't he have a wonderful sound in him, our Jock? He's one of the Catholic Scots from Antrim, John."

"Leave be," Liam said. "You knew that road was off-limits, Joseph. Why do you tempt McCrae and his rocket launcher?"

"To use up his ammunition," Herity said, a chuckle in his voice.

"Aren't you the funny man!" Liam said.

"Not as funny as you nor as sharp," Herity said.

"We've a sort of agreement with McCrae and you know it," Liam said. "Those girls down there must be preserved, no matter that they're in McCrae's dirty hands."

Father Michael moved suddenly, stationing himself beside John. "What're you saying, Liam Cullen?"

"Stay out of this, Priest," Liam said. He glanced at his cousin. "Go back and tell the others it's all secure here. They can inform Mister McCrae it's only innocent pilgrims on his road."

Jock turned away. His green-clad form appeared to melt into the pines. Soon, even the sound of him vanished.

Father Michael was not to be put off. "Dirty hands, you said, Liam Cullen. What have you seen?"

"Well, there's two of the older girls pregnant, and that's for sure," Liam said.

"Does McCrae have a priest with him?" Father Michael demanded.

"As to that," Liam said, "Mister McCrae no longer holds with your Church."

Father Michael shook his head from side to side.

Herity had watched this exchange with unconcealed amusement. He turned now to Liam: "Do you have a head count yet?"

"Not to be certain, but we've identified nine older women and there's maybe thirty of the younger ones."

"Where did they all come from?" John asked.

"Oh, that we know," Herity said. "Our Mister Brann McCrae scooped up the young ones at the first sign of trouble. The luck of the devil, he had. Not a sick one in the lot. As to the older ones . . ." Herity looked at Liam.

"They've been with him for years."

"What do you mean, scooped?" John asked.

"He told the parents they was to be hidden away safe from the plague," Liam said. "And that's true enough."

"Only the one man?" John asked.

Liam nodded.

"I must speak to him," Father Michael said.

"You've nothing to say to him, priest, that he wants to hear," Liam said. "McCrae and his women are followers of the Druid religion now, so they say."

"Another blasphemy!" Father Michael glared at Liam. "You said you've an agreement with him. You speak to him. You told Jock . . ."

"Was it a group marriage you planned to hold?" Herity asked. "Mister McCrae and all of his females joined in holy wedlock! What a fine thing!"

Father Michael ignored this thrust, keeping his attention on Liam. "Unless you arrange for me to speak to him, I'll give you the opportunity to shoot me in the back as I go down there. I'll not have their souls in hell!"

"Well, why not?" Liam asked. "The priest talking to Mister McCrae, that'd provide a bit of sport for my boys. It'll be on a field telephone you talk to him, and that at least five hundred meters from his perimeter. You can't go nearer. If it's only talk you want, we can provide the means. If y' mean to confront him in person, though, you'll get your bullet . . . in the back or anywhere else we care to shoot."

"When will you arrange this?" Father Michael asked. He sounded calmer.

"Tonight."

Liam turned away and strode toward the trees. "Keep your heads down as we come level with the road. We've shelter beyond the ridge where you can wait."

As the others followed Liam, John brought up the rear, dodging the whipping branches, ducking for the larger ones. Pine needles clung to his yellow sweater. He could feel them in his hair. Spiderwebs bridged some of the passages. He brushed them away, feeling then for the small pistol in his pocket.

While they were concentrating on the priest, another person might slip away and approach McCrae's château. This thought filled his mind with confusion. Herity would know for sure who John O'Donnell was then.

But who am I?

He heard a ringing in his ears and wondered if he was going to faint. John O'Neill wanted no women to survive in Ireland. There were women at the château.

He heard Herity and Liam Cullen arguing up ahead. Liam's voice lifted suddenly:

"You're a fool, Joseph Herity! Always have been. You've exceeded your orders the same way you did that other time. I've warned you before and I'll warn you again: You'll not endanger my charges!"

Herity replied in a voice inaudible to John, but John was not listening. *Orders? What orders?*

He felt an extreme caution. What was going on here? O'Neill-Within could be felt there, questioning, crouching, listening. This march across the Irish countryside was not what it appeared to be. How long had they been about it now? More than a month. Why so long to get from one place to another? Why the detours and the ramblings along byways with Herity saying they had to go only the safest routes?

Gannon had sensed something wrong. Was Gannon's assessment correct?

> *If we depend exclusively on defense measures, we shall increasingly behave like hunted creatures, running from one protective device to another, each more complex and costly than the one before.*
>
> **—René Dubos**

"THIS CASTLE'S haunted," Kate whispered. She shivered next to Stephen in bed, glad for once that the slight inward curvature of the mattress forced them to snuggle close together all night.

"Shush," Stephen whispered. "It's no such thing."

It was dark in the original pressure chamber from Adrian Peard's research laboratory and there was only an occasional shuffling of feet or a cough from the night guard outside.

"It is, I say!" Kate whispered. "My grandmother could tell when ghosts were about, and I've inherited it. This is an evil place."

"It's keeping you safe from the plague," Stephen said, his voice louder. He had given up trying to go to sleep for now. Kate in this mood would not be mollified.

"The ghosts want me," Kate said. "I'll not leave this place alive." She took one of Stephen's hands and placed it on her abdomen. "And this poor child shall not come alive into the world."

"Kate, stop it!" he said.

She went on as though she had not heard. "There's fighting

among the soldiers here, Stephen. Evil spirits cause that and we both know it!"

"We know nothing of the kind!"

"You heard about Dermott Houlihan and Michael Lynskey. Them raging because of the memory-sound!"

"We've asked them to stop using women announcers on the wireless," Stephen said.

"Dermott saying the woman on the wireless had the exact sound of his dead Lileen and Michael saying, no, it was the sound of his Peg. I heard Moone describing it, Stephen, and there's no escaping that! Them fighting there and rolling on the floor, bloodying each other, tears running down their cheeks all the while."

"But afterwards, Katie darling, they went off to the saloon bar arm in arm. Remember that. 'O, it was a grand fight,' they said."

"It's a madness," Kate said.

"That's as may be, Katie."

"Don't call me Katie! I'm not a child!"

"Darlin', I'm sorry." He put out a hand to soothe her but she thrust him away.

"It's ghosts," she said, her voice hushed. "There's no women now to lay out the corpses. The faeries are causing the ghosts. Oh, the faeries are getting many souls now."

"Kate, you must stop this. It's not good for the baby."

"This whole world's not good for my baby!"

"It's just the lateness of the hour, Kate. It must be three or four of the morning."

"The great cost, that's what'll do it," she said. "They'll tire of paying to keep us here and we'll be turned out into the plague."

"I'll crab the man who tries!" Stephen said.

"And how could you stop them? With that little pistol?"

"I'd find a way!"

"Stephen, what if there is no cure?"

"Kate, you're crazed," he said. "No cure? Why . . . why . . ." Stephen broke off, unable to call up a thing terrible enough to put down such a thought.

"They'll not even give me a fine funeral," Kate said. "There're no priests."

"There are priests."

"Then why can't they find one to marry us?"

"They'll find one. You heard Adrian. They're looking for this Father Michael Flannery right this very instant."

"The middle of the night, looking for a priest? They only do that when they need the last rites. And that's what I'll be needing before long."

Stephen remained silent. Kate in this mood daunted him. And her talking of faeries! She was almost a nurse. Faeries! What a nonsense.

"Where's the flying column can free us from this misery?" Kate whispered.

She was thinking about her father, Stephen realized. Flying columns! That had been her father's recurrent plaint, so she'd told him.

"We used to go to the horse fair whenever there was one near enough," Kate said. "Once, we went to the Dublin Horse Show. I was so small he had to hold me up in his arms for me to see. It was so exciting!"

She shouldn't be talking about the Dublin Show, Stephen thought. She knows what happened there after the plague and the quarantine. She'll be on to that next.

"They'll find a cure, Kate," he said. "And we'll be worrying about schools for our children, where best to send them."

"It's only one child in me, Stephen, and too early to be talking of schools."

"They're reconstituting St. Edna's school," he said. "Wouldn't that be grand, a child of ours at . . ."

"They're idiots!" she said, her voice fierce. "As though they could call up the spirit of Patrick Pearse to bless us. Beware when you call up spirits! That's what my grandmother always said."

"It's only a school, Kate."

"What a terrible fantasy to wish upon us!"

"I'll speak to Adrian again about the priest," he said.

"A fat lot of good it'll do. He has us where he wants us. He doesn't care if my soul burns in hell."

"Kate!"

"All that'll be left of me here will be one of those little brass plates on the memorial at Glasnevin—'to the heroines of Ireland, may their memory never die.' Only words, Stephen. Now, turn over and go to sleep."

How like her! he thought. *Fill me full of her fears, full awake, then we're to go to sleep!*

> *Ireland was warped by the Penal Laws. The English forbade us our religion, forbade us any form of education—then dared to call us uneducated! We could not enter a profession, not hold public office, nor engage in trade or commerce. We couldn't live in or within five miles of a corporate town! We couldn't own a horse of greater value than five pounds, couldn't own or lease land, nor vote nor keep arms nor inherit anything from a Protestant! We couldn't harvest from the rack-rented lands any profit exceeding a third of the rent. The law compelled us to attend Protestant worship and forbade the Mass. We paid double to support the militia that suppressed us. And if a Catholic power did harm to the state, we paid for it! You wonder we still hate the British?*

> —Joseph Herity

HERITY AND Liam Cullen stood in a clearing below the sheep-grazed meadowland that fronted Brann McCrae's great house, aware that they were watched by John about a hundred meters above. The two men appeared to be admiring the dusk as it crept down the hills toward the valley and the château. Swallows dived after insects in the orange light above the men. Somewhere off in the trees, a soldier could be heard playing a flute—a thin and haunting sound in the gloaming. The air smelled of pines and trampled grass.

"He's up there watching us right now," Liam said, his voice low.

"I saw him. You've posted good shots along the way?"

"You think I'm foolish enough to tempt fate the way you do?"

"They're to bring him down, not kill him, hear?"

"I'm one who obeys his orders, Joseph." Liam glanced back up at John, then looked at the valley. "Is he the one?"

"Sometimes I think he is and sometimes I'm sure he's not.

They've no help for us Outside, the Panic Fire and all. He could be the one and he couldn't. There's nothing left where he lived, that little town—the wart on a pig's ass, and no one remaining there to tell us."

"What makes you doubt?" Liam asked.

"He sleeps the sleep of the innocent, nary a quiver that I can see and I've watched."

"Then why do you think he may be the Madman?"

"Little things. There's something in his eyes when he looks at all this ruin."

"And you brought him here anyway!"

"I must say I was curious about this place myself." Herity shook his head. "How can you live with it every day?"

"We have our duty and the army obeys orders. We can't have people wandering through, carrying stories about our charges."

"Nary a word from our lips, Liam."

"So you say and you sober. But what about you and the drink in you?"

"Careful with your tongue, Liam. The IRA was the keeper of Irish honor when not even your army would lend a helping hand."

A faint smile touched Liam's lips. "Ahhh, but there's a story going around that it was you blew away O'Neill's family."

"There's lies told about many of us, Liam." Herity glanced at the automatic rifle in Liam's hands and his voice became silky. "Old friend, when we were jumping in the hay as lads, which of us could look to this day?"

"You were always fine with words, Joseph, but all I hear from your lips is that you think the Yank is really our Madman. Why is it . . . *old friend?*"

Herity looked toward the darkness gathering over the valley. Candles could be seen blinking in the château's windows. A cow lowed from somewhere down in the shadows. He spoke in a musing tone:

"That first day together, us tramping along the road, I turned our conversation to the terrorism, as they call it. The Yank said the IRA abandoned Irish honor."

"The very words of the Madman's letters, but everyone knows those words now. I'm not satisfied, Joseph. What do I tell Dublin?"

"Tell them I'm not sure . . . which means he's still the loaded bomb we cannot disrupt."

"You let him carry a pistol," Liam said. "Why?"

"To make him think I trust him."

"But you don't."

"No more than I trust you. Shall we be going along to that little hut with your field telephone?"

"I shouldn't let any of you leave here alive! I've my orders to protect McCrae's secret."

Herity whirled to confront him, face no more than a nose length from Liam. "The Yank is mine! You understand? Not yours to decide about life or death! He's mine!"

"That's what they're saying in Dublin." Liam spoke mildly. He turned then and led the way back up the trail to where John still stood.

John watched the two men approach and was astonished when Liam, without pausing, said: "You're coming with us, Yank."

Unable to hear what the men had said below him, John had filled his mind with conjecture. Herity was his guard, not his guardian, John had decided. He suspects. But what did he suspect?

He fell into step behind the men, wary and fearful. They picked up Father Michael at the guard hut, leaving the boy asleep on a pad in a corner. It was full dark by the time they entered a small wooden hut far down below the playing field beneath the château.

When they entered the hut, a match in Liam's hand scratched and a candle flared, illuminating the interior. It was all unfinished wood, a crude shed roof overhead. Only a single chair and table furnished it, a black field telephone and speaker in a khaki case on the table. A wire trailed from the telephone out under the eaves. There was the sound of footsteps outside and Jock's voice came to them:

"All in place, Liam."

Liam visibly relaxed. He indicated the chair for Father Michael. "I've arranged for McCrae himself to answer. He's anxious to have a theological discussion, so he says."

Father Michael, who had been silent for the whole trip down to the hut, took the telephone and put it to his ear. "Thank you, Liam."

"He'll answer or put a rocket into us right here," Herity muttered. "What could we do?"

"We could let him go hungry when he runs out of food," Liam said. "Now, be still! You've caused enough trouble!"

"Harsh words, harsh words," Herity said.

Once more, Liam ground the crank on the telephone.

"Why have we waited for night?" Father Michael asked.

"It's the way Mister McCrae always does," Liam said. "He likes for us to stumble around in the dark."

"And I'll wager he has a spotter scope with infrared," Herity said.

Silence fell over the room, a strange stillness as though a ghost had entered and put a hush on the life there.

Liam flipped a switch on the side of the khaki case. A soft humming came from the instrument. "We'll listen," he said, "but only the priest will do the talking."

Presently, there was a click from the telephone and a man's deep, carefully modulated voice asked: "Is that the priest?"

Father Michael cleared his throat. "This is Father Michael Flannery." He sounded nervous, John thought.

"And what is it you're wanting, Priest?" McCrae sounded amused, a cultivated, cultured voice being civil to an underling.

Father Michael straightened, pressing the telephone hard against his ear. "I want to know how those young women became pregnant!"

"Ahhh, the ignorance of the Romish priesthood," McCrae said. "Hasn't anyone ever explained to you the functioning of—"

"Don't get smart with me!" Father Michael snapped. "I demand to know if those girls are wed to the fathers of—"

"Keep a civil tongue, Priest, or I'll blow that hut out of this world and you with it."

Father Michael swallowed convulsively, then: "Will you answer my question, Mister McCrae?"

"Well, now, the young women are pregnant because that's the function of priestesses. They lay under the rowan tree at the full of the moon and I impregnated them. The blessing of the sacred rowan upon us all."

Father Michael took several deep breaths, his face pale.

John used the interval to edge his way toward the hut's single door. He hesitated there. Was Jock still outside? What had he meant, all in place? Both Liam and Herity were grinning, their attention on Father Michael.

"The rowan," Father Michael muttered.

"Our ancestors venerated the rowan and they were happier than the ones paying Peter's pence," McCrae said.

"Next you'll be worshiping Mithra or some other heathen statue!" Father Michael accused.

"Careful, Priest," McCrae said. "Mithra was an Iranian god brought along by the Roman legionaries. As a good Gael, I hate all things Roman, including your Roman Church!"

Herity chuckled: "Listen to them arguing like a pair of Jesuits! Oh, you were right, Liam. Rare sport."

John put his hand on the door latch and eased it open a crack. McCrae must be somewhere directly in front of Father Michael. The telephone line trailed out that way.

"Who's that talking there with you?" McCrae demanded.

"It's Joseph Herity," Father Michael said.

"Himself in the flesh? Ahhh, what a rare bag to tempt an old hunter. You've Liam Cullen there with you in the hut and one other. Who is that?"

"His name's John O'Donnell."

Herity suddenly thrust out a hand and covered Father Michael's mouth, shaking his head. The priest looked up at him, startled.

"Were you about to say more, Priest?" McCrae asked.

Herity removed his hand from Father Michael's mouth and waved a cautionary finger.

"We're on our way north to find someplace that'll accept us," Father Michael said, his voice faint. His attention remained on Herity.

"And there's no room at the inn!" McCrae chortled. "Which of you is pregnant?"

"Mister McCrae," Father Michael said, "I'm trying to save your soul from eternal damnation. Can't you—"

"That's not in your power," McCrae said. "We're druids here, worshipers of the tree, innocent as the first babes in the world. You can take your guilty god, you Romish impostor, and shove him where the moon cannot shine."

A burst of raucous laughter erupted from Herity. Liam chuckled.

John opened the door another few millimeters and slipped out into the darkness. The trail by which they had come led off to the right, he knew. He could not see Jock or anyone else but suspected there were other guardians around. Father Michael's voice could be heard from within the hut.

"Mister McCrae, you must put aside your evil ways, admit the error before it's too late! God will forgive—"

"I don't need forgiveness!"

There was madness in that voice, John decided. He crept around the corner of the hut and looked up at the château, a gray blob in the darkness, only two candlelit windows visible now. Bushes brushed his knees. He edged to the left, seeking a way through where noise would not betray him. The voices in the hut had been reduced to a murmur. As his eyes adjusted, he discerned a slope of low gray bushes between him and the château, gray patches on a darker background. Was there a way through? He moved forward, stumbled and would have fallen but for a hand that gripped his arm, dragging him back. John found himself suddenly hurled to the ground. The cold muzzle of a gun pressed against his neck below his right ear.

From the darkness behind the gun, Jock's voice asked: "And where was we goin'?"

John's head whirled with desperate thoughts. The gun pressed painfully against his flesh. His left cheek lay against sharp stickers.

"Answer him, Mister . . . *O'Donnell!*"

That was Herity's voice from farther back in the darkness.

"That crazy McCrae is going to shoot a rocket in here and kill us all," John husked. "You can stand around and wait for it but I . . ."

"McCrae always says that," Jock said, "but he'll not do it unless we try to approach him." The gun muzzle eased its pressure.

Herity cursed under his breath.

Liam's voice could be heard in the hut: "Party's over, Priest. You'll not convince the man."

Father Michael emerged from the hut, herded along by Liam. "God save the man," Father Michael prayed, "and those poor children with him."

"And him speaking of birth and rebirth," Liam taunted. "It has the look of truth under his rowan." He pushed Father Michael completely out of the hut and called to Jock. "Close it down, Jock. I'll douse the candles."

Darkness engulfed them.

Hands hauled John to his feet. He felt his arm released but he sensed others close around.

"Whisht now!" It was Herity close beside John. "Our noses are being ground into the realities, eh?"

"That's a terrible truth you speak." It was Liam just on the other side of John, a dim figure barely seen in the starlight.

"Except for McCrae up there," Liam said, "it's not a one of us can say he'll live in his children. Our descendants are cut off."

"Ahhh, don't say it, Liam." That was Jock speaking from behind John. "Those sweet darlings just up there and us outside never to touch."

"This is what we get for living only with our hatreds," Father Michael muttered. "We must stop the hatreds, Joseph! We must save that sinner up there!"

"It's a good man he is," Herity said.

"Evil!"

"Liam," Herity said, "you and Jock are such great companions. So helpful."

"Our duty is to guard that château," Liam said. "We obey our orders."

John could feel his trembling confusion subside as the others spoke. O'Neill-Within remained quiescent. *I tried,* John thought. People were moving around him. John felt a hand grip his right arm. Herity spoke close to his ear: "Was you really just trying to get away, John?"

"That was a stupid thing to do, putting us all in that hut," John said. "That's a crazy man up there. He could do anything."

"Madmen are like that," Herity said.

Liam spoke from the darkness up ahead. "Come along now. It's back to the cottage for all of us."

"Your duty," Herity jibed.

"That it is." There was relief and laughter in Liam's voice. "We all have our orders, Joseph."

John turned toward Herity beside him. "Who gave you orders to protect me?"

"Aw, it was the rowan tree," Herity said.

> *...reason abuseth me, and there's
> the torment, there's the hell.*
>
> **—Ben Jonson**

"BUT WHY do they call it the Literature of Despair?" the pope asked.

Pope Luke, who had been James Cardinal MacIntyre, sat in a rocking chair at the edge of his dining room with an angular view through the window beside him across Philadelphia's rooftops to the Old Harbor. The city's profile was outlined by the morning sunlight of a cold winter day.

The bathrobe he wore was a dark blue thing he had received as a gift while still a priest. It gapped over his mature bulk. Old brown house slippers encased his feet. His exposed shanks looked fleshy and faintly blue.

The pope, several observers had noted, looked remarkably like an opossum—that sloped-back forehead accented by baldness, the eyes that managed to appear both dull and intent at the same time. *Concentrated,* that was what one commentator had called the pope's eyes. They were the eyes of a dull animal seeking only after its dinner.

Pope Luke's question had been addressed to Father Lawrence Dement, his secretary, who stood near the sideboard where breakfast had been laid out. The pope had eaten sparingly but Father Dement, who never seemed to gain an ounce, had piled his plate high with bacon, four eggs, toast and marmalade, fried potatoes and a small steak.

"The Literature of Despair," Father Dement said. "That's just the Irish way."

He crossed to the table where he put down his plate and pulled out a chair facing the pope. "Is there any coffee?"

"We've run out again. There's tea in that silver urn."

Father Dement, who still looked like a graduate student at thirty-five, his blue eyes sharply aware, the little curl of black hair over his forehead, the wide mouth always ready to smile, Father Dement returned to the sideboard as though he had not a care in this world and poured himself a cup of steaming tea.

"Literature of Despair," the pope muttered.

Father Dement put the teacup on the table beside his plate and sat down to eat his breakfast. The pope's secretary, who had been one of the first to note the man's resemblance to an opossum, wondered: *What is it that has him focused on the new Irish literature?*

The bacon was undercooked as usual, Father Dement noted. He scowled and ate it anyway. There might be no opportunity for lunch. Despite the pope's bulk and that food-searching look in his eyes, the man seemed to exist on a minimal intake. Some wondered if the pope ate secretly in his room.

Pope Luke's attention that morning had been focused by a report on the restoration of two Irish abbeys, occupied now by lay brothers who devoted themselves to producing illuminated manuscripts in the ancient fashion, on vellum and magnificent handmade linen paper. Thus far, no examples of this work had been seen outside Ireland, and the verbal content was known only sketchily. Reports had concentrated on "the artistic quality" and the label being applied to such works: "The Literature of Despair."

"A renaissance of language," one report had called these works, quoting one short passage:

"We have all three martyrdoms in generous proportions: the Green, the White and the Red. The Green, that's the hermit's life and the solitary contemplation of God. The White is separation from family, from friends and from home because there can be no family nor home without a wife. And what is friendship if it does not grow from the most intimate of all sharings? And the Red martyrdom, that is the oldest of them

all: the giving of your life for the Faith."

Father Dement thought privately that Ireland had always fallen back on words when all else failed.

The pope's thoughts were more political, this being the native ground he understood best and the thing that he knew had worked most strongly to elevate him to his present eminence.

That and God's Grace, of course.

It was a gift. He felt that he had been elevated as the Church's most jealous guardian against schism. There were too many people in this world ready to sink into themselves, looking for mystic answers that the Church did not welcome. Holy Mother Church, the One and the Only, that was it. Mother Church. Pope Luke knew the problem this appellation raised in his plague-stricken world. When there were no women around, the title, Father, could take on cynical overtones. How could there be a Mother Church without Fathers? It aroused jealousies all dark and twisting in bereaved people. Pope Luke knew about the questionings.

"Tell me, Priest, how can you have a mother when I have none? How can you be called Father when I'll never have that holy privilege?"

And there were always those who demanded: "Where were you, Priest, when the blow fell? Where was your God when this thing happened? Answer me that, if you're able!"

Were these new abbeys in Ireland part of the new mysticism, spurred on by such questions?

Pope Luke was particularly disturbed by another passage from this new literature quoted by a commentator:

"Our young idealists lived too long in the rat-holes of conspiracy. They came to think of this as their natural habitat and they resisted anything that might bring them out of such an environment. But God has shown us the way out. Why will we not take it?"

What way? the pope wondered. The commentator had not said and the papal queries to Ireland were not being answered.

The pope arose presently and went down the hall to his bedroom where his robes had been laid out. He could hear the stirrings beyond his private quarters, all the trappings of the papacy being readied for another busy day. He longed for simpler times and often felt an active reluctance to leave a solitary station. Father Dement he tolerated because messages needed to be sent, words recorded and transmitted.

For his part, Father Dement dawdled over a fourth slice of toast generously spread with marmalade. The Philadelphia papacy's ovens produced a quite satisfactory loaf, he thought. And there was no point in rushing through breakfast, no need to hurry after the pope and help him. This pope did things for himself, preferred it that way. His confessor complained that the pope rushed too swiftly through the holy necessities.

Why had the pope questioned the name given by the Irish to their illuminated manuscripts? After all of these months with Pope Luke, Father Dement found he still could be surprised by the man's vagaries and twists of thought. Perhaps it had something to do with the ceremonies planned for this morning here in Philadelphia.

"We must find our happiness in God."

Those were the pope's words. Literature of Despair, that did cast a pall over things. But it need not enter this day's activities.

In spite of every effort to stop him, the pope was moving ahead with steady determination toward the goal of the Philadelphia Pilgrimage. Some of the new cardinals, especially Cardinal Shaw, had raised objections, siding dangerously with President Velcourt and other leaders who pointed out the problems raised by the plague. Not only were large movements of people, many of them probably infected, frowned upon by governments, but isolated populations tended to react with independent violence against strangers and others trying to enter or pass through sanctuary regions.

Pope Luke remained adamant. Father Dement shook his head to correct himself. No, it was more a quiet persistence than anything else. It was as though God had spoken to him directly and the pope moved in the sureness of such support. That was, of course, a thing internal to the papacy. Father Dement knew that the old belief could not be denied. He shared that belief himself. A pope consecrated moved thereafter within the special aura of God's concern. The unbroken line of holy succession—Christ to Peter to Pope Luke—carried an intrinsic promise of divine power and love. These very rooms here in Philadelphia, once part of the Church's regional government, possessed now that sense of divine power which the pope's presence assured.

Father Dement sopped up the last of his egg with a final bite of toast, drained his teacup and pushed himself away from the table, sighing. An acolyte housekeeper, his face properly subdued in holy awe, stepped from a doorway's shadows where he had been hovering, glided forward and removed the dishes. Father Dement scowled. The young man was efficient, but it was not the same as the old days, not the same at all.

This pope refused to have female help in the Holy See, however. Were it not the pope himself evincing this behavior, Father Dement would have diagnosed it as pathological. Father Dement shuddered at the thought of the trouble he knew was coming. The pope had yet to say publicly what he said privately, but that could only be a matter of time, perhaps at the culmination of the first Pilgrimage . . . if that Pilgrimage were allowed to occur.

"God has visited His judgment upon women for a divine purpose. The sin of women has been held up to our view. We have been told clearly to remove that sin."

Father Dement stood and squared his shoulders. The Red Martyrdom, as the Irish called it—that had always been an ultimate demand that the Church could make upon its people. Father Dement felt, though, that Pope Luke was inviting it. He was profoundly hostile to sexual union and no escaping that. He was antifemale. Father Dement dared to think it. The pope was listening too much to Father Malcolm Andrews, a Protestant minister who had joined the Church and risen to High Council.

Moving to the window where Pope Luke had sat, Father Dement looked out over the city. He sensed a pattern beginning to emerge—the Literature of Despair . . . the Irish trying to rebuild their old ways . . . Father Andrews and the antifemale movement gathering momentum around the pope . . .

Only yesterday, Father Andrews had said: "The poets once said we lived, loved and went to the grave in the sureness of posterity. That has been taken from us. One mortal blow and we are bereft, our descendants cut off. Mankind lives now in the immediate presence of the grave. No one can deny the message of this event."

And Pope Luke had nodded agreement.

Father Dement could hear the household gathering, the councillors, the cardinals, attendants. This day was about to have its official beginning. Sometime today, the pope would enter his private chapel and there pray for divine guidance. Only a handful of those around the pope, Father Dement among them, knew the nature of the crisis for which the pope would seek divine guidance. The argument between Pope Luke and

President Velcourt had been going on for some time now but last night's call from Huls Anders Bergen, secretary-general of the United Nations, had raised the issue to a new intensity. Father Dement, as usual, had listened on an extension telephone, making notes for Pope Luke's later review.

"I do not believe Your Holiness understands what the President is prepared to do should you defy him," Bergen had said.

Pope Luke had replied in a mild voice: "One does not defy God."

"Your Holiness, President Velcourt does not view the issue in quite that light. The President, with the backing of other world leaders, makes a distinction between the political papacy and the religious papacy."

"There can be no such distinction, sir!"

"I fear, Your Holiness, that in this new political climate there can be and there is such a distinction. The President's viewpoint, unfortunately, is the popular one. He has the political backing to take violent action should he so choose."

"What violent action?"

"I hesitate to . . ."

"Don't hesitate, sir! Has he intimated what he might do?"

"Not specifically, Your Holiness."

"But you suspect something."

"I'm afraid I do."

"Out with it, sir!"

While he made his notes, Father Dement thought he had never heard such firmness and purposeful command in the pope's voice. Father Dement had never been more proud of Pope Luke than in that moment.

"Your Holiness," Bergen said, "it is quite possible that the President will order a missile dropped on you."

Father Dement gasped. His hand slipped down the pen, creating a scrawl on his note pad. He recovered quickly and made sure he had the words correctly. This would take close review.

"He has said this?" the pope asked.

"Not in so many words, but . . ."

"But you have no doubt he might react that way?"

"It is one of his options, Your Holiness."

"Why?"

"There is rising clamor against your Pilgrimage, Your Holiness. People fear it. The President will react politically if you force his hand."

"A missile is a political reaction?"

Father Dement thought this response by the pope rather uninformed, but perhaps it was only the famous "Holy Naivete."

"President Velcourt is being petitioned to stop you, Your Holiness," Bergen said. "It has been suggested that the Philadelphia Military Command move in and make you a prisoner."

"My Guard would not permit that, sir."

"Your Holiness, let us be realistic. Your Guard could not hold out for five minutes."

"The Church has never been stronger than it is today! People would protest."

"The mood in Philadelphia, Your Holiness, is not universally shared. That is what makes a missile solution so likely, in my view. There is a finality about it against which there could be no argument."

"Did the President ask you to call me, sir?"

"He asked me to reason with you, Your Holiness."

"You are deeply concerned?"

"I confess that I am. Although I do not share your religion, you are a fellow human being and every one of these is precious to me."

Father Dement thought he heard true sincerity in the secretary-general's voice. Apparently the pope heard this, too, because there was real emotion in his reply.

"I shall pray for you, Mister Bergen."

"Thank you, Your Holiness. And what may I tell President Velcourt . . . and the others concerned?"

"You may tell them that I will pray for divine guidance."

God of mercy! God of peace!
Make this mad confusion cease!

—Dr. William Drennan,
"The Wake of William Orr"

IT WAS dusk outside the White House, that strange Washington dusk which lingered and lingered, blending finally into the brilliant lights of the Capitol's night.

President Velcourt, looking out at the dusk and the lights coming on, thought he had never before been this tired. He wondered if he had the energy to get up from his chair and go to the cot he'd had moved here into the Oval Office. But he knew if he once put his head on the pillow, necessities would flood his mind. Sleep would not come—only the fatigue and the heart-draining need for action.

What a day this had been!

It had started with Turkwood storming into the office, his expression black, to slide the morning report onto the President's desk. Sometimes, Velcourt wondered at the advisability of inheriting Turkwood from Prescott. There were occasions when you needed someone who would do the dirty work, but Turkwood seemed tainted, perhaps untrustworthy.

As Turkwood had started to leave, Velcourt had asked: "What's wrong with you?"

315

"I just had to fire someone in communications." Again, Turkwood moved to leave.

"Wait a minute. Why did you fire someone?"

"It's not your problem, sir."

"Everything here's my problem. Why'd you fire this person?"

"He was using the White House channels to talk to friends in the Mendocino Reserve."

"How the devil could he do that?"

"He got at the satellite code somehow and was just . . . well, rerouting to his friends."

"I thought that was impossible."

"Apparently not. We're questioning him right now to find out how he did it. He says he just worked it out."

"What's his name, Charlie?"

Velcourt felt his pulse quickening. A resourceful and independent mind right here in the White House.

"His name? It's ahhh, David Archer."

"Get him in here, Charlie! I want him here sooner than instanter."

Turkwood knew that tone. He ran out of the office.

David Archer was a pale young man with acne-scarred features and a hunted expression. His movement into Velcourt's office could only be described as slinking. Turkwood, wearing a grim expression, was right behind him.

Velcourt put on his most affable expression, his warmest tone of voice. "Sit down, David. Is that what they call you? David?"

"They . . . they call me DA, sir." He sat facing Velcourt.

"DA, is it?" Velcourt looked up at Turkwood. "You can leave us alone, Charlie. DA looks harmless to me."

Turkwood left, but there was reluctance in every movement. He spoke from the doorway before closing the door. "You have that nine-fifteen appointment, sir. The phone conference."

"I'll be right here, Charlie."

He waited for the door to close, then: "They've been pretty rough on you this morning, eh, DA?"

"Well . . . it was a stupid thing for me to do, sir." David Archer sounded brighter once Turkwood was gone.

"Do you want to tell me how you got access to the satellite code, DA?"

Archer looked at the floor and remained silent.

"Before you tell me, DA," Velcourt said, "I want you to know that you're back on my staff and I have a promotion in mind for you."

Archer lifted his chin and looked at Velcourt with an expression of incredulous hope.

His voice warm, Velcourt asked: "How'd you do it?"

"It was fairly simple, sir." Archer took on an eager expression as he warmed to his explanation. "I could see by the transmittals that it was ninety numbers and a random scrambler. I just programmed a random hunt with a confirming feedback. At off-hours I had the random hunt poking at the satellite channels. It only took about a month."

Velcourt stared back at the younger man. "You cracked it in a month?"

"My program was self-correcting, sir."

"What's that mean?"

"It seeks out its own internal channels to make the job easier. I made a ripple response confirming each correct bit in the code series and the program just made notes, ninety numbers at a time. Our system's fast, sir. I checked about a million different series every minute."

Velcourt felt that he had just heard something profoundly important but he couldn't put his finger on it. "They told me that code was unbreakable, DA."

"No code's unbreakable, sir." He gulped. "And you know there are other people sending private messages. I thought it would be all right. I wasn't using the channels when there was official traffic."

"What other people?"

"Well, Doctor Ruckerman, for one. He talks to somebody named Beckett at Huddersfield."

"Oh, that's official. Ruckerman's on Saddler's staff—science advisors."

"But he doesn't log them, sir."

"Probably too busy. Who else uses the system for personal communications?"

"I don't want to rat on people, sir."

"I sympathize. But you don't think you just ratted on Ruckerman, do you?"

"Well, he is calling Huddersfield."

"Right! The rest of the calls are probably just as innocuous. I'd like to know who they are, though."

"Mister Turkwood, sir. And Ruckerman calls his family out in the Sonoma Reserve. It's always things like that, sir—people calling family or friends."

"I'm sure you're right. I'd like you to make me a list of the names, though, and leave it with my secretary. Sign it with your new title: director of White House communications."

Archer had the good sense to know when he had been dismissed. There was a wide grin on his face as he stood. "Director of White House communications, sir?"

"That's right. And your job's a tough one. You are to make sure that when I send out a field order, it goes to the proper person, that it's confirmed, and that action is taken according to my order."

Velcourt recalled that conversation with pleasure as he looked out at the gathering dusk. It was one of the few pleasures in an otherwise unpleasant day. Even as he sat here staring with bloodshot eyes out the window, he knew Soviet bombers were diving once more across Istanbul. Satellite observation had detected a vehicle moving near the Stamboul end of the shattered Galata Bridge—whether shifted by some natural cause or driven by human hands the satellite could not determine. So the rubble would be stirred once more, the Golden Horn rocked by tactical nukes, with Beyoğlu and Osküdar getting an additional burning to make sure.

How long has it been since I slept, really slept? Velcourt wondered. He could understand how this office had killed Prescott so quickly.

After Archer, there had been the phone conference with the Russians, the French and the Chinese, then the briefing by Ruckerman and Saddler. Ruckerman had passed off the unlogged calls with a wave of the hand. Too damned much red tape! Velcourt had liked this response, but his mind still whirled with the briefing.

What the hell did Ruckerman mean when he said O'Neill must have found a way to produce Poly G in quantity? What the hell was Poly G? Their explanations had only clouded his mind.

And Saddler sitting there, shaking his head and saying that, given other circumstances, O'Neill surely would have qualified for a Nobel!

Sweet Jesus! A molecular biologist goes mad and sets the world on its ear.

Saddler and Ruckerman had sat right here in this office

arguing, Saddler demanding: "And where would he get the natural DNA to induce polymerization?"

"Obviously, he found a way!"

What the hell had that meant?

"Then how did he make his DNA biologically active?" Saddler had asked.

Velcourt had a memory that could replay such conversations word for word, but replay did not clarify what he had heard.

"Remember he was a pharmacist also," Ruckerman had said.

Pharmacist. Velcourt knew what that was. He cursed the fact that he had not seen fit to take more science courses in the university. Gobbledygook!

"It's fantastic!" Saddler had said. "This man was capable of dealing with polymers at the most delicate level."

"And don't forget," Ruckerman had admonished, "he found the placement sites, controlling the precise order in which the monomers were arranged. And we're talking about giant molecules."

"Listen," Saddler had said, "we have to find that man and keep him alive. God! The information in his head!"

Considering the provocation, Velcourt thought his interruption mild. "Would you two gentlemen mind including me in your discussion? You're supposed to be briefing the President."

"Sorry, sir," Saddler said. "But both of us are more than a little awed by how O'Neill obviously handled the peptide-bond formations in—"

"What in the hell is a peptide bond?"

Saddler looked at Ruckerman, who said: "It's a basic linkage in the DNA helix, Mister President. It proceeds much like a zipper, starting with amino acid valine at one end of the chain, closing bond after bond until the protein molecule is completed."

"I understand about one fourth of what you just said," Velcourt said. "Which means I don't understand a damn thing!"

They heard the frustration and anger in his voice.

Ruckerman frowned. "Sir, O'Neill tailored a special virus, perhaps more than one."

"Certainly more than one!" Saddler said.

"Most likely," Ruckerman agreed. "He created it to infect certain bacteria. When a bacterial virus infects bacteria, an RNA is formed that resembles the virus DNA and not that of the host. The sequence of the nucleotides in the new DNA molecule is complementary to that of the DNA in the virus."

Saddler, seeing the angry glint in Velcourt's eyes, held up a hand. "Sir, O'Neill identified the genetic message in humans that directs that the fetus will become a female. He formed a disease that bonds itself to that message."

That, Velcourt understood. He nodded.

"Huddersfield confirms that there are no asymptomatic carriers of this plague," Ruckerman added.

"It infects men and doesn't kill them, is that what you mean?"

"Yes sir."

"Then why the hell didn't you say so?" Velcourt drew in a deep breath to calm himself. Damn these bastards with their gobbledygook! "What're the symptoms in men?" he asked.

"We're not sure yet, sir," Saddler said. "Perhaps no worse than a bad cold." He emitted a nervous laugh.

"I don't think this is a subject for humor," Velcourt said.

"No, sir! No, sir, it isn't."

Ruckerman said: "The disease either masks or changes that sex-differentiation pattern in a lethal manner."

"How could he know it'd do that?" Velcourt asked.

"We don't know how he tested it. We don't know a great many things about it, but we're beginning to define a pattern," Ruckerman said.

"What pattern and how does it work?"

"I'm talking about the pattern of O'Neill's research, sir," Ruckerman said. "We know something about his original laboratory . . . before he went to Seattle. There were friends who visited him there. We know he had a computer."

"His chemical techniques must've been virtually flawless," Saddler said. "For example, he would've had to use bacterial enzymes derived we know not how, but we are forced to keep reminding ourselves that he had been at his DNA researches for about five years preceding the tragedy in Ireland."

Velcourt looked from one man to the other. "What kind of rotten fate would put such a unique man in the path of that kind of motivation?"

"The Bechtel people have run an analysis," Saddler said. "They say it was bound to happen sometime—sooner or later. O'Neill wasn't all that unique."

Velcourt was aghast. "You mean anyone could have done this terrible thing?"

"Not just anyone," Ruckerman said. "But a growing number

of people. The increasing spread of knowledge about how it was done, that and the simplification of techniques plus the availability of sophisticated equipment to anyone with the money . . ." He shrugged. "Inevitable, given the kind of world we live in."

"Inevitable?"

Ruckerman said: "Consider his original laboratory, especially that computer. He must've stored chemical fractions for later use. Any good lab would. And he'd use his computer for cataloguing and analysis. No doubt of it."

"He had no difficulty getting antibiotics, of course," Saddler said. "He took them off his own shelves when he sold the pharmacy."

"The antibiotics to which his plague is immune," Velcourt said. That part he remembered from earlier briefings when Prescott was still alive.

"Analysis of the equipment he is known to have used," Ruckerman said, "tells us he employed a delicate play of chemical kinetics to achieve his results."

"There you go again!" Velcourt snapped.

"Sir," Ruckerman said, "he used temperature control and enzyme cutting techniques at various stages, heat as a driving energy or lack of it as a brake."

"He used X-ray, temperature and chemical processes," Saddler said.

"We have a list of the publications to which he subscribed," Ruckerman said. "It's clear he was very familiar with the work of Kendrew and Perutz. He wrote notes in the margin of one publication on the enzymic dissecting techniques of Bergman and Fruton."

Velcourt recognized none of these names, but he heard the awe in Ruckerman's voice. There was also something on which a politician could focus.

"You have a publication that he used?"

"Just one. He had loaned it to a student and the student forgot to return it."

"This O'Neill sounds like a complete laboratory team all in one man," Velcourt said.

"He was multi-talented, no doubt of that," Saddler agreed. "Had to be to crack that code all by himself."

Ruckerman said: "The psychological profile suggests that some of his talents may have lain dormant until released by the driving passion ignited when his family was killed."

Saddler said: "Milton Dressler is now insisting that O'Neill was at least a latent schizoid and was driven into this genius mode by access to a different personality that lay dormant until that bombing in Ireland."

Velcourt had heard of Dressler—the psychoanalyst in charge of the Profile Team. The President said: "He went nuts, and the nut was the one who was capable of doing this."

"In a nutshell," Saddler said.

All three of them joined in a nervous laugh. Saddler and the President stared at each other afterward, abashed.

Velcourt had little time to review the briefing after the men left. Something they said, though, nagged at him. Something about breaking a code.

As the day's fatigue threatened to overwhelm him, he tried to recapture that elusive something. It was full dark outside by now and the lights of the Capitol bright against a cloudy sky.

I'll think about it tomorrow, he thought.

*Do not cry that I have been unfair,
you Irish and English and Libyans.
You chose your leaders or tolerated
them. The consequences were pre-
dictable. You pay now for the failure
of reason. You Irish, at least, should
have known better. Like a one-crop
society, you staked your survival on
violence. Is the lesson of the potato
blight grown so dim? As you sow, so
shall you reap.*

—John Roe O'Neill, Letter Three

It no longer bothered John that he was forced to leave the
vicinity of McCrae's château without spreading the plague there.
He knew now that he was being saved for more important
things at the Killaloe Lab. Nemesis remained true. Jock had
saved him from a terrible error. Herity was confused. Had John
merely been stumbling about blindly in the dark outside the
telephone hut?

By his intervention, Jock had also revealed Herity's purpose. Herity was looking for O'Neill.

This amused John. With Herity nearby, O'Neill-Within would
never reveal himself. John Roe O'Neill lay subdued, blocked
by a fear-anesthesia. The nightmare screams were temporarily
walled off. John O'Donnell could stride along with his three
companions, swinging his arms freely. He felt liberated.

Jock Cullen and four armed soldiers escorted them two miles
down the hill away from the château before returning their
weapons. Herity checked his machine gun carefully, then looped
its supporting strap around his neck. John merely slipped the
pistol and ammunition into a hip pocket and pulled the yellow
sweater over it.

323

They parted at a crossroads where a signpost still pointed the way to Dublin. Jock gestured to the sign with the rifle: "You know the way. Don't come back."

The consequences of disobedience did not have to be spoken. The escort turned and marched back up the hill, leaving John and his companions in the stone-bordered roadway. There were tall pines all around, but meadows could be glimpsed ahead where the road led down off the ridges.

John glanced at Herity. The man was like that Japanese toy, the little dumpling doll with weights glued into its rolling bottom: six times down, seven times up. He would always return to the upright position. John felt amused by the idea of Herity returning to a standing position though dead. Something bitterly tenacious in him. Dangerous. He might be confused, but he would not stop hunting.

"Let's be going!" Herity said. He waved them ahead and aimed a kick at the boy, which the boy dodged.

In that instant, John recognized the source of Herity's irritation with the boy. Here was a young lad's flesh, the shape and form that Herity could identify, but without animation except for that slumbering rage. The flesh was clumsy, like a mechanical toy left to run down and with its spring now almost unwound.

"Do something definite!" Herity was saying.

That was why Herity's anger had been subdued by the boy's attack at the wash house. Something definite.

Within a mile, they came to a Y-branch in the road, no signpost here. Herity took the right-hand way, but Father Michael stopped, the boy with him.

"Now just a minute, Joseph. That's the long way by a good many miles."

Herity didn't even pause. "We've been ordered to deviate via Dublin."

Father Michael hurried to catch up, but the boy lagged behind with John.

"Why?" Father Michael demanded. "Who said?"

"Jock said. Orders from Dublin."

Father Michael glanced back at John, then at Herity. "But . . ."

"Be still, you crazy priest!" There was frustration in Herity's voice. He quickened his pace, forcing Father Michael almost to trot. Their footsteps sounded muffled on the paving, enclosed by the border of thick trees and rock walls. John sensed a new tension in Herity's manner—quick glances left and right, the machine gun held ready in his hands.

Father Michael hitched his pack higher and fell back slightly. Herity eased his long strides, peering up and around.

John looked up through the trees: a peculiar light in the morning sky, as though everything came through a gray filter. Distances were muzzy in diffusion, everything caught up in a sea-driven mist from the east. The sky directly overhead spread out a dark silver shaded into lighter steel eastward.

Breakfast lay heavy in John's stomach—fresh beef and boiled nettles with potatoes. The château's guardians had set aside for their mess a small stone cottage of what had obviously been a substantial farmstead on a ledge cut off from McCrae's establishment by a long, slanting ridge. The cottage's interior walls had been crudely knocked out, opening space for a long table and rude benches. The food, cooked on a turf fire, had been served just after dawn, only John's group and the escort at table.

Herity had arrived last with Jock beside him, the younger Cullen uneasy and trying to avoid conversation. But Herity had been full of questions.

John had eaten quietly, listening. There were things to be learned here. Liam had been called away by his command duties. The other guardians already were posted for their day duty around the château.

The other soldiers at the table, sensing something different in Jock's manner, kept a quiet watch. Slowly, tensions began to mount in the stone-walled cottage.

Father Michael broke the silence: "God is putting us through a sore test."

The words sounded forced, leaving an even more intense silence behind them.

"Sure, Father, and which plague did you have in mind?" Herity asked. "Was it the plague of the papacy now?" He spoke with unswerving arrogance.

"What's the use of blame?" Father Michael asked.

"Him asking such a question!" Herity laughed.

"We've much to answer for," Father Michael said. "The British planted a bad seed amongst us, but I ask you now, where was that seed nurtured? Was it not ourselves seeing the fruit and plucking it from the branches?"

"Eve's apple it is!" Herity said.

"Only we called it the Provos of the IRA," Jock said. "A beautiful red apple with a bomb in it."

Herity's jaw clamped tight. A flush spread over his face. He put both hands on the table. Violence wavered in the air.

"Have done!" Father Michael said. "Are we not all paying the piper now?"

"Let us pay him then and have our little dance," Jock said. "Will y' dance wi' me, Joseph?"

"Enough!" Father Michael thundered. "I'll curse the first. one of you taking to violence!"

Jock swallowed convulsively, then in a low voice: "Mayhap you're right, Father. Best it were over and the world going on without such mischief."

Herity glowered at the priest. "I don't fear your curses, Michael Flannery. But I'll honor the truth in young Jock. He sees the way of things."

Father Michael sighed. "Joseph, you were a God-fearing man once. Will you never come back to the Church?"

Herity stared into his cold stew, oddly subdued by the sudden quenching of Jock's fire. "I've lost me faith and that's what huddles me, true enough."

"Then why . . ."

"Shut your fool mouth, priest! I've no more respect for clerics, not after Maynooth. I'd sooner melt their bells for drinking mugs than spend another minute in one of your churches!" He pointed a death's-head grin at Father Michael. "And if y' call that blasphemy, I'll tip y' into the first well we find."

Jock had led them down through the fields away from the château, dew drenching their pants. They could see the paved road ahead, a farm lane entering it. There was one last glimpse of the château as the party rounded the barrier ridge. It was a gray castle wall nestled in the trees. Faintly, they heard the sound of children shouting.

Jock looked over his shoulder at the distant sound, pausing by a stile while the others climbed over onto the farm lane. As John passed, Jock looked at him. "It was mostly the girls learned the Irish dances," he said. "They do their dances of a morning up there." He pointed toward the château with his chin. "If we lose those girls, we've lost it all—all of those beautiful dances. I think I can forgive McCrae anything if we don't lose that."

After Jock left them, John's thoughts kept returning to those words—the half-hopeful sadness in them.

Herity continued to march along at the point, an advance

scout with his machine gun at the ready. Father Michael trailed behind him. John and the boy kept pace at the rear.

The road made a sharp left turn up ahead out of the flanking trees. Straight ahead beyond the turn, grass tufted around a jutting mound of pale granite. Herity stopped, motioning the others to stop behind him. John looked past Herity, wondering what had spooked him. All he could see was two sheep on a grassy shelf below the rocks. The sheep stared up at them full of alarm.

"It's only some sheep," Father Michael said.

Herity waved a hand for silence. He studied their surroundings, the mounded hillocks below the outcropping, the empty valley beyond—a narrow place with a boggy stream down its middle.

"It's a wonder it is that you're not dead long ago, Michael Flannery," Herity said. "Whatever it is bothers those sheep should bother us."

"And what might be bothering them?" the priest asked.

"I wonder where Liam went this morning?" Herity asked. "Let us be goin' back a ways, and silent as the tomb about it."

Herity backed up the road, keeping his attention on the rock and the sheep. John turned and walked beside him, glancing backward occasionally. Father Michael and the boy went on ahead, not looking back at Herity.

"What is it?" John asked. He felt for the pistol in his hip pocket, but thought better of it and removed his hand empty.

"It's only men that's hunting the sheep for their meat nowadays," Herity said. "Something frightened those creatures before we came along."

"Probably just some of Liam's soldiers out foraging," John said.

"Foraging for what?" Herity asked.

Father Michael stopped ahead of them and turned. "Something passed between you and Liam Cullen," he said. "What was it?"

"Dublin gave him his orders to let us go safely on our way," Herity said, glancing once sidelong at John. "It wouldn't be like Liam to disobey such orders where there's others to see and inform."

"You're not serious!" Father Michael protested.

"Liam and me was wains together," Herity said. "I knew the child and I know the man. Who's to question if he does a bit of foraging here in this valley? Answer me that, Priest!"

They had stopped at a place where rocks had been tumbled from the top of the road's bordering wall on the valley side. Herity crossed to this place and peered over the wall into the trees. "A trail of sorts," he said. "I think we'll be going down this way."

Father Michael joined him. "You call that a trail?"

"It has great advantage for us," Herity said. "You can see by the marks on it that no one's passed that way today."

The priest shook his head. "I can't believe that Liam Cullen would shoot all . . ."

"Leave off, will you now! Liam's a soldier. Why is it, y' think, t' valley back yonder has no folk in it? Run off or killed by Liam and his boys. And in this valley, too. I know the inside of Liam's head. There's no stories to be carried if there's no one to carry 'em."

"But we knew about . . ."

"Knew? Rumors and little bird droppings from them as hears the Council's deliberations. We knew nothing!"

Herity lifted a foot over the wall and hopped across. Father Michael joined him. John and the boy followed. The trail was a dark hole down through mixed evergreens, the ground pocked by sheep hooves, but no sign of a human footprint. Tufts of wool clung to the low branches like the markers of a paper chase. The way was steep with exposed roots.

With Herity leading, they slid and clambered down, grasping limbs to slow their descent, clinging to roots in the steeper parts. The trail emerged from the trees onto a grassy ledge with man-made steps of rock down to a sloping meadow. A stone cottage with only half a roof sat in tall grass about fifty meters into the meadow. Beyond it, a series of rock-shelved terraces curved away to the right through closely bordering trees. A sunken, weed-filled wagon track ran along the terraces at the bottom. It led at an angle, left to right, through two gates that had been left standing open.

John brushed needles and dirt off him while he looked at the scene. It was like a still life, title: Dreams Abandoned.

"There's something you never saw in the Irish countryside," Father Michael said, his voice low. "Gates left open."

"Hush now!" Herity whispered. He moved down through the meadow to the house, drifting through the tall grass like a deer stalker.

John followed and heard the priest and the boy swishing through the grass behind him.

Herity headed for the first open gate into the wagon track. They passed the ashes of what probably had been a small byre with a pile of manure beside it. Grass grew thick on the manure and bushy weeds already were sprouting in the burned area. The wagon track sloped up to the right along the rock walls of the terraces, which stepped down from twice a man's height to only waist height about two hundred meters ahead. As they passed the second terraced step, the view was opened across stone-walled meadows and the road they had abandoned, then up the far side of the road to a castle ruin on the opposite ridge less than a mile away.

Herity stopped. "Ahhhhh," he said.

John stopped beside him. There was no sound of the priest and boy behind him. All were looking at the castle. It stood in a haze of trees and bushes with only the crenellated battlements fully exposed. Behind the screening growth, splotches of color could be glimpsed on the walls. Ruined turrets and buttresses stood out against the morning sky like illustrations in a tourist brochure. John found himself thinking how sure it was that castles, even ruined ones, transformed a skyline into something cruel—as though fangs had been exposed.

"I'll have the binoculars," Herity said, his voice hushed. He reached back toward Father Michael while keeping his attention on the castle.

Father Michael pressed the binoculars into Herity's outstretched hand. "What is it?"

Herity did not answer. He focused on the castle, sweeping his attention across it, then stopping. "Well, now," he whispered. "Slowly, all of you, back up into the shelter of the wall."

"What is it?" Father Michael insisted.

"Do as I say!"

Keeping his attention on the castle, Herity pressed them back up the wagon track until the terrace wall concealed them. He lowered the glasses then and smiled at Father Michael.

"It's Liam yonder with the mate to my little beauty." He patted the machine gun on its sling against his chest. "Now, I ask you, why would Liam Cullen be looking along that road with such a weapon in his hands? Ahhh, that sneaky man."

"What do you intend?" Father Michael asked.

"Well now, as to that—since he hasn't seen us, him being too intent on the road where he expects us to appear, I think I'll be coming up behind Liam to ask what he's doing there

away from his post at Mister McCrae's fine house." Herity
cleared his throat and spat on the ground. "Discouraging, it is.
I expected a better quality of soldiering from Liam."

"I'll go with you," Father Michael said.

"You'll wait here," Herity said. "You'll wait as a corpse or
as a living man able to guide Mister John O'Donnell into Dublin
should anything harmful happen to me."

Father Michael started to protest but stopped when Herity
produced a long knife from his boot. "And should I be forced
to silence you, Michael Flannery, I'll have to treat the boy the
same, him being without a protector then."

Father Michael stared wide-eyed at Herity. "I believe you'd
do it!"

"Ahhh, it's wisdom you're getting at last. Now, you'll wait
here where you cannot be seen." He looked at John. "Attend
to it, if you please, John."

Herity crouched, turned and scuttled along the low notch
of the terrace, straightening only when the wagon track dipped
far enough to conceal him from the castle.

"A terrible man," Father Michael whispered. "Sometimes
I think he's the devil incarnate." He looked at John. "Would
he really have . . ." The priest broke off and shook his head.
"I think he would."

"He's capable of it," John agreed and wondered why he
found this thought pleasing.

"Capable, yes. A fine word. And I keep forgetting that it's
you who're the important one here, John O'Donnell. You must
be brought safely to Killaloe. We must think always of the Lab
and the lives to be saved. But what of their souls? I ask you
that: What of their souls?"

John felt uncomfortable with this question. The priest's
voice—so gentle, but the violence under it. There was that
absolute arrogant certainty once more, the thing cemented in
belief that could not be questioned. How hesitant he sounded,
though, as though these words were spoken only out of a
remembered role.

"Then why are we going to Dublin?" John asked.

"They've a wireless back there." He nodded in the direction
of McCrae's château. "I suppose orders was passed along.
They'll be taking you to Killaloe in a motor car, no doubt."

John felt for his pistol in his pocket but did not withdraw
it. What if it was Liam up there intent on murder? What if

Herity got himself killed? John peered around them: open meadows with only a few stone walls behind which to hide.

"These are hard times," Father Michael sighed. "It's difficult to make decisions."

John looked to his right along the wagon track. Herity no longer could be seen there. *Could I risk looking around the terrace wall at the castle?* But Herity had taken the binoculars.

The boy slid into a sitting position with his back against the wall beside John.

Father Michael spoke in a hushed voice as though he had been carrying on a long conversation with himself and only now decided to share it. "I blame the English, I do. How can we blame the Madman? Poor soul crying out against outrage, and him here on holiday not wanting to hurt even a fly." The priest shook his head. "Why did the English ever come here? What good have they ever done?"

John spoke absently, his mind elsewhere. "They'd say they gave you law and constitutional government." Where was Herity? Should they wait here, exposed like this? Was Liam really up there intent on murder?

"English law!" Father Michael said. "Them speaking of tolerance! When were the English ever tolerant? Look at their bloody riots against the Pakies! They've always been bigots. It's them I blame for all of this."

John spoke dryly, trying to conceal amusement. "You were all forgiveness at breakfast."

"It's a Flannery family failing," Father Michael said. "We're full of the blather before the head's awake." He stared down the track where Herity had gone. "What's keeping the man? He's had time enough."

"Slow and silent," John said, but he felt his own stomach knotting at the question.

"More murder," Father Michael muttered. "I wonder did Joseph bring any of the poteen from Gannon's?"

John merely looked at him.

The priest sighed. "No people ever had better cause for turning to the drink than the Irish." Tears sprang from his eyes and ran down his cheeks. "My own little brother, little Timmy, telling me: 'The bottle is my salvation.' Him speaking the words of Jimmy Joyce: 'Ireland sober is Ireland stiff.' Ahhhh, my blessings on y' anyway, little Timmy."

Another great sigh shook him. He brushed the tears from

his cheeks and looked back the way they had come, his attention on a corner of the ruined cottage, the only part of it visible from this position.

"No one builds," he whispered. "Not anyone. Until the plague, we didn't realize why we built. It was for the children. Without the children there's nothing left of ourselves."

He fell silent, then: "Och! Where is that..."

The peculiar rippling burst of a machine gun sounded across the valley, the sound silencing the priest. John stiffened. Which machine gun? Herity's or Liam's? The boy stirred and looked up at them. John thought he might break his silence but he only wet his lips with his tongue.

Father Michael looked at John. "Was that..."

"It was."

"Which of them?" Father Michael whispered.

John stepped over the seated boy, noting the haunted gaze which followed him. The edge of a terrace wall lay directly in front of John. A weedy vine grew between the stones. Would there be more shooting? He eased his head out of the rocky shelter until one eye could look up at the castle.

"What is it?" Father Michael whispered.

John moved farther out, both eyes looking up at the ruin on the height. Nothing moved there except a gentle breeze stirring the screen of trees and bushes. No birds... nothing. He felt the stillness, a waiting for life to reveal itself. It seemed utter foolishness to be peering around the stone shelter this way.

Father Michael tugged at John's sweater. "What is it?"

"Nothing," John whispered.

"But that was a machine gun."

"It was, but which one of... Wait!"

Something had emerged on the eastern parapet of the castle ruin—a vague movement fuzzed by the intervening growth. Damn Herity for taking the binoculars!

"What do you see?" Father Michael demanded. He started to move around John but John pressed him back.

Something waved from the parapet. John recognized it abruptly—Herity's green jacket whipping back and forth in semaphore and... yes, Herity's straw hair below the arms that held the jacket up like a triumphant banner.

"It's Herity," John said. "He's waving for us to come up."

John stepped out of the concealment and waved his arms. The jacket on the castle described one more arc and was lowered. Father Michael came up beside John.

"What is that strange coloring on the castle's walls?"

"Let's go up and see," John said.

Father Michael hung back, reluctant to move. "It's blood," he said.

"Then you'll be needed," John said.

He led the way down the lane past the second open gate, hearing the priest and boy behind him. The track curved around a wall to another open gate and then up to the paved road. A paved drive directly opposite went up to a low wall below the castle, turning right there and up onto a flat parking area where the burned wreckage of a bus could be seen with one wheel over the wall. The whole vehicle, faded red-and-black, tipped at an impossible angle. Why didn't it fall? John saw it then: The front was wedged against a tree on the parking terrace. The tops of the trees grew tall, rising over a second terrace where the plantings had been allowed to run wild.

Father Michael came panting up beside John, dragging the boy by one hand. "I don't see him. Where's Joseph?"

"He's up there," John said.

He held his silence until they reached the road, where he stopped and looked left and right, then laughed at himself for the habit that had made him do this—as though a car might run him down here!

The drive up to the castle was paved with stones as black as the walls that lined the way. Moss and lichen grew on the stones. Grass straggled from beneath the stones and along the tops of the walls.

Herity's voice called to them from the concealment above. "Up here!"

John led the way across the parking terrace and into what revealed itself as a covered stone passage up to the castle yard. They emerged and saw the castle itself close up without its haze of trees and bushes. Someone had painted the keystones of the window arches in red-orange, the artificial color of plastic, of cheap hair dye.

"There's your blood," John said.

He lifted his gaze to the wall above the windows. The same paint had been used to write a scrawling message across the entire visible stretch of stone wall, crudely spattered letters in a child's block capitals:

"FUCK THE PAST!"

Herity emerged from a postern gate at the base of the wall.

He carried two machine guns now and another pack, military green. Herity stopped when he saw John, the priest and the boy staring at the castle wall above him. Turning, he read the words. A roaring laugh escaped him. "There's the new Irish poetry!" He swiveled on one heel and strode across to John, thrusting the second machine gun into John's hands. "There! Now, we're both properly armed and we may even win through to Dublin." He slipped the new green pack off his arm and pressed it into John. "Liam had the foresight to bring extra clips and plenty of ammo."

"It . . . was Liam?" Father Michael asked.

"Such a grand view from up there," Herity said, hooking his chin toward the castle parapet above them. "The entire road open to him. He brought too much ammo, though. He'd've needed only one short burst and we'd have been pig meat."

Father Michael shook his head from side to side like a wounded animal. He opened his mouth but did not speak, then, it was forced out of him: "Damn them!"

"That's right, Priest, a good curse now and then helps things along." Herity grinned conspiratorially at John.

"It . . . was . . . Liam?" Father Michael demanded, tears in his voice.

"You're using the proper past tense," Herity said. "Was! Liam is past imperfect." Herity chuckled at his jest.

"Dead?" Father Michael insisted.

"Haven't I said it? I crept up the back way and himself watching the road so close over that little weapon there he didn't hear me until it was too late."

"Where's the body?" Father Michael asked. He sounded infinitely tired.

"Save your empty praying for when we've more time," Herity said. "Unless you've a mind to bless the castle privy."

Father Michael stared at Herity. "What?"

"I tipped him in with the rest of the shit," Herity said. "It'll take 'em a little time to find him, should they come hunting." Herity took one of the priest's arms and turned him around, holding him where he was forced to look down at the burned bus. "It was full of people when it burned," Herity said. "A heavy military-type machine gun made those little holes below the windows. You can say a few words as we pass it on our way . . . *Father*. We're in a bit of a hurry just now and we'll have to be watching our backs for Jock as we go."

Herity released his grip on Father Michael's arm and strode

past him toward the steps down to the parking terrace. As he moved away from them, he exposed a dark stain down his back—the kind of stain that could have come from carrying a body from which blood still ran.

For as long as they continue to control life and death, aristocrats understand correctly that their power depends mostly on their families, and much less on the people who must be kept subservient. This is why marriage remains so important to the aristocratic clan structure. Power marries power. In this trait, aristocrats recognize each other immediately. They share a common behavioral pattern. Here is the clan-economics where the real bargaining occurs—in the still vital dower exchange.

—Jost Hupp, M.D.

BILL BECKETT stood looking out the window of Wycombe-Finch's posh office at the Union Jack whipping from its staff in front of the Huddersfield Administration Building. The smartly uniformed color guard who raised the flag every morning could be seen marching away toward their barracks at the perimeter station near the main entrance. A flock of wagtails flew across the marching men, turning to flash their white belly patches against the gray morning sky.

He could see his reflection in the window, a blurred shape much thinner than once it had been.

It's going to rain, Beckett thought. He heard the door open behind him, Wycombe-Finch's rasping voice, Joe Hupp's softly accented response. Joe was raising the issue of computer time. That was vital.

Beckett could still taste breakfast—oatcakes with a rasher of bacon. One thing to be said for Huddersfield: They ate solidly. It seemed to put no fat on him, though. Danzas obviously detested local food but had resigned himself to it. Beckett could hear Danzas and Lepikov entering the office.

Turning, Beckett affirmed that they were all here. The director had stopped beside the door. He closed it, turned his pale, veined face toward Beckett and nodded. The others were busy moving chairs up to the narrow table at one side of the office where the small conferences were held.

Beckett moved across the room slowly, thinking about the sales pitch he had to make. Some things did not have to be reaffirmed, he knew. Nucleic acids were the molecules upon which the genetic coding was written. *They* directed the manufacture of proteins. *They* held the key to heredity. Heavy polymers, like proteins. The DNA was actually a doubled molecule with one chain twined around the other in helical form, but they knew now that it was not merely a two-part structure written in four-letter code. Was Hupp right? Did the two dominant parts require the presence of an *igniter,* which interposed itself much like a snake crawling into a hole? That would fit with Browder's Maypole concept. It would require partial matches at each bonding point that would relax in the newly created medium and jiggle onward to the next step and so on and on until the moment of completion: total ignition. Contact!

But understanding such complexity required a sophisticated computer approach. And if Wycombe-Finch wouldn't give them the computer time, perhaps Ruckerman could pry it out of the new President. They were never going to break this code without such help.

Beckett took his seat beside Danzas, looking across the table at Lepikov and Hupp. The director pulled a chair up to the end of the table and rested his elbows there.

"We must make this decision today," Lepikov said. His full lips barely moved as he spoke but the heavy eyebrows compensated, lifting and falling with each word.

The director turned his head and looked at the stack of bifold computer printouts that Beckett had dumped on his desk earlier.

"That's about a third of last week's run," Hupp said. "But it's the important third."

Beckett said: "Wye, you must give us access to a great deal more computer time. It's slowing us down, this standing in line for—"

"You really think you're reproducing the structure?" Wycombe-Finch asked. He brought his pipe out of the side pocket of his tweed jacket, a sure signal that he was prepared to stand firm and make this a long session.

"We have a toe in the door," Beckett said.

The director knew this expression, but wondered at its accuracy. He filled his pipe and lighted it, watching the coal as it glowed under his lighter.

"Are we certain there are no women available for tests in all of England?" Danzas asked.

"Too early to face that problem, don't you think?" the director said. He looked at Beckett, pulse quickening at this turn. How close was this team?

"We'll need test subjects eventually," Beckett said.

"No women we can safely get at, I'm assured," Wycombe-Finch said. "Some will be provided, I'm certain, when the time comes. The Americans, perhaps? I'm told they have quarantine stations staffed with . . ."

"We dare not ask," Lepikov said.

Danzas stroked his long nose with a forefinger and nodded agreement.

"We've discussed this at some length," Hupp said. "The United States, the Soviet Union, China . . . there is nowhere we dare turn. They would know immediately that we had achieved a breakthrough."

"I'm familiar with that theory," Wycombe-Finch said, speaking around his pipe stem and a long curl of blue smoke. "But how close are we?"

Hupp shrugged.

"A toe in the door doesn't mean we've made the sale," Beckett said.

The director removed his pipe from his mouth. "Let us say that I do as you suggest, increase your access to computer time . . . by how much we will not estimate for the sake of this hypothetical consideration. But let us say I do it. What then?"

"If you give us enough time at the computer, you'd better start arranging immediately for test subjects," Beckett said.

"What about that woman in the tank at Killaloe?" Hupp asked. "Her husband called me recently, you know. I didn't raise the question with him, but it crossed my mind."

"Just exactly what is it you fear from the major powers?" Wycombe-Finch asked.

Beckett cast a long-suffering look at Hupp. They had been through this several times with the director. The man was stalling, weighing his options. *Hypothetical consideration!* It was one of Wycombe-Finch's more irritating characteristics: He refused to act swiftly and decisively. *Another damned bureaucrat!*

"If we let it be known that we have solved the plague," Hupp said, "the world's major powers would face several attractive choices, arguing from their individual and selfish viewpoints. First, each would assess how well its female population was protected from conventional attack. Once the females are immunized, they can be considered a national asset to be sequestered in protective custody."

"Under circumstances that would have been considered most unacceptable in preplague times," Danzas said.

"We could expect commando-style attack right here," Beckett said. "They'd want to control us."

"Even if they learn that we've achieved something," Lepikov said, "we cannot broadcast the solution widely. It must be confined to this facility."

"You're really serious about this," Wycombe-Finch said, a faint querulousness in his tone.

"The Soviet Union would consider the statistical advantage in knocking out existing and potential adversaries," Lepikov said. "If you can cure the plague, and especially if you understand the other implications in this, the first-strike becomes an exceedingly attractive option. Certainly, this establishment becomes immediately expendable."

Wycombe-Finch looked at Beckett. "You share this opinion?"

"Any atomic power becomes exceptionally dangerous to us under these circumstances," Beckett said. "It hinges on something we here cannot possibly know: how well they have protected their female populations."

"Any other population segment could be freely sacrificed," Lepikov said.

Hupp leaned forward. "They've already taken such losses that they're all operating from a reserve position. People backed against a wall tend to make dangerous decisions."

Wycombe-Finch scratched his jaw with his pipe stem.

"Military thinking," Lepikov muttered. "It is the same everywhere."

As was his pattern, Danzas cleared his throat and looked at each person at the table, signaling that he was about to make a pronouncement. "You must also consider what might be done by a nation such as Argentina or India, a nation whose potential for disastrous decisions does not have what Bill would call 'a sufficient track record' from which to predict behavior. Such a nation might ignite conflict between superpowers, hoping to sit on the sidelines and pick up the pieces."

Wycombe-Finch picked a fleck of tobacco from the outside of his pipe bowl. "An interesting theory. Mad."

"Madness is contagious," Hupp said, "as contagious as the plague itself. O'Neill has loosed a second plague upon our world—this madness."

"Governments are sure to think in terms of rebuilding the world's gene pool from their own stock," Beckett said. "And once they know how to manipulate the DNA the way O'Neill did . . ." He shook his head.

"More plagues?" Wycombe-Finch asked.

"Why not?" Hupp countered.

Danzas nodded his head, a curiously angular motion like the bobbing of a child's toy.

Wycombe-Finch reached behind him to a small side table and brought a large ashtray there into position before him. He knocked out his pipe in it and refilled the pipe. "What if it is O'Neill in Ireland?" he asked.

"And the Irish get him to cooperate?" Beckett asked, his voice weary.

"Indeed," the director said. He lighted his pipe and puffed at it.

"You heard my conversation with Doheny," Beckett said. "I say the odds are strongly against them getting O'Neill to cooperate . . . if that's really O'Neill. I mean, my God! They've had him how long? Four months?"

"But what if it is O'Neill and he has arranged other plagues for us?" Wycombe-Finch asked.

"The world will need facilities such as this more than ever," Lepikov said. "Why do we not recognize our worth, our great value?"

Wycombe-Finch said: "That seems to me the decisive argument against any attack upon us. What I fear is that someone else may achieve a cure before us."

"That's a different game, all right," Beckett said. He had been hoping the director would be the one to raise this possibility. "What about our computer time?"

Wycombe-Finch exhaled a cloud of blue smoke and stared down at his pipe. He had not reached his present position without understanding the interplays of political power, but the uses of that power had always filled him with disquiet. He knew such things as were being discussed here could occur . . . did occur. His own particular regimen, however, had always been to offer no threat to those immediately superior to him and, at the same time, to operate within a circle of steady, consistent achievement. He thought of this as the essence of the scientific method. Intuition, imaginative leaps—all such things he saw as threatening to the orderly march of science. Wycombe-Finch did not like to contemplate a disorderly world, but this, he realized, was unfortunately the nature of the world at present. O'Neill had thrown a spanner into the works. True men of science could only hope to restore order. And something would have to be done to limit the disruptive consequences of scientific discoveries, something none of the others at this table had even considered, he thought.

The members of the DIC team stared at him expectantly.

"I shall announce new apportionments of computer time in the morning," Wycombe-Finch said. He looked at Beckett. "We must proceed in an orderly fashion, old boy. Give me a night to study the situation." He gestured with his pipe at the computer printouts on his desk. "I daresay there's some food for cogitation in that lot."

Beckett sighed. It was not what he had hoped for but it was something. The director would give them a bone—more time in some form. It looked like the ball was in Ruckerman's court, though. Could Ruckerman do it without tipping their hand?

THE THIRD week out from McCrae's, Herity stopped them at nightfall beside a small, one-room cottage hidden from the road by a hillock. They reached it on an overgrown track through the inevitable granite walls. John found himself pleasurably anticipating walls and a roof overhead. They had spent the previous night fireless, crouched in an abandoned hay shed while wind drove the rain around them.

Inside, the cottage smelled of mildew, but the windows remained unbroken and the door sealed tightly. Herity came back from scouting the area to report there was no fresh food, not even chickens wandering in the yard to lead them to a nest of eggs.

A broken-leg table propped by a length of green limb stood in front of the fireplace. Father Michael found dry peat in an adjoining shed, kindling on a shelf beside it, and soon had a fire going.

"I haven't seen any signs of pursuit," Herity said, his tone pensive. "No assurance in that. We'll mount guard again tonight."

Father Michael went to his pack in a corner near the fireplace and extracted a package wrapped in plastic. "Here's that piece of pork," he said.

The boy sat down on the floor beside the fire and extended his hands toward the warmth. Herity put his pack next to John's beside the door, glanced at the machine gun propped against it and smiled. He looked around the room: no loft, only this one small enclosed space.

John went to one of the two windows opposite the door and stared westward at the darkening sky. Sunset through the clouds filled the air with a dim yellow light that disappeared even as he watched. Distant forks of blue lightning danced under the clouds like shapes drawn by children. The lightning appeared unreal until he heard the crumping detonation of the thunder. He counted the seconds between flash and thunder—ten and crump! The next count was shorter. The storm was approaching fast.

Father Michael opened his plastic package on the table. "It's cozy with a fire," he said.

Herity picked up his machine gun and, leaving his pack, ducked out the door.

"Now where's he off to?" Father Michael asked.

"Only one door in this cottage," John said. "He doesn't care for that."

"Windows on three sides," Father Michael said. "I suppose it's still a trap. Do you suppose, John, that he really killed Liam?"

John merely looked at him.

Father Michael sighed. He rummaged once more in his pack and brought out some of Gannon's cheese. "I'd not want Joseph's sins on my soul," he muttered.

There was a decayed, rancid odor from the pork, John noticed. Spoiled, no doubt of it. Didn't the priest know?

"I wish Mister Gannon and his little family well," Father Michael said. "I'll pray for them tonight."

John thought of Gannon. That single pistol shot. Suggestive. Gannon had been a man ready to die, anxious for it even. Too sensitive and deep for these times. How had Gannon judged the four strangers who'd taken over his household so abruptly and then left him? *Did he see a group personality in us?*

Father Michael went to stand near the boy, both of them staring into the orange glow of the peat fire.

Why are we together?

John tried to visualize Herity, the priest, the boy and himself as Gannon had seen them. Groups were supposed to have a social identity. A philosopher would try to fathom that identity.

Lightning struck nearby, the thunder close and loud. The darkness outside seemed thicker, more dense afterward.

They were four different people bound together for different reasons, John decided. The lack of symmetry in the group bothered John. There was a dangerous disparity here. Was it Herity-the-hunter who did not belong? It felt no better with him outside.

Rain began to pour onto the cottage roof. A leak near the wall opposite the fireplace produced a steady drip-drip-drip that splashed toward the packs by the door. John moved them under one of the windows, resting the machine gun firmly on the pack that Herity had taken from Liam.

It came to John that each of them was being carried along by an obsession. *I must do O'Neill's bidding.* The boy had his vow of silence. Herity was a hunter. And Father Michael, yes . . . the priest was looking for his religion.

The thing holding this party together contained something unnatural, John decided. Was it supernatural? He felt that it was important to fathom what held them all together.

The rain had become very loud on the roof but the thunder and lightning were moving off to the northeast. John recorded this with only part of his awareness. His musings were no idle fantasy, he thought. The old uncanny of this land, the supernatural of little folk and faeries upon which Herity constantly harped, were gone. They had been replaced by something inescapably real, naturally super.

I did that. I did it for O'Neill.

"Where is that Joseph Herity gone to?" Father Michael asked, a whine in his voice.

"Waiting out the rain in some shelter probably," John said.

"The rain seems to be slackening a bit," Father Michael said. "It's a mild winter. Should we wait for him before we eat?"

"If you wish."

Silence settled over the room with only the faint hissing of the peat fire in the background, the rain on the roof reduced to a light pattering. John became conscious of a second leak dripping near the first one. The boy snuffled loudly.

Abruptly, the door burst open and Herity entered swiftly,

closing the door behind him. He wore a light poncho, which dripped a wide wet stain on the floor. There was a wild look in his eyes. He shook wetness off his green cap.

"We're not followed," he said. He slipped the poncho over his head, dropping the cap to the floor with a damp plop. Under the poncho, the machine gun hung by its neck sling but their attention was caught by a string bag slung from Herity's left shoulder. It contained three white plastic bottles and a jumble of canned food, the preplague commercial variety with bright labels.

"Now where did you find that lot?" Father Michael asked.

Herity grinned. "Provender for those on the run. We've buried caches of it all over Ireland."

"You've been this way before, then," Father Michael said.

"That I have." He hung his poncho on a peg beside the door and plopped the string bag onto the table, sending it teetering precariously on its propped leg. "Gannon's cheese," he said, looking at the table. "A good supper that'll make but the meat's high. Would you be making us all sick, Priest?"

"I don't like to throw away food."

"Ahhh, we still remember the starvation times, don't we?" Herity said. He picked up the packet of meat in its plastic wrapping and dropped it onto the fire. The grease flared briefly, sending an acrid smell of rancid pork and burned plastic through the room. Herity peered across the room at John standing near a window. "You know what pork smells like burning, John? Same as we would."

John remained silent.

Herity took up a slab of hearth bread and covered it with cheese.

The priest and the boy came up to the table and followed Herity's example. Father Michael passed a slab of bread and cheese to John, saying: "Bless this food, Lord, for the keeping of our flesh."

John ate beside the window staring outside. The storm had moved across the hills taking the rain with it. The eaves still dripped glistening pellets of water visible briefly as they passed the firelight shining out the window. The cheese had a faint tobacco smell and it tasted sour. John felt rather than heard Herity come up beside him. Herity's breath smelled of the sour cheese and something else. John sniffed. Whiskey! John looked squarely at the man in the orange firelight. Herity's eyes were steady, no faltering in his movements.

"I've noticed, John, that you don't reminisce," Herity said, his voice even.

"Nor do you."

"You've noticed that, have you?"

"Is it something you're hiding?" John asked. He felt bold in this question, safe because O'Neill-Within would never show himself in this man's presence.

A lopsided smile twisted Herity's mouth. "The very question in me mind!"

Father Michael turned his back to the fire and stared across the room, his eyes in shadows. The boy returned to his position seated on the hearth.

"I've been, wondering," Herity said, "how you come by your knowledge of Ireland?"

"A grandfather."

"Born here?"

"His father."

"Where?"

"Cork."

John stopped himself on the point of repeating Grampa Jack's story of the seven hundred rifles. That might already have surfaced as part of the O'Neill background. A stillness came over his entire body as he thought about this. He knew there was a certain crazy prudence in his behavior. The reasoning evaded him, though. There was a connection between O'Donnell and O'Neill.

I know the things O'Neill knew.

They were related, he decided. It was a troublesome relationship whose connections were to be avoided.

"So your ancestors were half Irish," Herity said.

"Full Irish."

"Both sides. Isn't that a marvel!"

"Why all these questions, Joseph?"

"Call it me natural curiosity, John. I've been wondering, I have, where it was you did all your fiddling with microscopes and test tubes and the wonderful instruments of science?"

John looked at the firelight glowing around Father Michael's dark figure, the boy a motionless mound by his feet. They were like posed silhouettes.

"Well now, he's not answering," Herity said.

"It was the University of Washington," John said. That was safe enough. The region had been hit by the Panic Fire even before he had left France.

"And I'll wager you were an important man," Herity said.

"Very minor."

"How is it you escaped the troubles there?"

"Vacation."

Herity favored him with a long, measuring stare. "Then you're one of the lucky ones."

"Like you," John said.

"Have you personal reasons for coming here to help?"

"My reasons are none of your business!"

Herity turned to stare out the window beside them. His voice carried a reflexive undertone when he spoke. "You're right, Mister John O'Donnell." He aimed a twisted grin at the priest, a satanic look in the underlight from the fire. "Isn't that the Eleventh Commandment, Father? Thou shalt not pry!"

Father Michael remained silent.

"Will you be forgiving the poor country manners of an Irishman?" Herity asked.

John stared at Herity. Jock had as much as said Herity had been in the Provos. "There're all sorts of manners in our world," John said. "As Father Michael would say, you can forgive anything that doesn't cut the life out of you."

"A man of wit," Herity said, but his voice was bitter.

Father Michael shifted position, rubbing his hands in front of him. He looked first at Herity and then at John. "You don't know about our Joseph Herity, John."

"Be still, Priest," Herity said.

"I'll not be still, Joseph." Father Michael shook his head. "Our Joseph was going to be an important man in this land. He studied the law, did Joseph Herity. There was them that said he might be first among us someday."

"That was a long time ago and it came to nothing," Herity said.

"What changed you, Joseph?" Father Michael asked.

"All the lying and the cheating! And you there with the word of 'em, Michael Flannery." Herity put a companionable hand on John's arm. "It's a cold floor but a dry one, John. I'll watch until midnight and then you can stand awake until dawn. Best we start early and go overland instead of the road. There's trails, y' know."

"Hunted men always learn where the trails are," Father Michael said.

"And they learn to avoid men who talk too much," Herity said. He took up his machine gun, slipped his poncho over his head and looked distastefully at the wet cap on the floor. Rain no longer beat against the roof. He put the cap on the hearth near the fire and straightened, stretching. The machine gun made a sharp outline under the poncho as he moved. "Keep the fire," he said. "I'll do me watching from outside." With that, he crossed to the door and let himself out.

"We had grand hopes for him once," Father Michael said. Using his pack as a pillow, he lay down with his feet toward the orange glow of the peat fire.

The boy lay curled up like a hedgehog, his head in the anorak, a dark mound at a corner of the fireplace.

John followed the priest's example, his thoughts filled with Herity's sharp questioning. *You don't reminisce.* The man was carefully observant. John began reviewing their conversations, the things they said as they walked. Nothing casual came from Herity. John realized belatedly that the man was a trained interrogator, getting his answers from the reactions he saw as much as from the words he heard. *He studied the law.* The rough manners, the country accent—part of an elaborate pose. Herity went deep. John fell asleep wondering what he might have revealed to that watchful man.

Much later, John awoke thinking he had heard a strange sound. He groped for the machine gun on the floor beside his pack, felt the cold metal. He took a deep breath, smelling the close odors of themselves in the confined space—an attar of human sweat distilled from their long tramp and the fatigue that sent them sprawling into sleep whenever they could. He sat up in the darkness and shifted the machine gun to his lap.

A snort nearby. Snoring.

The fire was out.

The room was a black confinement that focused on a sudden sound of scratching. A match flared and John looked into Herity's face less than a meter away.

"You're awake," Herity said. The match went out. "You can keep watch from inside, John, should you prefer. There's not a sign of pursuit for more than a mile out."

John stood. There was starlight visible out the window.

"It's turned cold, it has," Herity whispered.

John heard him stretching out on the floor, the little movements of trying to find a comfortable position. Herity's breathing deepened, became slow and even.

The machine gun was a cold weight in John's hands. Why had Herity let him have this dangerous weapon? It could kill the three sleeping figures in seconds.

John went to a window and stared out into the starlit night, the pale silver of a winter meadow laid out against the dark backdrop of trees. He stood there, shifting occasionally from one foot to the other, thinking about this strange man, Joseph Herity.

The lying and the cheating.

Herity had been an idealist. He no longer was an idealist. Father Michael's question lay in John's awareness: *What changed you, Joseph? Change . . . change . . .*

John Roe O'Neill had been changed. No question about what did it.

Circumstances.

In time, the sky lightened to the east and a red-orange sun came over the treetops. It was a perfect Japanese Rising Sun for a moment, spokes radiating upward through a mist. Bird sounds came from the ring of trees beyond the meadow. The growing light cast a flush over the landscape, throwing into relief a dark track of crushed grass leading off through the overgrown meadow.

Herity spoke from the floor behind him. "There's no church bells to waken us anymore."

Father Michael coughed and there was a stirring from him as he sat up. "There'll be bells again, Joseph."

"Only to send their alarms over the towns and the country-side. Your Church is dead, Priest, just as dead as all the women."

> *In 1054, the patriarch of Constantinople and the pope excommunicated each other. That was the end of holiness for both churches. After that, they became instruments of Satan. I'm convinced of it.*
>
> **—Joseph Herity**

ON THE narrow trails and the back roads, across the bogs and through dank tree-filled hills, twisting and turning over the heights, sometimes camping cold, sometimes snug in abandoned cottages, Herity led his party toward Dublin. They were eighteen days reaching the Wicklow foothills, another nine days circling around to come in from the northeast where they were not expected. And hardly a soul to be seen in the entire passage.

To John, the trip became a constant careful sparring with Herity. The most casual conversation could be dangerous. One afternoon, they had passed a leaning signboard with one word on it: *Garretstown*. It had been cold with a wet wind whipping over the hills, and John had longed for something warmer than the sweater.

"There's things done for no reason in this land," Herity said suddenly, glancing sidelong at John. Both of them were heavily whiskered now, John's bald head a veined contrast.

"What things?" John asked.

"Like slaughtering the hounds of the Kildare Hunt. It was a mean thing, taking out on dumb animals the misery caused by irresponsible humans."

Father Michael spoke from behind them. "The Hunt was an English thing."

"I was there," Herity said. "And maybe there was a reason as you say, Priest. Provocation—the Hunt crowd not understanding how easy it is to expose the devil in your neighbor."

John nodded, submitting to an urge to prod at Herity. "The way someone provoked O'Neill?"

Herity did not rise to this bait, but he walked silently for a time. Father Michael moved up beside them as they came out onto a narrow farm road of unpaved dirt. The boy could be heard trailing along behind.

"I've thought the same thing!" Father Michael said. He looked full at John with an expression of amazement on his long face. "The foolishness of people is beyond understanding."

"Like wanting to resume the Dublin Horse Show?" Herity asked, his voice filled with slyness. He, too, looked at John, the men walking along, one on each side of John, both looking at him.

"That was trying to bring back the good things," Father Michael said, but he kept his attention on John.

"Business as usual!" Herity said, looking ahead. "As though nothing had happened to make it obscene. Tell us about it, Father. You was there."

They plodded along in silence for almost fifty paces before Father Michael responded. In that time, he took his gaze off John and stared at the ground in front of him.

"It was raining a bit," Father Michael said. "We came on it after the mob had mostly gone. I saw some of the last of them coming away. Carrying boots, some of them were. And bits of clothing. I saw one man with a fine coat over one arm and bloody jodhpurs over the other, a great grin on his face."

Father Michael's voice was low and remote, as though he recounted something seen in a foreign land, a wonder from some heathen place and not an event from civilized Ireland.

The four walkers were in a dip in the road now, a short bridge visible at the bottom and a boggy stream winding its way through reeds under the bridge.

"That mob, they didn't seem ashamed of what they'd done," Father Michael said.

"Ahhh," Herity said, "there's anger here just waiting for something to strike."

"There was bodies all over the grounds," Father Michael said. "Men . . . dead horses . . . gore. No way to tell Catholic from another. They'd taken away all the crosses for their metal. Not even a ring left. Fingers cut off to get them. I knelt in the mud and prayed."

"But who did it?" John asked.

"A mob," Herity said.

John looked at Father Michael, fascinated. He pictured the priest coming on that scene, staring down at bodies of Horse Show officials and audience. Father Michael's simple words conjured a vision.

"They even took most of the boots and stockings," Father Michael said. "Boots and stockings. Why did they do that?"

The vision of bare feet outstretched in that muddy carnage like a final gesture of lost humanity stirred John oddly. He felt deeply moved, far beyond the brutal facts being recounted in Father Michael's dull voice. Something besides life had gone out of Ireland with those deaths, John thought. He even felt an absence of glee from O'Neill-Within. Interest, yes—fascinated interest, but no particular joy. Perhaps it was satisfaction, O'Neill-Within felt—a feeling of contentment.

John realized then that there was a deep and telling difference between happiness and contentment. O'Neill-Within might be content with what had been wrought even while it brought him no happiness.

"How do you feel about this, John?" Herity asked.

"It brings me no joy," John said.

"A black day," Father Michael said.

"Would you listen to him now?" Herity asked. "The only Catholics there was the hostlers and the grooms, the hardworking folk. A pack of Protestant landlords answered for their misdeeds and the priest is upset."

Father Michael spoke more strongly. "They were murdered! Slaughtered like animals—with knives, clubs, pitchforks and bare hands. There wasn't a shot fired."

Herity looked at John. "Does this give you an idea atall, atall, what might happen should the Madman O'Neill appear in our midst?"

John sensed O'Neill-Within, silently watchful.

"All those deaths and no good reason," Herity said. "Oh, there was reason, but I'll agree with the priest that it was better not done." Herity leaned across John to address Father Michael. "But you were fascinated by all that death, weren't you, Priest?

A good reason to pray with your knees in the mud."

Father Michael plodded along with his gaze directed downward. He shuddered.

John glanced at the priest, sensing the darting accuracy of Herity's remark. Yes, Father Michael shared his Church's love-hate relationship with death. It was his source of power as a priest, but the man-within could not be denied, either. No more could O'Neill-Within. Death was the ultimate failure, the human weakness that went beyond illusion into illusion, that intervention whose absolute sway could not be avoided.

Herity saw concealed things!

"It's educational it is," Herity said, "listening to the voice of a man when you cannot see his face." Again, he leaned forward to peer across John at the priest. "I listened to you, Michael Flannery. You telling about that slaughter and not a sign to say you see at last why I spit on your Church!"

Father Michael did not respond.

Herity grinned and returned his attention to the road ahead of them. The boy could be heard behind them throwing a rock into the bushes. They had topped the rise beyond the stream now and looked down a long hill where the road entered a thick barrier of evergreens.

"You see, Priest," Herity said, "what is most difficult is to be abandoned by God. He left me. I did not leave Him. They have taken away my religion!"

Father Michael's eyes glistened with unshed tears. He thought: *Oh, yes, Joseph Herity, I understand about that. I know all the psychological things they taught in the seminary. You would say the Church is my substitute for sex. It's the love I could never find from a woman. Oh, yes, I understand you. It's a new Church you think we have and not a woman for any of us.*

Without knowing why, Father Michael felt strength entering him from Herity's words.

"Thank you, Joseph," he said.

"Thank me? What is this you're saying?" Herity's voice was filled with outrage.

"I thought I was alone," Father Michael said. "I see that I'm not. For that, I thank you."

"Crab the man!" Herity said. He fell into angry silence, replaced presently by a sly smile. "You're confused, Priest," he said. "There's none of us together."

John saw the look of amusement on Herity's face. And

Father Michael . . . confusion? Herity obviously took malicious enjoyment from another's confusion. Did he enjoy Ireland's confusion as well? No . . . that went contrary to Herity's *Cause*. The plague had upset the untouchable. Recognizing this, John realized with an abrupt shock of awareness that he had the key to Herity, the thing that would undo the man.

Destroy his belief in his Cause!

But that was the very thing Herity was trying to do to Father Michael. How could that be a weakness in Herity and . . . yes, a strength in Father Michael?

"What're your politics, Joseph?" John asked.

"Me politics?" He grinned. "I'm a liberal, I am. Always was."

"He's a godless Marxist," Father Michael said.

"Better than a godless priest," Herity said.

"John, d'you know about the war of indefinite duration?" Father Michael asked.

"Close your fly trap, Michael Flannery," Herity said, his voice even and venomous.

"Never heard of it," John said. He sensed a poised stillness in Herity.

"That's the Provos," Father Michael said. He returned Herity's black look with a smile. "Prevent any settlement, kill the ones who'd compromise, terrify the peacemakers, prevent any solution. Give the people only war and violence, death and terror until they're so sick of it they'll accept anything in its place, even the godless Marxists."

"You'll recall," Herity said, "that this priest mourned the Prod landlords at the Dublin Horse Show. The greedy capitalists!"

"They were greedy, right enough," Father Michael said. "I'll grant you that. It's greed that drives the conservatives. But it's envy driving the liberals. And these Marxists . . ." he hooked a disdainful thumb at Herity ". . . all they want is to sit in the seats of the mighty and lord it over everyone else. The intellectual aristocrats!"

John heard a new strength in Father Michael's voice. The man apparently possessed powerful roots and he had found them. He might be beset by doubts, but the strength he gained by struggling against his doubts accumulated. It grew day by day.

"Now that I know how to pray for you, I shall pray for you, Joseph Herity," Father Michael said.

John looked from one man to the other, sensing the deep currents between them.

A malicious grin came over Herity's mouth but did not touch his eyes. He patted the machine gun on its strap at his chest. "Here's me soul, Priest. Pray for this."

"There's a demon loose in our land, Joseph," Father Michael said.

Herity sobered. A wild look entered his eyes. "A demon is it?"

"A demon," Father Michael repeated.

Still with that sober look, Herity said: "Mercie secure ye all, and keep the Goblin from ye, while ye sleep." His wolfish grin returned. "The words of Robert Herrick, Priest. Y' see the advantages in a classical education?"

"There's advantages in fearing God as well." Father Michael's voice was calm and assured.

"Some things we fear because they're real, Priest," Herity said. "Some things're only illusion. Like your precious Church and its pretty words and its fancy rituals. A poor substitute for living as a free man."

"Are you a free man, Joseph?" Father Michael asked.

Herity paled and looked away. He spoke with his gaze directed at the side of the road. "I'm freer than any man present." He whipped his gaze around to focus on John. "I'm freer than this John Garrech O'Donnell and him with something terrible hidden deep inside him!"

John's mouth clamped shut. He felt a jaw muscle twitching. *Damn the man!*

"There's illusions and there's illusions," Herity said. "Sure and we all know it."

John kept his attention directed straight ahead. He could feel the pressure of attention upon him from both sides. Was it only illusion after all?

"A substitute for life," Herity said, a terrible pressure in his voice.

John looked to his right, seeking help from Father Michael, but the priest kept his gaze on the road at his feet.

"D'you find your illusions comforting, John?" Herity asked. "As comforting as the illusions of the priest there?"

John felt the stirring of O'Neill-Within. *How did I come by this thing?* he wondered. Was there ever a place where it could be identified? He felt that the acquisition had been slow . . . like a growth, perhaps, or a new skin. Steadily constant, casually demanding but never importunate. It was the self intrinsic and the memories were real.

Father Michael wrestled with his own demon, feeling it aroused by Herity's words even though he knew these words were not directed at him but at the poor soul walking with them. Was it truly the Madman in this quiet American?

How do we come by what we are? Father Michael wondered. He remembered a basement room in his village church. Ballinspittle, a name the Yankees made joke of, but it was his own. The church with its plaster neatly applied by a local artisan as a service to God.

Remembering gave Father Michael an anchor in his past.

Clean and white the plaster had been. Framed pictures spaced along it—Sacred Heart of Jesus...Holy Mary, Mother of God...a whole row of popes, a blessed medal draped on its chain against red velvet, all in a heavy frame under glass and with a brass plate underneath telling whoever looked that it had been blessed by Pope Pius himself. There were benches in the basement room. Father Michael remembered sitting on a bench, his legs too short to reach the floor, his eyes fixed on a plaque nailed to the back of the bench ahead of him:

"To the sacred memory of Aileen Matthews (1896–1931). Presented by her loving children."

How remote it all felt now.

John felt tormented by the silence of his companions and by their very presence. He wanted to run away, to dash off into the fields and bury his face in concealing grass, never to rise again.

But Herity was too dangerous!

Anything I do, he can see it and see through it.

"Well, perhaps I shouldn't pry," Herity said, his voice light, "that being a commandment of these times."

John's throat felt parched. He longed for a drink of water... or something stronger. What was it Herity carried in those small plastic jugs? He often had the smell of whiskey on his breath, but he wasn't sharing it. John looked off to his right— a hill there, the barren silhouette of a dead pine on its flank with ivy climbing the wooden corpse. The ivy was a winding cloth on the stark witch-shape.

"We'll be stopping here," Herity said.

Obediently, they all stopped.

Herity was looking off to his left, a tiny cottage there only a few meters from the dirt road. There was a plaque on its closed door: "Donkey House." A small stream ran past the door, no more than a handspan wide, flowing silently over black rocks.

"Donkey House," Herity said. He shifted his gun to the ready. "Now wouldn't that be a fine place for the likes of us to stop and rest? It being unoccupied of course." He hopped the stream and peered in a corner of the one window beside the door.

"Dirty but empty," he said. "And doesn't that sound like a fitting description of some who're known to us?"

KATE HAD developed a mental game of her own for the times when she felt that Stephen wanted no more of her, those times when his attention submerged into his books and he refused to answer her simplest question.

She played it now in the morning quiet of their confinement, her eyes closed, her feet tucked under her on the chair. Stephen could be heard where he sat across from her, the pages of his book turning with an irritating rhythm.

Only a few minutes ago she had said: "My back aches, Stephen. Will you rub it, please?"

Stephen had grunted.

She hated that grunt. It said: "Don't bother me. Get away from me."

And she had no place to go except into her own mind.

It was a fascinating imaginative game.

What I will do when we have come through these times.

Safely into her own imagination, she could live without any doubts of her personal survival. The rest of the world might be reduced to rubble. One hand would emerge from that rubble, pulling a survivor out of the ruin. She would be that survivor.

They were changing the guard and servicing one of the compressors outside the pressure chamber. Metal clanged occasionally on metal. Voices exchanged bits of trivia. She tuned it all out of her awareness, sinking deeper and deeper into the world of her own creation.

I will wear fine jewels, she thought.

This avenue did not attract her now. She had played the possession game too many times: jewels, designer clothing, a beautiful home. . . . Sooner or later, the retreat into future possessions found her in her own dream home but that was frustrating. She could not truly fill out such a home, not even furnish it in the way she knew it might be furnished. Her image of a perfect home had been fixed on Peard's cottage at the lake. She knew there were grander homes. Films had let her glimpse mansions. She had visited the magnificent residence of a retired doctor near Cork once, going there with her mother to visit the housekeeper, who was an old friend. The friend had led them through quiet, unoccupied rooms—a library, a music room, a solarium . . . a great cavern of a kitchen with a massive peat stove.

The peat stove definitely would not do. It would have to be gas . . . just as in Peard's cottage.

Poof! There went the entire dream fabric. She did not have enough experience upon which to construct an acceptable fantasy.

Whatever, it would be a home with Stephen, of course, because they were bound together now as surely as man and woman could be united.

Our children will be with us, she thought. *And Stephen will . . .*

No! She did not want that dream. Stephen was always there somewhere and she was angry with him now. He might die, though. That shocked her, but she held to it, feeling guilty and suddenly without roots. Stephen could be killed protecting her. She did not doubt that Stephen would give his life for her. How sad that would be, living with the memory of such a sacrifice.

I would be a lonely widow.

Nagging awareness interrupted: *"A lonely widow? In a world with thousands of men for every woman?"*

It was an exciting thought, making her gasp. Sad it might be . . . but the power in it! Who might she take as a second husband? Somebody important, certainly. She knew herself as no raving beauty, but still . . .

Abruptly, with part of her mind, she knew this was not merely idle speculation. This fantasy had touched something live and real. It was almost palpable and she found this both magnetic and terrifying. She knew then that she had opened up something more than just a dream. This was a channel where fantasy might educate . . . or at least prepare her against strange possibilities.

Kate focused hard on that external world then—that place outside the pressure chamber where new relationships were developing. It was a crucible out there with agony and wrenching loss. Any fantasy she attempted from now on would have to consider the strange realities that she saw only as reflections from the words of the guards and the images on the telly.

When they have found a cure, I will step out into that world, she thought.

This was a profoundly disturbing realization and she felt angry at her own fantasies for leading her into such a predicament. She still did not doubt that she would survive; fantasy protected her there. But right at the edge of her dreams there lay goblin actualities, which leered at her. Frantic, she grasped for a protective dream.

An island! That was it! She and Stephen would find their own island and . . .

"What're you thinking, Kate? Your face is all screwed up as though you'd swallowed something bitter."

Stephen's voice intruded at the moment she found her fantasy breaking on more impossibilities—what island? How would they get to it? She found herself thankful for the interruption. Opening her eyes, she saw that Stephen had put down his book and was preparing to bake bread. Odd, how he liked to do that, a bit of domesticity in him that she had never suspected. All the ingredients came in sterilized cans, though, and he had fastened on this as a way to add interest to their lives.

"I was wondering what'll become of us when we get out of here," she said.

He turned a wide grin of pleasure toward her. "There's my girl! Never doubt for a minute that we'll make it, darlin'."

"Will we, Stephen?"

Without her dreams, she found herself plunged back into a world beset by doubts.

Please, Stephen, tell me something reassuring.

"We're perfectly safe here," he said. But there was a ring of insincerity in his voice that she had come to recognize immediately.

"Oh, Stephen!"

Kate dissolved into sobs and all thought of bread baking was gone for the moment. His hands still dusted with flour, Stephen came across the room and knelt beside her, holding her tightly around the waist and his cheek pressed against her abdomen.

"I'll protect you, Katie," he whispered.

She clutched at him, holding his head against her. *Oh, God! He might die trying to protect me!*

> *The hand that signed the paper*
> *felled a city;*
> *Five sovereign fingers taxed the*
> *breath,*
> *Doubled the globe of dead and halved*
> *a country;*
> *These five kings did a king to death.*
>
> **—Dylan Thomas**

HERITY FOLLOWED an even more circumspect route as they neared Dublin, leading his party in across the pasture lands to the northwest of the city and avoiding the traveled ways to the interior where, it was said, bands of land pirates still lurked.

John remained a mystery to him, but there was no doubt in Herity's mind that the man concealed something dark. He might be the Madman. Then again, he might only be another lost one with his own sins on his mind, his own griefs and reasons for coming here. He might even be sincerely desirous of helping Ireland in its hour of testing.

As he marched across the fields toward Dublin, Herity prodded and listened to every word John uttered. It was maddening. How could this be the Madman? There was emotional betrayal in him, but betrayal of what?

Father Michael remarked on the absence of cattle as they neared the city.

"Men still eat," Herity said.

"But they leave a lot for the birds," Father Michael said.

The boy took on an intense look of concern as Father Michael mentioned the birds. An ancient stone ruin stood off to the side of their track, rooks soaring around it. Beyond it, they could see the hills to the south of the city. Barren trees devoid of all green fanged the heights. Somewhere over there lay Tara, Herity knew. There where kings had lived, not even cattle grazed now.

"Isn't it strange," Father Michael mused, "so many of the ancient lyrics mentioning the blackbirds." He stared at the birds wheeling over the ruin.

John also watched the flock, thinking how those particular birds haunted this landscape, realizing that this must always have been the case. He said as much, noting how sharply the boy looked from one speaker to another when the birds were mentioned.

Herity kept his gaze rolling over the landscape around them, a mounting tension in him. Green copses off there and burned houses, the meadows like moats with the weed-grown lanes through them. A burned patch in a meadow off to the left showed ugly mounds in it—suggestive shapes drawn there in charcoal and yet washed away by the rains. Bodies?

A dark line of rain could be seen sweeping across the fields and copses—black as the wings of the soaring birds.

Seeing undamaged buildings ahead, they hurried to beat the storm. Their lane came out on a narrow paved road with an intact shed beside it, glass on the ends of the shed, a long bench at the rear, an empty wooden pocket there for timetables on a no-longer-existent bus line. The squall swept overhead as they reached this shelter and they were only dampened by it as they huddled in the rear. Rain pelted the roof and bounced off the macadam, bright pellets of water beating all around. The temperature dropped sharply.

As quickly as it had come, the storm passed. It left long lanes of blue in the sky. The hills to the south stood out clearly in the rain-washed air, ridges lighted by the lowering sun. Green there with patches of yellow furze, the trees clumped along the ridges like spears planted there by the ancient kings who had ruled from that place.

John stepped out of the shelter and stared around him. There was an emerald brilliance to the land, a beauty that he thought had been near enough to this for eons... something to ignite in the human breast a love of the earth beneath the feet. He felt that it was a thing deeper than patriotism, because it infected Gaelic descendants who had never seen this land. People caught up in that kind of love identified with it. They became bound to it in a way that could make them happy if they could only go into a grave covered by such beauty.

Was it possible, John wondered, to love a country without caring very much for the people who put their mark on it? Possession might not be nine points of that law, after all. When you considered it carefully, possession was transient, no more than the right to carve your initials in a length of cliffside . . . or to build a wall that eventually would melt back into the earth.

Herity came around from behind the shed zipping up his fly. "Let's be moving along. We'll not be in Dublin by nightfall but there's shelter ahead and a bit more civilization. We're inside the Dublin pale here at last."

He strode off. John fell into step beside him. Father Michael and the boy brought up the rear.

"Despite what Joseph says, don't expect civilization here," Father Michael said. "This is a brutal place, John. It may be that the centers of government were always this way and now we've merely pulled off the mask, exposing the truth of the matter."

"Brutal?" John asked.

"There's stories of torture and madness and proof enough to confirm them."

"Then why are we going here? Why aren't we going directly to the Lab at Killaloe?"

Father Michael nodded toward Herity's back. "Orders."

John felt his palms wet against the machine gun, which hung from its neck strap next to his chest. One little flick of a finger to remove the safety the way Herity had showed him. He could run off by himself and find his own way to Killaloe. Or could he? Three bodies to dispose of . . . and no telling who might come to investigate the shooting. He glanced at the boy.

Could I do it?

He felt his fingers relaxing from the gun's hard metal and that was answer enough. Something had changed among the four of them here on this road. O'Neill's revenge had been accomplished upon these people. John knew then he could not bring his companions more agony.

"What do you mean . . . torture?" he asked.

"I'll not speak more of it," Father Michael said. "There's things bad enough in this poor land." He shook his head.

The road led into a tall stand of evergreens and they were

almost into the trees now. John glimpsed buildings off to the right through the dark trunks of the evergreens—white stone and black roof. It was a large building with several chimneys. Smoke drew vertical lines from two of the chimneys.

Herity whistled as he walked. Abruptly, he stopped whistling and held up a hand for them to stop. He cocked his head, listening.

John grew aware of singing, the sound of choristers in the distance, toward the building. It was a lovely sound of harmony, reminding him of holidays. His memories began to play—Grampa Jack, firelight and stories, music from the radio. The singing grew louder, extinguishing the memories. Illusion vanished as he recognized the choristers' words.

"Listen to the little bastards, will you?" Herity exulted. "Listen to 'em, Michael Flannery!"

The sweet young voices sang with inescapable clarity:

> *"Fucking Mary we adore,*
> *Fucking Mary, Jesus' whore.*
> *And when we all ejaculate,*
> *That is why we masturbate!"*

Father Michael clapped his hands over his ears and failed to note that the singing stopped. Now, there was only a grunting chant from off in the trees, a Gregorian parody: "Hut, hut, hut, hut . . ."

Herity threw back his head in laughter. "Now there's memorable blasphemy for you! There's blasphemy to conjure with, Priest." He grabbed Father Michael's right arm and pulled it away from the ear. "Ahhh, now, Michael, I wish I'd thought of that little song."

"Somewhere you still have a conscience, Joseph," Father Michael said. "I shall find it yet though it lie beyond the bottomless pit."

"Conscience, you say!" Herity blared. "Is it your Church's old guilt game again? Whenever will you learn?" He turned and strode off down the road, the others close behind.

Father Michael spoke in a conversational voice. "Why do you speak of guilt, Joseph? Is it something on that conscience you profess not to have?"

It was clear to John that the priest was maintaining better control. Herity's anger mounted with every step. His knuckles were white on the stock of the machine gun. John wondered if the man might turn that weapon against the priest.

"Why will you not answer me, Joseph?" Father Michael asked.

"It's you that has the guilt!" Herity raged. "You and your Church!"

"You keep harping on the Church," Father Michael said, his tone reasonable. "If one person says you're guilty, yourself saying it of yourself, that's a sore problem, Joseph. But the collective guilt of a whole people—that's another matter."

"You're a dirty, lying priest!"

"Hearing you rant has brought me to some hard thinking, Joseph." Father Michael quickened his pace until he walked beside Herity. "It occurs to me, it does, that it's hard for a collectivity of people to accept the awakening of its conscience."

Herity stopped in the center of the road, forcing Father Michael to stop also. John and the boy halted a few paces back and watched the antagonists. Herity regarded Father Michael with a silent scowl, his forehead creased in thought.

"The Church could administer to the individual," Father Michael said, "but not to the people. That was our failure. Where is a people's conscience?"

A look of bland superiority erased the scowl from Herity's face. He stared at the priest. "Has the mad priest finally come around to sanity? Do you see at last the world you've made?"

"All I'm saying is that it's hard for people to feel guilty together," Father Michael said.

"Is that all of it?" There was glee in Herity's voice.

Father Michael turned and looked back the way they had come, staring past John and the boy at the road climbing out of the trees toward the meadows. "No, Joseph, that's not all of it. Before the people will accept guilt, they'll do terrible things together. Better the bloodbath, kill the innocents, ignite the war, lynch and murder . . ."

John felt the priest's words like a physical lash. What was this? What had Father Michael said to produce such feelings? John knew his face must appear frozen. He could not sense O'Neill-Within anywhere. He had been left alone to face this thing, whatever it was. He felt shattered, broken away from essential ground.

"So you're sorry for all the pain you've spread?" Herity

asked. John felt the question. He thought it had been asked of him directly, although it was obvious the words were directed at the priest.

"Sorry?" Father Michael looked squarely at Herity, forcing the man to meet his gaze. It was as though Father Michael saw Herity clearly for the first time. "Why should I be sorry?"

"Blather!" Herity sneered. HIs voice sounded weak, though. "Father Michael says this. Father Michael says that. But Father Michael is a notorious liar, trained in it by the Jesuits!"

"Joseph, Joseph," Father Michael said, pity in his tone. "John Donne's bell can toll for the one but not for the many. I shall pray for your individual soul, Joseph, and for the soul of any individual I can identify. As to the many, I see that I must think on it."

"Think on it! Is that all you can do, you silly old fool!" Herity turned his glare on John. "And what're you staring at, Yank?"

The boy stepped clear of John's side, stopping a pace away.

John tried to swallow in a dry throat. He knew his inner turmoil must be transparent.

Herity appeared not to notice. "Well, Yank?"

"I . . . I was listening."

"And what did you hear, you there with your ears stuck out like the wings on a bird?"

"An . . ." John cleared his throat. "An intellectual argument."

"You're another liar!" Herity said.

"Now, Joseph," Father Michael said, his voice mild. "I think John was merely mistaken."

"Stay out of this, Priest! This is between the Yank and me!"

"No, Joseph, it is not. I aroused your anger and you could not best me. Now, you attack our guest."

Herity turned a look of disdain on Father Michael. "Could not best you?"

"It was not an intellectual argument," the priest said. "On that I do agree." He looked benignly at John. "We Irish don't really like an intellectual argument."

Herity opened his mouth and closed it without speaking.

"I know we often say an intellectual argument is the darling of our desires," Father Michael said. "But that's not true. We much prefer passions. We like to fan the burning in the guts. We like to parade our agonies."

"Is this you speaking, Michael Flannery?" Herity asked, wonder in his voice.

"That it is. And I'm saying it's only a short step across the pits of hell, one step to take us into the deliberate creation of agonies to parade."

"Can I believe my ears?" Herity asked the air. He leaned toward the priest, peering up under the hat brim as though trying to determine if this were truly Father Michael. "Can it be yourself saying such wonderful things?"

A wry chuckle shook the priest. "We've had the time for a spell of thinking on this tramp, haven't we, Joseph?"

Herity did not answer.

Father Michael turned his attention on John and John wondered at the pain of that gaze: so mild and so accusing. He felt it like the cutting of a knife in his chest.

"The most intellectual pursuit of the Irish," Father Michael said, "is the pursuit of the sardonic." He glanced at Herity and Herity recoiled. sniffing and rubbing at his nose. "A pity we always stop short of laughing at ourselves, a thing we should be doing when we face up to our more bitter truths."

"You wouldn't know a truth if it kicked you in the balls and you not having a one," Herity accused.

"Then all is peace and tranquillity in our poor land, is it?" Father Michael asked. "Sweet agreement everywhere—as it's always been."

"Whatever hurt we've had," Herity said, "comes from our enduring devotion to the superstitions of the Church and it sapping the strength out of us for all these centuries."

Father Michael sighed. "Joseph, I think your worst vice may be that you haven't it in you to be magnanimous."

"It's God's own truth you've stumbled onto there," Herity said. "Magnanimity isn't the most celebrated Irish virtue, as some poor bastard is supposed to've said. I'll own to it, Michael Flannery, because I know we must hold to our hates. Where else do we find the strength to go on?"

"Thank you, Joseph," Father Michael said. "There's hope for you yet and I'll continue my prayers." The priest turned on a heel and strode off down the road.

John realized in that moment that something in the argument had completely restored Father Michael's faith. What had Herity said to accomplish that? John stared at the priest's receding back. So strongly he walked, so firm and assured.

Herity, too, stared after Father Michael.

"There y' go, Priest!" Herity called. "Running away." He looked at John. "See how he runs?" But the weakness in Herity's voice was an admission of defeat. He had tried his best to kill the priest's faith and he had failed.

The boy ran after Father Michael. Catching up to the priest, he grasped the man's hand.

"No hope for either of them," Herity said. "Well, come along, John. My friends have been watching us . . ." he gestured with the machine gun as two men came out of the woods ahead of Father Michael and the boy ". . . and here they are now."

Herity reached across to John as they began walking and slipped the machine gun and its sling over John's head. "They might not understand. Will you be passing me the little five-shooter, as well?"

John stared ahead as though in a dream, obeying Herity without really feeling the pistol as he rid himself of it.

One of the two men coming toward them was Kevin O'Donnell, still wearing the Aussie hat he'd worn that night on the pier at Kinsale.

Romans corrupted the Gall and that produced the Englishman. They took to Roman ways like a hog to the trough. Roman tactics are direct: make your families hostage. They enlisted us in their armies because that was our alternative to starvation. They corrupted our religion with greed. They replaced cheap, easily understood law with law that's expensive and mostly impenetrable to common folk. Legalized robbery is what it's all about.

—Joseph Herity

"THEY REFUSED to confirm or deny whether they actually have O'Neill in custody?" Velcourt asked.

Charlie Turkwood raised both hands, palms upward. There was a saturnine look in his dark eyes. His thick lips appeared poised on the edge of a smile.

They were in the Lincoln sitting room of the White House, a room Velcourt had set up as his private study. He glanced at his wristwatch. "What time is it over there right now?"

"About nine A.M., sir," Turkwood said.

"Strange," Velcourt said. "How the hell did they find out that we have those dental charts and fingerprints?"

Again, Turkwood produced that negative shrug of the hands.

Velcourt was hungry and he knew this made him short-tempered. He struggled to control himself. "You know what I'm thinking, Charlie?"

Turkwood nodded. The thing was obvious.

"If they've broken the code on that plague," Velcourt said.

"They could have us all by the balls," Turkwood said.

An odd look of withdrawal came into Velcourt's eyes. He spoke in a musing tone: "Code."

"What's that?" Turkwood asked.

370

Velcourt leaned toward the speaker phone on his desk and depressed the key: "Get me Ruckerman. I want him in here as soon as you find him. And DA, too."

The speaker burped a question.

"Yes, I mean Asher!"

Another question.

"I don't give a damn where Ruckerman's gone! Send a car!"

Turkwood stared at the President with a puzzled frown.

"What're the odds that the Irish have rockets?" Velcourt asked. He leaned back in his chair.

"The Pentagon thinks the odds are high, sir. They think the Continent's vulnerable, at least."

"A new plague made in Ireland," Velcourt said.

"That's what they're suggesting, sir."

James Ryan Saddler, the science advisor, slipped into the study, saw Turkwood standing near the small desk, Velcourt seated in a comfortable swing chair behind it. "You're trying to find Ruckerman, Mister President?" Saddler asked. He cleared his throat. "Anything I can do?"

"Don't you knock before coming in here?" Velcourt demanded.

Saddler paled. "Amos was right outside, sir. He said . . ."

"Okay, okay." Velcourt waved a placating hand. Again, he leaned to the speaker phone. "Amos, prepare a message for my signature. It goes directly to the Irish government in Dublin— no named recipient. It will point out the number of people we lost getting those fingerprints and dental charts out of the plague area. Repeat our demand to know whether they have someone in custody they suspect is O'Neill and, if so, demand to know why they suspect this. Tell them we want an immediate reply and say we are still considering whether to send them copies of the fingerprints and dental charts. Immediate reply, got that? The consequences of a failure to reply will be left to their imaginations."

The speaker said: "Yes, sir."

Velcourt returned to his position leaning back in the chair, both hands clasped behind his head.

"Is that wise, sir?" Turkwood asked.

Velcourt did not respond.

"What's going on?" Saddler asked.

"There appears to've been a shakeup in the Irish power structure," Turkwood said. "We think the military is still in the saddle but they've delegated authority to a split premiership—equal power to the secretary of plague research, Fintan Doheny, and to the head of the Finn Sadal, Kevin O'Donnell."

"What do our agents over there say about it?" Saddler asked.

"We don't have one we can depend on."

"Just when we need them the most," Velcourt said.

"Why're we putting on the pressure, sir?" Turkwood asked. "Barrier Command's sure to ask. An *immediate* reply? I'll have to tell them something."

"Tell them zilch. I'm talking to the Irish. They'll think we're up to something nasty, maybe looking for an excuse to nuke them. It'll throw them into a tizzy or it'll produce an exposure of their hand. If they have a real threat, they'll have to make that known to us."

Saddler said: "Sir, I'm sure you know of the scenario that says we'll nuke anyone who admits they have O'Neill."

"Let 'em worry. They can't do a fucking thing except answer and their answer will tell us a bundle."

"What about the possibility O'Neill has set up a dead-man switch with another plague?" Turkwood asked.

"The Russians and the Chinese say they're ready to risk it," Velcourt said. "That's what the Joint Chiefs and I discussed last night. We're inclined to agree."

"But sir," Saddler said, "that could mean the Russians and Chinese have a cure!"

Velcourt shook his head. "They can't manufacture an aspirin without our knowing about it."

Turkwood looked at Saddler. "What about our query to the Biochemical Society?"

"Their records were computerized and lost," Saddler said. "A few of the surviving members remember O'Neill, but . . ." He shrugged.

"We have very few cards and we have to play them right," Velcourt said. "The big ones are those fingerprints and dental charts. We don't dare just give them away."

"I still think I'll have to tell Barrier Command something," Turkwood said. "If I refuse to answer . . ."

"What the hell is this sudden worry about Barrier Command?" Velcourt demanded. "Who cares what that Canuck admiral thinks?"

Turkwood swallowed and looked grim. "Yes, sir."

Velcourt stared hard at Turkwood before speaking: "What about that other little job you're supposed to be doing, Charlie?"

Turkwood shot a worried glance at Saddler before looking at the President. "It's in hand, sir."

"I'm holding you responsible that it isn't botched!"

"I'd better be getting back to it now. Is there anything else, sir?"

"No. Keep me posted. You stay, Jimmy."

When Turkwood had gone, Velcourt asked Saddler: "How well do you trust Ruckerman?"

"An honorable man, sir."

"He's been having unmonitored conversations with Beckett at Huddersfield. No record of what they said."

"I'm sure it was all technical, sir. Plague-related."

"That's what he says."

"Ruckerman doesn't lie, sir."

"Everybody lies, Jimmy. Everybody."

Saddler frowned but remained silent.

Velcourt glanced at a scatterd pile of reports on the small desk. "Our situation gets no better. Hong Kong's a write-off Chaos in South Africa. War of extermination against their black neighbors. The Soviets are voting to nuke the whole region." He slid one sheet from the papers and glanced at it before dropping it onto the pile. "And now, Brazilian Israel has just declared itself independent of its host. Not that I blame them. CIA says the Brazilians were starting to make an identity list of all Israeli women 'for later use.' The Brazilians were planning to trade surplus women to devastated areas! My God!"

Saddler swallowed, then: "Sir, I need to discuss that last message from the Chinese Research Center at Kangsha. They are asking for updates on computer-oriented study of the plague. I hesitate to . . ."

"Stall them. What's the latest satellite report on that area north of Kangsha?"

"Some indications of Panic Fire, sir, but they have a disproportionate number of fireproof buildings. Even with augmented photos we're very uncertain of what's happened there. We think maybe they tested a plague cure and it failed."

Velcourt leaned to the speaker phone. "Amos, I want an agency report on Kangsha within the hour." He returned to his position leaning back in the chair. "I'm going to tell you something, Jimmy. It must not leave this room. I'll give you my reasons later."

Saddler's face went solemn and fearful.

"Because of the places they've had to burn out," Velcourt

said, "the Soviets right now are weaker than wet shit. Their suicide rate has become astronomical. And we have to pretend we don't know this and we'll have to continue this pose just as long as they have plenty of TU Twenty-nines and Backfire Threes and other instruments of total destruction. Do you understand that?"

Saddler nodded silently.

"The Australian Outback Reserve is still intact and we've armed it," Velcourt said. "That's an ace-in-the-hole, but it could backfire. The Aussies can be goddamned independent at times."

"But they know their future is with us, sir."

"Do they?" The President looked at the door through which Turkwood had just left. "And now we come to Charlie Turkwood. He's been seen cozy-cozy with Shiloh Broderick."

"I don't understand, sir."

"Don't you know about Shiloh?"

"Well, I . . . uh . . ."

"I thought everybody knew about Shiloh and his gang."

"Pretty reactionary, sir, so I hear."

"Reactionary? You wanta know what's worrying them? World commerce is practically at a standstill. They're getting impatient."

"There's a lot of that going around, sir." It was a weak jest and Saddler was sorry he'd attempted it as soon as he had spoken.

But Velcourt grinned and said: "Thanks, Jimmy. That's one of the reasons I'm trusting you. We have to hold on to our sanity any way we can."

"Sir, the search for a cure has to be our only priority."

"At least our top priority. Which brings me to my reason for dumping all this on you—Ruckerman."

"What about him, sir?"

"You're going to send him to Huddersfield."

"Sir! They're contaminated in . . ."

"Which will give him a really strong motive to make good over there. If he fails, he'll never see his family again."

"Why're we doing this, sir?"

Velcourt looked at the papers on his study desk and abruptly swept them onto the floor. "This goddamned job! Every time you turn around, another fucking distraction!"

"Sir, what—"

"I had this in my head weeks ago! All the pieces! But they

don't give you a moment's peace to think!"

"But about Ruckerman, sir?"

"You are sending him to Huddersfield, Jimmy. Not me. You. I have nothing to do with it except to authorize your request."

"If you say so, sir, but I—"

"You know David Asher."

"DA? A bright young fellow, sir, but what . . ."

"I don't dare send him because Shiloh would hear about it and he's bright enough to start poking in the wrong places. Everyone knows DA was using the satellite code to talk to his friends out in Mendocino."

"People are wondering how he did it, sir. Did he find a copy of . . ."

"He did it with a thing he calls a computer search program. I know just enough about it to believe it could be adapted to breaking the plague code."

"The Chinese!" Saddler said. "Could they . . ."

"They could or they could have an independent approach."

"But why send this to Huddersfield, sir?"

"After we get it to Beckett we'll spread it around to our own facilities, but I don't have much confidence in them. Atlanta is a bunch of plodders. They couldn't find water if they crawled out of a submerged submarine. And Bethesda!"

"They're trying hard, sir."

"Trying and plodding aren't enough. You have to be inspired. Beckett's my man. I can smell a solution, Jimmy. Always could. Which is why we're making sure this thing gets to Beckett at Huddersfield. There're those who'd try to prevent this, Jimmy. And Ruckerman's the right messenger. He's savvy with computers."

"I know, sir. He's been trying to get the Rocky Mountain Facility to shift over to a—"

"I saw the report. Damn! I saw the report and didn't even tumble to. . . . Well, we're doing it now!"

"How much do I tell Ruckerman?"

"You tell him to keep his damn mouth shut! He talks only to Beckett. Ruckerman's cover is that he's there to make an on-site inspection and report to me. We're sending him because he was accidentally contaminated."

"Yes, sir, but . . ."

"So he's got to be accidentally contaminated! And that will be as soon as possible after DA briefs him, which briefing will take place right here in my study. Details I will leave to you but I have a suggestion. There's a young pilot named Cranmore McCrae living in Woodbridge just outside our perimeter. He's contaminated. He has made several requests that we allow him to fly to Ireland, where he has an uncle. The uncle's some kind of a nut but rich as hell and still powerful, apparently. I've had a full report on young McCrae. A fairly bright boy. He flew with the CIA air force in Vietnam and did a few other jobs for us. Resourceful and reliable."

"Why wouldn't this McCrae just go to Ireland once he was outside our..."

"We tell the Canuck admiral to shoot him down unless he goes directly to England. After he drops Ruckerman, then he can go to Ireland, where Barrier Command will do the usual with his aircraft."

"But what if the English won't—"

"They will cooperate because you will tell them it would anger us exceedingly if they don't. If he fell into Irish hands, they might just cut his throat. The English are a bit more cautious."

"If you say so, sir."

"What have they got to lose? I mean, my God! He's one of my science advisors!"

Saddler's mouth felt as though it were filled with sawdust. All of this cloak-and-dagger intrigue! He felt like a nonperson in the White House. The President trusted him but this was not why he had entered government service! He thought then of the pressures he would have to put on Ruckerman and it made his stomach turn sour.

As though he read Saddler's mind, Velcourt said: "You're Ruckerman's closest friend here, Jimmy. I think you're the only one who could get him to do this."

"It's not as though he had his family right here," Saddler said. "His wife's caught out there in the Sonoma Reserve, you know."

"I know."

"I'll have to tell him quite a bit, sir."

"I don't really care how much you tell him; just make sure Turkwood doesn't get wind of it. It'd go right straight to Shiloh. I don't trust those bastards at all. I mean, Jimmy, Shiloh's people are a bunch of real nuts. Let me tell you—their latest thing is they want to kill the pope!"

In the long sweep of history, revenge is such a bore. The insane and the young idealists get caught up in it, though. The young want the Old Man to be guilty. That makes it easier to depose him. Young idealists are a danger in every age because they act without looking deeply enough into themselves or into the problems they address. They're driven mostly by their own hot blood. It's largely a sexual thing. They want control of the breeding stock. And the tragedy lies in the fact they mostly perpetuate new dreams of revenge for the next generation of young idealists . . . that, or they create a super madman, a Hitler or an O'Neill.

— **Fintan Craig Doheny**

"YOU UNDERSTAND," Doheny said, "that we are necessarily concentrating a great deal of our effort on sex chromatin bodies."

"That doesn't surprise me," John said. "I presume you have facilities for fluorescent microscopy?"

"Oh, yes."

They sat in Doheny's office high in the administration wing of Kilmainham Royal Hospital. It was a white-walled room about six meters square. Framed photographs of country landscapes and city scenes decorated the walls. John paid little attention to them after a first glance. Doheny sat in a comfortable chair behind a large desk. He was a wispy-haired troll with eyes that pinned down whatever they saw.

John sat in a wooden chair across from Doheny. There was a yellow settee with a coffee table against one wall of the room. A bookcase filled the wall behind Doheny. Two windows on John's right looked out across the park-like grounds to Kilmainham Jail where, he was told, Kevin O'Donnell had gone, that being his headquarters.

They had come down to the city in armored cars—Father Michael, the boy, Herity and Kevin O'Donnell riding in one, John and Doheny alone with a driver and one guard in the other. The cars had parted on Inchicore Road, the one carrying John turning to sweep under the arch into the hospital grounds. Doheny had led John up a short flight of steps, moving swiftly for such a heavy man. They had gone down a long hall of closed doors into an elevator and up three stories, down another hall to this glistening white room. A small man in a green smock had followed them inside and had taken John's finger-prints.

"You don't mind, do you?" Doheny had asked.

That had been almost an hour ago.

John glanced down at the dark ink that solvent had failed to remove from his fingers. Why had they taken his finger-prints? John could feel the stirring of O'Neill-Within. Danger here!

He had felt immersed in peril since the encounter on the road above Dublin. Doheny had been the man with Kevin O'Donnell—a curly fuzz like baby hair covering his round head. The face was benign—wide blue eyes, a short and thin nose, rather flat lips with smile creases. Jolly, that was the word for Doheny, but he radiated threat.

Kevin O'Donnell had been the first to speak.

"I see you found warm clothing, Yank. Permit me to intro-duce Fintan Craig Doheny. Doctor Doheny is here to decide whether you live or die."

Doheny had remained silent.

Not looking at Kevin, John had pressed his lips together tightly to keep them from trembling. Herity and the others stood back, silent observers.

"We know who you are," Kevin said.

For an instant, John thought his heart had stopped. He kept his attention on Doheny. The latter studied John with bland intensity. John understood then: Doheny was the hunter waiting at the water hole, gaze unwavering, every sense concentrated on the kill. What bait had he staked out here?

"Have you nothing to say?" Kevin asked.

John found his voice, an astonishingly level tone emerging from icy calm. "What am I supposed to say?" He allowed himself to look at Kevin and met an eager stare. "Of course you know who I am. You saw my passport."

"You're John Roe O'Neill!" Kevin accused.

John created a smile, forming it with exquisite slowness, his lips turning up, mouth slightly parted.

"Would you be telling us what you find humorous?" Kevin demanded.

John took a deep breath. He could hear it in Kevin's voice: bluff, all of it. There was no bait at this water hole.

"A lot of things have become clear to me," John said.

"You'll be explaining those words," Kevin said.

John glanced at Herity standing there with a quizzical expression on his face, Father Michael looking withdrawn and pained, the boy huddled against the priest, then back to Doheny. "Let's not play stupid games. You've had Herity interrogating me all this time and you—"

"He's a heavy-handed fellow, our Joseph," Kevin said. "That amuses you?"

"I'm just relieved to understand finally what's been going on," John said.

Kevin leaned forward on the balls of his feet. "Then you're denying . . ."

"You're all being stupid!" John said. "Ireland's the last place in the world the Madman would come."

Kevin looked squarely at John. "We've thought on that. Were I the Madman, I should want to play God. I should want to see what I had wrought. This is the Madman's seventh day, this is. How can he not come here and admire his work?"

"That's mad," John said.

"And aren't we talking about a madman?" Kevin asked.

As John started to respond, Doheny raised a hand for silence. John understood then: Doheny was the Grand Inquisitor. Someone else put the questions and applied the pain. Doheny observed and judged.

John studied the man. What was his judgment?

For the first time in this encounter, Doheny spoke, a deep and compelling voice. John was surprised at the gentleness of it—velvet, that voice.

"Let's bring him along," Doheny said. "I'll need his fingerprints and we'll want a dentist to look in his mouth."

John felt his mouth go dry. Fingerprints and dental pattern! O'Neill-Within could be felt squirming. What evidence did the Irish Inquisitor possess? Nothing had been left at the college. Surely not at the house. Had it? Panic Fire had been used there.

He had heard it on the news while still in France.

From that point, John had allowed himself to be moved along like a puppet, concentrating on presenting a bland expression—bored. Long-suffering.

The first half hour in Doheny's office had been bad. Waiting . . . waiting. What would the fingerprints reveal? When would they take him for a dental examination? Then a telephone had rung. Doheny had lifted it from a hook beside his desk, speaking one word into it.

"Doheny."

He listened, then: "Thank you. No . . . nothing else."

The charade had been played out, Doheny thought as he replaced the phone on its hook. *This John Garrech O'Donnell had not broken.* He now understood Herity's confusion. What was it about this John O'Donnell?

Doheny swiveled his chair and looked out the window toward Kilmainham Jail. Should the suspect be turned over to Kevin? The jail was a slippery place where men had died for no better reason than a whim. The present regime was only reinforcing that reputation. *Why did we choose that place for a seat of government?* Doheny wondered. *A terrible place, a monument to uncounted griefs.* He knew the answer.

Because it's large enough and small enough. Because it's in Dublin. Because we had to bring ourselves back together. Because we needed a symbol. And there's one thing to be said for Kilmainham: It's a symbol.

"You say you're a molecular biologist?" Doheny asked.

"That's right."

For about twenty minutes then, John submitted to questioning about his knowledge, particular emphasis on recombinant DNA. Doheny displayed a considerable knowledge of the subject, but John had sensed the limits quite early when the questions lapsed into the area of educated guesses. John detected easily the areas where his own knowledge went far beyond Doheny's, especially when they got into synthesis interphases. The trick was to limit what was revealed in the answers.

Doheny tipped back in his chair, hands behind his head. "Where would you consider yourself most valuable?"

"My micromethodology is considered to be very good."

"That's what you concentrated on at this University of Washington?"

"Among other things."

Without tipping his head, Doheny lowered his gaze to his bare desktop. "You've had experience with mitotically active small lymphocytes?"

"Oh, yes."

Doheny leaned forward, elbows on the desk, hands clasped loosely in front of him. "I suspect you're more conversant with the subject than I am. We have made some discoveries, however."

John felt his pulse quicken. There was a sense of questioning from O'Neill-Within.

"I'm anxious to know about your progress," John said.

"I want to caution you about your approach to this plague," Doheny said. "As a medical researcher you will tend to have a bias about disease. The plague ignites a particular susceptibility to that mistake."

John took a moment to respond. What was Doheny saying? Was he stalling? Had the Irish discovered nothing significant after all this time?

When John failed to speak, Doheny said: "You are required to face absolute termination immediately. To the traditional researcher, diseases are things that run their course. Life goes on even if a particular case is not cured."

John nodded and held his silence.

"We expect immunities to develop," Doheny said. "Or we expect some other natural process to intervene. But the plague will terminate mankind unless we solve it."

O'Neill-Within whispered in John's mind: *They've found out about the long dormancy phase.*

It came to John then that Doheny was still probing, subtly and expertly seeking after O'Neill. As he thought this, John felt O'Neill withdraw, deep within. Doheny was more dangerous than Herity. What had happened to Herity, the priest and the boy?

"Quarantine will not work forever," Doheny said.

John found that he was taking short, shallow breaths. He tried to breathe deeper but his chest pained him.

"Have you confronted the fact that we may face an unsolvable problem?" Doheny asked.

John shook his head. "There has to be a . . . solution." He thought about his own words. It had never occurred to him that O'Neill's revenge might be an ultimate failure for mankind. Every problem could be solved! He knew how the plague had been created: The form of it lay there in his mind, an internal movie that he could play at will. No cure? That was insane!

"Have you noticed that we're not creating any hopeful new myths here in Ireland?" Doheny asked.

"What?" Doheny's words bounced around in John's awareness. What was the man saying?

"Only the old myths of death and destruction," Doheny said. "It's fitting we should originate the Literature of Despair."

"What has that to do with . . ."

"What greater proof of ultimate defeat?"

"Have you given up?"

"That's not the point, John. May I call you John?"

"Yes, but . . . what are . . ."

"Recognizing ultimate defeat does terrible psychic damage, John. Bitter, bitter consequences . . ."

"But you yourself just suggested . . ."

"That we may have to swallow the bitter pill."

John stared at the man. Was he insane? Was this a variation on the mad priest at the clothing hut?

"What do you say to this, John?" Doheny asked.

"Where're Herity, Father Michael and the boy?"

Doheny looked startled. "What's your concern about them?"

"I . . . just wondered."

"They're not Ireland, John."

Yes they are! John thought. *They're my Ireland.*

Revenge had created them, shaped them like clay on a potter's wheel. The silent boy loomed large in his mind. What would the boy be if there were nothing fragile or pathetic about him? There must be strength in him somewhere. John tried to visualize the boy maturing—those faun's eyes. A heartbreaker should any mature female ever get to know him. But that would never happen if Doheny's suspicions proved true!

No more agony for that boy, John thought. *It's enough. O'Neill-Within is content.*

"We're not defeated," John said.

"And that's what I'm warning you about, John. Look around you. Defeated people always try to compensate with myths and legends."

"We're not talking about myths and legends!"

"Oh, but we are. We're talking about the retrospective curtains that hide unacceptable facts. Not disaster but heroic tales! No people has ever been more accomplished at myth creation than we Irish."

"No more hope," John said, his voice low, remembering

Grampa Jack and the magic stories beside the fireplace.

"The devil's own truth," Doheny said. "Imagine it, John. Everything in our history conspired to strengthen the Irish faculty for the heroic myth to soften defeat."

"Tell that to Father Michael!"

"Michael Flannery? Aw, now, even the Church did stalwart duty with its myths. Defeat reduced to divine justice, God's revenge for past misbehavior. The English even had a hand in this. With a kind of unwitting perversity, they outlawed our religion. Prohibition always strengthens what it bans."

John's thoughts whirled in confusion. What lay behind Doheny's words?

Doheny patted his bulging stomach. "The starvations were a peculiar Irish trauma, a lesson we've never forgotten. Compulsive eating is our most common response to adversity."

John decided this must be mad rambling. No real point in it, no reasoning behind it.

"I'm one of the few fat men in Ireland these days," Doheny said.

"Then you haven't given up."

"I may be the only mythmaker left to us," Doheny said. "Inspired research, that's what we need right now."

John shook his head, uncomprehending.

"I've been sitting here composing a myth about John Garrech O'Donnell," Doheny said. "Garrech." He rolled it out in that velvet voice. "John Garrech O'Donnell, a fine old Irish name. It demands a special myth, it does."

"What in the hell are you talking about?"

"I'm talking about John Garrech O'Donnell, a Yankee descendant of strong Gaelic stock. That's what I'm talking about. You've come back to us, John Garrech O'Donnell. You've brought us a sensational new approach to the plague! You're a vision of hope, John Garrech O'Donnell! I'll put it about immediately."

"Are you nuts?"

"People will admire you, John."

"For what?"

"For your vision. The Irish always admire vision."

"I'll not be a party to . . ."

"Then I'll have to turn you over to Kevin for immediate disposal. We've plenty of lab technicians. What we need is inspiration and hope."

"And what happens if I don't . . ."

"If you fail? Ahhh, then that's the end of you right there. We're not very tolerant of failure, we aren't."

"You mean you just kill off..."

"Oh, no! Nothing so bloody or simple. But Kevin has a short temper and a quick gun."

"Then I'll have to hide my mistakes."

"Not from me, you won't!" Doheny pushed himself away from his desk. "We'll be sending you along to Peard at Killaloe. I suggest you work out your sensational new approach to the plague before you arrive."

John's gaze followed Doheny as the man arose. "Do or die?"

"Isn't that the nature of our problem?" Doheny asked.

John forced his gaze away from Doheny. The way the man stood there, accusing!

"You see, John," Doheny said, "there's new pressure from the plague. The thing is mutating. It's into the mammals of the sea: the whales, the porpoises, the seals and such. No stopping the spread of it now."

John knew his face was a frozen mask. Mutation! There was something he had not considered. It had gotten out of hand. The thing was a wildfire.

"If you'll just wait here," Doheny said, "I'll go and lay on your travel arrangements."

He let himself out into the hall. Kevin already was there, emerging from the adjoining office.

"You're a fool, Doheny!" Kevin whispered. "What if he tries to destroy our work at Killaloe?"

"Then you'll have to kill him," Doheny said. "Have they sent the fingerprints and dental charts, yet?"

"They're playing it cautious! *Why do we want them? Do we have a suspect?* Why else do they think we'd ask?"

"It was dangerous to ask, Kevin."

"It's dangerous to live!"

"Kevin...if that's O'Neill in there and if I've motivated him correctly, he'll solve the thing for us."

"You as much as told him it couldn't be cured!"

"That surprised him, you know. He was shocked. Never thought about it before. Typical researcher. Eyes on the goal."

"And what if you're right?" Kevin asked. "What if it's O'Neill and *he* fails?"

"Then hope is dead for sure."

> *A doctor says: "Sir, it would be better to die according to the rules than to live in contradiction to the Faculty of Medicine."*
>
> —Molière, speaking to a patient who recovered with unorthodox treatment

WILLIAM RUCKERMAN'S first meeting with his pilot was on the field at Hagerstown, Maryland. Dawn opened a thin crack of light along the eastern horizon. It was cold, it was misty wet and Ruckerman was nursing a nervous stomach. He had been staying in a military-run hotel near the field for two days before Weather said it was safe to make the trans-Atlantic flight. The two days had been a sniffy, headachy period in which he had experienced the growing certainty that he was suffering the benign symptoms of the plague, realizing with an empty feeling that he was now a carrier.

Someone from the Washington power elite had to do this, though, the long-term stakes being what they were. Beckett's little cabal had really nailed down the potential but they were crazy if they thought they could control it by themselves.

Cranmore McCrae, the pilot, turned out to be a short and rather stout young man with an oversized head—a head so large that Ruckerman decided it must be the result of hormone imbalances. McCrae, standing just inside the plane, appeared deformed: small blue eyes set widely apart over a flat nose, long mouth with thick lips and blocky jaw which moved on a hinge far back against his neck.

The plane was a small twin jet of a model Ruckerman did not recognize. It looked like an expensive executive aircraft—sleek and fast with its nose jutting far out over the front gear. The door folded down to become stairs.

The sergeant who had driven Ruckerman to the field stood at the foot of the stairs, damp wind whipping his coat, until McCrae closed the door and sealed it. McCrae strapped Ruckerman's bag into an empty seat, then led the way forward, beginning the oddest interrogation Ruckerman had ever experienced.

"Tell me, Doctor Ruckerman," McCrae asked, "is there any reason Charlie Turkwood might want you dead?"

Ruckerman, who was seating himself in the right-hand side of the cockpit and beginning to fasten his seatbelt, stopped and stared at McCrae. What a strange question. Ruckerman wondered if he had heard it correctly.

"Fasten your seatbelt there," McCrae said. "We're getting the hell outa here."

"Are you suggesting Charlie Turkwood might want me dead?" Ruckerman asked, clipping the lock of his seatbelt.

"That's the general idea." McCrae donned a headset and adjusted a microphone close to his lips. He thumbed a switch on the control wheel.

"This is Rover Boy," he said. "Ready to taxi."

"Clear to taxi, Rover Boy." The metallic voice from the tower came from an overhead speaker. Ruckerman looked up at the grille.

"I have no idea what you're talking about," he said. And he wondered what Jim Saddler had gotten him into—people wanting him dead! He mused on this as McCrae cleared for the runway, taxied into position and aimed the aircraft down the long field.

McCrae looked at him then. "I sure hope you're right."

He pushed the throttles to the firewall. The plane gathered speed, slowly at first, then pressing Ruckerman back into the cushions. Lift-off was smooth, followed by rapid climb out over the low overcast. Ruckerman blinked in the bright sunlight reflected off a fleecy ocean of clouds.

"About six and a half hours estimated flying time," McCrae said.

"Why the devil did you ask that question about Turkwood?" Ruckerman demanded.

"I was a CIA pilot and I still have a few friends who tell me things. Can I call you Will? I hear that's what your friends call you."

Ruckerman spoke stiffly: "Call me whatever you like, just so long as you explain this, this . . ."

"Well, Will, my friends say Turky is bad news. I've been nosing around, you know? Trying to find out if there might be some jokers in this deck . . . some other reason for our little trip."

"What other reason could there possibly be?" Ruckerman looked out at the cloud cover, a changing landscape without any safe referents. He wondered if they had assigned him a mad pilot.

"You really think the Irish have that Madman O'Neill?" McCrae asked. "They want me to look into that after I drop you off."

"I'm sure I couldn't say," Ruckerman said.

"I know that sergeant who drove you out to the field," McCrae said. "An odd-job man. What'd you two talk about during the drive?"

"He wondered who had arranged for me to do this. I . . . I told him I thought it originated with the President himself."

"Christ on a crutch!" McCrae said.

"Will you tell me what this is all about?"

"Look, Will," McCrae said, "we're at thirty-two thousand right now and things look pretty smooth here. I'm going to put this bird on automatic while I go back and have a look around. You just sit tight and don't touch anything. Sing out if you see any other planes. Okay?"

"Look around? For what?"

"I'd feel a lot better about this flight if I was sure we weren't packing something that'll go boom."

"A bomb?" Ruckerman felt a tight sensation in the pit of his stomach.

McCrae had unbuckled his harness and slipped out of it. He stood bent over, looking back at Ruckerman.

"It could be just my native caution." He turned away and left the compartment but his voice was still audible to Ruckerman. "Damn! I should've demanded to make my own inspection of this bird!"

Ruckerman turned and looked out the windscreen. Their

flight path was taking them diagonally across a deep chasm in the clouds, a gray glimpse of ocean through the screening mists far below.

This was insane. This whole trip did not ring true, suddenly. He was tempted to tell McCrae to turn back. But would McCrae obey him? And even if McCrae agreed, would they be allowed to return?

"This is a one-way trip until we find the cure," Saddler had said.

Ruckerman thought of the deep banks of antiaircraft missiles around Washington. One MUSAM with its multi-headed heat-and-motion-seekers . . .

McCrae slipped back into his seat and buckled his harness. "I can't find a damn thing." He checked his instruments and looked then at Ruckerman. "How'd they rope you into this?"

"I was the obvious choice."

"Yeah? For what?"

"I have the confidence of the President and his chief advisors. I have the scientific background to, well, assess . . . things."

"My friends say you may be a patsy."

"What do you mean?"

"There's a lot of hate going around against science and scientists. How'd you get contaminated, anyway?"

Ruckerman swallowed. This was the tricky part. "I . . . it was a stupid thing. I went through a wrong door at one of the quarantine stations. They should not have left that door unlocked!"

"And maybe you should've been more careful."

Ruckerman searched in his mind for a way to divert the conversation, then: "How were you chosen as my pilot?"

"I volunteered."

"Why?"

"I have an uncle in Ireland, a real oddball. Never married. Rich enough to pay off the national debt." McCrae grinned. "And I'm his only living relative."

"Is he still . . . I mean, alive?"

"He has a ham radio. Ham operators have been passing along his messages. Uncle Mac's got himself a private estate over there. And this'll get you. He's reviving the religion of Druidism—tree worship, the whole magilla."

"He sounds crazy."

"Not crazy, just weird."

"And you're his only heir? How can you be sure of that or that inheritance will . . . Things have changed, you know."

McCrae shrugged. "Uncle Mac and I are look-alikes. He was always pretty fond of me. Things being the way they are, what better thing do I have on my plate than to go over and look after my own interests?"

"Well, I wish you luck."

"You, too, Will. You're gonna need it."

"I still don't understand what made you suspect a . . . bomb?"

"I know things about Turkwood that most people don't even whisper."

"You know him?"

"From before the plague and since then . . . by phone. That's what worries me, Will. I know things he might want erased. You, though, I can't figure why he might want you out unless it's just another write-off."

Ruckerman tried to swallow in a dry throat, remembering how cautious Saddler had been. Not a word of what he carried in his case, the special search program from DA, none of that must get to Turkwood. That had been the reason for the ridiculous charade at the quarantine station. Accidental contamination!

"You okay?" McCrae asked. "You look sorta peaked."

"This is insane," Ruckerman muttered. "It's vital that I get to England! And you must get to Ireland, find out if they really have O'Neill. My God! If it's O'Neill and he could be persuaded to talk!"

"If," McCrae said. "If they really have O'Neill and if the son-of-a-bitch is still alive. I dunno, Will. If I were in Ireland and I had that guy in my hands . . ."

"They know how important it would be to preserve him!"

"Do they? And what difference does it make to them? What've they got to lose?"

McCrae released his harness. "I'm going back for another look around. Same drill. Don't touch anything, Will."

"Mister McCrae?"

"Call me Mac."

"Yes, well, Mac . . ." Ruckerman shook his head. "No, it's too wild."

"Nothing's too wild. What's making you nervous?"

"Both Doctor Saddler and the President were very anxious that . . . ahhh, this trip be kept secret from Turkwood, that is, until . . ."

"Secret? Why?"

"I, uh, don't know."

"You do know but you're not saying. Christ! I've got myself another hot cargo!"

"I'm sorry, Mac, but this is all probably just our active imaginations. These are times for..."

"These are times for active imaginations." He stared at the instrument panel. Presently, he touched a white button above the throttle console. A red light went on above the button. "That could be because we're going too fast," he muttered. He disengaged the autopilot, grasped the throttles and eased them back.

Ruckerman watched the airspeed indicator crawl back into the green band, stopping at 120.

Again, McCrae touched the white button. Again, the red light flashed.

"Could be a circuit malfunction," McCrae said.

"What're you doing?" Ruckerman asked.

McCrae pushed the throttles forward, checked their course and restored the autopilot. They were out over open ocean, only a thinly scattered cloud cover underneath. The sun was bright, throwing white sparkles off the waves.

"There's a little barometric gadget that's been used a few times," McCrae said. "My friends once said Turkwood likes it. It's attached to a wad of plastic explosive and the whole thing's seated in a landing gear compartment. It's armed when you lower the gear and, if you go below a set altitude, ka-powie!"

"What... what set altitude?"

"Maybe a couple hundred meters. Right down there when you're on final, the field in front of you and not a damn thing you can do about it. No time to jump out with a parachute, provided you even have a parachute, which we don't. Right down there where you're sure to smear yourself all over the landscape. Real helmet-funeral stuff."

"Helmet funeral?"

"They recover just about enough of your body to fill a standard flight helmet."

"What evidence do you have that..."

"That little red light there. Emergency confirmation circuit. Green says gear's up and seated, or down and seated, whichever shows on this indicator up here." McCrae pointed to another switch above his right knee. A green "gear up" light glowed above the switch. "When I test, the light says gear's not up, but we're flying as though everything's in order."

"Could there be some other explanation?"

"Circuit malfunction. But Jesus! A whole platoon of mechanics checked out this bird."

Ruckerman thought about this for a moment. He took a deep breath and shook his head. "It's paranoid!"

"With Turkwood? That's the safest way to go."

Ruckerman felt anger taking over. It was an emotion he loathed. The mind did not work clearly with any strong emotion. Rational thought—the world's only future lay in rational thought. Science failed when rational thought failed. The anger continued to mount.

"What the hell can we do about it?" he demanded. "How can we be sure your suspicions are even..."

"Let me think about it, Will." McCrae checked his instruments and the autopilot, confirmed their position and leaned back in his seat. He closed his eyes.

Ruckerman watched him, embarrassed by the angry outburst. *A patsy!* McCrae's suspicions were all fantasy. The computer program, the summations of other projects, all of the material back there in that bag . . . and O'Neill possibly in Ireland! God! He might even get a chance to interview the man personally. What could be more important than that? The President might do many things to stay in power and keep his world in order, but he certainly would *not* jeopardize the efforts to find a plague cure.

Slowly, Ruckerman grew aware of a strange sound. He looked at McCrae. The man was snoring! The bastard was asleep! How could he sleep after . . . after . . .

McCrae snorted and sat upright, opening his eyes. "They've got lakes in England," he said. "A high lake . . . or maybe even a high field." He reached down to his left, fingered through a series of charts there and extracted one, opening it in front of him. He scanned it, his lips working. "Yeah. Yeah, a nice high one right up there above Aberfeldy." He restored the chart to its place beside him. "We fake engine trouble and . . . swoosh."

"How far will we be from Huddersfield?" Ruckerman asked.

"Don't worry, Will," McCrae said. "You're a VIP. They'll wheel you around in a limousine. Me, I'm small potatoes and few in the hill. I gotta find a way to get back to Ireland and then to Uncle Mac's place."

McCrae turned and grinned at Ruckerman, a wide toothy

expression in that lantern-jawed face. "Besides, I'm captain of this here ship. I say where she goes."

Ruckerman scowled at him, then turned away. Insane suspicions! But . . . a few more hours' delay . . . What did it really matter? Just as long as McCrae was satisfied. The selfish bastard! Harebrained! Another thought crept into Ruckerman's mind. He turned toward McCrae.

"Granting that there's an explosive device on this plane, what if it's set to go off after a certain time?"

"Then we feed the fishes," McCrae said.

> *Up the long ladder*
> *And down the short rope—*
> *To hell with King Billy,*
> *To hell with the Pope!*

—Songs of the New Ireland

JOHN SAT in the far back of the armored car with only a slit in the steel beside him through which he could see the passing countryside, everything green upon green in the morning light. It was cold outside and the steel chilled his skin when he touched it. The seat was not padded. Father Michael and the boy occupied the seat in front of him, the boy curled up asleep with his head against the priest. The driver and an armed guard in front were a taciturn pair, ruddy-faced youths in military green, dark-haired both of them, with an oddly cynical alertness in their manner, as though they listened to some unseen speaker who warned them of terrible things to come.

Another armored car went in front about a hundred meters away, and two more followed, all three fully manned. There was a rocket launcher on the car in the van.

There had been no sign of Herity since that last glimpse of him heading off for Kilmainham Jail, and Father Michael nor any of the others could or would say where he had gone.

Father Michael leaned forward, dislodging the boy beside him and arousing a sleepy moan from him. The priest spoke to the driver, the words not audible to John, but the driver's answer carried clearly to the rear.

"We go by the way that's reasonably safe, Father. The long way is often the shortest these days."

Father Michael nodded and leaned back.

The armored car bounced and jerked in the rough spots. The road went winding up through hills, giving an occasional glimpse down through lanes of conifers toward the Irish Sea with houses and smoking chimneys—touches of glistening ice wherever John could see fresh water in the breaks. It was scenery of such ordinary splendor that it produced a sense of electric disturbance in John, stirring O'Neill-Within to cavernous whimpers, small cries and always that awful scream waiting there in the caves of his mind. The view down to the sea should not appear untouched. There should be signs on the land that the old Ireland had vanished. Otherwise . . . what was the purpose?

The driver turned to his companion and said something. John heard only the two words at the end, spoken louder as the rumblings of the armored car increased on a steepening climb.

". . . but now . . ."

Those two words at the end of a statement, the recurrence of those same two words and nothing spoken after them, struck John as a verbal mark of the new Ireland. This thought soothed O'Neill-Within and left John alone to reflect.

". . . but now . . ."

A more descriptive expression of the times might not be found. *Nothing* came after now. Men had thought once they could solve any problem, scientific or otherwise, if they set about it with scrupulous persistence and good will, with a patience that cared nothing for time. At least, that was the scientific way to think. But now . . .

What could he do at the Killaloe Facility? Were Doheny's darkest fears to be proved true? That could not be! He thought about his departure from Doheny that morning. It had been dark before dawn, cold in the office. The light over Doheny's desk had been a yellow island in the gloom. Doheny had been busy signing a stack of papers, passing them to an old man who waited beside him—a stoop-shouldered old fellow who took the papers in a knobby-knuckled hand, straightening them on the desk before departing with them. Not a word spoken between the two men the whole time.

John had busied himself moving around the office, looking at the photographs on the walls, peering closely at them in the dim light. He stopped at one, caught by the mystery of a partly defaced sign on a brick wall. He tried to make out the wording.

"IF   Y   HAVE   FORMA   AB   UT   MURD   EX-
P OS NS , IN MIDATI N , OR TER ORIS , IN
CO P ETE CONF ENCE CAL BE AST 65 155 ."

Seeing John's attention on the photograph, Doheny said: "I keep that as a reminder. It was mostly useless, words instead of actions. Nothing but words and very little action. The message is there, though, and the rulers in Ulster put great store by it. The thing is an interesting comparison with our present problem. When the missing parts are restored, the sign reads:

"If you have information about murder, explosions, intimidation, or of terrorism, in complete confidence, call Belfast 65-155."

John turned and looked down at Doheny, feeling a surge of turmoil at the man's words. Terrorism!

"The Madman sent us a message with missing parts," Doheny said. He nodded at the photograph. "That sign was in Derry. Belfast was the central point for gathering intelligence."

John spoke slowly while staring at the photograph. Terrorism. "Intelligence about men like Joseph Herity?"

"And about the Prods, too. There was little to choose between them if you were a target for the bullets and the bombs."

John turned slowly, reluctantly. Doheny gazed up at him benignly, a glint of cynical humor in the dark eyes. The man appeared so like a fuzzy-haired doll there under the yellow light, the morning painting gray on the window behind him.

"We had something close to sixty thousand souls there then," Doheny said. "Now . . . I'd say no more than four or five thousand men living in and around. A city dies without its women."

John cleared his throat but did not speak.

"Trade it is that keeps a city going," Doheny said. "But trade's a dependency of the home. A city . . ." He flicked a glance at the photograph behind John. "A city is a place for artisans, for shopkeepers, deliverymen and the like. But women are at the heart of a city's trade. Men alone are forced back onto the land, grubbing their food from the dirt and rediscovering what it means to be a husbandman. Strange word, that."

John looked at the top of the windowframe, unable to meet Doheny's stabbing gaze.

"That color photograph to the right of the sign is of the same sign from across the river," Doheny said. "That little white spot there, you can't read it from that far away even if it's complete."

John turned and looked at the photograph, a study of the old city of Derry, its rock walls chipped and scarred by the conflicts of centuries... dirty brown rocks rising above the River Foyle... and low to one side, the little white rectangle with its black lettering.

"The men who're still there won't leave," Doheny said. "But there's no meaning to the wage packet anymore. They'll be gone soon enough. It's the wage packet, y'know, John. The foundation of the family presence, source of housing, food, clothing, entertainment. Now, I ask you straight, John, how many sources of wage do you suppose could be found today in Derry?"

John turned back to Doheny and that pinioning stare. "Not... many."

"What good are incomplete messages?" Doheny asked. "But it's our literary fantasy to persist."

John moved away from the wall, going around the desk to the stiff wooden chair. Something in those photos had contaminated him! The chair was cold and hard beneath him. Doheny's gaze followed him, expression unwavering.

As he stared out the slit in the armored car, John thought about that conversation. The convoy was crossing a long stretch of high bog with newly cut turf ricks neatly thatched, a patch of dark plastic at each peak weighted there by stone. It was such an ordinary scene that he could feel it once more arousing O'Neill-Within.

Father Michael turned suddenly and stared at John.

"They're still cutting turf," John said.

Father Michael spoke in a low voice, not to disturb the boy beside him. "The hydroelectric dam at Ardnacrusha was blown away early. We've only the peat-burning stations now and not many men as will cut the peat for them."

John noted that the priest had put on a V-necked gray sweater with white buttons under his black suit. He had exchanged his hat for a black watchcap. The sweater was close to the color of one worn by a toothless old guard in the hospital courtyard. Doheny had left John there alone with the man, going away "to see what's keeping the cars."

The old man's sweater had been hand-knit, thick yarn and

the slight imperfections that only the hand could impart. John had stood on the stones, aware of the damp cold in the morning. There were patches of blue overhead, the mist lifting. His attention kept coming back to the old man standing there so watchfully silent, the thin chest under the gray sweater.

His wife's hands made that sweater, John thought. Even as John thought this, the old man pulled the sweater close around him against the chill. The thing gapped with a missing button at the bottom. The knitting had a begrimed look as though it had never been washed, and John thought: *The old man wants that second-hand touch of her in this garment that her fingers worked.*

He heard the whisper of O'Neill-Within then: *"Is there nothing left that Mary touched?"*

Tears burned his eyes.

The old man looked away at some noise outside the courtyard, bent his head to listen and, when he turned back, his watchful stare was gone. It was a withered face, a witless eye and a mouth where the teeth were no more—and that was all. He spoke in a cracked voice:

"You're t' one come in wit' t' priest?"

"That's right."

"Warn that one not t' start up t' Church and t' Mass here!" the old man said. "I'll wind his cassock around his breathpipe if he tries."

John was astonished at the bitter strength in the old voice, a strength that did not move up to the eyes nor touch the mouth, as though that toothless hole were only a mechanical speaker for a message from deep within.

"You don't want Father Michael celebrating the Mass?" John asked.

"Celebrating!" The old man spat on the courtyard stones, then spoke in a weak voice as though the one word had used him up. "I'm an old man wit' all me nimble days gone, most of me power spent. There's no more quickness in me and I'll go no more to Mass because I think too much there of me Fiona kneeling and praying." Fire returned to the cracked voice. "What have her prayers brought except t' loneliness?"

John felt O'Neill-Within, a silent watcher, fascinated by the toothless mouth and its bitter words.

"I was born at midnight and can see t' shades of t' dead," the old man said. "If I squints me eyes proper and if I stares at one place long enough, I see me old woman there at t' fire, just as real as life, cooking me breakfast porridge."

The old man squinted his eyes and peered across the inner spaces of the courtyard. His voice fell almost to a whisper.

"It's not like t' memories of old pains. They can be made gone, y' know. This is t' pain that goes not away. This is t' pain you can feel wit'out t' knowing. It's in t' skull, it is, and it won't stop short of t' grave." He shook his head feebly. "Mayhap not even there."

Doheny returned then, striding across the stones from the arched entrance, a strangely vigorous walk in such a heavy man. The old man gave him a limp salute as Doheny stopped.

"They're picking up Father Michael and the boy right now," Doheny said. "Be along in a minute. Has old Barry here been whiling away your time with a story?"

John nodded.

Doheny patted the old man on the shoulder. "Get along out to the entrance, Barry. Wave a hand when they come up. We'll join you then."

Doheny spoke to John while keeping his attention on the old man walking away from them. "Some among us live in the hope of revenge." He cast a quick glance at John. "Some in despair and some lost in whatever pleasures they can find— drink, drugs, hideous parodies of sex with no hope of progeny." He nodded toward the old man who had taken up station in the middle of the entrance arch, his attention directed to the right. "Barry there wants only to meet the Madman and ask one question: 'Are you satisfied with what you've done?'" Again, Doheny glanced at John. "We're most of us beyond fatigue." He cleared his throat and John thought he would spit, but Doheny swallowed. "We have our various ways of avoiding reality. If you forced us to face it every moment of our days we'd all go mad."

The rumbling of several vehicles could be heard at a distance on the street outside. The old man bent forward to stare in that direction.

Doheny said: "O'Neill's revenge was, I suppose, his way of not facing his reality. And the terrorists who outraged him, the bomb, that was their way of avoiding their reality." Again, he looked at John, a fixed stare. "You'll find even a bit of sympathy around for that poor Madman, O'Neill."

John rubbed his throat, unable to turn away from Doheny's gaze.

"If you have no alternative to despair, you may explode,"

Doheny said. "We had only the role models of our fathers, the examples in the Church and State and family—violent and angry and painful." Doheny turned toward the entrance. "Ahhh, there they are now."

John looked up to see the old man waving to them. An olive-green armored car was visible in the archway beyond him.

"When you get to Killaloe," Doheny said, "make them give you some fresh clothing, stuff that fits. You should be comfortable at least."

Riding toward Killaloe in the armored car, John returned again and again to that strange scene in the hospital courtyard . . . the old man, Doheny. It had been like theater prepared only for him. To what purpose? Was it a fishing expedition aimed at O'Neill?

O'Neill-Within remained quiescent. No sighs, no whispering, not even the echoes of screams nor the howling like that of a bereft dog. That was the most terrible sound of all—the howling.

The old man in the courtyard remained bothersome. John felt sympathy for him. It was the sympathy he felt for O'Neill. Both had suffered tragic bereavement. And what could the poor old fellow do about it? Guard a doorway? Run errands for Doheny, perhaps. Fill out his days until he died . . . alone. John had not imagined old men like that in Ireland, nor for that matter any silent boys.

Tears slid down John's cheeks. He closed his eyes against them and when he opened them, found Father Michael staring across the back of the seat at him.

John patted the seat beside him. "Father, please join me."

Gently, not to awaken the sleeping boy, Father Michael disengaged himself from the cradled head and slid over the seat, clumsily bumping into John and lurching to the position beside him as the car turned a sharp corner.

"What is it, John?" the priest asked.

"Will you hear my confession, Father?" John whispered.

It has come at last, Father Michael thought. He had suffered premonitions of this moment since first seeing John beside the lake—that strangely depilated head, the tortured face now covered by a beard . . . but the eyes still burning with terrible fires.

"Yes, of course," Father Michael said.

John waited while the priest found his case under the seat and arrayed himself for the ancient ritual. John felt calm, calmer than he could remember since...since...He could not remember ever being this calm.

Father Michael leaned toward him. "How long has it been since your last confession, my son?"

The question confused John. He had never been to confession. John Garrech O'Donnell had never said the words that lay now on the tip of his tongue. He uttered them:

"Forgive me, Father, for I have sinned."

"Yes, my son. How have you sinned?"

"Father...I have John Roe O'Neill within me."

A blank expression swept over the priest's face. He whispered hoarsely: "You...you are O'Neill?"

John stared at him. Why didn't the priest understand? "No, Father. I'm John O'Donnell. But I have O'Neill within me."

Father Michael's eyes went wide, a glazed look of fascination. He had learned his psychology from a good Jesuit, Father Ambrose Dreyfus, a doctor and an expert in Freud and Jung and Adler and Reich and the permutations between. The concept of schizophrenia was not foreign to Father Michael. But this! The enormity...the danger...

The habits of the confessional preserved him.

"Yes, my son. Please continue."

Continue? John sat in bewilderment. How could he continue? He had said it all. He felt like a raped woman carrying the rapist's child and being asked by a male gynecologist: "And what other symptoms do you have?"

When John remained silent, Father Michael asked: "Does O'Neill wish to confess through you?"

John sensed the terrible stirring within, the start of the howl. No! He pressed his hands against his ears, knowing as he did it that nothing would keep out the sounds of that awful anguish.

Father Michael sensed the dismay and said in his most calming voice: "You wish to confess for yourself?"

John held himself still for several long heartbeats, lowering his hands only when he sensed the calmness returning.

"For myself," he whispered.

Father Michael lurched into John as the armored car negotiated a rutted turn, growling loudly in reduced gears. The priest glanced forward: The driver and guard appeared unaware of the drama in the rear. The boy still slept.

His mouth close to the priest's ear, John whispered: "It's a terrible burden, Father."

Father Michael felt that he had to agree. An awesome sense

of compassion swept over him. The poor man! Driven insane...yet coming here in the shy and persistent identity of John O'Donnell. Wanting to help. A maddened creature within him trying to undo the terrible wrong.

"Help me, Father," John pleaded.

Father Michael placed a hand on John's head, feeling the neck muscles stiffen at the touch and then relax as John bent his head.

How could such anguish be relieved? the priest wondered. *What penance could possibly be assigned?* He sensed the other persona, O'Neill, waiting for him to speak.

"Please, Father!" John whispered.

Father Michael went into automatic, whispering the familiar absolution and benediction. Only the penance remained. What could he assign? How could anyone help this poor creature?

God help me! Father Michael prayed.

The solution filled his awareness and he felt blessed calm as he spoke.

"John, you must do everything in your power to find a cure for this plague. That is your penance." He made the sign of the cross on John's forehead, feeling that he had personally assumed John's burden. What priest had ever before been asked to keep such an awful secret under the seal of the confessional? Perhaps only Christ Himself had known such a weight. Father Michael could not tell.

John sat in silent withdrawal, his eyes closed tightly, fists clenched in his lap. Father Michael sensed the man's disturbance but could not hear the howling.

One of the key characteristics of an elite corps is its susceptibility to those more powerful than itself. Elite power is naturally attracted to a power hierarchy and fits itself neatly, obediently into the one that promises the most personal benefits. Here is the Achilles' heel of armies, police and bureaucracies.

—Jost Hupp

RUPERT STONAR, political watchdog on Huddersfield's plague research, stood directly under a spotlight in Hupp's working lab. Light glistened off glassware on the table beside him; it picked out lines of red in his unruly sandy hair. His expression had been carved in rock.

It was past midnight but Hupp did not know how much past. He had left his watch on his bedside table when answering the summons and had not been given time enough even to glance at it. A tough Royal Marine, someone Hupp had never seen before, had escorted him to the lab and left him about a pace from Stonar. There was no one else in the room. Hupp felt at a disadvantage in a bathrobe.

As the Royal Marine left, Stonar said: "Post a guard and let no one else in here."

"Yes, sir!"

Hupp decided he did not like the disdainful stare in Stonar's pale blue eyes. There had been a great many military types around in the halls and on the grounds—and Hupp did not like that, either, but he kept his feelings to himself.

"What is happening?" Hupp asked.

402

"You are at a critical stage in your researches," Stonar said. "How critical?"

How had Stonar found out? Hupp wondered. He said: "Wouldn't it be better if you talked to Wycombe-Finch or Doctor Beckett?"

"Why do you not suggest I talk to Doctor Ruckerman? After all, has he not recently made a thorough study of the work at this facility?"

So Stonar also knew what Ruckerman had brought, Hupp realized. This could get sticky. He said: "Ruckerman would be a good choice. Where is he?"

"He'll be brought to me when I'm ready for him."

"But why me?" Hupp asked.

"I must be certain to get the truth. Your family is closer and more accessible to us. Consequences of a lie would be extremely painful to you."

All of this was uttered in a flat monotone, knotting Hupp's stomach with fear. *Genine! The boys!* Hupp knew only too well how precarious was their safety in the Dordogne Reserve.

"What have you achieved?" Stonar asked.

"We are approaching a precise biochemical description of the plague," Hupp said.

"Would you stake your life on that?"

"Yes." Hupp stared back at Stonar, thinking how appropriate was the man's nickname: *Stoney*. Those eyes had been chipped from sapphire.

"Does this mean that presently you will be able to reproduce the plague?"

"Or an . . . antidote."

"Convince me."

Hupp glanced down the length of his cluttered lab. Not a chair in sight. This was not the place he would have chosen for an interview—too much evidence of his own volatility.

"It's quite complex," Hupp said.

"Simplify it."

Hupp groped in his robe pocket for his glasses, anything for a prop. The Royal Marine had not allowed him time to dress and now Hupp remembered that his glasses were with his watch on the bedside table. His feet were cold, protected only by slippers from the hard floor.

"The intertwining helix bends back and forth on itself," Hupp said, "You see this, for example, in the gene for botulinus or cholera toxin, and even for ordinary enteric organisms."

"Enteric?" Stonar asked.

"Things that can live in the small intestine."

"Are you saying O'Neill could have changed an ordinary organism into something like cholera?"

"Could have . . . yes. But he didn't. The plague is no ordinary viral genome. It is something nature could not have produced without human intervention. Do you understand the general recombinant DNA procedure?"

"Assume that I know nothing."

Hupp blinked. Stonar must know quite a bit about the recombinant process by now. He shrugged, then: "It's a kind of cut-and-paste procedure using enzymes mostly. You cut up the plasmid DNA and introduce foreign DNA before reinserting the plasmid in the host. A plasmid is a kind of miniature chromosome, a circlet of double-stranded DNA present in bacteria in addition to the bacteria's main, single chromosome. The plasmic replicates each time the cell divides."

"Go on."

Hupp started to speak but was interrupted by a disturbance in the hall outside. He recognized Wycombe-Finch's voice and someone else saying: "Leave or you will be removed bodily."

Stonar seemed not to notice. He asked: "What does the new genetic material do to the host?"

"It carries new information, permitting the cell to do new things, but it isn't essential to the cell's life except under unusual circumstances."

"As in the plague."

"Exactly. O'Neill created an exquisitely balanced set of genes that enter an ecological niche never before occupied by a disease organism."

"You have not completed your biochemical description and you already know this?"

"We deduced it quite a ways back. The plague not only binds up bodily mechanisms that might battle such an invasion, it also blocks vital enzymes, creating a very swift, pseudo-aging process. And most terribly, it locks itself in one place."

"That zipper idea."

"Something like that."

Stonar glanced around the lab—messy damned place! It was from just such a place that this hideous plague had originated. He returned his attention to Hupp, a man he considered to be *a wily little frog.* They all lied!

"Can it be disengaged from its locked position?" he asked.

"We'll be able to answer that question more definitely once we know its exact shape but we're already pretty sure it can be."

"You're not really sure," Stonar accused.

"Mister Stonar, these things are strings of amino acids. Each string ends in a single chain, a condition not generally found in nature because the reproduction process would tend to weed them out."

"Why is the plague not weeded out?"

Hupp took a shallow, trembling breath. He longed for Beckett's presence. Bill was much better at this sort of thing.

"O'Neill created a living factory," Hupp said. "It reproduces his pathogen and is dependent upon that reproduction for its continued existence."

"Are you telling me that you will not be able to answer my question until the very moment when you can reproduce this plague?"

"I warned you it was complex!"

"And I warned you to simplify it." There was death in Stonar's voice.

Hupp tried to swallow in a dry throat. He said: "The genetic information for a protein that can be made in one kind of cell must be transferred to another kind of cell. Before O'Neill, we believed we could change only a few characteristics by recombinant procedures, nowhere near enough to achieve a dramatic new disease in new guises. O'Neill's pathogen is no ordinary spinning-out of a simple amino acids strand. The enzymic and other splitting procedures are extraordinary. We are learning remarkable things from him. Remarkable." Hupp's voice trailed off into a musing tone, then: "I don't think he realized."

"What didn't he realize?"

"Our discoveries may be of far greater value than . . . they may far outweigh the effects of the plague."

Stonar regarded Hupp with a baleful stare, then: "Of course, your family is still among the living."

Hupp was brought up short by realization of how much Stonar must have lost to the plague. He spoke quickly. "I don't mean to make light of the plague. I'm trying to take a longer view. Humankind has taken an agonizing step, I'm saying the gigantic nature of that step has yet to be recognized."

"You're not suggesting history may look back on the Madman as a hero!"

"Oh, no! But he has led us into a new understanding of genetics."

"Fahhh!" Stonar said.

Hupp, lost in his musings, did not hear. "We have been lifted to new horizons. I am in awe of what I see."

"You scientist types scare the bloody hell out of me!" Stonar said.

Hupp heard this and was shocked to an abrupt remembrance of the power in Stonar's hands. Hupp said: "I must point out, sir, that it was not scientists who drove O'Neill insane. A violent extension of politics unfortunately struck a man who was competent . . . Mother of Christ! What an inadequate English word! Not *competent,* but unusually gifted in this dangerous field."

"You'll let me know when you're ready to admit O'Neill to your august ranks?"

Now alert to the tones in Stonar's voice, Hupp heard the derision.

"Pandora's box has been open for a long time," Hupp said. "There's no way to prevent such things as this plague unless we find a way to prevent political insanity—including insane terrorism and the injustices of police states."

"You haven't the vaguest idea of the extent to which government can go in suppression," Stonar said. "However, I did not come here to discuss political philosophy. I think that's beyond your competence."

"You believe you could have prevented an O'Neill by some . . . some kind of . . . of surveillance?"

"We will return to the matter at hand," Stonar said. "Which is your description of this plague. How do you achieve this?"

"It's based on a lot of clues, some supplied by the Irish and others . . ."

"Brought here by Doctor Ruckerman."

"He's helped, yes," Hupp admitted. "As I said earlier, the intertwined helix of DNA bends back and forth upon itself. This bending is extremely interesting. We have now discovered that the shape of submolecular elements in the DNA can be inferred from these bends and twists. It dawned on us that O'Neill had developed a new field desorption mass spectrometer technique, a soft technique for analysis of the products from the pyrolysis of DNA."

"What?"

"He used stereoisomers—left- and right-hand. He...he *burned* them, superimposed the spectrometer images and deduced the submolecular shape from the...from the...It's like seeing a shadow on a shade and deducing the shape that must have projected that shadow."

"You see?" Stonar said. "You can simplify when your life depends on it."

Hupp did not reply.

"Doctor Ruckerman has told his President that you are almost ready to do amazing things," Stonar said. "Does Wye agree?"

"Doctor Wycombe-Finch?" Hupp scratched his head, stalling for time in which to think. "I think he'd like to give us carte blanche to explore the disease template we're producing."

"But he has other people and their projects to consider?"

"That's about it. We're already talking about half the available computer time."

"You're sure you can't yet tell whether your plague...ahh, template, will lead to a cure?"

Hupp shrugged, a gesture that Stonar found offensive.

"You don't know?"

"We'll be able to answer that after we've achieved our biochemical description of the plague."

"Would it help if you had more of this facility's resources at your disposal?"

"Perhaps, but only after we've—"

"Achieved your description of the plague! Yes! Understand me, Hupp. I don't like you. You're the kind of person who created this disaster. You—"

"Sir!"

"It is not my suggestion that you are insane enough to try following in O'Neill's steps. At any rate, you'll be carefully watched and that will not be allowed. I consider it unfortunate that we need you at all. I caution you not to overestimate the extent of that need."

You are the undoubted son of a Montmarte whore! Hupp thought. He remained silent.

A faint smile touched Stonar's lips and was gone. He turned on a heel and went to the door. Opening the door, he said: "Bring in Ruckerman."

Will Ruckerman had been awakened in much the same way as Hupp, but he had been allowed to dress and then had been held under guard in an equipment storage room across from Hupp's lab.

Something had gone wrong, Ruckerman knew, but he could not guess what. The increased military presence on the Huddersfield campus had been inescapable, however. In spite of the chill in the little storage room, he had perspired heavily, a fact noted by his unresponsive guard.

Everything had been going so well! Velcourt's plan to get him into Huddersfield had worked and not even Saddler had suspected the real reason. Only Turkwood had smelled something wrong and had tried a typical Turkwood response. Ruckerman thought about their arrival in England.

McCrae had grinned at him in the small jet's cockpit, bringing the plane around in a tight circle over the lake above Aberfeldy in Scotland. "You are about to see an artist at work," he said.

"Why can't we find an airport above the..."

"Look up there." McCrae hooked a thumb at the Barrier Command jets circling high above them. "This is an emergency. If we suddenly go hunting around for another place to set down, they're going to smell mousie. You can bet they have orders to shoot at the slightest suspicion that all is not kosher here."

"That lake looks awfully small."

Ruckerman stared ahead of them at the approaching water. A low mist curled above it.

"The trick is to set us down at precisely the right spot," McCrae said. "We'll skim a bit but not much."

Gently, bucking slightly as it hung on the edge of a stall, the plane dipped down into the valley at the end of the lake and leveled off.

Ruckerman gripped the edge of his seat with both hands. McCrae was going to kill them! Those hills at the far end of the lake were too close!

McCrae was talking as much to himself as to Ruckerman: "Nose up a little." He pulled the wheel toward his chest. "A little more."

Ruckerman stared in terror at the hills looming higher and higher ahead of them. There wasn't room to do this! He started to shout a protest when the tail touched water. He felt it slap, then the nose came down sharply in a shuddering, bucking screech of protesting metal that threw him against his safety harness. Solid water covered the windscreen in front of him, hiding his view of the shore. Something grated and rasped under the nose. Water cascaded off the windscreen. The nose came up and the plane stopped. Ruckerman saw a thin line of leafless trees directly in front of him, a field with sheep cropping the grass beyond.

"Yayhooooooo!" McCrae's mouth opened wide in a shout of joy. He said something else but it was lost in the thunder of three Barrier Command jets screaming past close above them.

Ruckerman felt deafened by the sound. He was a moment recovering, then something gurgled and creaked behind him.

"Look at that, will you?" McCrae demanded. "The nose is on dry land!"

McCrae popped the cockpit's emergency exit and swung away a triangular section of windscreen beside him. He unharnessed and stood on his seat with his head outside to peer around them. "Let's get our asses out of here," he said. He stepped over the edge of the cockpit and slid down the plane's side to a pebbled shingle with spiky reeds growing through it. Presently, Ruckerman leaned out above him.

"What about our bags?" Ruckerman asked.

"If there's a bomb," McCrae said. He shook his head. "Better get out and wait a bit."

Ruckerman frowned. Probably no bomb at all! Just a grandstand play by this young jerk. Ducking back into the plane, Ruckerman made his way to the rear, wading through water over his ankles. He retrieved his bag and McCrae's lashed in the seat behind it, then returned to the emergency exit where he tossed both bags to McCrae.

"C'mon!" McCrae said. "Get outa there!"

Moving slowly to emphasize his disdain, Ruckerman followed McCrae's path to the ground. There he took his bag and followed the pilot up the pebble shingle toward the trees.

"That was a damned fool, harebrained thing to do!" Ruckerman said. "There was no—"

He was interrupted by a thumping explosion at the plane behind them. Both men whirled at the sound. The plane's left wing had been cut away along a jagged line near the fuselage. The severed portion of the wing had been driven sideways about six meters and lay upended in the reeds.

"One thing you can say for Turkwood," McCrae said. "He's neat."

Ruckerman stared at the scene in gape-jawed horror. My

God! What if that had happened in the air? He was still staring at the plane when a Land Rover came growling over the hill above them and sped down to the lake.

"We have visitors," McCrae said.

As he stared at the military guard in the little storage room opposite Hupp's lab, Ruckerman thought about poor McCrae. The English were adamant about not sending him to Ireland.

"We've no facilities for holiday jaunts," the regional commander had said as he arranged Ruckerman's transportation to Huddersfield. Poor McCrae had been shunted off to something called "The Holding Center for Foreign Nationals."

Someone rapped on the storage room door. Ruckerman's guard opened the door. Someone said: "Bring him."

Ruckerman found himself presently standing beside Hupp. Stonar regarded them both as though they had been scraped off with slime from the underside of a damp rock. Ruckerman, who had met Stonar only briefly at one of the latter's regular inspections, knew he was in the presence of Authority and now could complain.

"What is the meaning of this?" Ruckerman demanded. "Do you realize who I am?"

"You're a spy," Stonar said. "We've been known to shoot spies." He glanced at Hupp. "The frog here has just told me an interesting story. He will keep his mouth shut now while you answer a few questions."

Fat's in the fire! Ruckerman thought. Well, the President had warned him he was on his own at Huddersfield. The United States government could take no official action to protect him.

"We thought your recent report to President Velcourt rather interesting," Stonar said. "Beckett and his team are going to do some amazing things. What amazing things?"

"They're very close to a complete description of the plague," Ruckerman said. He cleared his throat. "I resent being called a spy. Everything I've done—"

"Has been monitored by us," Stonar said. "By *amazing,* did you mean they will produce a cure?"

"How can we tell until we have the complete picture?" Ruckerman asked.

Hupp nodded.

"Stay out of this, frog," Stonar warned.

But Ruckerman now had the clue he needed. Hupp had not let the cat out of the bag, not to this turd!

"You are not helping our efforts by this attitude," Ruckerman said. "There is a high likelihood that we will be able to produce a . . . cure, if you will."

"But you used the word *amazing*."

"The President is impatient," Ruckerman said. "And it's my informed guess that we will succeed. As a scientist, however, I cannot tell you flatly right now that we will be able to nullify the plague. All I can say for sure is that we'll have a complete picture of it quite soon."

"How soon?"

Ruckerman glanced at Hupp as though to say: "This is too much." Hupp shrugged.

"Weeks, perhaps," Ruckerman said, a sigh in his voice. "And maybe only days. We are tracing out an extremely complicated organism for which there is no precedent. It is absolutely new, man-made."

"You told your President that you've given Hupp and his team 'a complete picture.' A complete picture of what?"

"I brought with me some new software, a computer search program, which has speeded up our efforts remarkably. The President knew I was bringing this."

"Why didn't you inform us of this immediately?"

"I didn't think you would understand it," Ruckerman said. "I was given to understand that only Beckett's team was sufficiently advanced to employ this software effectively."

"Given to understand? By whom?"

"By Beckett himself, among others!"

"And the reports of your spies!" Stonar accused.

"Mister Stonar," Ruckerman said, "the search program is in Huddersfield's computer system where anyone can have access to it. If you wish to examine it, please feel free."

Stonar glared at him. The bastard, Ruckerman! He knew computer software was beyond the inspector's competence! Scowling, Stonar stepped to the door and opened it. "Send in General Shiles." Stonar waited to one side of the open door.

Presently, a brigadier general in a superbly tailored field uniform strode into the room. He nodded once to Stonar. Shiles was a tall, skinny figure, monocle in right eye, swagger stick under left arm. He had weathered skin and a hawk's-beak nose above a tight little mouth and square chin. The eyes were pale blue and the one behind the monocle gave off a glassy sheen.

"You heard the entire conversation, General?" Stonar asked.

"Yes sir." Shiles's voice was brusk and clipped.

"I must be getting back to base immediately," Stonar said. "I'll leave you to lay out the conditions to everyone here. You can start with the frog and his friend, the spy."

"Very good, sir."

Stonar passed a baleful stare across Hupp and Ruckerman but did not speak. Turning, Stonar left the room. A uniformed hand reached in from outside and closed the door.

"I have a full brigade plus the original guards in position around this establishment," Shiles said, speaking to a position between Hupp and Ruckerman. "No one from here will be permitted to leave. No more going down to the village pub of an evening. There will be no outside communication without my personal permission. Do you understand?"

"Sir," Hupp said. "I think I can . . ."

Ruckerman placed a hand over Hupp's mouth and shook his head. Shiles regarded Ruckerman with astonishment. Lifting a notepad and pencil from Hupp's lab table, Ruckerman scribbled a few words and passed the tablet to Shiles.

Time for the carrot, Ruckerman thought. *The stick sure as hell would not work with this man.*

Shiles gave him a momentary cold appraisal before taking the tablet and reading what Ruckerman had written. The monocle dropped out of Shiles's eye. He replaced it before finding the pencil and writing beneath Ruckerman's message: "How can this be?"

Ruckerman took the next page in the tablet and wrote: "What we have discovered leaves no other conclusion."

Shiles glanced at the door through which Stonar had gone, then at Ruckerman.

Ruckerman shook his head, took the tablet and wrote: "He can deliver death; we can deliver life."

General Shiles tore off the used pages of the tablet and stuffed them into a side pocket. He tapped his left thigh with his swagger stick. Ruckerman could see decision forming in the man. That was a rich carrot displayed on the pages of the tablet. A long, long life and perfect health. And Shiles was a man to believe in scientists. Were they not the ones who had given him atom bombs and rockets? He must know this prize was worth the gamble. He would want to control it.

"Damme!" Shiles said. "It would appear I've been given charge over the golden egg."

"Remember what happened when the farmer killed the goose," Hupp said.

"You're quite bright for a frog," Shiles said. "Just don't forget that I'm the farmer."

"I presume you will use discretion," Ruckerman said.

"Indeed," Shiles said. "I will leave you two to your scientific devices now. I trust you'll explain the new rules to your teammates? Leave Wycombe-Finch to me."

Ruckerman waved a cautionary finger.

"Yes, quite," Shiles said. "The fewer who know the better." Turning on one heel, he strode to the door, flung it open and left them.

Hupp heard heels clicking outside and imagined the snappy salutes. The British were very good at snappy salutes.

"It could be worse," Ruckerman said.

Hupp nodded agreement. Ruckerman had been right to silence him. There were listeners behind every wall. And Ruckerman was correct to bring Shiles into the picture. There was plenty of power to go around. Shiles had the look of a man who enjoyed power, the more power the better.

"Wycombe-Finch is off the hook and we're on it," Ruckerman said.

Perhaps our greatest crime was this devotion to violent fanaticism. It led us to kill off or otherwise silence moderation. We destroyed our moderates, that's what we did. And look what it brought us!

—Fintan Craig Doheny

JOHN TOOK an instant dislike to Adrian Peard at the Killaloe Facility. The man was all decked out in lovat green tweeds, standing at the entrance to greet the new arrivals. He was a caricature of the great seigneur, that brown face under the courtyard's intense lighting.

The Lab had been visible in the fading light as John's armored car had come down out of the hills. It was not actually at Killaloe, their driver had explained, but farther north. The name was a deliberate bit of confusion, which they were not to expose. The facility was a large stone building that once had been a castle. The daub-gray stone lay within the crooked arm of a hill like a malignant growth that had extruded several feelers toward the nearby lakeshore.

"It doesn't belong there, that's what you're thinking," the driver had said. "Everyone thinks that. But it's better inside. From the inside, you cannot see the place."

"Welcome to the Killaloe Facility," Peard said after introducing himself. His handshake was dry and perfunctory. "Your fame has preceded you, Doctor O'Donnell. We're all quite excited."

John felt anger. Doheny had made good his threat to create

a John O'Donnell myth! Father Michael and the boy were assigned a guide and directed to "the other wing." The priest avoided John's eyes as he left. Father Michael had been silent and withdrawn ever since John's confession. O'Neill-Within had ceased howling, though, and John felt somewhat calmer. Confession had helped. The mental confusion that had followed confession lay in a walled-off limbo. All John wanted now was food and rest, a time to think.

"We've laid on a small meeting of top staff," Peard said. "Hope you feel up to it. Time presses."

John blinked at him, anger suspended in fatigue.

Peard thought the man looked tired and confused, but Doheny had said to give no time to reflect. *Keep him off balance.* Still . . . *this* was supposed to be O'Neill?

The courtyard air smelled of lake dampness and mildew with overtones of exhaust fumes from the departed armored cars. John was glad to leave it. Peard escorted him inside the great double doors, some standing open with people visible inside at various occupations—computer terminals, a centrifuge whirling, the hiss of steam from a sterilizer. John recognized blue laser light in one room. The impression was of well-intentioned but largely senseless industry. There was much bustling about, intent examination of culture dishes and test tubes and even an electron microscope. The hum of a powerful electric motor came from behind one closed door.

There was a curved stairway at the far end of the hall. It took them up to a landing where Peard flung open a heavy oak door and escorted John into a library. Old portraits lined one wall above bookcases and stacks and a wheeled ladder. A small fireplace of Italian marble with carved cherubs decorated the end of an open space where chairs and one heavy table had been set out. The room smelled of pipe smoke and old books. John found himself being introduced to at least ten men. He lost count after the third. They were mostly tweeds and turtleneck pullovers, a few cardigans. There was a Jim somebody, a Doctor Balfour "of whom you've heard, of course." When John had shaken the last hand, a free-standing chalkboard was wheeled out from the stacks and placed near the fireplace.

Peard gestured at the chalkboard, thinking that his people had behaved quite well. They had been carefully briefed, of course. Their expressions betrayed only anxious curiosity.

John stared from the people now seated looking at him to

the blank surface of the chalkboard. It had been scrubbed clean, not even a hint of what had been written there before. Empty, dark-green surface. What was he supposed to do with it? Abruptly, he recalled the penance assigned him by Father Michael. Would that arouse O'Neill-Within?

"Doheny says you have a remarkable new approach to the plague," Peard prompted.

John reached for the chalk on the ledge below the board. O'Neill-Within did not object. The hand was a fascinating thing to watch: It moved of itself. His body had taken on another life. Turning to Peard and the others with a calm smile, John spoke in a firm voice.

"Everyone naturally agrees that a virus must have been used as the specialized structure with which to inject the nucleic acid into the cells of this new bacteria. I assume that the phage approach needs no explanation in this room."

Several dry chuckles greeted this.

John turned and stared past the chalkboard for a moment, appearing to gather his thoughts. His gaze fell on the fireplace and a portrait above it: an Elizabethan dandy with form-fitting dark coat and lace at the neck and cuffs, cruel eyes, the face of a predatory bird.

"Synthetic hereditary information was incorporated into the DNA complement of the virus," John said, shifting the chalk from one hand to the other and back.

How intently they listened, hanging on every word.

"There has to be another necessary characteristic of the phage," John said. "That the virus in its parasitizing of the new bacteria must possess DNA with only a single chain at its end— an incomplete helix designed to lock into the receptor DNA. It is a complementary message being inserted into the host. I assume that the synthetic DNA must adhere to the viral DNA in such a way that it causes the virus to manufacture more of the desired form."

What a remarkable thing his voice was, John thought. It went on almost of itself, steady and informative. Heads were nodding agreement all around him.

"But what if the phage were created with more than a single dangling chain?" John asked. "Certain human cells have receptors for testosterone, for example. Females have estrogen receptors. There are many similar receptor sites. There also must be a message pattern that determines whether the fetus will be either male or female. The pattern will be different for each sex. The nucleic acid blueprint that directs the creation of proteins must possess a shaping force that can direct substances into locked positions."

He turned to the chalkboard and watched that remarkable self-directing hand sketch a series of three-letter combinations:

UCU—UCC—UCA—UCG
GGU—GGC—GGA—GGG
GCU—GCC—GCA—GCG . . .

He watched the hand at its work until it stopped after completing five rows of the triplet series, then it went back and added identifying labels opposite each series—Ser, Gly, Ala, Thr, Pro.

A pipe-smoker in a hand-knit blue pullover at John's left gestured at the board with his pipe stem. "It's incomplete," he said. "Incomplete series."

"I'll give you the rest of it presently," John said. "I want you to think in groups of five. Order is important, as you indicate. But the choice of five, I believe, is essential. The transmission code is broken into groups of five, allocations being matched to the available chemical bonds at the receptor sites."

"Those sex-determining sites you postulate?" the pipe-smoker asked.

"Yes. I ask you to imagine flagella, the fibers in a single chain and incomplete, reaching out and locking into living receptors—a penta-plug, you might say, designed for a specific receptacle. It can only be plugged in at a particular site. But when it is plugged in, it will not drop out."

Peard's staff hitched chairs closer, peering up at John.

"Why five?" someone asked.

"Each of these quadratic stacks . . ." John gestured at the series he had written on the board ". . . has an open end, a fifth segment that can be allocated as you wish. You shape it to fit."

"Good God!" the pipe-smoker said. He gave John a look of awe. "Shuts off the living process. How did you hit on it?"

"The simplest required form," John said.

"Given the plague's symptoms," Peard offered.

"How do you determine the side groups?" someone demanded.

"Between the DNA and the RNA, the only chemical difference is the fourth base, thymine for one and uracil for the other," John said. "The different sequences can be determined by comparing the FD mass spectrums, using stereoisomers, of course. The different shapes of the DNA helixes will tell us the submolecular shapes within them."

"You're saying Crick's Central Dogma is not true," Peard said.

John nodded. Peard had a quick mind, anyway. He obviously had leaped ahead to the implications in what had already been revealed.

Questions began to bombard John from all sides. ". . . more than one amino acid substitution? . . . of the peptide bond? Yes! The carboxyl group and the amino group . . . But doesn't it have to be a high polymer? Wouldn't the phage disintegrate?"

Peard jumped to his feet and waved a hand for silence.

"There has to be feedback from the cytoplasm," John said, "just as Doctor Peard suggests."

John put the chalk on its ledge and rubbed a hand across his brow, closing his eyes. He had the beginnings of a headache and his shoulders trembled with fatigue.

Peard touched John's arm. "Long drive, eh? I'd say a bit of food and rest are indicated."

John nodded.

"Fits, dammit!" someone said. "Makes all sorts of sense."

"We'll meet again tomorrow after Doctor O'Donnell has rested," Peard said.

John allowed himself to be led off by Peard. He could still hear the people talking in the library, excited voices, some arguments. Was Doheny right after all? Did it only take inspiration? But he had given them an accurate briefing. The penance demanded it.

Peard led him into a brightly lighted kitchen where sandwiches and milk were provided by an old man in a white apron. Peard took him then to a small bedroom with its own bath. A single window looked out across the moon-bathed lough. John heard the door close and the snick of a bolt. He tested the door. Locked. He extinguished the room's lights and returned to the window. There was a stone-enclosed cattle booley next to the lake, boggy ground with high reeds beyond the enclosure.

I'm a prisoner, he thought. *Doheny's doing?*

He let fatigue rise up within him as he watched the moonlight pour across the lough and the bogs. What did it matter if he was a prisoner? The moonlight out there was a haunted thing, he thought, the light out of lovers' past pouring itself away where no love could be. Bits and pieces of the long ride to this place tugged at his awareness. They had driven interminably in the long twilight, a timeless, droning eternity.

When O'Neill's howling had ceased, he had felt the removal of a weight. The steel slit in the side of the armored car had framed a view of a hilltop bathed in orange sunset, remnant black shadows up there where an ancient ring fort, a rath, had stood. That had been a place of life, he thought. Now, it was a silent relic. He felt that the occupants of the armored car might fade just as easily into empty relics, bones and rusty metal. The ride was far different from the tramp over the countryside.

Sparring with Herity had become almost an instinctive thing in the months of their slow passage. Doing their laundry in running water, digging food out of buried caches, killing feral pigs and cows. What a land it was! John recalled a small stream at his feet, water winding through reeds, the ground boggy along the edges. The current had tipped the reeds in a careless rhythm—down, up, down, up...It had been movement like their walking feet. There had been freedom in it. Yes—freedom: their possessions on their backs. An odd feeling: He had been liberated there with Herity, the priest and the boy, experiencing a freedom from the things of the world that perhaps only the migratory hordes of the nomad ages had known—those people of foot and horse and tents. Not until oxen and carts had possessions begun to subdue that kind of freedom. It was a thought John felt he would have liked to discuss with Gannon.

We took only what was useful to a nomad's life....

As John stood in the darkness of his room staring at the moonlit lough, he grew aware of movement below him. A dark figure had come out of the shadows on the other side of the original castle ramparts. John recognized Father Michael from the walk. The priest moved aimlessly out to the edge of the paved area and then onto the lawn at the top of the lake. The priest there reminded John of the penance—help them find a cure. He faced away from the window, turned on the room's lights and undressed for bed. Help them find a cure. Yes, he would have to do it.

Father Michael was facing the building when John's light went on. He glimpsed John's profile, the vague movements, saw the light go out.

John's confession had left a paradoxical residue in Father Michael—an awful weight and a sense of emptiness. The priest was reminded of the moment when he had bid goodbye to another period in his life—the years when he had occupied a corner house in Dublin's Coombe, serving as spiritual advisor in the Catholic school. He had seen the very house that morning from the armored car when the driver detoured out of the city— the row houses all sadness, everything gone to weed and empty windows. The Church school had been reduced to a granite ruin, its interior emptied by flames.

What he missed most, Father Michael decided, was the boys and girls spewing forth from the school, the noisy romping of their play in that interlude of freedom between classrooms and home. Whenever he closed his eyes and thought about it, Father Michael could summon back their shouts, the loud calls of derision and display, the brief gatherings of faces, the outcries with plans for later, the complaints about chores.

Father Michael looked up at John's darkened window recalling the effect of the silent boy upon that poor man up there. Doheny had constructed that effect with efficient malice. The boy had been a good choice. He represented an essence of something to be seen in the few boys to be glimpsed in this Irish world. None of the old vigor remained. Was it that boys did not make as much rumpus in the absence of girls? There had been a special kind of happiness under all of that noise that Father Michael feared this world would never again experience. It was not just the boys who had lapsed into something reminiscent of those stone-faced houses in the Coombe—each individual ultimately hidden behind a blank exclusion that tried to betray no hint of the griefs concealed within.

John's confession changed nothing, Father Michael decided, unless it led the man to right in some small way the terrible wrong that had been done.

And what if there is no cure?

Father Michael felt that his own thoughts had betrayed him. It was an unprincipled thought, not worthy of him. God could not intend such a thing! This was one more example that the old principles were gone, erased by one man's actions. Father Michael's newly restored faith stumbled.

Principles!

That was one of those words like *responsibility*. Such words were private passions exposed, like a corner of yard goods on a shop table, not revealing at all what lay under the stack.

Synonyms for things quite different, they were. Faith went about disguised as Principle.

Faith.

It was a grab-bag word, one of those little red-and-black signs bought at a cheap shop. It said: *Keep Off the Grass*. It said: *No Trespassing*. It said: *Restricted Area—Authorized Personnel Only*.

Father Michael buried his face in his hands.

God, what have we done?

They had destroyed innocence for all time, he thought. That was what they had done. He realized then that there must have been an innocence about John Roe O'Neill before tragedy shattered him. Not a perfect innocence, because even then O'Neill had played with terrible powers, the Sorcerer's Apprentice trying an incantation while the Master was absent. Was God not in His heaven then? Was the loss of innocence God's intent? There could be no going back from such a loss. That was the most terrifying thing of all. You could not return to virginity.

Father Michael knelt on the wet grass below John's window then and prayed aloud:

"God restore us. God restore us. God restore us."

Peard, returning from conferring with Doheny, heard the voice from the lakeside and paused in the shadows between the buildings to stare out at the kneeling figure. The moonlight was bright and Peard recognized Father Flannery. The priest had not yet been told about the little marriage chore in wait for him. Peard debated whether to go out and bring up the subject immediately, but the priest obviously was praying. Peard was of that school which thought of prayer as an extremely personal thing, not to be shared with others. Watching someone pray embarrassed him. Whenever he was in church he only mouthed the prayers silently, aware of all the listeners around him.

It'll wait until morning, Peard thought.

He hurried off to his quarters, his mind full of what had passed between him and Doheny. It had been a fascinating conversation. Doheny had already been in his office, having sped the short route to Killaloe in a fast convoy with motorcycle outriders. He had been on the phone, talking to Wycombe-Finch, an oddly one-sided conversation with the Englishman apparently not speaking much. Doheny had written on a pad for Peard to read: "Something's happening over there. Someone's listening to us and Wye is upset by it."

"I tell you, Wye, the man's personality changed in front of our eyes." Doheny pointed to Peard and gestured at the TV monitor on the corner of the desk, its cameras still focused on the library and the position where John had performed at the blackboard. Doheny's lips formed the words silently: "I watched it."

Peard nodded.

Wycombe-Finch apparently said something noncommittal or disagreed with Doheny. The latter scowled at the phone.

"The driver watched in the mirror," Doheny said. "The priest heard his confession, yes. Whatever it was, Father Michael's absolutely crushed by it."

Doheny motioned for Peard to take the chair across the desk from him. Peard obeyed, wondering why Doheny dared share this information with the Englishman. It was dangerous. Anyone could be listening.

"Five, yes," Doheny said. "He says the base series continues to be divisible by four."

Doheny listened for a moment, then: "What's unnatural about it? We've had it right from the horse's mouth."

Wycombe-Finch apparently said something that Doheny found amusing. "Why should he trick us? Anyway, this is beautifully simple: five single extensions to the double helix, all set to lock in at the receptor sites. It's quite elegant. I tell you, Wye, the man standing there explaining all this to us knew what the hell he was talking about."

Doheny sounds British when he's talking to Wycombe-Finch, Peard thought. *He was so damned open about this collaboration! It does smack of treason.*

Doheny listened, rolling his eyes, then: "Yes, the implications are mind-staggering. Talk to you later, Wye." He replaced the phone in its cradle before looking up at Peard. "Adrian, have you really considered the kind of tiger we have by the tail?"

"What do you mean?"

"Have you considered where this knowledge may lead?"

"We can put the world back together," Peard said.

Doheny aimed a lidded gaze at the shadows beyond Peard. "Back together? Oh, no, Adrian. Humpty Dumpty is broken beyond repair. Whatever we put together, it won't be our old world. That one's gone. Forget it."

"Two generations, three at the most," Peard said.

"Don't talk stupid, Adrian!" There was anger in Doheny's

voice. "Knowledge has always been power but never before to this extent. If we're not careful we may create a world that'll make these plague times seem like a country fair by comparison."

Peard blinked. What did Doheny mean? The world would be short of women for a time, certainly. But if they cured this plague, many diseases might be erased. A black shadow could be removed from mankind's future.

"I'm for some sleep," Doheny said. "Our guest is all safely tucked away for the night?"

"Locked in and a guard posted."

"If he asks about the lock tell him I ordered it," Doheny said. "The guard isn't obvious, is he?"

"All very normal. In mufti and an excuse for being in the halls."

"There're some restrictions on his movements during the day," Doheny said. "He goes nowhere near the safe-tank down there with Kate and Stephen. Somebody has to be with him at all times. Close watch and alert and keep him on the grounds. Unsafe beyond our perimeters. He'll understand that."

"What about the priest and the boy?"

"No restrictions there. I want him to run into them frequently. Is old Moone around?"

Peard glanced at his wristwatch. "He's in quarters right now."

"Have him bug O'Neill's room during the day tomorrow."

"You're sure he's O'Neill?"

"Sure as gold in the bank."

"If he discovers he's being bugged, won't that make him suspicious?"

"Moone knows how to do it. Tell Moone to put a recorder on the bug and let me have the tapes daily."

"You're staying?"

"I'm staying. You couldn't get me away from here."

Peard's mouth drew into a tight line. He did not like this development. Peard liked his own little empire, his own powers. Doheny's presence diluted those powers.

"I want no slip-ups," Doheny said. "No repetition of Kevin O'Donnell's stupidities. If this fails, it's on my shoulders. That being the case, my orders will be followed to the letter and I'm staying to see to that."

Peard nodded, finding this to be expected. If it failed, Doheny could only blame himself.

"Am I billeted in the same room?" Doheny asked.

"Yes."

"Come along now," Doheny said. "Let's get our rest. Tomorrow's a busy day."

"I still have the supply lists to go over," Peard said.

Doheny smiled, but Peard noticed that the smile went no farther than his mouth.

"Very well, then," Doheny said. He left the room.

Peard waited for several minutes before picking up the telephone and placing a call to Dublin. When it was answered, he identified himself and said: "I think we have Doheny's ass."

*Until this plague, it was little ap-
preciated how technology, scientific
research and development included,
speeds up both success and disaster.*

—Samuel B. Velcourt

HULS ANDERS BERGEN, not feeling at all like the influential
secretary-general of the United Nations, slammed the door of
his office and strode across to stop, then leaned with both fists
on his desk.

This can't go on, he thought.

It was almost dark outside, the end of a foggy spring day
in New York City oddly similar to what it had been for more
than fifty years—people hurrying to get off the streets before
nightfall. Busy streets at this hour had been a mark of the city
for as long as Bergen could recall. He could hear the traffic
sounds even at this height. New York had always been a noisy
city at nightfall, he thought.

Activity still buzzed, too, in the halls and offices outside
Bergen's doors. The UN was a ferment of reports and rumors.
The Chinese at Kangsha were not denying that they stood on
the edge of an important medical announcement. A brilliant
new research team in Brazilian Israel had just that morning
made cautious revelation of a cryogenic suspension technique

425

that preserved the life of an infected female indefinitely. The Swiss were reporting "mixed success" with a dangerous chemotherapeutic approach to the plague.

Trust the Israelis and the Swiss to produce brilliantly unorthodox techniques to meet this problem, Bergen thought. They were alike in this, closing ranks and turning inward for their superb strength.

And what was happening at Huddersfield?

Bergen straightened and flexed the sore muscles of his hands. Bad habit, that, making fists when he was upset.

On top of what had happened this morning in Philadelphia, the British action shutting down all but the most essential communications with the Outside filled Bergen with disquiet. He moved around his desk and seated himself in his fine Danish chair. The traffic sounds were particularly clear in this position.

The differences from BP New York had been mostly accepted, he was told—checkpoints every few blocks, identification scanners, apartment wardens who were supposed to know every occupant by sight. How quickly the outrageous became routine!

Very little partying these days, Bergen knew. More's the pity. A good relaxing, old-fashioned party was exactly what he needed right now. Take his mind off the problems before him, especially this new one demanding that he make a decision.

Too many unknowns lurked just at the edges of awareness, Bergen thought. Why had Ruckerman been sent to England? Bergen did not buy for a moment the story that an advisor to the President of the United States had been accidentally contaminated. Velcourt was up to something. A canny fellow, Velcourt. Look how quickly he had appeared to jump on the pope's bandwagon, speaking out against "unbridled science." Of course, that stand would be reassessed in view of what had just happened in Philadelphia.

Explosion of a gas main followed by an uncontrolled fire— and the pope and nine cardinals were dead. Accident? Bergen thought not. It had the smell of a contrived incident. Too many people were on the streetside rumor mill saying it was God's judgment for the pope's attack on scientists. This had been planned and executed by a master assassin with almost unlimited resources. Velcourt's doing?

Well, the streets were a dangerous place to play that game, as the Soviets had learned to their dismay. Get people used to mobbing up and the many-footed animal could turn against you. Get people accustomed to spreading rumors and the rumor system took on a life of its own. False reports and quack cures were rampant in the streets all over the world, Bergen knew. It required special teams to chase them down and quiet them or . . . God help them! find that one had been confirmed.

Vinegar baths, for the love of heaven!

There was no doubt at all that the plague was mutating and spreading into animal populations, both feral and tame. Velcourt had said privately that he already was taking actions to preserve certain key species—cattle, pigs, dogs, house cats. Other nations surely were taking similar steps or would be soon. The UN's "Private Alert" system had spread the word quietly, but it surely would be public knowledge within hours.

What can we do? Will we have to write off all wild species?

Africa was a lost cause. No hope there at all. Some Indian elephants might survive, especially in places like the Berlin Zoological Gardens, which remained intact thanks to the Soviet Union's Iron Ring buffer zone. The Iron Ring was being hailed as a superb, self-sacrificing Soviet intervention. Bergen shook his head. Only a few years back the Iron Curtain had been generally cursed. Now, the Iron Ring was a boon to mankind.

Bergen leaned his head into his open palms. How scattered his thoughts were! Any diversion at all was welcomed to put off the moment when he had to make his decision. The question was not: Should they try to save the world's feral populations? It was: *How do we break the news that such an effort is impossible?* The animals of the sea would not survive. Finis the whale. Finis the gentle porpoise. Finis the amusing sea lion. Finis the happy sea otter. Finis, finis, finis!

Wolf, coyote, badger, prairie dog, kulon, panda, civet cat, hedgehog, antelope, deer . . .

Good God! he thought. *The deer.*

Bergen had visions of hunters, already bridling at confinement away from their annual forest orgy, reacting to announcement that the deer was finis. And the elk . . . the bison.

No more Groundhog Day!

The concept "Endangered Species" had become ridiculous. How could he concern himself with tigers, jaguars, leopards and sea cows when man was now among the world's most endangered species?

If only people could be united to . . .

Bergen straightened, holding to this thought, sensing something valuable in it. A volunteer project? Contributions? People would laugh at a financial effort to save wild animals. Collecting for such creatures while humans remained in peril! There would be outcry against bleeding hearts. But the wild animals were valuable—to science, to genetics especially, to research. Scientists might be reduced to using only humans as guinea pigs. That carried very nasty overtones in its effects on morality.

Morality, yes.

Bergen thought about the report he had been handed only a half hour ago, the thing that had angered him so deeply. He had known for some weeks that elements close to the centers of power in the U.S. Capitol were fomenting unrest among American Muslims. Rumors of a secret base in the Sudan were rampant. There were stories that Muslims from the Sudan were prepared to launch an infective jihad, breaking out of their confinement to kill infidels with sword and knife . . . and to kill the women merely by breathing upon them.

What had happened to the old human values?

Bergen felt that he fought a lonely battle to preserve something of the old human values—concern for your neighbor, the Golden Rule.

The report he had been handed before storming into his office had identified the source of the local Muslim unrest. Shiloh Broderick! Bergen had come to look upon Broderick as a satanic figure, the essence of all that must be suppressed that the world might be restored to some semblance of its former order. Broderick's agents were at work in New York City and in five other key centers, including Philadelphia. The report made this undeniable. Had it been Broderick behind the death of the pope? Bergen was prepared to believe it.

How to save the best of human morality in the face of such men?

Bergen could feel the new surge in plague research. They were on the verge of momentous things. Announcement could come momentarily. The good things from the past had to be preserved!

Save the animals.

He began to see the shape of it then: a rallying cry, a diversion to occupy embattled people and get them past this last bad time until the researchers provided a plague cure. The idea gave Bergen something restorative and opened up an answer to his other problem.

Should the report on Broderick be shared with Velcourt? Bergen was not free of the suspicion that the President might somehow be involved with Shiloh Broderick. They said the two hated each other, but that was an old ploy. Broderick might be a very handy tool to people such as Velcourt. No matter. Knowledge that the secretary-general of the United Nations knew about Broderick's latest incursion might put a damper on further violence from that source. And Bergen knew he had an upbeat note on which to end the exchange.

Save the animals.

Bergen reached for the red telephone in his desk drawer and had actually touched the phone when a change in the noises outside his office caused him to hesitate. Something crashed out there. He could hear a difference in the human sounds— shouts, distressed cries...some of them cut off abruptly. He removed his hand from the red telephone and stood up, was standing there undecided when his door burst open.

A man in a dark ski mask and carrying a silenced machine gun stood there. The burst of bullets that cut across Bergen's chest stitched a pattern of holes in the window behind him.

The gunman uttered a wild cry, the last human sound that Bergen's ears reported: "Imsh Allah!"

O King that was born
To set bondsmen free,
In the coming battle
Help the Gael.

—old Irish prayer

IT WAS three horsemen racing along the lough from the south—black movement in the fading light. John saw them at a distance, hearing at the same time the movement of many heavy vehicles on the hills above the Facility. The horses were lathered, he saw, but still responding to the crop. John watched them from a position on the lawn fronting the lough where he had gone to be alone after a harried day. He knew he was not really alone; there were men watching from a doorway behind him. He did not have enough emotion left even to resent this. He felt drained, incapable of any strong movement.

Questions . . . questions . . . questions . . .

There had been hardly a moment this day when someone was not picking at him. And the answers poured from his mouth without conscious volition—another voice, another personality, which acted from within, rising out of an alarming source of independence.

Was it O'Neill-Within?

He could not even be sure of that.

The horsemen were still at some distance but not slackening their pace. John noted that the riders did not look back, which he interpreted as meaning they were not someone's quarry. The

430

urgency of their movement struck him then. Something about them . . . He felt the coldness of impending disaster.

The sound of approaching vehicles had grown louder but he could hear the beat of horses' hooves now. His chest felt tight. Then he recognized two of the riders— Oh, God! It was Kevin O'Donnell and Joseph Herity beside him, a stranger close behind. The horses plunged onward against a backdrop of stone-pocked hills, a landscape that darkened by the second as the sun dipped toward the western hills.

Why were Kevin O'Donnell and Joseph Herity coming here . . . and on horseback? He watched the men gallop past him up the lawn. Herity gave John a devil's grin as he passed but the others did not even turn. They drew up at the courtyard formed by the two lakeside wings of the building, dropped their reins and strode inside past John's watchers without a word.

Arrival on horseback: Why should that be threatening? John wondered. As the sun dropped behind the hills, leaving his world in the long twilight, it grew colder. John shivered. He had been nine weeks here, seeing the slow shift from senseless industry to a new vitality. They had the best equipment in the world, all of it sent in on the free boats via the Finn Sadal, and it was beginning to focus correctly at last. John had felt the excitement all day, another reason he was drained.

They had kept him in the south wing most of the day, introducing lab technicians to advanced computer techniques, showing them how to bring automation into their efforts. Another week, two at the most, and they would have the plague pathogen in their hands.

After that . . . what?

Once during this day, John had thought he glimpsed Doheny at a distance across the grounds. There had been a great deal of activity over there at the old castle structure, the central core of this complex. A big flatbed truck had backed into a newly made hole in a brick wall there. It had emerged after a time with a large black tubular thing lashed to its bed. It had looked to John like a big steel tank. The truck had been joined by armored cars and a whole convoy, which had taken the turn for the road to the northeast. He had been told earlier that Kells was in that direction and Dundalk on the Irish Sea, places he knew he probably would never see.

Old Moone came in then and asked John to come along to the culture lab and check the setup for its automation changes.

Moone was a fixture around the Lab, John realized. The old man shuffled along in his decrepit way, purposeful but lacking a necessary élan. Many of the researchers here had shown that same lack of vital independence until John's revelations had fired them. Perhaps Moone did not know what was happening at the tiled benches and esoteric equipment he passed by so often. The man betrayed no awe of the scientist. If anything, he seemed disdainful toward all around him.

It was an old pattern, John thought. Scientists earned this response. He recalled the few famous scientists he had met, realizing how different they had seemed from ordinary mortals. The minds of scientists differed from the minds of other humans, John thought. The scientist rode at a higher elevation. He saw farther across the landscape. People expected from such men the behavior of the cavalier, of the romantic leader.

John looked out across the lough where everything had gone to gray. *I was a scientist,* he thought.

It was a strange thought, foreign, forcing him to reassess these differences he had sensed. Those differences were far more telling than the old romances would have it, he realized. He had worked with a narrowed vision, that was it. Even the near reaches were denied him. It was a gaze that could sweep past the individual without a change of focus.

Abstract dedication to the project.

Not even hope was allowed, only the immediate result.

John began to see a new sense in the things Doheny had said back at Kilmainham. No more myths? The people here had been wandering through their own despairs until John's arrival. They had gone through the paces out of habit. Training had given them patterns they could follow but the patterns would not deviate from known tracks.

Can they really see what I've given them? John asked himself. It was a desperate thought rising from that lost place within him. He could reconstruct the plague. He knew that. But the cure?

He turned back toward the buildings and, picking up his watchdogs, made his way up to his room. Supper sat heavy in his stomach and he knew he would not sleep soon, but he was glad to hear them throw the bolt and seal him into this place. He left the lights off and watched the darkness settle over the lough.

There was a pounding somewhere—clump! Clump! As though awakening from a dream, John realized the pounding was feet running along the hallway. His door was flung open and Doheny darted into the room, blinking at the gloom after the brightness of the hall. He turned on the overhead light, closed the door and stared at John.

"You must listen to me very carefully and do what I say," Doheny said. "We haven't much time."

There was shouting outside the building and more sounds of heavy vehicles. John stared at Doheny.

"It's the curse of Ireland," Doheny said. "We are doomed to repeat ourselves endlessly."

"What's happening?"

"Kevin O'Donnell has seized control over this region," Doheny said. "I've known for two days he was going to do it. Alex warned me..." Doheny shook his head. "Kevin and Joseph have worked some devil's agreement between them and they've come to see it done."

"But why have you come running in here like this? What's this have to do with me?"

"They're interrogating the priest and the boy," Doheny said.

John felt a constriction in his chest.

"If they threaten the boy," Doheny said, "Father Michael will break the seal of the confessional. I know him. What will he tell them, John?"

John opened his mouth but could not speak. His voice refused to perform.

"Kevin and Joseph are the same kind of man," Doheny said. "Extremists and fanatics! It's all the same, anything's an excuse for getting high on their own adrenaline. It's a dope and they'll do anything for a fix. They'll keep after the priest until they've emptied him and filled themselves."

John closed his mouth, still unable to speak.

"Who are you, John Garrech O'Donnell?" Doheny asked. "Who are you, really?"

"I've told you," John gasped. The words hurt his throat.

"Did you tell the priest, as well?"

John hunched his shoulders, leaning forward. The pain in his chest and throat demanded relief.

"They've found his fingerprints and dental charts in the States," Doheny said.

"Whose..." It was all John could speak.

"O'Neill's, of course. They're playing it cagey, the bastards, but we'll have them in time. What will those fingerprints and dental charts show us, John?"

John shook his head from side to side, once more mute. He could not feel O'Neill-Within. He could only feel a great emptiness there.

"You're a queer specimen and that's no mistake," Doheny said. "Do you have real feelings?"

John stared back at Doheny, locked in place by those questioning eyes.

"We're that close to victory," Doheny said. "That close." He held up thumb and forefinger of his right hand, a tiny gap between them. "And now this!"

John managed a whisper. "What's . . . happening?"

"The thing that always destroys us," Doheny said. "Victory. We cannot take victory. It sets us against each other, a victory does. Like dogs over a bone. That's what every Irish victory becomes—a bone polished by our own teeth! And no meat left on it at all. In the end, we throw it away for the useless thing it is."

John's lips once more formed the words: "What's happening?" There was no voice behind it.

Doheny cocked an ear toward the door. There was a faint slamming sound in the distance. He said: "The truth is, we Irish, preferring to make epics out of disasters, could find no victory to serve the same function. We may say otherwise, but our actions give the truth to my words. We prefer disasters."

John backed away from Doheny, stopped by the side of the cot. His knees trembled.

"You're going to be put on trial, John," Doheny said. "And they'll have me along afterwards to stand in their dock." He grinned. "Because I've denied to Kevin the real prize he sought here—little Katie Browder!"

Feet could be heard running in the hallway.

"Listen to me, John!" Doheny said. "You must demand Father Michael for your defense counsel."

John found a hoarse whisper with which to speak. "Defend me from what?"

"Promise me, you fool!"

John's head nodded agreement on its own.

The door behind Doheny was slammed open with such force that it crashed into the wall.

John stared out at a cluster of armed men framed in the open doorway. Joseph Herity stood in the forefront grinning at him.

Rachel, Rachel, I've been
thinking
What a fine world this would be
If the girls could be transported
From beyond the deep blue sea.

—Songs of the New Ireland

For Kate O'Gara Browder, the flight from the research facility was a nightmare from beginning to end. Doheny had given them little time to think or question his decision.

"It's for your own safety."

"But where are we going?" Stephen had asked. He had peered out at Doheny through the same small port where Father Michael Flannery had stood the previous morning to perform the marriage ceremony.

"To Dundalk for now," Doheny said.

Even as he spoke, there had been no turning back. It had begun with the stopping of the air pumps, that constant reassuring noise that told them the chamber's pressure was higher than the pressure outside, that nothing of the plague might creep into this sanctuary. They had lived with the sound so long by then that they no longer noticed it, but the absence!

"Stephen! The air pumps have stopped!"

He leaped to his feet and dashed to the main porthole, which commanded a view of the enclosing area outside and some of the equipment

"What do you see?" she demanded, pressing close behind him. A sense of engulfing terror gripped her. *Please, God! Not now.*

"There's no one out there," Stephen said. He went to the communications panel and thumbed the microphone switch. "Hi, out there. What's going on?"

There was no response.

They heard it then, many footsteps, the sound curiously localized by the speaker above the port. There was a dragging noise with the sound of footsteps . . . heavy dragging and the sound of metal scraping on stones.

"There's Doheny," Stephen said.

She squeezed in beside Stephen to peer out at Doheny. He looked flushed. His fuzzy hair was more disarrayed than usual. Doheny took up the outside phone.

"It's all right. The pump will not be off long," he said.

"But what's happening?" Stephen demanded.

That was when Doheny said they were being moved for their own safety, being taken to Dundalk. *Why Dundalk?* Kate wondered.

"Be sure to take your supply of the antiseptic in with you," Doheny said. "And that rope you used for a safety line when we moved you from the barn—rig that again. You may be tossed about a bit."

Doheny's instructions were uttered in an intense monotone that they had never before heard from him. They were to take everything they thought they would need and stow it securely in the original chamber from Peard's barn. Stephen was to paint antiseptic around the tank's entry port. And hurry! Men with cutting torches were waiting to burn away the metal juncture between the original tank and the one built there.

"We can't move both of them," Doheny explained.

"But why are we doing this?" Stephen persisted.

"Because I've convinced some friends in the army that we cannot keep Kate alive here!"

"Where's Adrian?" Stephen asked.

"He's under guard in his quarters. Adrian's joined the enemy. Keep your pistol with you, Stephen. Kevin O'Donnell's coming and there's no stopping him. He's insane and he wants Kate."

"But why Dundalk?" Kate asked.

"Because we hope to get you completely out of Ireland. We've enough of the army and others loyal to us that we can get you safely to Dundalk. From there . . ." Doheny broke off.

"Where?" Stephen demanded.

"To England, we hope. Everything depends on Barrier Command." Doheny returned to his original instructions then. "And it would not hurt to drench a sheet with the antiseptic. Put it over the inside of the access port after you've closed and sealed it." .

"The air pressure," Stephen said.

"We'll have a pump going again soon as we put you onto the lorry. You'll have positive pressure again. Best get into the little chamber as rapidly as you can."

Nylan Gunn, commander of the Killaloe guard, had come down then to take over from Doheny, telling the latter he was needed in communications. Gunn was a slender, dark Galway man with slightly bowed legs and a face with small features. He had been a commander in the constabulary before the plague.

"Don't worry, lass," he told Kate. "We'll not let the mad O'Donnell have y'."

Moone had been right behind him "to say goodbye."

"Trust Fin Doheny and Nylan here," he said. "They'll save you. And don't have any more truck with Adrian Peard!"

"What has Adrian done?" Stephen asked. He felt that the ground was being cut away from beneath him. Adrian betraying them? How? What had he done?

"I've had a leetle microphone in the bastard's office for months now," Moone said. "He was too slick for me! Sure enough, he's unlocked the door for Kevin O'Donnell to come and lord it over us."

Stephen had heard the stories of Kevin O'Donnell and the Beach Boys. He glanced at Kate.

"Do what Nylan tells you," Moone said. "Goodbye, Katie. Have a brave child even if y' are married." Chuckling, he left them.

It was all mad movement then, loud conversations and the sound of heavy equipment outside, the outer wall being breached. She and Stephen entered the small chamber finally and Stephen sealed the inner port, drenched a sheet with antiseptic and fastened it over the port. The small space reeked with the acrid smell of the antiseptic.

Kate sat close to Stephen on the bed, clutching him tightly when she heard the burners cutting away the outer chamber, even tighter when the cables went around their container and it swung free to settle with a thump onto an unsteady support on the lorry. The lashing cables rang against the chamber's steel when they were dropped into place and tightened. The end port gave them a view of the new opening through the bricks that had been put there such a short time ago to enclose their containers.

The sound of the compressor returned, soothing them somewhat. They could hear the generator motor chugging loudly behind them near the lorry's cab.

The lorry began to move so gently that they did not feel it at first, then they saw the opening into the castle receding and felt a wheel lurch into a rut. There was the sound of other vehicles, several of them. Stephen peered outside. "A lot of armored cars," he said. "Must be ten or twelve of them."

Nylan Gunn's voice came to them then from the little emergency speaker near the head of the bed. "Everything all right in there?"

Stephen found the microphone and keyed it. "It seems to be okay. How long will we be like this?"

"No telling, lad. But I'm up here with the driver. Sing out if you need me."

Stephen looked at Kate. She appeared pale and her forehead was deeply furrowed. "Why don't you stretch out and try to sleep, darling?"

"I couldn't sleep!"

"But you'd be safer if you were on the mattress there."

"No, I wouldn't. This is not safe." She closed her eyes. The baby felt so heavy in her abdomen. And she needed to void her bladder. There was nothing for it but the little toilet they had used at first. She made Stephen turn away while she crawled to the *convenience* and used it.

She was hungry then and all Stephen could provide was canned fish and beans, both cold. He insisted she take her vitamins before he would give her the food. He could be so callous, she thought. Studying his medical books at all hours! Never looking up even when she stared at him, needing him. He had no idea at all about her absolute longing for a crisp stalk of celery cold from the garden . . . fresh green lettuce. Oh, how she longed for it. Or a raw carrot. Surely by now they should have devised a way to sterilize fresh foods for this chamber!

She lay back after eating and watched Stephen crouched there by one of the ports, staring out at the passing landscape. She had no desire to look at it with him. It would only remind her that she was confined and could not go out there to walk through the fields, breathing fresh air that did not smell of a chemical toilet.

What would he do if she screamed at him? she wondered. She felt like screaming. What a dumpy little prison this was. More than six months confined like this! And when she complained, all Stephen could do was remind her that this chamber preserved her life.

Kate had heard descriptions of the plague's effect on women. Terrifying. She held to a tempting fantasy, though. There must be an island somewhere free of the plague. She and Stephen would go there and walk freely in the open once more. Perhaps that would happen even now. The most awful part of this confinement was the absence of a door out of it. She stared at the sheet covering the sealed port. But they had a door now.

Something rolled against her left elbow, dislodged by the lorry's movement. She looked down and saw the little television that had been provided them at the Facility. She put down an urge to break the thing. It was like the portholes. When it was not providing views of the unattainable, it showed them bad news.

If it weren't so confining and boring in here! Stephen always reminded her they had plenty to read. Their keepers could sterilize books but they couldn't sterilize fresh fruits and vegetables! That was because they could use caustic antiseptics and heavy ultraviolet on the books, as Smarty Stephen would point out if she raised the issue.

Damn Stephen! He made me pregnant and now he won't even talk to me when I need him!

"I want out," she whispered.

Stephen did not hear her above the sounds of the lorry, which reverberated in the chamber's confinement.

Kate tried to imagine what it would be like to step out of the chamber. She would live for a little while, she knew. But it was no longer the world out there that she had known. This world was not the world of before O'Neill. The Madman had changed it. Because of a woman. They killed his wife. Kate knew there had been children killed, too. Two of them. But it was more romantic to think of this having been done for love of a woman.

Would Stephen do such a thing for me?

Madman O'Neill had completely changed their world because they killed his wife. Changed. She had heard the news summary from Continental BBC the previous night: in all the world, five thousand men for every surviving woman. This had fascinated her, but Stephen had appeared worried when he looked at her.

The announcer's report of the disproportionate numbers had been prelude to comment on a new phenomenon.

"The Lysistrata Syndrome," he called it.

Kate remembered his words exactly: "Women are clamoring for positions of power. Who is to deny them this? Will the Church now refuse to enroll them as clergy?"

Women priests, Kate thought.

"As the Catholic Church struggles to choose a new pope in the wake of the Philadelphia tragedy," the commentator said, "it must also confront the need to recognize a change in the roles of men and women. This world is moving away from its past at a rate never before seen. The new pope, whoever that may be, will be required to make momentous decisions. Every day that we are denied a cure for the plague only makes it more apparent that we, mere mortals, have judged wrongly in the past." The commentator had cleared his throat, then: "This is George Bailey from the Continental BBC, Paris."

Stephen's only comment had been: "The haves and the have-nots—that has a new meaning now."

She knew what Stephen feared would happen: every woman with a dozen or more husbands. Chattel. Women owned by their husbands.

The motion of the lorry lulled her and Kate fell asleep after a time. Stephen glanced down at her, his expression worried. Poor Kate. It was beginning to get cold in the chamber. He found a blanket and spread it over her. She stirred restlessly under his touch but did not awaken. She remained asleep even when Nylan Gunn spoke again from the lorry's cab.

"We've just had a signal from Barrier Command, Admiral Francis Delacourt himself. He has our request under advisement but he says also his orders are to assist in any legitimate undertaking associated with plague research. He sounds like a pompous ass."

Kate awakened after a while only to use the *convenience* and inquire if she had heard Gunn speaking or "was that a dream?"

"Barrier Command's been asked to provide us with passage to England," Stephen said, extracting the sense from Gunn's words.

Her voice was sleepy as she returned to the bed and pulled the blanket up to her chin: "Why would they send us to England?"

"I think there's going to be another civil war in Ireland," Stephen said. "Doheny wants us in a safe place."

"Men," she muttered.

The lorry stopped at dusk below the crest of a hill. Stephen, looking out a port, saw eight tanks parked beside the road. A helmeted figure stood out of the lead tank's hatch and called to the lorry:

"We've the situation in hand! Go straight down to the docks. There'll be a jeep to lead you at the next intersection."

The lorry eased ahead in low gear, topped the hill and gathered speed. Burning buildings could be glimpsed out the ports. They passed a cluster of sprawled bodies beside a shattered wall. Darkness curtained the view by the time they rolled out onto the pier and stopped, but orange spots of fire could be seen on the surrounding hills.

It was cold on the pier and getting colder. Stephen found a flashlight and pointed it at Kate. There was a glassy look of fear in her eyes.

"Shut that off! Please, Stephen!"

He turned off the torch and crawled under the blankets beside her. They could hear the cables being moved and adjusted against the chamber's metal. There was a grinding engine sound. Voices called out commands.

Nylan Gunn's voice intruded from the speaker: "Barrier Command's providing you with passage to England. They've sent in a barge and a tug. Not to worry. It's going to be all right. Now we're going to disconnect the compressor again to lift you off. It'll join you on the barge in a few minutes. Bon voyage!"

They heard the compressor go silent, more movements of the cables, more engine sounds.

Metal rapped sharply against the side of the chamber and a voice called out: "Hold on in there! We're going to lift you now."

The chamber lurched and they felt it swing. Stephen put an arm over Kate to steady her. The end port gave them a blurred view of bright spotlights and dark water, orange gouts of fire, then a swinging glimpse of dock buildings.

"Steady the thing, you idiots!" a voice shouted.

The swinging stopped. There came a sickening drop. Kate

emitted a small shriek. The descent stopped, then resumed at a steadier pace, ending abruptly with a thump.

"Pass a line over both ends!" someone shouted. "That's it! Then around here. Make it fast. Now, the netting. There's going to be a lot of pitching about out there."

Kate wondered about that remark as they got under way. She heard the rumbling surge of powerful engines, then smooth movement detected mostly by watching the spotlights at the dockside recede. Stephen busied himself securing loose objects, tucking them in around the edges of the mattress, wedging them with books under the bed's plywood base, securing the safety lines.

The smooth movement changed suddenly to a steady fore-and-aft tipping. Stephen leaned across her to peer out a port on her side. He could see only the dark side of the tug, an edge of a red running light. Within minutes, the tipping became a lifting and dropping with definite pounding of water near the head of the chamber. Spray washed past the ports. Kate tasted a sourness in her throat. This new motion shifted suddenly to a heaving pounding craziness, a twisting at the end of each drop. Stephen wedged himself against the side of their bed and held firmly to Kate.

Only yesterday, Kate thought, she had been complaining because nothing changed in their quarters. The temperature had always been kept so annoyingly warm. She had used much of the morning to sort and fold their few items of clothing. A lucky thing. It had made the move into the little chamber much easier.

She gripped Stephen's arm as the barge under them took that moment to make a particularly sickening descent into a wave. As they came up out of the trough, she felt something warm seep down both legs, then a gush of liquid.

"Stephen!"

"It's all right, love. They'll get us across."

"Stephen, the baby's coming!" she wailed. She tried to sit up, steadying herself with a hand against the wooden lip that Stephen had added to their bed, but the barge under them was dropping down into another trough, pitching her onto her back.

It was all wrong, she thought. Weren't there supposed to be pains first, contractions? And it was too early! The baby wasn't due for more than a month.

Stephen groped for the torch, found it and snapped it on. Kate had kicked off the blanket and lay now in a puddle of

amniotic fluid. He left her for an instant to rip the sterilized
sheet off its covering position over the lock. She helped him
draw the sheet under her. It was still damp and smelled awfully
of the antiseptic.

"Weren't there any contractions?" he asked.

"Nothing but the water breaking. Something's wrong, Stephen." Her voice degenerated into a wail. "I'm afraid."

He wedged the torch beside the mattress, pointing it upward
to reflect off the metal above them. His face appeared calm,
but she knew he had only book knowledge of pregnancy and
birth. She felt him taking command, though. He had the ropes
rigged around his shoulders now and another rope across her
chest. The bed pitched and twisted terribly with the sea's movements. She heard the keening of the wind, the sodden slosh of
water against the tank. The torch fell from its position. Stephen
recovered it and wedged it more tightly.

"I can feel the contractions," she gasped. "Ohhhhhhhhh!
Not now!"

"Be calm, darling."

"Why couldn't it wait?"

Another contraction brought a cry from her. "I don't know
what to do," she wailed. Perspiration ran off her body.

"I know what to do, darling. Let the contractions come."

What was he doing down there? She tried to lift her head
and look down at him where he crouched between her legs.
He pushed her back.

"Stay flat! Hold on to that rope."

"It's too soon! It's too soon," she wailed.

She could feel the pitching of the barge as it drove Stephen
lurching against her legs. Another contraction gripped her.
Another.

"I'm timing them," Stephen said, a hand on her abdomen.

"First baby," she gasped. "It may be slow." At least that
was what the nursing manuals advised, she remembered.

Another contraction. Another. She felt her world devolve
into crazy motion and the periodic contractions.

"I can see the head," Stephen said. "That roll of dry blankets
beside you on the left. I'll need one. See if you can reach it."

She was grateful for something to do. Between contractions,
her clutching hand found the blankets and stripped one off. A
pitching roll of the barge banged her head against the hard edge
of the tank. She cried out but kept her grip on the blanket.

Stephen did not look up. She felt his arms against the insides of her thighs. Another contraction set her moaning, but she remembered her training. Bear down with it! She felt the baby slide out.

"The blanket!" Stephen shouted. He jerked it from her hand. She saw him wrapping the baby in it. "I've tied off the umbilicus," he said.

"Is . . . is it alive?" she gasped.

"It's a girl and she's alive!" There was joy in Stephen's voice.

"Is she . . . all right?"

"Her fingernails aren't complete but she's got hair and she's breathing. We have to keep her warm now."

"What about the afterbirth?"

"Everything's out."

"It was so quick!"

"She's very small, darling." He loosened one of the ropes holding him and put the blanket-wrapped infant beside her. "Hold her there with one hand while I move these ropes. We're pitching worse than ever. Can you still reach the blankets?"

"Yes."

Kate stared at a tiny face poking from the blanket beside her. It was an *old* face . . . so wrinkled. There was a little puddle of mucus at the nose. It bubbled as the baby breathed.

"It's too cold in here!" Stephen said. He passed a rope across Kate, moved the torch to a position nearer her head and dragged more blankets across her. Presently, he cinched the rope down tightly and lay beside her, holding to the rope. He made a tent of a blanket over their heads. "We'll warm the air with our breathing and our own bodies."

"She's almost two months early, Stephen. She needs more than this blanket over her."

"I know." He extinguished the torch. "But it's all we have."

Kate began to cry softly. "What a terrible way to enter the world. What a terrible world."

"It's the only world she has, darling."

The baby made a tiny hiccoughing noise.

Stephen flashed the torch on her face. The baby's lips were moving in and out. He sensed a hunger for life in the motion.

"Let me see her," Kate said. She raised herself on one elbow and stared down into her daughter's face. "She hasn't been named," Kate said. "We've not even thought about a name."

"There's no hurry."

"Stephen, if the cables break, this iron tank will sink like a stone."

"The cables aren't going to break. They've even put a net over us."

"I'll not have my daughter dying without a name!"

He stared at Kate in the dim torchlight, feeling the wild motion of the sea, aware of the wind sounds, the waves shocking against the barge. Morbid thoughts were easy to have here, but they helped nothing.

"They've taken every precaution," he said.

"It's a girl, Stephen. Don't you understand? It's a girl. The plague . . . something awful is going to happen. I know it!"

He could hear hysteria in her voice.

"Kate! You're going to be a nurse. You're my wife and I've just delivered our first baby."

"It's dirty in here," she said. "Sepsis."

"We'll not let you die of a fever, I say! Now, stop this." He extinguished the torch.

"Dervogilla," Kate said.

"What?"

"We'll call her Dervogilla," Kate said. "Gilla for short. Gilla Browder. It has a nice sound."

"Kate! Have you a mind to the name you'd saddle this poor babe with?"

"You're thinking of the curse on the original Dervogilla."

"And on Diarmud, the man she ran off with."

"We're running off."

"It's not the same."

"Dervogilla and Diarmud," Kate said, "the two of them to wander Ireland and never find peace, never to be together until one Irishman forgives them."

"I'm not one to believe too much in luck," he said, "but that's a name to tempt fate."

Kate's voice was firm. "It's the curse of poor Ireland, as well. Don't speak against it, Stephen. I know why this plague was laid upon us. Because we refused to forgive Diarmud and Dervogilla."

"You heard that somewhere. The old men nattering back at the castle."

"Everyone says it."

"You're daft."

"You must forgive them, Stephen, and say you approve this name for our daughter."

"Kate!"

"Say it!"

Stephen cleared his throat. He felt on the defensive against this new Kate, this virago. He realized abruptly that she was a mother defending her child in the only way she knew. He felt a wash of tenderness for her and for their daughter.

"I forgive them, Kate. It's a pretty name."

"Thank you, Stephen. Now, our daughter will live."

He felt her moving the baby and turned the torch on her. She was trying to bring the baby to her breast.

"I don't think she'll suckle yet, Kate."

"She's moving her mouth."

"It's when she breathes."

"Gilla," she said. "A pretty name."

Stephen once more extinguished the torch. It was getting dim. They might need it.

Kate closed her eyes. If this terrible motion would only stop. Darkness made it worse. And the wild noises outside. The sourness arose once more in her throat. Abruptly, with barely time for her to put her head out of the blanket shelter and turn away from the baby and Stephen, she vomited. The smell permeated the chamber.

"It's all right," she gasped, reaching for his hand to stop him from turning on the torch. She did not want anyone seeing her like this. "Take the baby." She rested her cheek against the hard edge of wood beside the mattress, heaving and heaving. It was going into the books under the bed, she realized. The smell was awful. She heard Stephen taking deep breaths to keep himself from being sick. She tried to do the same but her stomach was knotted too tightly.

The nightmare went on and on, absorbing all of her energies. It was only gradually that she grew aware of a change in their motion. The barge was rocking only slightly now. Kate wiped her mouth on a corner of the blanket and thought she might live. There was a roaring of the tug's engines beside them and they felt their motion reversing, then a crunch against pilings. The accents of British dock workers could be heard out there.

"Have a care, y' bloody sod! Precious packet, this one. Get the lorry in closer."

Once more, the compressor went silent. They felt the chamber being lifted, steadier here. There came the expected thump as they were settled onto a lorry.

Stephen found the microphone and keyed the switch. "Hello, out there."

There was no answer.

"Do you smell that?" someone outside asked.

"Bloody puke!" someone else said. "Look under the thing!"

The compressor started up then. Someone pounded on the side of the tank. "Hullo, in there! I think you've been breached! It's low down to the end here." The hammering continued to locate it.

Stephen grabbed up the torch and crawled out of the restricting rope toward the sound. The light was very dim, but he saw what he thought was a dark crack beneath the head of the bed. He looked around frantically for something to cover the place. Pressure was building in the chamber and he heard a faint hissing—vomit being forced out of the crack. His books! He had packed some of them in a box wedged behind the toilet. Grabbing the first book off the top, he began tearing out pages and stuffing them over the crack.

"Get a welder over here!" someone outside shouted.

Another voice called something that Stephen could not make out. Paper and vomit were making a crude patch but, as pressure built up in the chamber, he knew the patch would not hold.

"I don't care if you have to break his bloody door down!" someone out there shouted. "Get that welder!"

We've been breached, Stephen thought. *The plague.* It happened while the compressor was off. He looked up and met Kate's staring eyes, shadowed holes in the reflected glare of a spotlight coming through the ports. She held Gilla in her arms.

"You've fixed it, haven't you, Stephen?" she whispered.

"Yes, love."

"I knew you would."

Faith, he thought. *It resists all reason.*

A molecular biologist who dreamed of becoming famous because of a dramatic contribution to the fine chemistry of DNA—that was a thing not considered by this world's power brokers.

—Jost Hupp

JUST AFTER noon on the fifth day after Kevin O'Donnell took over the Killaloe Facility, John was removed from the basement storeroom where he had been imprisoned. The prison chamber was one of three dark, stone-walled rooms beneath the old castle tower, a noisome place with slime on the walls and a damp floor. The barred windows on the three identical doors suggested this had been the castle's original dungeon keep. Doheny had been kept for a time in one of the other rooms, but he had been removed earlier. The priest and the boy occupied the third cell. The overhead joists of the outer chamber dripped with cobwebs. The wall opposite the three prison chambers was piled high with a jumble of old discards: broken sofas, warped tables, rusty electric lamps, a gas stove with three legs, odd lengths of iron pipe, an automobile wheel with flaps of rubber clinging to its rim. A rotted stack of planking lay piled against a corner.

Two uniformed guards came for John. He did not know their names, but they were the ones who had brought meals to the prisoners. John thought of them as Slim and Baldy. They told him to strip and, when he obeyed, they kicked his clothes into a corner and handed him a clean-room smock from the Facility. It was more gray than white. He was allowed to keep only his shoes.

It was a cold gray day and a wind blowing when they escorted him into the castle courtyard. He shivered under the thin smock. A thick cloud cover made the courtyard a gloomy place. Through the arched gateway to the lakefront he saw the wind whipping a froth on the water. The wind wrapped the inadequate smock around his shanks.

"Where are you taking me?" John asked.

Slim said: "Shut up, prisoner."

The castle proper lifted a stark monolithic shape in the gray light, with a few spots of yellow in the narrow windows to indicate where lamps had been turned on against the darkness. There were streaks of white blossoms on the window ledges, though, and the air smelled clean after the rotted odors of the dungeon.

Slim and Baldy kept firm grips on his upper arms as they hurried him across the courtyard into the administration wing, then down a yellow corridor and up the stairs to the castle library.

Every light in the library had been turned on. The crystal chandeliers danced with brilliants. Spotlight sconces focused on a raised platform that had been built near the fireplace out of plywood nailed to heavy timbers. A trestle table had been placed on the plywood and leather armchairs set up behind it. Kevin O'Donnell and Joseph Herity occupied two of the chairs. Father Michael sat at the end of the table, the boy standing beside him. Fintan Craig Doheny stood in front of the table, his back to John. Six chairs had been arranged at one side in what looked like a jury box. A dock fashioned of water pipes had been bolted to the floor near Doheny. John's guards manacled him to this stanchion before retiring two paces.

John stared around the room. There were people standing packed in the library stacks peering out at him. He recognized Adrian Peard in his lovat green tweeds in the forefront. Peard would not meet John's gaze.

Doheny and Kevin O'Donnell were conversing in low voices when John entered. They paid no attention to the prisoner's arrival but went on with their conversation. Herity was sipping from an open bottle of whiskey. Several folders of papers lay loosely on the table between Kevin and Herity. A large paste-board box sat on the chair to Kevin's right.

John found himself enduring chiaroscuro shifts of mood as he awaited whatever ritual they had prepared for him here. The scene was at once ludicrous and moving in the trappings it borrowed from deadly courtroom games.

Father Michael stared fixedly at the table in front of him, not moving when the boy nudged him at John's entrance. The boy stared at John with an unreadable expression.

John directed a thought at O'Neill-Within: *They mean to kill me because they think I'm you.*

O'Neill-Within did not respond.

Kevin suddenly raised his voice: "The boy is a witness and he'll speak his piece when I say!"

The boy turned his head and looked at Kevin. In a high voice on the edge of hysteria, he screamed: "You're a shit! Your mother thought she was having a baby! She had shit instead!"

Nervous laughter sounded from the stacks. Kevin merely smiled. "Let him be," he said. "We know he has a full line of talk and most of it taken from the gutter."

Herity tipped up his whiskey bottle and took a long swallow from it. He placed the bottle carefully on the table in front of him and stared at it. The bottle was almost half empty.

Father Michael looked up at Kevin and Herity. "You're evil men. An oath means nothing to you—your own or another's. I ask you, Joseph, when you knew they had the fingerprints and dental charts in America, why did you threaten this boy and force me to break the seal of the confessional? Why?"

"I did it to make the boy talk, not you," Herity said. "No one should go through life like a silent ghost!"

"I pronounce you anathema," Father Michael said, his voice low. "You are cursed through all eternity, Joseph Herity, and you, Kevin O'Donnell. I give you the burden of your terrible sin and may it grow heavier with every breath you take."

"Your curse means nothing to us," Herity said. He took another pull from his bottle.

A hint of nervousness in his voice, Kevin said: "Life and death are in our hands, not yours!"

Father Michael looked at John: "Forgive me, John, I beg it of you. They would torture this poor boy. I cannot permit that. I have broken the seal of the confessional. Forgive me."

Turmoil gripped John's breast. Seal of the confessional?

How could that be important? Perspiration poured down his brows, burned his eyes.

Kevin O'Donnell grinned and opened the box on the chair beside him. He lifted a large sealed jar from it and placed it on the table beside him. John stared at the bottle. It was filled with amber liquid and there was something floating in the liquid. O'Donnell turned the bottle slightly, and John saw a face there.

It was a head!

The eyes were closed but the lips were slightly parted. John thought he recognized the third horseman who had arrived with Herity and Kevin.

"Meet Alex Coleman," Kevin said. "Pickled in whiskey at last and that his dream of paradise, I'm sure." Kevin focused a wide-eyed stare on John, motioning for Doheny to stand aside. "This was the traitor whose warning let Fin here spirit away from us the pride of Ireland."

Doheny said: "Kevin, you—"

"Don't interrupt! You're here under sufferance and only so long as you live up to our agreement!"

Six men came out from the stacks then at Kevin's signal and took seats in the row of chairs, seating themselves with a noisy scraping of the wooden legs on the floor, coughs and low-voiced comments.

Kevin rapped once on the table with a small block of wood. He lifted the wood.

"I have in my hand a bit of the roof timber from Cashell. It is a token that Irish Law prevails here." He lowered the wood gently to the table. "We have ridden here on horseback as did the kings of old, it being the mark of a conqueror. The Brehon Law will be restored." He glanced once around the room. "Is there another O'Neill present?"

No one moved.

"The prisoner's family has deserted him," Kevin said. "The prisoner stands alone." He tapped the bottle beside him. "But the triumvirate is present and the trial will proceed." Kevin let his gaze wander over the others in the room, settling at last on Herity. "It's time, Joseph."

Herity put his bottle aside gently and lifted a sheet of paper from the stack on the table. He read from it, glancing occasionally at John.

"We say first that you, prisoner, are John Roe O'Neill. We say you are the author of the plague which has outraged our poor land and much of the world besides, making an exception for the British and the heathens to whom it was a just punishment. We say you had no cause to harm us in this cowardly fashion. And how do you plead, John Roe O'Neill?"

John stared at the head in the bottle. It was speaking to him in the voice of O'Neill! "What was my crime?" it asked. "I was wronged. That priest knows! I was grievously wronged."

Who can deny that? John thought.

"What did I ever do," the head asked, "that those terrorist killers whom the Irish tolerated and openly abetted—what had I *ever* done to deserve the callous murder of my family?"

"It was a terrible provocation," John whispered.

"Is the prisoner speaking?" Kevin asked.

John did not hear him. The head was speaking: "It's the Irish who should be on trial here! They're the ones who fed the disease of terrorism!"

• John nodded silently.

Father Michael glanced sidelong at John, wondering at the sudden odd stillness in the man, as though he had locked himself into some secret place where no sound could penetrate.

Doheny turned then and looked full at John. *Sic semper Irish honor,* Doheny thought. *What will this poor Madman think when he learns that I'm his prosecutor?*

What a price to pay!

But Kevin O'Donnell would surely destroy this lab if his orders were not obeyed. Even Adrian Peard would suffer, damn him! But they had to continue with what the Madman had given them. A cure for the plague, that was the only priority. Ireland might yet do it alone!

Kevin glanced at Father Michael. "Have you an opening statement, Priest?"

Father Michael coughed and lifted his attention to John. "Whatever the Madman did, it's plain there was no malice in him before he suffered outrage."

"We will refer to the prisoner as O'Neill!" Kevin said.

Herity smiled slyly and took another swallow from his bottle.

Father Michael said: "Even malice is not the word to describe his intentions. O'Neill appears to have been motivated by blind rage rather than any other emotion. He wanted to strike insanely in the vicinity of those who had destroyed his world. We must admit his aim, in this respect, was accurate—not totally, but perhaps sufficiently so for his mad rage."

John rattled his manacles against the pipe, staring at the head in the bottle. The head remained silent. Why wouldn't O'Neill come to his defense?

"I do not argue that O'Neill acted from any principle," Father Michael said. "I presume he knew full well who was responsible for his act and for the outrage which was committed against him. If there was any faith involved it was only his faith in his ability to strike us down."

Father Michael stood and turned to look at the jurors. The boy stepped back a pace.

"Passion there was and no doubt of that!" Father Michael thundered. "Passion against the authors of his agony! Against us!" He lowered his voice to a gentle monotone. "He has given us passion as well. What will we do with it?"

Father Michael returned his attention to Kevin. "If it's revenge we're after, then let us call it by its rightful name. If we are to ignore the holy injunction against passing judgment, then let us judge with revenge in mind and thereby expose ourselves to the consequences."

Herity sneered: "Judge not lest ye be judged."

"Let him speak," Kevin said. "I have promised that we will suppress no line of defense."

"Yes!" Father Michael said. "We swore a holy oath on the sacred honor of Ireland! Truth and justice, that is what we swore by Almighty God to uphold!"

"Almighty God," Herity said. He took another pull from his bottle.

"Joseph Herity reminds us," Father Michael said, "of the holy warning. Christ intended it to be the thorn in our side. It raises the terrible question: Who judges? Dare we pass judgment on the judges? If we say that only men can be judges, we deny God. Do we deny God?"

"I do!" Herity said.

"Shush, Joseph," Kevin said. "Let him rant."

Father Michael sent a burning stare around the room. "We were civilized in Ireland when the rest of the world was a pagan mudhole. Let us act like civilized men." He directed his stare at Doheny, who stood in front of the table with a glowering look of displeasure.

"If we make any pretense at being a court of Irish Law, as *Judge* Kevin O'Donnell says, then let us have no hypocrisy in our court. Let us not soothe ourselves with illusions. Let us not pretend we are the purely good and this poor Madman . . . Mister O'Neill, is purely evil. That is the issue which our oath forces us to address."

"Must we?" Herity asked.

"We must!" Father Michael shouted. "What is this man charged with?"

"Charged with?" Herity repeated in mock solemnity. "He's only charged with destroying the flower of Irish beauty."

"He was certainly insane at the moment!" Father Michael said.

"Moment?" Herity demanded. "Surely it took more than a moment!" He glanced at Peard, who stood now just out of the stacks. "Have you anything to say to that, Doctor Adrian Peard?"

"He's behaved sanely every time I've seen him," Peard said. "And I've watched him carefully ever since being alerted that he was O'Neill."

"And what has he done here?" Father Michael asked.

"Pretended to show us how the plague was created," Peard said.

"For the love of heaven, man!" Father Michael protested. "He's revealed everything we need for us to find a cure."

"I see no cure," Peard said. "I think we'll find one, but not because of him."

"Ahhhhhh." Father Michael nodded. "And the cure will be the work of Adrian Peard. Oh, I see it now." He looked at Doheny, who refused to meet his gaze. Father Michael turned once more to look at the jurors, thinking they were a motley lot, giving every appearance of boredom. Had they already consulted with Kevin and Joseph and arrived at a verdict? Was this trial only a sham?

"The ultimate conflict is between good and good, not between good and evil, is that our contention?" Father Michael asked. "I say to you that in this room, we are exposing the conflict between evil and evil. Does evil have the right to judge evil? You may ask: 'Who could know it better?' But I warn you to face this with clear heads and a full understanding of the admission you make when you judge!"

Father Michael returned to his chair and sat down. The boy came back to his side.

John stared at the head in the bottle. Would the head speak? That head was the true judge in this room. John held this thought close to him, warming himself on it.

Kevin looked at Doheny and nodded, finding a restorative amusement in the thought of how Doheny had been forced into assuming the role of prosecutor. How that must gall the man!

Doheny noted the quickening of interest on the faces of the jurors. Judgment was a foregone conclusion, as Kevin had made clear by his private instructions to those men chosen from among his own forces. But the taste for tragic spectacle had not vanished from Ireland, Doheny thought. The attraction of the capital trial could not be denied. We throng to the spectacle of agony and the course of death. We throng to Golgotha. He girded himself with this thought as he prepared to speak.

My task is a simple one, Doheny thought. *I must merely give them sufficient words of justification before they announce the judgment.*

In his most reasonable voice, Doheny addressed the jurors. "I have no desire to humiliate O'Neill. I agree that he could only have been mad when he did this thing. But that is no excuse. Granted that insanity has been lodged as excuse for other heinous crimes, this goes beyond anything in our history. It ranks only with the crucifixion."

Doheny shot a glance at Father Michael. Raise the religious issue, would he?

"Passion, the priest says," Doheny intoned. "It is the ultimate passion of humankind. Can humanity show mercy to O'Neill? Can we face the obvious fact of his insanity, saying this was a mitigating circumstance? I say we cannot! There are crimes for which insanity is no plea! There are crimes, the very contemplation of which, demand that the insane be judged guilty!"

Doheny turned to look at O'Neill. Why did the man stare so at the head of poor Alex? The Madman made no response to this trial other than a low hunching of the shoulders, but his gaze remained fixed on the head in the bottle.

"The priest says: 'Judge not lest ye be judged.' A tempting quotation and one I expected to hear. But whose judgment do we deliver here? Are we to assume that God approves of O'Neill's crimes?"

Doheny glanced at Father Michael, thinking: *Let him return to his insanity plea now!*

Still looking at the priest, Doheny said: "Only the devil himself could approve of O'Neill's crime. And perhaps this is the devil's seventh day when he rests to admire *his* work. I do not admire his work. I cannot say: 'Let God judge this man because we mere humans cannot judge.'"

Doheny returned his attention to the jurors, noting that they had lapsed into boredom. Had he already given them enough justification?

"God knows best. Is that our judgment?" Doheny asked. "Do we assume that we, mere humans, cannot know what O'Neill has done? Have we no powers of observation?"

One of the jurors, a man with a red scar down his right cheek, winked at Doheny.

Doheny turned away, feeling that he had somehow joined in a crime. His voice was low when he continued, prompting Kevin to order: "Speak up, man!"

"I say to you," Doheny said, starting over, "that the judgment is ours. We are the survivors of outrage. It is up to us to clean the slate. It is not evil against evil in this room. We are warring against evil! War! This is a principle that we must recognize and apply!"

In what he hoped was a dramatic gesture, Doheny pointed at John.

"What denial does he make? His puny explanation is that it was not he but another who lives within him. But we here know the truth that we swore to uphold."

Again, John's manacles rattled against the pipe that confined him. And the head in the jar spoke to him! The voice was surely O'Neill's: "What are these fools doing? I did what I had to do. I was driven to it. And why do they have you here, John Garrech O'Donnell? Because no one was closer to me than you. Because you knew me best!"

"Does the priest have anything to add?" Kevin asked. "I'll have no man saying we silenced you."

Father Michael stood slowly, shot a glance at Doheny, then said: "Law and, presumably, this Irish court pretend to share an ethical principle with science. Truth! We must have the truth no matter what follows. Truth though hell should bar the way."

He turned and swept his gaze along the row of jurors. "All I've said to you is that if you once assume this principle, you abandon it at your peril. I am happy to hear *Judge* O'Donnell say he will not suppress any line of defense. Whenever we silence a line of inquiry that might lead to unwanted disclosures, we do disservice to truth. We have embraced the principle of open disclosure and no legal excuse may be used against it."

Father Michael passed a mild gaze around the room. The jurymen still appeared bored. Well, they would not be bored in a moment! There was no telling what went on in Kevin O'Donnell's muddled head. Doheny was listening carefully, as though he suspected where this might lead. And the Madman had looked up, staring around him with a confused expression.

"War?" Father Michael asked. "Is this a principle that I have overlooked? Is there such a thing as a principle of war! If so, do we dare confine this principle only to nations? Or to political societies such as the Provos and the Finn Sadal? If such a principle exists—as Mister Doheny suggests—it must be able to stand by itself or it is no principle at all. Is it a principle? One man alone can embrace a principle. Any man can do that. May we rail against his choice or denounce his choice of weapon?"

Kevin raised the length of Cashell roof timber, but lowered it gently.

"Was the plague a weapon in a war?" Father Michael asked. "Do we dare rail against it? Well might *he* rail against the bomb!" Father Michael turned and stared up at Herity, who had just drained the last of his whiskey. "Joseph Herity's bomb!" Father Michael thundered. "Can he sit there in judgment when it was his bomb that killed O'Neill's wife and wains?"

The jurors perked up, glancing from the priest to Herity. Kevin's face held a look of secret glee. Herity appeared not to have heard. He stared at his empty bottle on the table in front of him.

John glanced wildly around the room. He could feel the words still leaping about him, live things. The head in the jar spoke to him then, commanding: "Well, speak up! It was Herity who killed Mary and the twins!"

John fixed his gaze on Herity. A voice came out of him, high-pitched and twittering: "How do you like your war now, Joseph Herity?" He giggled, rattling his manacles, his head weaving from side to side as though there were only infant muscles in the neck.

Father Michael looked at John, then across the room at Peard. "Sane is it, Adrian?"

Peard would not meet the priest's eyes.

Kevin brought his block of timber crashing onto the table. "Enough! We are not on trial here! The issue of sanity has been laid to rest."

"May I not speak about this question of war that Mister Doheny has raised?" Father Michael asked, his voice soft. He saw that some of the jurors were grinning. The grins disappeared as Kevin looked at them.

When Kevin did not respond, Father Michael continued:

"This man, O'Neill, wedded before God, lost his whole family to men who bragged that it was war, that they acted in the name of the people. War, the Provos called it."

Once more, Kevin brought the wood crashing onto the table. "I said that was enough!"

"Ahhhhhh," Father Michael said, smiling at Doheny, who was looking fixedly at the floor. "At last we find a line of inquiry which cannot be allowed. Here is a truth we dare not confront!"

Kevin looked at Herity, who now lifted a bleary expression to the room. "Do you hear what he says, Joseph? Will you not speak up?"

"It gnaws at you like a worm, Joseph," Father Michael said. "You'll not set that burden down."

Herity got unsteadily to his feet and leaned on the table. "We'll foll-follow any . . . any lu-lunacy so long as it . . . it has dash! Dash is what we . . . we love." His face solemn, Herity looked at Father Michael. "We don't say . . . say aud-audacity. We say . . . we say audashity! That has . . . has both shit . . . shit and dash in it!" He began to laugh weakly, then sobered, turning his gaze to Kevin. "You put something in me drink, Kevin. What'd you put in me drink?"

"You're drunk, Joseph," Kevin said, smiling.

"Not so drunk that I've lost all reason." He slumped back into his chair. "M-m-me legs! Th-they d-d-d-don't w-w-work!"

Abruptly, Herity's head lolled to the right. His mouth opened. He gasped once and was still.

Peard darted out from the side and mounted the platform. He pressed a hand against Herity's neck, looked up at Kevin, then: "He's dead!"

"I knew the drink would get him eventually," Kevin said. "Well, leave him be. The triumvirate is still present."

Father Michael moved to approach Herity.

"Stay where you are!" Kevin shouted. He lifted a pistol from beneath the table.

"Pistol justice is it?" Father Michael asked.

"Back to your place, Priest," Kevin said, waving the gun.

Father Michael hesitated.

"Do it," Doheny said.

Father Michael obeyed, sinking into his chair. The boy pressed close to his side.

Kevin put his pistol on the table in front of him and looked at Doheny. "Thank you, Mister Doheny. We must keep order.

Will you speak now to O'Neill's guilty knowledge?"

Doheny swept his gaze past the dead figure of Herity. He gestured Peard off the raised platform. Peard returned to his place at the stacks.

"O'Neill employed guilty knowledge of medical matters," Doheny said, sounding as though he recited a memorized piece. "Guilty knowledge is anything that should have been suppressed at conception. When such things infiltrate our peaceable lives, the guilt is obvious."

Father Michael opened his mouth and closed it, realizing this was something Kevin had ordered Doheny to say. What devil's pact had been signed between those two?

Kevin was staring at the priest.

Father Michael got to his feet, pushing the boy aside. "What was this guilty knowledge? A medical matter, perhaps? The sole province of medical doctors? Then why do doctors publish? Is it their illusion that only they understand the language of their discoveries?"

"Anyone who uses guilty knowledge is guilty!" Kevin roared.

"And O'Neill learning about such matters confirms his guilt?" Father Michael asked.

Kevin nodded, grinning.

That man should know better than to argue with someone trained by the Jesuits, Father Michael thought.

He turned to the jurors and asked: "What happens when we suppress such discoveries? Think about the various means of suppression and who may be permitted to employ such means. Immediately, you must face a disturbing realization. Suppressors are required to know what it is they suppress. The censors must know! You have, in fact, suppressed nothing! You have only confined the knowledge to a special elite. I ask you: How do we select that elite?"

Father Michael turned and smiled at Kevin.

"It is an unanswerable question," Father Michael said. "Do we suggest that O'Neill conspired with guilty knowledge to bring down our world?"

"That's it!" Kevin snapped. "He conspired!"

Father Michael looked at Doheny, but the latter had turned away and was watching John. John had returned his attention to the head in the jar, cocking his ear toward it, nodding as though the head spoke to him.

"Let us remind you of the Latin that you appear to have forgotten," Father Michael said. "Conspire! That Latin which

law loves so much says conspire means 'to breathe together.'
There was no breathing together here! He did it alone!"

Father Michael turned on his heel to face the jurors, giving
them time to absorb this.

His voice almost inaudible, Father Michael repeated it:
"Alone." Then louder: "Can you not grasp the awesome significance of that singular fact?"

The jurors were looking at him now, no signs of boredom
in their faces.

Father Michael almost sang it to them: "He did it alone.
How do we manage our affairs in the light of such knowledge?
How do we judge our own behavior now? Where is the guiltless
to hurl the first stone?"

"This is bootless!" Kevin said. He rapped on the table with
his pistol. "Mister Doheny, would you put these matters to
rest?"

Doheny looked at the pistol in Kevin's hand, knowing that
no mistake would be permitted now.

His voice sad, Doheny said: "We have identified the author
of our misery. We do not need his admission or denial. This
is O'Neill." Doheny pointed, then lowered his hand. "He makes
all previous murderers appear amateur. Warfare becomes a
minor affliction. The priest finds it interesting that I refer to
the plague in terms of war? Is he saying that every Irish soldier
who fired a shot in anger is guilty?"

Shockingly, John tittered and shook an admonitory finger
at the head in the jar.

Doheny crossed to stand in front of the jurors, intensely
aware that Father Michael was above and behind him. Why
had Kevin done that, placed the priest at a higher level?

"O'Neill is amused," Doheny said. "He is not embarrassed.
He is not penitent. He is defiant." He turned and stared at John.
"Look at him."

John's gaze was fixed on the head in the jar. The head
spoke: "How do you like Mister Doheny's defense?" The head
emitted a banshee scream that John felt echoing in his own
skull. John pressed his palms against his ears.

"He does not want to hear," Doheny said. He turned back
to the jury with what he hoped was a look of sincerity. This
was not a pleasant role, but the need was great. "The priest
says O'Neill did it with provocation. I agree. You find that
surprising? The act says he was provoked. But how did he
select the targets for his plague? The priest says we declared

war on O'Neill. I do not recall such a proclamation, but no matter. Perhaps war needs no proclamation. The priest asks us to be clear-headed, though. What does he mean by this? Should we be remote, cool and, perhaps, detached about our misery? Are we to anticipate a defense on the issue of sweet reason?"

The jurors chuckled.

Doheny thought then about the points he and Herity and O'Donnell had gone over before assembling here. Had he touched them all? Insanity . . . reason . . . justified provocation. Doheny decided he had said enough. There remained only the confrontation with the boy. That could be held to the end. He walked back to his position near John, passing his gaze over Herity's body. Why did no one question Joseph's death? Was everyone terrified of Kevin and his killers? Poison, it must've been. Herity had been a man who could hold his drink.

Doheny's glance fell on John. The Madman was staring once more at the head in the jar. What did he find so fascinating about poor Alex's head? It was just one more death in a room full of it!

The head was speaking to John: "Why do they question? All the answers are in the letters."

"But I was only trying to silence O'Neill's screaming," John said.

Father Michael leaped to his feet. "Did you hear that? He was trying to subdue O'Neill's agony!"

Silence settled over the room.

Father Michael sighed. He turned and looked at the jurors. What was the sense talking to more death's-heads? he wondered. Might just as well address Alex's head there in that terrible jar. He had to try, though.

"There is a pattern here," Father Michael said. "A clear pattern woven inextricably into other patterns—into the Battle of the Boyne, into the Penal Laws, into Caesar's heavy foot on Britain and even in the fact that the wind did not blow when Rome's galleys met the Celtic fleet off Gaul."

These were Irishmen, Father Michael thought. They would know Celtic history.

"Are you summing up?" Kevin asked.

"If you want to call it that," Father Michael said. He rubbed the side of his nose as he swept his gaze along the six jurors. "I speak of a pattern which ranges from Stalingrad to Antioch, from Bir ain aba to Mai Lai, and much farther because it is not always found in momentous battles, but sometimes in very small conflicts. Ignore this pattern and we slay this world finally with ignorance. Recognize it and our values change. We will know then what to preserve."

Father Michael fell silent for a moment and glanced back at the boy, who stood staring at him with a look of wonder. Could that young lad understand? Was this the only mind in the room worth addressing?

Doheny felt himself deeply moved by the priest's words. God! The man was an Irish orator from the old tradition. The jurymen were obviously disturbed by him. They had planned this so carefully. Bring in the boy at the end, put it to him: Would he kill O'Neill? There was justice in it. What had that boy ever done to O'Neill? Kevin said the boy had agreed privately: He would pull the trap and do it with a curse. He would light the match, pull the trigger... anything.

The door behind Doheny burst open with a crash. A uniformed member of Kevin's guard came rushing across the room. "Sir!" he called even before stopping in front of the table. "The word is out that we have O'Neill! We've had to close the gates! Thousands of people—there must be ten thousand all around us! They want O'Neill! Listen."

They all heard it then, a sullen chant from outside the castle grounds:

"O'Neill! O'Neill! O'Neill!"

Abruptly, the Madman roared with laughter, then: "Why don't you give them O'Neill?"

Despair creates violence and the Brits were past masters at creating despair among the Irish. There's a widespread belief in England, you know, that the Irish, like women and Negroes, are essentially children, incapable of governing themselves. But no people can be truly free until they rid themselves of their inherited prejudices. The English and their Ulster satellite have been slaves to their Irish prejudices.

—Fintan Craig Doheny

"HAVE THEY been contaminated?" Wycombe-Finch demanded.

"It's too early to tell," Beckett said.

It was almost midnight and both men spoke in loud voices to override the construction sounds in the big warehouse where they had brought the pressure chamber containing the Browders. The thum-thum-thum of the chamber's air pump formed a background noise that intruded irritatingly on the other sounds.

The chamber had been lowered onto a wooden cradle near the center of the warehouse and a space cleared all around it. Tall stacks of canned food and pallets of other supplies had been moved back against the walls. A swarm of carpenters and other volunteers labored near the chamber, building a plywood and plastic room to which the chamber could be attached.

Wycombe-Finch and Beckett stood about six meters from all this activity but they could still smell vomit in the air being cycled out of the chamber. It was a repugnant odor, especially when mixed with the aromas created by the emergency welding, and that had been done hours ago on the landing stage at the coast near Ellesmere.

"Are you sure acids will sterilize the larger chamber?" Wycombe-Finch asked.

"The real problem's the fumes," Beckett said. "We'll have to clear the air in there before letting them enter the new chamber."

Wycombe-Finch stooped to peer at the new weld under the chamber, then straightened. "It must be hellish in there," he said. "Have you told them how close you are to a cure?"

"I've told them we're working as fast as we can to produce enough for the mother and baby." He shook his head. "But you know, Wye, if they're contaminated . . . we'll be lucky to get enough of it in time to treat the baby, let alone the mother."

"How certain are you really that the serum will be effective?"

"Certain schmertain!"

"Are you suggesting it might not work?"

"It works in the test tube." He shrugged.

"I see. Well, if it doesn't perform outside the glassworks, Stoney will be rather put out."

"Fuck Stoney!"

"You Americans! You're so gross under pressure. I believe that's why you've produced so few really good administrators."

Beckett clamped his mouth shut to suppress an angry reply. Abruptly, he strode away from the director, dodging two workmen with a sheet of plywood and coming to a stop at a port on the end of the pressure chamber. It was dark inside, all the lights turned off. *Could they be asleep?* he wondered. He did not see how they could sleep in the presence of all this construction din.

The temporary speaker above the port crackled and Stephen Browder's voice demanded: "How much longer must we endure this? The baby really needs oxygen!"

"We're filling a small tank right now," Beckett said. "We had to find something that would go through the supply lock."

"But how long?"

"Another hour at the most," Beckett said. He could see Browder's face near the port now, a pale shape in the tank's gloom.

"They're building with wood?" Browder said. "How can you sterilize . . ."

"We've acids that should do the job."

"Should?"

"Look, Browder! We've identified the pathogen and we've killed it outside the human body."

"And how long before you have the serum?"

"At least thirty-six hours."

Beckett heard Kate's voice then demanding: "Stephen! What're they saying?"

"They're getting the serum, love," Browder said.

"Will it be in time?" she asked.

"There's no certainty you were contaminated, love! They got the weld patch on very fast and the heat, well no germ could live through that."

But it spreads in the air you breathe, Beckett thought. He said: "We're working as fast as we can."

"We're extremely grateful," Browder said.

Wycombe-Finch touched Beckett's shoulder then, shocking him because the construction noise had concealed the man's approach.

"Sorry," Wycombe-Finch said. "I've just had word that Stonar's on the telephone. He insists on talking to you."

Beckett looked out to an open door of the warehouse, a wide space filled with Huddersfield staffers peering in at them.

"They're hoping for a glimpse of the woman," Wycombe-Finch said, seeing the direction of Beckett's gaze. "Shiles has posted guards to keep them out."

"Yeah." Beckett started to move toward the door, but was stopped by the director's hand on his arm. "Bill, go very gently with Stonar. He is a dangerous man."

"I will." Beckett nodded toward the staffers at the door. "We'll have to let them see her sometime soon—a schedule of viewing or something."

"Shiles has it in hand."

"Better have the viewers searched to make sure no one brings a hammer to crack the viewing port."

"You don't really think . . ." He sniffed. "This is England! We've put out the word that all nonessential personnel must stay away. At any rate, there'll be nothing to see except a big wooden room and a small metal cylinder."

"What phone can I use for Stonar?" Beckett asked.

"The Ad Building security office just across the way is probably the closest. First on your right after you go through the entrance."

Beckett strode toward the doorway, where he was delayed by the press of people demanding: "Do they really have a woman over there?"

"And her husband and her daughter," Beckett said. "You'll

have to stay away from there for now, though."

"My God, man!" someone said. "Don't you know how long it's been since we've seen a woman?"

"There's no way you can see her just yet," Beckett said, pulling away. He strode quickly across the grounds, leaving the crowd at the doorway, but not before he heard someone say: "Bloody Yanks!"

His way was lighted by the constant pathway-illumination that made the Huddersfield Establishment look like a busy factory complex at night. A great many people were up and around, he noted: More of the curious coming to peer into the warehouse.

The security office also was brilliantly illuminated. A guard sat behind the single small desk in the room, his attention on TV monitors overhead. At Beckett's request, he pushed a telephone across the desk but kept his gaze on the monitors. The operator put Stonar on the line immediately.

"Where did they have to go to get you?" Stonar demanded. "Land's End?"

Stonar on the telephone was no more pleasant than Stonar in person, Beckett thought. "I was in the warehouse where we've lodged the container with that Irish couple."

"Is it true she had a baby on the crossing?"

"Yes, a daughter. Premature. It's going to be touch and go."

"Two guinea pigs for your serum, though."

"Truer than you think. They may have been contaminated."

"Well . . . I imagine we'll scare up quite a few women when we announce your serum."

"You announce nothing until we've tested it!"

"Of course, old man! Of course." Stonar sounded almost pleasant. "You're pretty confident of the thing, aren't you?"

"We have our fingers crossed. Those last bits from the Irish really put us over the top. Quintuplicate series in the messenger code, by God!"

"They must've gotten that directly from O'Neill. The Irish could never have come up with it on their own."

"It's true they have O'Neill himself?"

"Doubt it not, old fellow. Bloody fecal matter hitting the bloody fan, too. Our informants say they're on the edge of civil war. One lot's holed up in their research facility, hoping that'll keep them safe from direct attack. Another lot got most of the northeast coast and quite a few places inland. Typical Irish dust-up!"

Beckett looked at the back of the security guard's neck, wondering at Stonar's manner. The man sounded almost chatty, even friendly.

"Where do they have O'Neill?" Beckett asked.

"At that research facility, we're told. Say, Bill, I'd like you to put me thoroughly in the picture, if you will? I've a meeting coming up with the prime minister and the king. Bit of technical jargon, that sort of thing." Stonar actually chuckled. "Everyone's quite excited. What is it you're doing, actually?"

Beckett nodded to himself. The picture had become exceedingly clear. Dangerous man, indeed. He wanted something to impress the brass!

"Our approach is to give a disease to the disease," Beckett said. "You know that the twenty possible amino acids are sequenced by the genetic code. The plague interferes with that sequencing. It inserts a new message to control the biochemical activity in the cells. The coding of the cells by which they perform their special functions is addressed by the plague, specific messages to specific types of cells. Are you getting all this?"

"Recording it, old chap. It'll be typed off for me. Do continue, if you please."

"Use the spiral staircase analogy," Beckett said. "It's a genetic disease, attacking the DNA helix at critical places in the staircase."

"Quite." Stonar managed to sound elated but dry.

"When the new message is injected into a transmitting cell, instead of a quadratic form, it's carried in a series of fives—"

"That thing they passed along from O'Neill."

"Quite." Beckett took delight in imitating Stonar, but apparently the man did not notice. "We knew O'Neill must've used a virus as his messenger into the bacterial host," he said. "And there was that tantalizing clue of the similarity to granulocytic leukemia."

"And what does that mean, old chap, if they should ask?"

"It indicates a disruption of the normal genetic coding. The structure of the DNA was certainly changed."

"Quite. And why doesn't it attack men?"

"There's no biochemical niche where the plague pathogen can lock itself in and do its dirty work. It's broken down by the bodily mechanism that regulates the rate of cellular growth."

Beckett smiled to himself, realizing he had just passed along all of the essential information that would alert a knowledgeable person to the other things they would be able to do: no more mitotic disease, an end to cancer. They would be able to control the energy-building activities of related RNA. And much more.

"That's splendid!" Stonar said. "You did a lot of work on the old computer, didn't you?"

Oh, yes, Beckett thought. *Have to bring in the great new tool of science!* He said: "We had two things going for us there—a superb new search program developed by a young American plus the image enhancement techniques that NASA produced to improve pictures sent back from space. We were able to see things within the genetic structure never before seen."

"O'Neill must've seen them," Stonar said.

"Quite," Beckett said.

"That search program, that was the thing your man Ruckerman brought over?"

"Yes."

"I've had him brought down here, you know? King requested it. Quite a lot of chin-chin to go through about the new world setup."

Beckett crossed his fingers. "I imagine so."

"Ruckerman representing your President, the king there, the prime minister—very high-level."

And you think you're right in the middle of it! Beckett thought.

"Oh, by the by," Stonar said. "You may be interested to know that Kangsha is making a guarded announcement about a cure."

"The Chinese?"

"They're giving no details but the signal is clear enough, old chap. They use the word *cure.*" Stonar cleared his throat. "The Japanese and the Soviets are still silent about their progress but Jaipur is saying now that it will be accepting bids within a month for a chemical treatment of the plague that has produced remarkable results. Their words."

"That is interesting, especially about the Chinese."

"Pass it along to Wye, will you, old chap?"

"Of course. Give Ruckerman my regards."

"Certainly. We're getting along famously, you know? But

I must say he'll never be able to say *quite* quite as well as you do."

The connection was broken with a definite "click."

Before Beckett could hang up, Shiles came on the line. "Wait there, will you, Bill? I'll be right over."

Beckett put the phone back on its cradle. Shiles had been listening. What did that mean? Probably nothing much. Everyone took it for granted that all conversations were monitored. But Shiles himself on this one!

A white-smocked figure thrust open the security office door then, ignored Beckett and addressed the guard monitoring the TV screens. "Hey, Arley! There's a woman in some kind of isolation chamber over in the warehouse!"

"I know," the guard said. He kept his gaze on the screens above him.

The door slammed as the informant left. They heard his feet running down the hallway.

Beckett looked up at the screens then, realizing that the one on the far right showed a close-up of the end of the Browders' pressure chamber. Faint movement could be seen through the glass of the port.

Shiles entered presently, his usually neat uniform appearing a bit mussed. He took in the situation in the room and said: "You can leave, Arley. Take over on the upstairs monitors."

The guard left with one last longing look at the far right screen.

When the door closed, Shiles said, "We were wrong not to let Wye in from the first. He was in my office this evening making guarded allusions to 'some extremely exciting spinoffs' from your breakthrough. 'Give us a handle on no end of things,' he says."

"Some bent nose coming up," Beckett said.

"We could blame it on your frog friend," Shiles said.

Beckett stared at him with a dawning realization. The English had it bred in the bone never to trust anyone from beyond their shores. And that would include Bill Beckett, Danzas and Lepikov as well as Hupp. How the hell were they supposed to put this world back together in the middle of that kind of shit?

"If there's any blame, I'll take it," Beckett said.

"Awfully decent of you," Shiles said. "But do you have any real appreciation of the forces we're holding in check? Blame can be quite dangerous."

Beckett looked at Shiles with care now, thinking about the sullen, volcanic potential simmering out there, most of it held back poorly by the hope that a cure for the plague might someday be produced. And what was the last estimate on the ratio between the sexes? Eight thousand men for every surviving woman. And the ratio was growing more outrageous by the day.

"Don't want to have Wye throwing you to the lions," Shiles said.

How could Wycombe-Finch throw anybody anywhere? Beckett wondered. What was happening here?

"I thought we had an agreement, General," Beckett said.

"Oh, we do, old chappy! We certainly do. Big necessities coming up, though. Who gets the serum and who doesn't? Who gets the women, etcetera, etcetera . . ." He broke off, hearing the door behind him opening slowly.

Wycombe-Finch peered in. "Oh, there you are, Bill. And General!" The director let himself into the office and closed the door. "Thought I might find you two here."

"What is it, Wye?" Shiles asked.

"Well, actually, it's rather embarrassing." He glanced at the monitors, then back to Beckett. "Must bite the bullet, I guess."

"Please do," Shiles said.

Wycombe-Finch took a deep breath. "Been listening to your conversation," he said. "Not for the first time. Bad habit of mine. Always has been. Curiosity, y' know."

Shiles glanced at Beckett with an "I-told-you-so!" look.

"Stoney and I have shared our views on these matters," Wycombe-Finch said. "He'll be bringing the king and the prime minister into the picture tonight, most likely."

Shiles rubbed at his neck, his attention fixed on Wycombe-Finch's mouth, a slow flush mounting from beneath his collar.

"Stoney can be quite obtuse at times," Wycombe-Finch said. "Good political head, though. Knew that when we were in school. Afraid we've taken the bit in our teeth, you two."

"What've you done?" Beckett managed.

"Well, very early on, Fin Doheny and I concluded we might need a means of emergency communication. Radio's a hobby of mine, y' know? I've an American product, CB, you call it. I've, ahhh, changed it a bit, of course. More powerful. Antenna in the attic. That sort of thing. Barrier Command popped onto us quite early but they didn't seem to mind so long as we spoke in the open. I tried to reach old Fin earlier. Can't raise a peep. Bad show over there, I'm afraid. But Barrier Command now has your serum formula and the jolly old biochemical picture, all that. It's Stoney's view that they'll pass it along to America and all the others."

"Bloody hell!" Shiles said.

"Don't want any violence, y' understand?" Wycombe-Finch said. "Awfully attractive prize. Have to share it, don't y' see? Can't have people coming in here with guns and things, taking it."

Beckett began to laugh, shaking his head. "Oh! Wait'll I break this to Joe!"

"I do believe Lepikov's already told him," Wycombe-Finch said. "Amusing fellow, the Russian. Quoted me an old Russian saying: 'Whoever starts a conspiracy plants a seed.' Very good, what?"

"You never know what the seed'll produce until it comes out of the ground," Beckett said. He looked at Shiles. The flush had completely covered the general's face.

"Government couldn't permit a small group to control the fruits, y' know," Wycombe-Finch said.

Shiles found his voice. "I swear to you, sir, that my concern was to form a distribution system to make sure it was apportioned equally."

"Of course it was, old chap!" Wycombe-Finch said.

"There'll be plenty for everybody," Beckett said. He looked at Shiles. The general had begun to regain his composure. "And you're still in command of a sizable chunk of the military, General."

"But I shall have to obey the government," Shiles said. "It's what I was trying to explain to you earlier."

> *The Irish always seem to me like*
> *a pack of hounds dragging down some*
> *noble stag.*
>
> —Goethe

THE COMING of the mob ignited a strange new personality in Kevin O'Donnell. Doheny glimpsed it only briefly as he and the other principals of the trial were taken out under guard, ordered locked up in the rooms under the castle's tower. Kevin turned first to the jury and told them to find weapons. They no longer were jurymen but "soldiers at Armageddon!" A distant look of dreaming took over Kevin's face. He gestured broadly with his right hand and took up the jar with Alex Coleman's head, saying:

"Come watch it, Alex! This is the moment for which I was born."

Herity's corpse he ignored except to topple the chair and body as he left the room, striding along, Doheny thought, *like God Almighty*.

As his party was rushed across the courtyard by the guards, Doheny noted that the gates had been closed, shutting off the view of the lough. The cries of the mob were loud in the courtyard, though—an all-male animal demanding its due. Some were screaming: "The cure! Give us the cure!"

Now what had made them think a cure already had been produced?

The guards hustled Doheny into the bailey behind John, Father Michael and the boy, but not before he glimpsed Kevin once more striding along the parapet of the old castle. Kevin did not deign to glance down at the mob that was shouting out there. His manner said he considered them a pack of brutes hungering for the food of the gods, the manna that only he controlled.

"Give us the cure! Give us O'Neill!"

Doheny and his companions were herded to the door at the head of the dungeon keep. The guards thrust them through the door and slammed it behind them, not bothering to lock them in their individual cells. They stumbled down the long stairs to the chant of the mob, which had returned to its original demand: "O'Neill! O'Neill!"

They stopped in the room of jumbled discards at the bottom of the stairs. Father Michael brushed cobwebs off his face. John returned to his cell and entered it. The boy climbed up on the broken sofa trying to peer out of a barred window high on the wall. The mob sound was loud there. John emerged presently wearing the clothing the guards had made him discard. It was damp and marked with patches of slime, which he tried to wipe away with the lab coat.

"Why did they take away my clothes?" he asked, his voice distant. "Was it because the priest had a knife?"

"It's all right, John," Father Michael said. He put a hand on John's shoulder. There was a deep trembling in the man.

The boy was clambering across the stack of lumber in the corner, still unable to reach the barred window.

"Give it up, lad," Doheny said. "You'll fall and hurt yourself."

A great roar came from the mob. There was a quick burst of automatic weapons fire, then silence. Even the chanting stopped.

"What do you suppose they're doing out there?" Father Michael asked.

"Sharpening their scythes, their pruning hooks and pitchforks, most likely," Doheny said. "Preparing for the jacquerie."

The last word was almost drowned in another mob roar that shook the room.

John seemed not to hear it. He was staring up at the boy on the stack of lumber, remembering him as he had been during their tramp across the countryside. There was a feral energy in the boy now, a tension and purpose about him.

"Father Michael!" the boy called, his voice low and intense. "There's a tunnel back here!"

"A tunnel is it?" The priest scrambled over the discards toward the boy, pulling boards aside and peering behind him. He lifted his head and spoke to Doheny: "There's fresh air! It's a way out!" He pulled out more boards, exposing a low opening. "Bring John!"

Doheny took John's arm. "Come along."

"I can't," John said. "O'Neill doesn't want to go." He swept a wild gaze around the dark room. "Why have they come? I don't . . ."

The rest of it was lost in another roar from the crowd and more gunfire. The mob sounds became a rhythmic assault, no words, just hoarse and inarticulate noises—a gigantic grunting that filled Doheny with terror. Father Michael darted across the junk and took John's right arm.

"I think we'll have to drag him," Doheny said.

"Come with us, John," the priest said. "We're trying to save you. Aren't we, Fin?"

"We are that."

"Will you take O'Neill, too?" John asked.

"Of course!" Father Michael said.

"But where is he?" John asked. "He was in the jar on the table. I don't see him."

"He's already gone on," Doheny said.

"Oh."

John allowed himself to be led in a stumbling scramble across the junk and around the stacked wood. The boy awaited them there in an arched passage of moldy stone. The floor underfoot was slippery with slime and there were upturned stones, puddles of water. The smell of sewage seeped through the cracks.

Doheny listened to the mob sounds overhead. The thumping of many feet could be felt. The gunfire had been reduced to a few scattered shots. Father Michael pushed John down the passage ahead of him. The boy led. There was faint light ahead, but it was dark and odorous in the tunnel. Presently, they saw patchy daylight ahead framed in bushes and partly blocked by an iron grating. Father Michael waved them all to a stop at the grating, listening. The mob was a dim sound behind them. No more gunfire. Doheny realized they had stopped in a small stone hut piled on both sides with rusty gardening tools—hoes, rakes, shovels, trowels, hand cultivators.

Rows of earthenware pots had fallen from rotted shelves and the broken shards ground underfoot with bits and pieces of wire and rust-eaten cans. Daylight leaked through chinks in the stone and through a doorway partly blocked by a gate of rusty iron and thick shrubbery.

John closed his eyes and hugged his arms close. He breathed in shallow gasps, flexing and tensing his fingers.

The boy crept out under the shrubbery and could be heard moving around the hut.

Doheny touched one of John's hands and was rewarded with an abrupt upward jerking of the head, eyes wide open and glaring.

Father Michael waved for Doheny to stay and went after the boy. He returned in a moment to say: "This hut sits beside an old glass house and there's an overgrown trail that seems to go out to the road. The boy's gone on ahead to scout it." The priest nodded at John. "Is he saying anything?"

"It's fascinating," Doheny said, caught up in clinical observation of John. "Controlled displacement of identity, I think. He knows there's another persona present and may even talk to it but I doubt he can overcome the dissociation."

Father Michael shuddered. "Whatever shall we do with him?"

At Father Michael's words, John squatted on the filthy floor and hid his face against his knees, crouching like a hunted animal in its den.

It would kill him to restore him to O'Neill, Doheny thought.

Where had that boy got to? A sudden chilling thought welled up in Doheny's awareness: Kevin had said the boy was ready to spring the hangman's trap under O'Neill. Had the boy gone to alert Kevin or the mob?

A noise at the doorway brought his attention away from John. The boy slipped through the opening. He appeared subdued, more like his silent self. He gestured for them to follow him and went back outside. The bushes swished with his passage.

"There's a sweet lad," Father Michael said, "and his soul guided by the Sacred Heart."

I hope you're right, Doheny thought.

"Up we go, John," he said, and helped John to his feet.

Father Michael ahead and Doheny behind, they got John

out of the hut into the open air. It was an overgrown park with tall evergreens all around, a glimpse of the lough through the trunks. A narrow stone-flagged walkway with bushes overhanging it led away from the lough. The boy was not to be seen.

Single file with Father Michael still leading and Doheny bringing up the rear, they forced their way along the flagstone walk. Bushes constricted the passage; limbs whipped at them. Father Michael turned his back on the obstructions and pulled John along, feeling for the flagstones with cautious steps. Doheny held a warding arm in front of his face.

They emerged presently through a hedge screen onto a narrow macadam roadway, its surface pocked with jagged potholes. The boy waited for them at the hedge and, as they emerged, he turned and set off to the left away from the castle.

Doheny hesitated, listening. There wasn't a sign of the mob, nor a sound. The silence felt sinister.

"Come along!" Father Michael whispered.

He feels it, too, Doheny thought. Well, flight was the only sensible thing at this moment.

Father Michael trotted off after the boy, who was almost a hundred meters ahead now. Doheny and John followed. John appeared willing to go, Doheny guiding him with a light grip on the left arm, but there was a slackness in him as though he had no volition except that imparted by his companion.

The road turned at the end of a long, tree-lined avenue and began to climb away from the lough, turning sharply back and forth into the hills. They came after a panting climb to a lookout point with a weed-overgrown rock fence and the sign still standing. Its arrow directed them to Bally . . . and the rest of it defaced.

"That'll be Ballymore, I believe," Father Michael said.

The boy had gone out to the edge of the lookout where he stared back toward the lough. The others joined him, passing a screen of tall trees and gaining, at last, a view down to the castle. Flames leaped from windows and roof. Smoke drew a vertical column in the windless air. Father Michael shuddered at the sight of the smoke, remembering the smoke at Maynooth. And there was a mob here, too.

All four of the watchers stared silently off across the treetops toward the castle, perhaps a kilometer away. A solid mass of people filled the grounds, a moving carpet of people. They were pressed body to body and the movement above them was hands waving, the glistening of weapons. The skin-crawling thing, though, was the silence. Not a shout . . . no outcries, no chanting . . . just that silent movement.

"Saints preserve us," Father Michael breathed.

The boy crept close to Father Michael and held the priest's arm.

John, noting the priest and the boy, thought them familiar figures. Yes, they had come a long way over the countryside. He turned to his left and saw an unfamiliar face.

"Who're you?" John asked.

"I'm Fin Doheny."

"Where's Joseph?"

Doheny understood and said: "I'm taking Joseph Herity's place."

"Where're we going now?" John asked.

Before Doheny could answer, Father Michael held up a hand and said: "Listen!"

They all heard it then: horsemen coming down the road from above them. A group of horsemen came around a bend in the road. In the lead rode a tall, bearded man carrying a rifle across the pommel. He lifted the rifle for his followers to stop when he saw the group at the lookout. The bearded man stared a moment at the people below him. His companions remained behind the screen of trees, only the noses of two horses exposed. Seeing no display of weapons from the party at the lookout, the bearded man lowered his rifle. He spoke over his shoulder: "Wait here." He rode down then and stopped at the edge of the road.

Doheny noted foam at the horse's bit. These men had been riding hard.

"What's happening off there t' th' castle?" the bearded man asked, gesturing with his chin.

"We were just looking at it ourselves," Doheny said. "Looks like a mob."

"And who might you be, if I may make so bold as to ask?" the horseman asked.

"My name's Fintan," Doheny said. "And this is Father Michael and—"

"A priest now!" the bearded man said. "Would y' be bound for Ballymore? It's God's own truth about th' miraculous cures from our spring water."

Father Michael looked up the hill, his expression saying: "Why not?" He nodded. "Yes, we'll be drinking the waters at Ballymore, God willing."

"A miraculous thing it is," the bearded man said. He leaned forward in the saddle and peered at John, who ducked his head and closed his eyes at this attention. "And what's t' matter wit' your friend?"

Doheny wet his lips with his tongue, catching a fearful glance from Father Michael. Before either of them could compose an answer, the boy stepped forward and took John's hand. "We're going to your spring, Mister. This is my father. He's been this way since my mother died."

The horseman straightened. His voice sad, he said: "There's many that way, God help us all." Turning in the saddle, he shouted to his companions: "Des! Bring t' packet of bread and cheese!" He turned to Father Michael. "I notice you carry no food. It's a ways to Ballymore. We'll share and pray you'll stay wit' us at Ballymore." He nodded beyond the castle. "We've business down in Killaloe. Could y' be tellin' us how t' get t'rough yon mob?"

"Business in Killaloe?" Doheny asked.

"I'm Aldin Caniff, t' leading man of Ballymore," the bearded man said. "We're escorting Erskine McGinty down to Killaloe where it's said they have a wireless t' talk across t' waters. Erskine's had a vision commanding him t' tell t' new pope about our waters!"

"I don't know about any wireless at Killaloe," Doheny said.

"It's well known," Caniff said. "T' new pope, y' know, is called Adam for t' new beginning! Himself as was David Shaw. Imagine! A simple priest one day, a cardinal t' next, and now! Now, he's t' pope!"

"If you're bound for Killaloe, I'd stay off the roads," Doheny said. "Mobs are a dangerous thing."

"Good advice, Mister Fintan," Caniff said. "It's Aldin Caniff himself as thanks y' for it."

A horseman came from behind the screening trees and reined up beside Caniff. The second horseman was a slender youth with straggling black hair. It framed a thin face with a gap-toothed smile. He carried a rifle in his left hand, which also held the reins. A leather bag was in the other hand. He lowered the bag to Father Michael.

Caniff looked at his companion. "Go tell t' others t' head back t' way we come. You mind t' path we saw? Wait for me at t' path. We'll be leaving t' road."

The other horseman reined around and returned behind the trees.

Caniff looked at Father Michael, who stood clutching the leather bag in both hands.

"T' way's secure t' Ballymore, Father. You'll find it marked by stones, piles of seven and a pointer t' t' way. Just you be careful crossing t' N-Six and stay away from Moate. Evil men in Moate. If anyone stops you, say you're under t' protection of Aldin Caniff!"

"Go with God," Father Michael said.

Caniff kicked his horse, reined it around and soon was hidden by the trees. They heard the clatter of departing horses.

Doheny waited for the sounds of the horsemen to fade. He looked at Father Michael then. The priest nodded. They both understood. If any of Kevin O'Donnell's people had survived the mob, John and his companions could be identified. Word could get out that a priest, a boy and two men had been seen on the road to Ballymore.

"We dare not cut across to Dundalk," Doheny said. "They'd expect us to head for my friends."

Father Michael looked at John, who stood staring off at the lough. The boy still held John's hand, a penetrating look on the young face as though he were trying to peer into John for the answers to strange questions. They would have to name the boy soon, since he would not reveal his original name. A new name—the boy wanted a second baptism, admitting that he had been blessed in the Church. But that was all he would admit.

"We've a rare cargo to protect," Father Michael said.

"I'm hungry, Father Michael," John said. "Did Joseph leave us any food?"

"We'll eat soon," Doheny said. "We should be getting off this road. We've been lucky in our encounter but there's danger depending only on the luck of the wayfarer." He turned and led them up the road, hearing the others follow. When he glanced back, he saw the boy guiding John, still holding his hand.

Nightfall found them far along a narrow path winding through thick evergreens. Doheny knew the kind of track they followed—a woodcutters' way, and there would be shelter of sorts along it. Plenty of firewood around, as well, to keep them through what promised to be a cold night. They had crossed several country roads and once had waited, peering out of the bushes, before running across a wider paved highway. Doheny did not know precisely where they were but he had marked the position of the sun and knew they had headed generally east. If they could avoid the Beach Boys...

John followed with the docility of fatigue. He walked alone now, the boy and the priest bringing up the rear. John seldom looked up from where he would put his next step.

Shelter was more or less where Doheny expected to find it, just over a rise into a small swale that would protect it from the west winds. It was a lean-to built of poles and caulked with mud and moss. The door was more poles held by three sets of crosspieces and hung on leather hinges with a stick latch. There were no windows, but a small hole penetrated the roof near a corner with a firepit beneath and a stack of wood stored nearby. The interior smelled of forest duff and smoke.

John flopped to the floor and sat with his back against a wall. Father Michael dropped his leather sack and stared around the gloomy interior. The boy joined John.

In the last of the daylight, Doheny started a fire and squatted in front of it warming his hands.

Father Michael closed the door and propped a stick of wood against it. The boy crept around the wall behind the fire, taking advantage of the reflected heat. John got to his feet and moved aimlessly around the confined space. Father Michael watched him carefully.

John stopped suddenly and spoke: "O'Neill doesn't like it here."

Father Michael glanced fearfully at Doheny crouched by the fire. Doheny stared back at the priest and motioned him closer. Father Michael edged around John and stood with his back to the fire looking down at Doheny. Steam started to rise from the damp places on the priest's clothing.

"Will O'Neill say why he doesn't like this place?" Father Michael asked.

Doheny waved a hand to make him stop. Did the priest not understand? O'Neill could not be brought out of this human shell. The man had seen too much of the terrible consequences brought on by his plague. Revenge he might have wanted, but this!

Father Michael stared down at Doheny with a puzzled frown.

John remained silent, his head cocked to one side as though listening.

Only an amoral monster could live with this Ireland on his conscience, Doheny thought. Everything they had learned about O'Neill said he had been a man of conscience—at least before Herity's bomb.

John straightened his head suddenly and spoke: "O'Neill says this world is not safe." He looked down at Doheny. "Did Joseph leave you one of his guns?"

"No need of guns here," Doheny said, getting stiffly to his feet. "Is there any more of that bread and cheese, Father?"

"Enough for the night and the morrow," Father Michael said.

The boy came around from behind the fire and joined them. His clothing smelled of steamed wool.

"O'Neill's right," the boy said, a pensive adult quality in his thin voice. "Guns and bombs make a crazy world and that's not safe."

Madmen and children speak the truth, Doheny thought.

"Precious Trinity, will we ever see a sane world?" Father Michael asked.

"Where a man can tell his lies with impunity," Doheny said.

"That's a cruel thing to say, Mister Doheny!"

Doheny turned his head and listened to the wind soughing through the trees around the hut. The fire flickered in a draft that swept through the scanty poles. Shadow monsters danced upon the walls.

"Cruel, yes," Doheny said. "But change is often cruel and that's what's happening: change. We haven't been living close enough to what our world's doing."

"Close enough!" Father Michael was shocked. The killing! The savagery!

"I believe I am a realist," Doheny said. "Most people lived in a four-sided world with guardians at all the gates—doctors, preachers, lawyers, elected demagogues—to keep away the surprises of change."

"Then how is it this terrible plague surprised the guardians?" Father Michael demanded.

"Because they got caught up in that world, too, a universe bounded by the weekly pay packet, the nightly television schedule, the annual holiday and an occasional dispensation of goodies and circus."

"I still don't understand how it could happen," Father Michael said, his voice barely above a whisper. He looked fearfully at John, who had walked to the door and stood peering out through a crack by the hinges.

"Because we listened only to the rich Americans!" Doheny said.

"I didn't know you hated Americans," Father Michael said.

"Hate them? No, I envied them. But so few of them ever lived close to what the world's doing!"

"You keep saying that," Father Michael protested. "What does it mean?"

"It means the very poor who know they may starve. It means sailors and farmers and woodsmen who walk close to nature's ever-ready disasters. It means the prophets who scourge themselves until they can see past the pain."

Father Michael looked at the boy, who stood listening to them, an avid expression on his face. The night sounds of wind and forest pressed close around them. What could John see through that crack by the door? It was only woods darkness out there.

"The guardians were false guardians," Doheny said, his voice low and thoughtful. "They said they would let only good surprises come through—packages from Father Christmas. Nothing would be allowed to disrupt the smooth world that the four-square inhabitants believed they possessed."

John turned and met Father Michael's gaze. There was an odd look of alertness and wonder in John's eyes, the priest thought.

"Where are we?" John asked.

"It's a woodsman's shelter," Doheny said, not looking up from the fire.

John focused on Doheny. "And who are you?"

Doheny shook his head, still not looking at John, half lost in his own deep thoughts. "I've the name Fintan Craig Doheny and I'm no better guardian than any of the others." He turned then and saw in the flickering firelight the strangely alert expression on John's face.

"How did we get here?" John asked.

His voice low and hesitant, Doheny said: "We walked."

"That's odd," John said. "You sound Irish. Am I still in Ireland?"

Doheny nodded.

"I wonder where Mary and the twins are?" John said.

Father Michael and Doheny looked at each other. The boy asked: "What's happening?"

Doheny shook a finger at him for silence.

"I'm John Roe O'Neill," John said. "I know that. Have I had...amnesia? No...that can't be it. I seem to remember...things."

Doheny lifted himself on the balls of his feet, poised for any response to sudden violence from John.

"Who brought me here?" John asked.

"You were brought by John Garrech O'Donnell," Father Michael said.

John shot a startled look at the priest. "John...Garrech..." His eyes went wide with shock. He stepped back until he was pressed against the wall by the door. His gaze went from Doheny to Father Michael to the boy, lingering there, and they could all but see the memories whirl behind John's eyes.

Doheny raised a hand toward him.

John's mouth opened, a round hole in an agonized face. "No-o-o-o-o-o-o-o-o-!" It was an eerie wail from that open mouth. He took a step toward Doheny, who stiffened. John whirled then and hurled himself against the door, smashing it open.

Before anyone could prevent it, John was outside, running and screaming, crashing through the trees.

Doheny put out an arm to prevent Father Michael or the boy from following. "You couldn't catch him. And even if you did..." He shook his head.

They listened to the sounds from the darkness—the wailing screams, the thrashing of underbrush. It went on for a long time, fading away at last into the distance, at one with the wind in the trees.

"Someone must find him," Father Michael said. "Someone must give him shelter. The Madman's a special charge upon us all and he should..."

"Oh, shut up!" Doheny snapped. He went to the doorway and restored the door, propping it in position against the night. When he turned back to the fire, the boy was staring at him, listening to the faint sounds from the darkness. Could the youth's young hearing still detect those screaming wails?

"It's the banshee," the boy whispered.

But such a form as Grecian goldsmiths make
Of hammered gold and gold enamelling
To keep a drowsy Emperor awake;
Or set upon a golden bough to sing
To lords and ladies of Byzantium
Of what is past, or passing, or to come.

—William Butler Yeats

FATHER MICHAEL did not like living in England. He especially disliked being confined to Huddersfield, although it was an exciting place these days with important people from all over the world passing through to learn about the cure for the plague. He accepted Doheny's reason for sending him to Huddersfield. Kate O'Gara Browder was an Irish national treasure and, more important, was sure to become a potent political implement.

"The Woman in the Tank!"

Father Michael thought her a rather silly young woman, but there was a tough core of self-determination in her, a thing Father Michael thought of as a "peasant quality." There had been a fair amount of this quality in Father Michael's own mother and he had recognized it immediately in Kate. She would be stubborn and even cruel where her own interests were involved. Give her a bit of power and she could become terrifying—unless her actions were leavened by a firm belief in God's wrath.

Doheny had said: "You will go to her to be her spiritual advisor, and that's true enough. I know you for a good priest,

Father. But you also will be there to see that she does nothing foolish that could be hurtful to Ireland. I do not trust the Brits."

"What could they possibly do?"

"That's for you to discover."

And here he was in the bosom of the Gall and had been for more than two months. As he walked across the campus toward his regular morning visit with Kate, Father Michael could feel the power of this place. A dangerous thing—yes. There were dangerous currents here—plots and strange devisings. He was glad he had come, even though he detested the British *flavor* of everything that happened here. His own motives for accepting Doheny's assignment had begun with simple curiosity but had been hardened by the need to get The Boy out of Ireland.

Father Michael still thought of the silent boy as The Boy, although the lad now said he could be called Sian. No last name. He refused to say anything about his family. It was as though The Boy had walled them off in some secret grave where only he could mourn.

The Boy was determined to enter the priesthood. That was a consolation. Father Sian. He would be a strong priest, Father Michael thought. A compassionate priest. Perhaps even a cardinal someday . . . and the possibility of pope. There was that.

Father Michael waited at a motor crossing for a long convoy to pass. It was going to be a sunny day, he thought. Hot, even. The convoy, he saw by the labels on the sides of the lorries, was part of the Wildlife Rescue Force. The telly was full of this good work—men shooting hypodermic darts into whales and porpoises and seals and wolves and bears and other creatures. It was a marvelous thing.

Yes, The Boy was far better off here than in the unrest of Ireland with its Finn Sadal holdouts roaming the countryside. No doubt of the outcome now, though. The death of Kevin O'Donnell at the hands of the mob had robbed the Beach Boys of a mystical force. They had fought with brutal ferocity for a time but without any central guidance.

The devil himself, Father Michael thought.

It was not the United Nations assistance to the army that had beaten the Finn Sadal; it was when they lost the guiding hand of Satan. Kevin had been Satan personified.

The convoy passed and Father Michael crossed the roadway, to be almost run down there by a speeding jeep that came careening around a corner and dashed off after the lorries, the driver shaking a fist and screaming at the black-clad priest in his path.

Some things never change, Father Michael thought.

But it was better that The Boy lived here now and was getting a fine education at the special school set up within the Huddersfield perimeter for selected students. They had ac-. cepted The Boy because he was Father Michael's ward and Father Michael had official status as an envoy of the Irish state. Yes, a fine scientific education, which could be reinforced later by the Jesuits in some safe place like America.

Sian was going to be important someday. Father Michael had begun to sense this that day on the road above the besieged castle when The Boy had taken John O'Neill's hand and told the white lie to protect the poor man. Given the obvious things there must be in The Boy's background urging him toward revenge, it had been a grand gesture, a true turning of the other cheek. Doheny had thought it merely clever and guileful but Father Michael had known better. It had been *right*.

There were a great many people on the Huddersfield campus this morning, Father Michael noted. Rushing about, brushing past him. The place got more cluttered with people every day. Some of the passersby recognized Father Michael and nodded. Others smiled vaguely, knowing they had seen him somewhere.

Y' saw me right here, y' Sassenach fools!

Immediately, Father Michael put this thought down as unworthy of him. He must learn magnanimity from The Boy.

Strange, the rumors and stories coming out of Ireland about O'Neill. He was seen here; he was seen there; but never a confirmation. 'Twas said that people were putting out food and drink for him the way they had once done for the Little People. Ahhh, there was no accounting for Irish behavior. Look at the hero they were making of Brann McCrae and him with twenty-six of those young girls pregnant!

"But he saved almost fifty Irish women!" they were saying.

Saved! What good was it saving their flesh if their souls were lost?

It was not as though McCrae were the only one who had saved women from the plague. They were saying it would be generations before all the stories were told of how women had been secreted and protected by their clever men. Not enough saved, though. But efforts would be made to bring them all back to God . . . even the poor girls at McCrae's château. It had not been their doing. They had been caught by the troubled times.

As he neared the Administration Building, where Kate and her husband were quartered, Father Michael saw the usual long line of men waiting to be threaded past the viewing window where Kate could be seen. Just to see a woman was a magnetic thing, so powerful that the authorities could not deny the demands. Too dangerous, they said. And what harm did it do?

It harms Kate, Father Michael thought. Just showing herself was bringing about changes in the woman that Father Michael feared. Was this the thing Doheny had warned against?

Father Michael made his way past the waiting men, hearing the bits of conversations:

"She's a pretty thing, I hear."

"And with a baby at her breast."

Father Michael saw resentment in the faces of the men he passed. They knew he had a right to push ahead, but there was a jealous awareness here that he could go in and talk to Kate, even touch her.

The line of men wound in a long serpentine up the stairs inside the building. Father Michael ignored the stairs and went to the lift at the center of the long corridor. The guard at the lift opened the door for Father Michael and punched the button for the top floor.

Father Birney Cavanagh was waiting outside the lift as Father Michael emerged on the top floor. There was no getting around the man and Father Michael was forced to stop.

"Ahh, there you are, Father Michael. I've been waiting for you."

Where had the Brits found this priest? Father Michael wondered. Oh, Cavanagh was a Catholic priest, right enough. That had been confirmed. But he had been too long with the Gall. He even spoke with the accents of an Old Etonian.

"What is it you want?" Father Michael demanded.

"Just a word or two, Father."

Cavanagh took Father Michael's arm and almost forced him into a corner beyond the lift.

Father Michael stared down at the other priest. Cavanagh was a cherubic little man with pale cheeks. There was an insecurity in his blue eyes, which seemed always to be looking for an avenue of escape. *Did he ever comb that gray hair?* Father Michael wondered. It always seemed to have just come through a whirlwind.

"A good Irishman," he claimed to be. And wasn't he out of St. Patrick's College, Maynooth, the same as Father Michael?

Had he gone through the troubles there? Father Michael had inquired, seeking to trap the man in a lie.

"No. I was sent out ten years before."

And that had proved to be true enough.

But Cavanagh was seeing Kate and talking to her. And Father Michael did not like the mood of the woman when Cavanagh had gone. The man was thick with the papal envoy who had come over from Philadelphia, too, and Father Michael did not like what he heard about *that*. There was talk of an accommodation with "the demands of these changing times." Father Michael knew what that meant: backsliding! Nothing good would come of it. There might even be a new schism. How could anyone respect a Catholic Church with its administrative seat in America? Things would not get back to normal until Rome was restored.

"You cannot go in to Kate just now," Father Cavanagh was saying, his eyes avoiding Father Michael's. "She has an important visitor."

"Who is it now?"

"The admiral over all the Barrier Command, the one who saved her by permitting the channel passage."

"God saved her!" Father Michael protested.

"Of that there is no doubt," Cavanagh agreed. "But it was the admiral's command that gave her passage."

"The channel would have parted if God had wanted it," Father Michael said.

"I agree," Cavanagh said, "but the admiral has his powers and we cannot disturb him just now. It's for her own good, I assure you."

"Why is he seeing her?" Father Michael demanded.

"As to that, I'm not at liberty to say."

Father Michael put down a surge of anger. He knew Cavanagh sensed it, because the man released Father Michael's arm and stepped back defensively.

"What is happening in there?" Father Michael asked, keeping his voice under careful control.

"There's guards on the door and you'll not be permitted to enter," Cavanagh said. "I promise you, there's no harm coming to her."

Father Michael sensed truth in Cavanagh's words and wondered if it would be right to force the issue. *I am an envoy of the Irish state!* But that had its strictures, too. An envoy must behave with proper decorum. He sensed Doheny's fear coming true. That silly woman was famous all over the world. "The Woman in the Tank!" Something about her had caught the public fancy. It was the press doing it, of course! All of those sensational stories. And the baby being born during the storm of the channel crossing.

"When will I be permitted to see her?" Father Michael asked.

"Perhaps this afternoon sometime. Would you care to wait in my quarters, Father. They've given me digs just down the corridor here."

Father Michael felt a hollow hardness in his stomach. Something bad was happening and he was to be kept out of it. Well, he would fight! Before he could speak, though, three armed naval officers came down the corridor, their attention on him. Father Michael knew then that he was to be a prisoner and these were his guards.

Our world undermines at its peril the individual's own sense of worth, that force at the root of human strength. This is our survival we undermine, our ability to deal with challenge. It is an inborn capacity without which there can be no humanity.

—Fintan Craig Doheny

KATE LIKED to sit by the window of her new room on the top floor of Huddersfield's Administration Building when she nursed her baby. She knew the big mirror across from her was actually a window permitting the lines of men passing in the outside corridor to peer in at her. She had only to look up into the mirror to see what the passing viewers saw. She found it odd that she felt no embarrassment to know men watched her suckling Gilla at her breast.

What a beautiful infant Gilla was becoming—the way her feet kicked, the wrinkles smoothing out, the look of alertness beginning to appear in her eyes. She was going to have red hair, fine and silky the way Kate's own mother's hair had been. How precious this infant was!

There had been a bad few days when they brought the serum and told her their decision. So cold-blooded they had sounded, and she had screamed at the hulking Doctor Beckett, that ugly, lantern-jawed man with his gigantic mouth and the awful words coming out of it.

"You and your husband can have many daughters, Mrs. Browder. You've already demonstrated that, and, with our new

490

techniques of genetic control, we can insure that you have *only* daughters."

Men in white coats had been holding her all through this, keeping her away from Gilla, not even letting Stephen be with her.

Beckett, an angry light in his eyes, had shouted at her: "We've only enough serum for you, Mrs. Browder!"

"Give it to Gilla!"

"No! If your blood picks up fast enough, we can give your blood serum to the baby. We may be able to save her."

"May be!" she had screamed.

But there had been no resisting the strong men and that was the way it had been—her arm strapped down, a needle in it. She had lived through dreadful days, rocking Gilla and sobbing, fearing every moment that she would see the terrible plague symptoms in the infant.

After the injection, Stephen had been permitted to come to her. Sounding almost like a priest, he had pleaded with her to "be calm and accept whatever God gives us." Stephen and the drugs had tried to be soothing but she could still think back to that time and feel the awful tremors in her stomach.

Gilla at her breast restored the calm. The blood serum had been produced in time. And now, everyone was giving blood serum. It was spreading out across the world like a wave.

The door behind Kate opened and she heard Stephen enter, the cautious movements. She saw him in the mirror, the way he looked at the mirror, not liking it but accepting the necessity. He had seen the long lines out there, the avid eyes peering in at mother and child. Stephen was resisting extensions of the viewing time but Kate was not sure this was right.

In the whole world, the ratio of men to women was said to be ten thousand to one or worse. Here in England, of course, it was worse, although women saved by resourceful men were still being found and inoculated. A great new barracks establishment had been set up at Aldershot where the women were being protected. Kate wondered how those women felt about her own special status—the first one saved. The Woman in the Tank. She knew there was pressure to get her back to Ireland, but she and Stephen were agreed that it was not yet safe. There were still Beach Boys with weapons roaming loose. And there were even women survivors being found in Ireland, although the stories of their tribulations filled Kate with horror.

Troubles! That was all Ireland ever seemed to experience.
I was lucky.

She sensed the power in her position. She was a symbol in a world agog with the announcements being made from Kangsha and Huddersfield. Despite her nurse's training, she found some of the things being said almost too much to accept. Was it possible that she and Gilla might live five thousand years or more? They were saying that they could assure from conception whether a baby would be male or female and that the female birth ratio was going to be held at "very high levels" until the balance had been restored.

Kate found the thought of a five-thousand-year lifetime difficult to imagine. Five thousand years. What would she do with all of that time? There would have to be more than producing babies, although she knew this would be her duty for years to come. Duty! Hard from the mouth of a priest, it was a male word . . . a legal judgment. There would be no escaping it. She and Stephen must produce more daughters.

There were compensations, though. Kate found she rather liked her present female eminence, sensing that she must take advantage of it while she could. It would not endure in the face of this new genetic science. While it lasted, it was exciting. The men paying court to her! That was the only way to describe it: courting. Not flirtation or simple attempts at seduction; the men were serious and it enraged Stephen.

Kate saw in the mirror that Stephen had taken a chair by the smaller window behind her, the one looking out over the Huddersfield campus. The way he pretended to sit there reading his book! He was making a statement to the passing viewers: "This one is mine!"

She liked that. Kate could feel the love of Stephen, a warm current all through her body. A bond of terrible strength had been welded between them in the confinement of the isolation tank. She knew tiny detailed things about him now, weaknesses and strengths.
He saved my life.

Each suckling movement of the baby drawing life's own milk from her breast amplified the waves of loving heat she felt for Stephen. She sensed it deep in her abdomen.

The courting men were interesting, though, especially the Russian, Lepikov. What a charming man. Old World charm. How amusing he was, lifting those thick black eyebrows at her, rolling his dark eyes. Poor man. His entire family dead somewhere in the Soviet Union. She felt so sad when she thought of it. How she wanted to cradle his head on her breast and comfort him. Stephen would never permit that, though.

Its stomach full, the baby turned away from her breast and drifted into sleep, a tiny bubble of milk on her lips. Kate smiled down at her daughter, taking her time about covering herself. Gilla was such a fascinating person to watch: the miniature face in innocent repose, that little dimple on her left cheek. What a blessing. What a miracle.

Kate glanced at her wristwatch: 10:10 A.M. She held the watch to her left ear. It still ran perfectly after all this time. She thought sadly of her mother presenting the watch to her the day Kate had gone off to nursing school.

Ahhhh, Momma, I wish you could see your own grand-daughter, your own flesh and blood, alive and happy.

Perhaps it was a blessing, though, that Momma could only look down from heaven at this scene. A terrible price was being asked of women. Secondary husbands . . . and even more. Kate felt a thrilling shiver at what she might be asked to accept. And how strange it was that the two priests disagreed on this question. She dared not even raise the problem with Stephen. She knew how he would react. The tiny steel chamber with its ever-sounding airpump had created a singleness between them, though, and she suspected that Stephen knew what she was thinking.

"The priest's here," Stephen said.

Just from his tone and before she looked up, Kate knew it was Father Cavanagh and not Father Michael. Stephen liked Father Michael and barely tolerated Cavanagh. Kate found this difficult to understand. Father Michael had married them back in Ireland, but he was such a hard man, that horse face never smiling. Father Cavanagh, however, was jolly and soothing. He spoke of a happy God who wanted pleasant things for his flock. Father Michael was stern and threatening. He liked to talk philosophy with Stephen. It got so boring at times.

Father Cavanagh brought up a chair and seated himself in front of Kate, their knees almost touching.

"And how are we today?" Father Cavanagh asked, his voice booming. "Gilla's looking as fine as a sunny day and it full of spring flowers."

Kate could see in the mirror how Stephen sneered at this. She knew what he was thinking. Cavanagh was a bit absurd with his Irish phrasings uttered in that odd English accent.

The priest leaned forward and tweaked one of Gilla's toes. The baby made a scowling face but resumed her innocent sleep when he removed his hand.

"Now, Kate," he said, "there's a rare light of health in your face. Have you need for anything special today? Is your heart at peace?"

"I never felt better, Father."

"It's what comes from the cure," Father Cavanagh intoned. "It strengthens the body. Look how the injections have helped your little Gilla overcome the effects of being born prematurely."

"It's a miracle," she agreed.

"God is bountiful." He patted her knee and stood, letting his hand linger until he was upright.

"Are you going so soon, Father?" she asked.

"They asked me to make it short today. There's an important visitor waiting to see you. Isn't that a wonder? You're a very special person, Kate. I remember you and Gilla in the Mass every morning."

With a stiff smile for Stephen, Father Cavanagh left them.

"A visitor?" Kate asked.

Gilla whimpered. Kate bounced her gently, keeping her attention on Stephen.

"I haven't any idea," Stephen said. He looked at Kate. "They haven't said a thing."

Kate shuddered. She sensed danger, aware of a difference. Yes...there was no more sound of people shuffling past the mirror-window. The air in the room smelled suddenly stale and full touched by faint tobacco aroma that the priest always left behind.

The door where the priest had gone opened suddenly and Rupert Stonar entered with a stranger in a naval uniform. The stranger had wide shoulders and long arms. His face was extremely narrow, with an enormous Roman nose that overshadowed a small mouth and sharp chin. His eyes were set too close together, Kate thought, but the lashes were long and curved. She knew Stonar, though, and looked a question at him.

"May I introduce Admiral Francis Delacourt?" Stonar said. "The admiral, as you may know, is the chief of Barrier Command and, since the outrage in New York, is effectively head of the United Nations. It was Admiral Delacourt who saved you by sending a barge and tug when the Irish civil war started."

"We are very grateful," Stephen said. He shook hands with the admiral, feeling a brief muscular grip in a dry hand.

Delacourt turned to Kate then and bent over her hand, kissing it. "Charmed," he said.

Kate blushed and looked down at the baby. Gilla took that moment to empty her bladder. "Oh, my!" Kate said, passing the baby to Stephen. "Would you change her, dear?"

Stephen took the baby, feeling the warm dampness.

"The nappies are in the other room," Kate said. She smiled up at the admiral. "I've never met a real admiral before."

"I'll just go along with you, Stephen," Stonar said, taking Browder's arm. "The admiral has a request to make of Kate."

"What request?" Stephen asked, feeling a sudden chill in Stonar's manner.

"The request is of Kate O'Gara, not of you," Stonar said, pressing Stephen along.

"That's Kate Browder! I'm her husband." Stephen planted his feet and refused to be moved.

"Oh, I guess you haven't heard," Stonar said. "Women will no longer take a husband's name. Matrilineal descent has been made a matter of law, the father's name being secondary."

"What law?" Stephen demanded.

"The law of this world. It's a United Nations thing," Stonar said, trying to press Stephen out of the room.

"I'm not leaving!" Stephen said. "Let go of my arm!"

"Be careful!" Kate cried. "You'll hurt the baby!"

"Let it be," Admiral Delacourt said. "He should be present even though the request is of the lady."

Stonar released Stephen's arm but remained standing beside him.

"What request?" Stephen asked.

"I lost my entire family in the plague," Delacourt said. "My request is that this lady give me a child."

Stephen started to move toward him, the baby held foolishly in his arms, but Stonar restrained him with an arm across his chest. "Be careful of the baby, you idiot!" Stonar grabbed Stephen's arm and held it firmly.

"Why does such a request shock you?" the admiral asked, looking at Stephen. "Surely, you must realize it is the norm now . . . there are so few women. It's just that I do not wish my line to die out."

Kate got to her feet, brushing at her skirt. A glance in the mirror told her there was a big wet spot from the baby in the middle of her lap. She looked pale, she saw. "Are there no other women to . . ." She couldn't complete it.

Stonar spoke while still holding Stephen, who permitted it for fear of harming Gilla.

Tell him, Kate! Stephen thought. *Tell him to get the hell out of here with his evil request!*

Stephen grew aware gradually of what Stonar was saying: So few women being sent to the devastated areas!

"China, Argentina, Brazil and the United States are the only nations that have consented, by local option, to share their breeding women," Stonar said. "England will get little more than a thousand of them."

Like cattle, Kate thought. She looked at the admiral. He was a powerful man, the head of Barrier Command. That meant warships and the backing of the United Nations. Accepting him could keep worse things from happening. She looked pleadingly at Stephen. Couldn't he see it? Her resolution of only a few minutes ago now seemed like a silly, schoolgirl thing that she had suddenly outgrown.

"Could you return in about a half hour, please, Admiral?" she asked. "Stephen and I need a little time to talk." She smiled at Stonar. "Mister Stonar, could you change Gilla for us? The nappies are in that little cabinet at the foot of her crib."

Stonar took the baby from Stephen's unresisting hands. The admiral smiled at Kate and bowed over her hand. He had already heard her answer in her tone of voice. She was a sensible woman, almost French in her manner. Perhaps they would have more than one child together.

In the other room, Stonar dropped the side of the crib and placed the baby on it. Gilla kicked her feet at him and gurgled with delight as he removed the wet diaper. The admiral helped him, both of them smiling at the thought of this scene—the two of *them* doing a nanny's work.

"She's going to accept you," Stonar said.

"You heard that in her voice, too." The admiral lifted the baby and smiled at her. Was that a smile in return or just gas, as they said?

"I could almost pick her myself," Stonar said. "But I could never forget that she's Irish."

"Good God, man, you aren't still harping on . . ."

"My only son was killed during the Bloody Amnesty in Belfast . . . after the plague. He was a paratroop officer. They tortured him to death."

"Oh, I *am* sorry!"

The admiral put the baby over his shoulder and patted her, feeling very fatherly. He had been well briefed on the troubles in Ulster. An Irish-Canadian had spent several hours at it.

"What was really at the root of it in the North was the Ulsterman's fear that the Catholics would institute just reprisals for all the oppressions of the past."

Two generations a Canadian and the man had still sounded like an angry Irishman as he handed the admiral a copy of an Ulster pamphlet signed by someone named William Boyce, commander of the Belfast Brigade:

"Now, these were the things we rightly feared should the Catholics of the South prevail over us—divorce prohibited, contraception illegal, no health plans, all of the things you find in the Eire Constitution. We know about the Catholic families, at least twelve children in every one, all of them living in hovels and slums, beggars in the streets, the whole dirty lot."

"Do you think we'll really be able to outlaw contraception?" the admiral asked.

"Of course! With the Church behind us, how can we fail?"

> *The failure of civilization can be detected by the gap between public and private morality. The wider the gap, the nearer the civilization to final dissolution.*
>
> **—Jost Hupp**

BILL BECKETT sat alone in the VIP lounge of Air Force One, insulated from the jet sounds by expensive soundproofing. The place smelled of leather and good whiskey. He glanced at his wristwatch: 10:28 EST. The parade was scheduled to start at 1:00 P.M. in Washington, D.C. He stared at all the empty seats around him, thinking of what this privileged isolation really meant. Ruckerman, who slept now back in the private bedroom, had chortled at sight of the plane.

"Número Uno, by God!"

The President had sent this plane especially for the two of them, a full general to escort them and brief them on the ceremonies awaiting them in Washington: a parade, addresses to the joint session of Congress, medals, a banquet in the White House. The general, a Walter Monk, had looked too young for the job—all smiles and white teeth but cruel eyes, ruthless.

Beckett sighed.

It was all true what Marge had babbled to him over the telephone.

"You're a hero, I tell you!"

What a strange conversation, the girls squealing and crying, telling him how much they loved him, how famous he was, then passing the phone back to Marge with: "Mother has something real important to tell you."

"There's talk of running you for President," Marge said.

My God! He couldn't absorb it all. He had been too close to the plague project for too long, his vision restricted to the day-to-day demands of their research. And Marge springing the next revelation on him with never a hint to prepare him, not one single clue in any of their few scanty telephone and radio contacts—it had almost overloaded the system.

"Bill, I don't want you to worry. You're my Primary and always will be."

Primary! How quickly the jargon took over. But he knew then what she was about to announce. The Secondary Marriage between Kate O'Gara and Admiral Francis Delacourt had set the pattern.

"You'd better know it before you arrive, though, darling," Marge said. "It'll be so obvious when you see me. I'm pregnant."

He could hear the girls behind her, chattering: "Tell him about . . ." The rest was lost as Marge continued.

"Didn't you hear me, Bill?"

"I heard you."

"You sound all tight and angry the way you do. Bill, you've got to accept this!"

"I accept it."

"The father is Arthur Dalvig, darling. *General* Dalvig. He's our regional military commander. You'll like him, I know you will."

"What choice do I have?"

"Bill, don't be that way. He's been very good to us. The girls love him. And, darling, he *has* made a great many things possible. When things were at their worst, he protected us and . . . and everything. Darling, please. He knows he's only my Secondary, that you'll always be first with me. He accepts that. Arthur admires you, Bill. He's one of those saying you should be President."

And why not? Beckett thought. *A President in the family can be a powerful career advantage for a military officer.*

"I love you, Bill," Marge said. And the girls squealing behind her: "Tell him about . . ."

Again, it was lost, whatever the girls wanted told, as Marge said she would save the rest of it until he arrived. Then: "Oh, girls! All right! They want me to tell you about all the men who're courting them, but they're too young. They'll have to wait until they're at least fifteen. And that's final!"

He was going home to a very different world than the one he had left, Beckett realized.

And so was Joe.

Poor Hupp. His dreams of being a power broker dispensing the scientific largesse with a careful hand—all gone. A cruel awakening into this new civilization.

"We are cows," Hupp had said.

This had brought shocked silence to the other members of The Team, all four of them holding their last meeting, parting finally in the impersonal crockery, tile and chromium of Huddersfield's main cafeteria. There had been much noisy activity out beyond their corner table. Huddersfield had become a world crossroads, every facility overloaded.

"Joe is upset because our old team is breaking up," Lepikov explained.

"Joe is right," Danzas said.

"You were not raised on the land as we were, Sergei," Hupp said. "You would not understand about poor, dumb cows. You never walk up to your cow and abuse it with your anger."

Danzas nodded sagely.

"You talk sweetly to your cow," Hupp said. "You feed it well. You brush it and clean it and give it the best medical care. You treat it gently, but firmly, just the way Stonar and his friends treat us. They know about cows. When the cow's head is in the stanchion, you lock the head there. Then you draw out the lovely, rich milk, being careful to strip out the last of the milk at the end lest the poor creature get sick on what is left in it."

Beckett had recounted this to General Monk during the first part of the flight, watching the amusement and speculation in the man's eyes. How was a possible President of the United States taking to such an insight?

This was one cow who was going to be bullish, Beckett thought. After Monk left him alone, Beckett began framing a campaign speech.

"We need a scientist in the White House. We need someone who knows the real dangers facing our world. We need someone capable of assessing the true nature of what our scientific laboratories produce."

Yes—give them the idea that the plague might not have occurred had there been a scientist President. That would do it.

"A woman for every man!"

It was a good slogan and might be an attainable goal. The idea carried dangerous undertones of ownership, though. Were women to be hostages to a human future?

Hupp had been absolutely right about one thing: *They need us, damn them!*

There was mounting evidence that O'Neill had created more than he knew in that crude laboratory of his. Now that people were once more moving about, crossing the old borders and the new ones, diseases never before observed were beginning to crop up. O'Neill had probably been a walking factory of infections. They could trace his path by where the new diseases were appearing.

God! One man had done this.

Was O'Neill still wandering insane in Ireland? It was possible. A form of that primitive respect for madness had come over the Irish. They were perfectly capable of harboring him, feeding and protecting him. The stories coming out of Ireland could not be discounted—rumors, myths. Cottagers were putting out dishes of food the way they once had done for the Little Folk. But now it was for the Madman. And the stories they told, and the press repeating them:

"I heard this screaming at night. Away down in the vale it was and not a human sound at all. It was the Madman sure! The milk I left out for him was gone in the morning."

EPILOGUE

The objective of some who have proposed regulation of recombinant DNA research is to use the power of government for the suppression of ideas that may otherwise flow from such research. That would take us back to an era of dogmatism from which mankind has only recently escaped. And it would be a feckless task. In the long run, it is impossible to stand in the way of the exploration of truth. Someone will learn, somewhere, sometime.

—Philip Handler, President,
National Academy of Science